THE VOW

CLUB INDULGENCE DUET
BOOK TWO

MAGGIE COLE

PULSE PRESS INC

This book is fiction. Any references to historical events, real people, or real places are used fictitiously. All names, characters, plots, and events are products of the author's imagination. Any resemblance to actual events or places or persons, living or dead, is entirely coincidental.

Copyright © 2023 by Maggie Cole

All rights reserved.

No part of this book may be reproduced in any form or by any electronic or mechanical means, including information storage and retrieval systems, without written permission from the author, except for the use of brief quotations in a book review.

WARNING

Warning: This series is a dark romance that has graphic sexual scenes both in and out of Club Indulgence which may be disturbing to some readers.

Mature audiences only.

1

Blakely Fox Madden

Sunlight streams through the small slits of the shades. It's barely morning. I've tossed and turned all night, with stale air in my lungs, hardly able to breathe. Now, all I can think about is Riggs fighting the waves on his surfboard and the calm chaos twinkling around him.

What am I going to do without him?

Is this really it for us?

It has to be. What he did was unforgivable.

I turn the burner phone on, cringing as I scroll through the messages for what feels like the hundredth time. No matter how often I listen to my voice, see risqué photos of my body, or read the taunting messages, it doesn't change my reaction. Every second is another slap in the face.

The picture of me in my wedding dress blowing Riggs a kiss, beaming with happiness, almost kills me. Riggs claimed it was his favorite, and everything about that moment makes me start to cry again.

I thought my entire life was complete when he snapped that photo.

Was it only to make my father angry?

No, Riggs loves me.

Does he?

Everything I thought I knew about Riggs and our relationship shatters into smaller pieces. The longer I stare at the moment I thought I had it all, the more betrayal seeps into my bones.

I tear my eyes off the photo and reread the messages. My father's angry threats and Riggs's taunting ones become blurrier. When I can't see the screen through my tears, I toss the phone on the bed and force myself to get up and shower, standing under the water in a haze until it turns cold.

I dry off, get dressed, and fight the urge to get back into bed, hoping Noah's not awake. He wouldn't stop pushing me to tell him what Riggs did, but I couldn't. How would I even begin to explain what my husband—the man I committed forever to—did?

Cringing again at my new reality, I go out into the main room. Noah's drinking coffee, working on his laptop, and a pain shoots through me. I always loved walking into the room and seeing Riggs working. Looking at Noah is another reminder I'm far from our Malibu beach house, and everything I thought about my marriage is now in question.

Noah looks up, questioning softly, "Hey, are you okay?"

I straighten my shoulders and lift my chin. "Yeah. What time is it?"

"Barely five."

"Why aren't you still sleeping?" I ask, trying to keep him off the topic of my issues with Riggs. Plus, I didn't expect him to already be working. I'm used to Riggs being up early, but I know he doesn't sleep well. The image of Riggs calling out in his sleep over his nightmares pains me, and I wince inside.

Noah shrugs. "I don't sleep too many hours."

What is it with these men who barely sleep?

I need tons of it. And lately, I need even more. Except last night when I couldn't rest, I've never slept so many hours. I'm always exhausted, but I assume it's from all the work at the studio and Riggs's relentless sex drive and dedication to wearing me out.

Noah demands, "Blakely, I need you to tell me what happened between you and Riggs."

I'm unsure why I don't want to divulge anything to him, but my gut's telling me not to answer him. So I respond, "It's not a big deal. I'll figure it out."

A stern look appears on his face. His voice matches his expression, and he claims, "I'm here to help you, Blakely. But in order to do that, I need to know what I'm protecting you from. So tell me what's going on."

My emotions creep up, and I fight my hardest not to cry again. I claim, "There's nothing to protect me from."

"Yes, there is," he insists.

"No, I'm fine," I assert, shaking my head.

He scowls. "What did that bastard do to you?"

"Don't talk about my husband like that," I scold, then my cheeks heat. I look away. My heart races faster.

Why am I sticking up for Riggs?

Tense silence fills the air. I can feel Noah peering at me.

I find my confidence and lock eyes with him, forcing myself to ask, "Do I have any money coming in yet?"

Noah's eyes turn to slits. "You don't have access to a bank account?"

My cheeks turn hotter. I lift my chin and lie, "We talked about going to the bank but we hadn't gotten around to it yet. Things have been too busy."

"Sure he didn't," Noah says in disgust.

Embarrassment and shame fill me. I let myself be in this situation. I allowed myself to give Riggs all the power. Even the contract I signed said he would fully provide for me, and as hard as I worked to escape my father's grasp, I didn't blink twice to hand my independence over to Riggs.

Noah gives me a pitying look and shakes his head. He informs me, "It'll be a few months before royalties kick in."

I look away, scrunching my face. *I'm so stupid. How could I have been so stupid?*

Noah stands up and walks toward me. He grabs my hand. "Blakely, you can stay here as long as you need to. And don't worry, I'll take care of you."

I pull my hand away from his. I don't want anyone taking care of me. That's how I got into this situation. I never should have let Riggs take care of me like he did.

I loved him taking care of me.

Look where that got me.

"I should have known he would try to steal your earnings," Noah declares.

Fire lights in my belly. I snap, "Riggs would never steal money from me. He did everything in his power to ensure my contract was in my best interest."

"Then why do you have no access to money, Blakely?" he questions.

Shame pummels me. I scold myself for not staying independent. I knew better than to trust anyone after dealing with my father.

Still, I continue to stick up for him and confess, "Riggs gave me cash, and I knew where in the house he kept it. I could grab whatever I wanted at any time. He never let me go without anything. He always took care of me."

The image of Riggs telling me to take money to the studio, even though everything was always provided for me, hurts.

He didn't try to keep me penniless. There's no way he would have given me cash when I didn't even need it if that were his intention.

There's only one instance I even used the cash. I had Rhonda from Naked Pipes run out and buy me a box of pregnancy tests.

Oh shit. I never took the pregnancy test.

A whole new set of fear and anxiety hits me. A week ago, I realized I hadn't had my period in months. So I secretly asked Rhonda to get the tests for me.

The notion I could be pregnant left me feeling anxious. I didn't know how Riggs would react if I had a baby growing inside me and we were together, much less if we were apart. He made it clear in his contract that he didn't want me getting pregnant, but we're also married, so would that change his mind about having a child?

Plus, the challenge of launching my record while knocked up didn't exactly seem like a good idea. So I kept putting off taking the test, trying to convince myself that no matter what, Riggs and I would figure it out.

Why did I not take the test?

I've got to get another one.

I can't ask Noah.

Oh God, I don't want him to know.

Noah interrupts my thoughts, interrogating, "Did you sign a prenup?"

"What? No!" I blurt out, offended he would think Riggs would make me do that. One thing Riggs has always been is generous with his money.

"So he can steal yours," Noah mutters.

"Stop it! He doesn't need my money," I declare.

Noah's face hardens.

I cross my arms and hug my chest, feeling overwhelmed.

Noah repeats, "Don't worry about money, Blakely. I'll get you a divorce attorney. You can take Riggs to the cleaners."

Offended, I assert, "I don't want his money, and we aren't getting divorced!" My pulse creeps up. I have no idea how I would ever forgive Riggs or get past this, but the idea of divorcing him just hurts too much.

Noah's eyes widen. "Don't be stupid. You're young with your entire life in front of you." His phone buzzes. He glances at it and clenches his jaw. Then he stares at me and roughly answers, "Matt, what is it?"

Goose bumps pop out on my skin.

Noah declares, "Ban him from the building."

More bad feelings fill me. There's no doubt he's talking about Riggs.

He's here.

I struggle not to run out of Noah's condo and go find him.

A moment of silence passes, and Noah barks, "I don't care if he threatens to have the cops raid the place. His wife isn't his property. He's not coming near her, and tell him if he attempts to, I'll file a restraining order."

My mouth turns dry. I put my hand over my stomach, feeling ill again.

Is this what I really want?

To never go near Riggs again?

To never see him and not talk to him?

What he did wasn't right, but I've always known Riggs was screwed up. I should have known he was capable of using me.

Maybe, this entire thing is my fault. Besides, he never lied about wanting to destroy my father. Perhaps I'm the stupid one for not making him tell me how he would execute my father's demise.

Noah hangs up the phone, warning, "He's not coming near you, Blakely." He walks to the window and glares through the glass.

I follow and look down, my gut churning faster. Riggs is fighting off three security guards, shouting as they push him away from the building. I put my hand over my mouth, and tears fall rapidly down my face.

He looks like he hasn't slept. His hair's a disheveled mess. He's so angry, and I'm scared he'll do something stupid with long-lasting consequences. One thing I'm not is oblivious to Riggs's temper. "Noah, please stop them," I beg.

Noah gives me a shocked look, then denies my request. "Absolutely not."

"They're going to hurt him," I claim.

Noah grunts. "Will serve the bastard right."

"He's my husband!" I cry out.

He turns to me. "And what did he do to you? You ran from a charity event through a sea of reporters and then you fled with me. You had me take you to your house so you could fill a suitcase of barely any of your possessions. So tell me what he did to you because that's a pretty extreme reaction."

I glance back down at Riggs. My entire insides shake.

He's finally backing away, but he's still pointing and shouting at the men, and I can only imagine the threats he's giving them.

"Tell me what he did," Noah pushes again.

More warnings not to tell Noah anything fill my head, swirling with too many other questions. I haven't even processed everything that I discovered.

Noah slides his hand on my back, and I jump away.

He holds his hands in the air. "Hey, I'm on your side, Blakely."

I step farther back, saying nothing. I have to get a pregnancy test. I need to figure out what's going on.

If I'm pregnant, that doesn't change what Riggs did. It's still unforgivable.

Noah tries again. "Blakely—"

"I don't want to talk about it."

"But—"

"Look, I need to go to the studio for my session," I interject.

"We can cancel it," he states.

I shake my head. "No." I spin and go into the bedroom, toss my cell and the burner phone into my purse, then return to the living room. I ask Noah, "Can you arrange a ride for me, please?"

"I'll take you. But are you sure you really want to go?"

"I do," I insist, needing to get out of this house and away from Noah and all of his demands and questions. In some ways, he's just like Riggs, yet he's the exact opposite.

Noah finally caves and leads me out of his condo. We go to the parking garage and he opens the door to his Mercedes.

I slide inside and cringe. It feels pompous, like my father's car. I've gotten used to Riggs in his Porsche. It just fills me with more sadness. It hasn't even been a day, and I miss him so much, yet I'm still so hurt and angry with him.

I'll never get past what he sent my father.

If I'm pregnant, I'm going to have to deal with him.

I'll raise the baby on my own.

Another pain hits me. My parents neglected me in too many ways. I always assumed if I was pregnant, I'd give my child everything, including two parents who were together. Now, it can't happen.

I'm not pregnant.

Why haven't I gotten my period, then?

The image of my parents at the event fills my mind. They looked horrible. I know it's been a few years since I've seen them, but I have no doubts that Riggs did that to them.

I try to remind myself that my father's awful and my mother is an out-of-control alcoholic and not much better. But still, she looks like she's a few steps away from dying from her alcoholism or wasting away from not eating, and it was shocking to see her in that state.

Can I ever be okay with Riggs going to the extreme lengths of destroying them, even if they've always been toxic and never had my best interest at heart?

They're evil.

They're my blood.

Would he use our child if he was okay using me?

The ache inside me grows. Our love seemed real, but how can it be if he was okay using me as a pawn in his retaliation against my father?

Noah tries to talk to me in the car, stating, "Listen, I know things are—"

"I don't want to talk right now. Please let me ride in peace," I interject.

He clenches his jaw.

I turn away and stare out the window. He stays quiet the remainder of the ride.

When we get to the studio, I pull Rhonda aside and into an empty office.

She gives me a sympathetic look. "Honey, are you okay? Your eyes are bloodshot."

Embarrassment rears its ugly head again. I fight through it and glance behind me, ensuring we're alone. "I need a favor from you."

She arches her eyebrows. "Sure. What is it?"

My shame grows. I admit, "I-I don't have any money, and I promise I'll pay you back."

Pity fills her expression. She steps closer and lowers her voice, asking, "Blakely, what is it? Just tell me what you need."

I close my eyes for a brief moment, then lift my chin and look at her. "I need a pregnancy test. I never took the one you gave me."

She glances at my belly, then nods. "Okay. Don't worry. I've got you, girl." She gives me a hug, squeezing me tight.

It feels maternal, and I almost lose it again, but I control myself.

She retreats, stating, "I'll be right back."

I wait for her to walk away, then try to compose myself as best as possible before moving toward the recording studio.

Ears steps out of his office a few feet from the door. He shoots me an uncomfortable expression and my stomach flips. He tries to cover it up, booming, "Hey, superstar."

I force a smile. "Hey."

He briefly studies me, then says, "Look, I don't want to get involved in your business, but I've known Riggs a long time."

My stomach curls. I put my hand on it and lean against the wall, closing my eyes.

"Blakely, you okay?" Ears questions.

Tears fill my eyes. Something about Ears feels safer than Noah. It shouldn't, knowing he has a long history with Riggs, yet I admit in a shaky voice, "No."

He shifts on his feet, lowering his voice. "He's losing his shit. Why don't you talk to him?"

I swipe at my cheeks, confessing, "I-I can't right now."

"You want to tell me what he did?" Ears asks.

I open my mouth and then shut it, shaking my head.

Silence grows until I break it. My voice cracks, and I demand, "Keep him away from me. I mean it."

Ears takes a deep breath, then exhales. "Okay. But, Blakely, you can't stay with Noah. Riggs will kill him."

"I would never do anything with Noah," I snap.

Ears's eyes widen. "Didn't say that."

"You insinuated—"

"No, I said that Riggs will kill him. You, of all people, know how possessive he is," Ears states.

I can't argue, but I don't know what else to do right now. I have no money. I firmly declare, "Noah's been kind enough to let me stay in his guest bedroom. Until my royalties come in, I have no other options."

Ears tilts his head, the crease in his forehead growing.

"What is that look for?"

"Riggs will give you money. He wouldn't want you to not have any," he claims.

"I don't want his money."

"You're married. It's yours too," Ears insists.

I put my hand over my face and breathe, trying to stop the queasiness in my stomach.

Ears suggests, "Let me talk to him for you."

I lock eyes with him. "And say what?"

He sighs. "You need money, superstar. You can't stay with Noah."

"I don't want to stay with Noah, but I have no other options," I assert.

"Let me work on your housing situation, then," Ears says.

I'm too drained to think. I finally nod. "Okay. Thank you."

"Great. Why don't you go into my office and try to sleep? I can pull the sofa out into the bed," Ears offers.

"No, thank you. I'm going to do my job," I assure him, then push past his large frame, not wanting to talk anymore. I go into the studio and into the recording booth.

For over an hour, I try to throw myself into my work, but it's almost impossible. My voice doesn't sound right. I'm unable to follow the directions I'm getting from Ears and Noah.

Rhonda finally comes into the studio and knocks on the window. I excuse myself and leave the room with her.

She says, "It's in the bathroom in the cabinet."

"Thank you," I reply gratefully.

She hands me a bottle of water.

I take it, go into the restroom, then close and lock the door. I find the box of pregnancy tests, take a deep breath, then down the bottle of water.

My pulse throbs so hard in my neck that I think I'll have a stroke. I follow the directions and unwrap the test. I pee on the stick, place it on the counter, and then set my timer on my phone.

Too many worries plague me. I pace the bathroom, trying to get Riggs's face out of my mind, but I can't. The alarm blares through the air, and I freeze.

This is it.

Please don't be pregnant, I chant to myself with my eyes closed at least a dozen times, with images of a little boy who looks like Riggs filling my mind and making my heart hurt more.

I force myself to look down at the stick, then pick it up and stare at it, with too many emotions exploding inside me like it's the Fourth of July.

2

Riggs Madden

My fist curls so tight I might break my knuckles. All I wanted to do was rush into the studio and pummel Noah in the face. He put his hand on my pet's back and escorted her into the studio as if she were his. If Ears's security guys weren't there and he hadn't already warned me that I wasn't allowed to get out of the car, I would've done it.

Even though it's been over an hour, I still can't relax my hands. And I'm trying to give Blakely the space Ears told me to give her, but it's borderline impossible.

After she disappeared inside the studio, I pulled in front of the building. Rhonda came out and gave me a dirty look. I don't know what Blakely or Noah told her, but she quickly trotted down the street, returning with a plastic bag.

Too anxious to continue waiting, I call Ears.

"Riggs, go home."

I reply, "I'm not going home. Send my wife outside, or I'm coming in even if I have to get out my gun and shoot up your security."

It's not a threat. Every minute that passes makes me think crazier thoughts. I know I'm unhinged right now, but there's nothing I can do about it. Until my pet is in front of me, I'm not going to be able to calm down.

The line goes dead. I call Ears again, but he sends it to voicemail, then rushes out of the building.

He crosses the street, yanks the door open, then slides inside my car, accusing, "What are you doing here? I told you to go away."

"I'm not leaving my wife," I bark.

His eyes turn to slits. "I told you to give her space. Go home, Riggs."

"Do I need to remind you how long we've been friends?" I threaten.

"Don't you dare pull that bullshit with me. What the fuck did you do to her anyways? She's a mess in there."

Guilt fills me. I scrub my face and lean against the headrest, closing my eyes as exhaustion sets in. When Hugh showed up at the charity event, I knew it was about to get ugly, but I had no clue my marriage would be the bullseye. I thought he'd make a scene, but it didn't occur to me he'd out me to his daughter.

I've never been so ignorant.

When Blakely looked at me as if I betrayed her, I wanted to die. Of all the things I've done to her, she's never looked at me like that. Watching her leave with Noah, not once but twice, gave misery a new meaning.

Ears sighs and softens his tone. "I have your back, but you gotta respect Blakely's wishes. We talked about this earlier."

"Did she tell you what happened?" I ask.

He furrows his eyebrows. "No. She won't talk. But she's upset."

"Did she tell Noah?"

"Not to my knowledge."

"Don't lie to me," I warn.

Ears holds up his hands. "Noah doesn't know anything. At least, that's what he claims, and I believe him. But he's only a friend to her."

"Bullshit. He's loving every minute of this," I claim, but I hope it's true she didn't confide in him. The thought makes me queasy. The last thing I need is for her to get closer to Noah.

Ears snarls, "I wouldn't lie to you."

The thought of Blakely spending the night at Noah's creates new rage inside me. I curl my fist again, seething, "Why don't you send Noah out here, and I'll ask him?"

Ears groans. "What are you going to do? Beat him up? What's that going to solve?"

I scowl. "My wife isn't staying with him. And he has no right sticking his nose into our business."

Ears grows angry. "Don't fuck up my business, Riggs. And don't interfere in your wife's career. You don't play around with Noah. He's not some low-class agent. He's going to take her to the top, and he's just helping her out."

"Bullshit. He wants my wife," I restate.

Ears shakes his head in disapproval. "Don't let your personal affairs cloud your judgment."

"My wife is not staying with him another night. I mean it, Ears. If she steps foot into his house again, I'll kill him. You know I'm not talking shit either!" I growl.

"Calm down, Riggs," he cautions.

"She is not staying with him!" I shout.

Ears's face hardens. He announces, "She needs money. You've given her nothing."

I jerk my head back. "I've given her nothing? What are you talking about? I've never withheld anything from her."

He pushes his fingertips together. "She has no money. Where is she supposed to go with no money?"

"I'm not keeping money from her. I would never—"

"She has nothing, and I can tell she's embarrassed. What is she supposed to do? Live on the street?" he interjects.

I beat myself up. I didn't intentionally not give Blakely access to our bank accounts or a credit card. Things have just been crazy. Besides, she knew where the cash was in the house. I reply, "There's been a lot going on. This isn't intentional. You know I wouldn't do that!"

Ears nods. He relays, "I told her you would give her money until her royalties get paid out."

"Of course I'll give her money," I say, and my gut churns.

Women having no money only reminds me of my mother's situation. It makes them do things they wouldn't normally do and have no independence. I add, "I would never do that to Blakely. You know how I feel about that kind of shit."

Ears's understanding expression turns to one only someone who grew up like we did and got out can understand. "I know, man. Seriously though, what happened between you two? Tell me so I can help smooth things over."

My queasiness grows as my stomach flips faster. I can't believe this happened. My perfect marriage has now blown up in my face, and I don't know how to get it back. Yet where do I even start to explain to Ears what I did?

Over the last twelve hours, it's hit me more and more that what I did was super fucked-up. Yet I was so deep into my revenge with Hugh I couldn't see that utilizing Blakely to get at him could hurt her. And I never thought she'd know what I did. I thought I could get away with it. But I was stupid and should never have sent anything about her to Hugh. I should have just taken him down with Jones and kept Blakely out of it.

Ears asserts, "Stop keeping me in the dark. I can't help you if you do that."

I mutter, "I fucked up."

"How?"

I sigh, confessing, "I let my need to take her father down cloud my judgment."

"Any more details in that?" he pushes.

I snap, "That's all you're getting, and my wife is not staying with Noah. She's coming home with me."

Ears shakes his head. "No, she's not. Whatever's going on, she's insistent that you stay away from her. Do yourself a favor and respect her wishes."

"Whose side are you on?" I ask him again.

He groans. "Yours, dumbass. But hers too. And Blakely was clear. Give her some space."

"With Noah? Fuck that," I bark.

"Stop with the Noah crap!"

"No! I know what he wants, and that's my wife. He might have you fooled, but I'm not," I declare.

Ears crosses his arms, ordering, "She needs a place to stay. Book her in a hotel if you don't want her at Noah's, but she's not going home with you today."

Everything inside me quivers. It feels like someone's squeezing my heart to the point I can't even breathe. I can't fathom the thought of Blakely not in my bed and not waking up to her every morning. It makes me sick, and the uncontrollable feeling I have only snowballs.

Ears questions, "What hotel is it going to be?"

My mind spins. I finally answer, "My wife's not staying at a hotel. She needs somewhere secure."

"Then where?"

I quickly review which of my properties are available and secure, and there are only two places. Everything else is rented or has a lower level of security than what I'm comfortable having my pet stay in. She needs somewhere nobody can get in or out unless they're welcome there.

The only two places are my L.A. place and Apartment Thirteen. So I answer, "Tell her she can stay at the L.A. apartment."

"You have to stay away," Ears warns.

I fight my internal battle.

Stay away from my wife?

How am I even going to do that?

As if Ears can read my thoughts, he repeats, "You can't go near her. I need your word."

I cave. "Tell her I'll take her to the apartment and then stay away."

Frustration fills Ears's expression. "Man, she's not going to be okay with that. You can't take her anywhere."

"Tough shit. No one goes in or out of my two places except me and now her."

"Then get her some transportation, but she's not going anywhere with you. She doesn't want to talk to you right now. You need to respect that," Ears asserts.

Groaning loudly, I pull at my hair. He's right, but I don't want to accept it.

"Get her a car," Ears orders. "Then she can come and go."

I close my eyes. Anything can happen to her and especially now that her single has dropped. I need to protect her. So I say, "I'll make sure she has a driver, but I'm not getting her a car. She needs to be safe."

Ears studies me a moment. He's known me longer than most people. He gets my fears. He finally says, "Okay, but you get cleaned up. You look like shit. Get some sleep, eat some food, and stay away from your wife until she's ready to talk to you."

The chaos inside me only grows. I hate it. I know it's not going to go away anytime soon. At any moment, I'm capable of snapping and completely losing it. Until Blakely's back in my arms, there's no way I'll rest easy.

Ears questions, "What are you going to do about giving her access to money?"

Guilt reappears. I pull out my wallet and take all the cash from the billfold. It's a few thousand dollars. I hold it out toward Ears. "Give this to her. I'll have a credit card issued for her today."

He takes the cash and reaches for the door handle.

I grab his arm and stop him. "Tell Blakely I found her secret box."

Ears turns back to me and arches his eyebrows. "Secret box? What does that mean?"

I sniff hard, fighting the anger building inside me.

Why didn't she tell me she thought she might be pregnant?

Does she already know?

Is she carrying my child?

I will not be a deadbeat father like mine. We're raising this baby together.

If she's pregnant.

All the questions I felt when I first discovered the pregnancy tests pummel me. "None of your business. Just tell her and let her know. Be clear that we need to talk about it sooner rather than later."

"Give her time, man."

"Just tell her," I reiterate.

Ears shakes his head again and lets out a deep exhale. He orders, "Have your driver here at two o'clock." He gets out and slams the door.

I squeeze the steering wheel until my knuckles turn white, watching him walk into the building, fighting the urge to follow him and beat the shit out of Noah.

I'm starting to hate that guy. The last thing I need is Blakely getting close to him. And I regret letting her decide on her agent. She wanted me to pick, and I should have.

That's what I get for trying to do the right thing.

Noah's probably eating this up. I don't put it past him to have already tried to do something with her.

My pulse pounds between my ears, and the air turns stale in my lungs. The thought of them in a bed together makes more bile rise in my throat.

I'll kill him if he laid a hand on her.

I debate about staying in the parking lot and finally get a text from Ears.

> Ears: Go take care of your shit and get away from my studio.

> Me: Did you tell her?

> Ears: Not yet. She's finishing a song.

> Me: I'm not leaving until you tell her what we discussed.

Twenty minutes pass until Ears messages me back.

> Ears: She said she wants to go to Apartment Thirteen.

Shock fills me. Why would she pick Apartment Thirteen? I thought she hated that place.

> Me: The L.A. apartment is better. She'll be more comfortable there.

> Ears: She doesn't want to go there. She said she'll only go to Apartment Thirteen if you promise to stay away.

More confusion fills me. I debate it, but Apartment Thirteen is as secure as my L.A. apartment. It's the only other property I own besides my Malibu house that has the same security measures. I know she'll be safe there.

> Me: Fine. Tell her she can go there.

> Ears: She wants a car too.

> Me: I said I'll send a driver.

> Ears: She doesn't want your driver to know her every move.

Anger seeps through me. What will she do that she doesn't want me to know about?

Divorce.

She's going to try and divorce me.

New panic sets in. I bang my head against the headrest. She's possibly pregnant with my child. No way this is happening.

> Me: No. Tell her I said her little secret is exactly why she needs a driver, never mind that she's in the public eye. It's not safe, and her safety is my priority. I'm not budging on it. Tell her she either gets in the car with me today or gets my drivers, whom I deem safe.

Ten minutes pass and my heartbeat never slows. The notion of my pet driving around L.A., where anyone could harm her, scares the crap out of me. The beating only seems to go faster until pain shoots through my chest. I'm clutching it when I text again.

> Me: If she tries to fight me on this, I'm coming in so we can discuss her little secret.

Another minute passes.

> Ears: Fine. She'll take your driver but wants her stuff moved from the beach house to the apartment.

It's another blow. The thought of all of Blakely's things not in our walk-in closet, where I can see them, as if she's never coming back, is cruel.

> Ears: She's not budging on it.

I groan out loud again.

> Me: Fine. I'll have it sent over in the next few days.

> Ears: Good. Go home. Get away from my building.

Feeling defeated but semi-relieved that she won't be at Noah's, I finally pull away. I arrange for two of my trusted drivers, who are also bodyguards, to be at Blakely's beck and call. I order them to send me reports on where she is at all times. The last thing I'm going to do is not know my wife's location.

Then I go to Apartment Thirteen and pace, looking around, trying to understand why Blakely wanted to stay here instead of the L.A. apartment. I can't figure it out, but I order groceries and wait for them to arrive. I put them away and then write her a note.

> *Pet,*
>
> *Are you pregnant with my child?*
> *You can't avoid me forever, and this living arrangement's temporary.*
> *You and I are tied together forever. There's no escaping our love, and you know it.*
> *Forever yours,*
> *Riggs - Your husband, in case you forgot.*
> *P.S. I'm sorry I hurt you. It was never my intention.*

I PUT THE NOTE ON HER PILLOW AND BEGRUDGINGLY LEAVE, vowing that I'll do anything and everything and stop at nothing to earn her forgiveness.

For the first time in my adult life, I'm scared I might lose. And my wife isn't replaceable. She's not a deal, money, or some other thing.

She's my life.

The fear reminds me of how I spent my childhood, and I curse myself for the stupidity that got me here. I'm unsure how to fix this, which only deepens the growing panic inside me.

3

Blakely

$\mathcal{T}$he metal doors to Apartment Thirteen open, and the L.A. skyline lights up against the afternoon sun, making the room appear different than the one night I was here. Anxiety grows as I glance around.

Why did I choose to come here?

I can't go to the L.A. apartment. It's another one of Riggs's homes.

Part of me expected to see him here when I walked inside, even though his Porsche wasn't in the garage. Disappointment and relief play an evil tug-of-war within me, adding to my overly exhausted state. And I told him not to come, but it's another slap of reality about what's happened.

The black leather furniture almost feels cold without the warmth of the candlelight flickering against it or the soft music playing in the background. The silence is deafening, expanding my loneliness. And somehow, I feel exposed. To who or what, I don't know, but a shiver runs down my spine.

I go to the window, taking in the city's chaos below. It's a constant reminder of how I've lost everything I thought I had.

How could I have believed the lie I was living?

All I wanted was Riggs's love. I assumed if I loved him, faults and all, nothing could break us. Yet the one person I trusted the most broke my entire world. And I loved being his wife.

I still am his wife.

I swallow the thick lump in my throat. I don't know what I'm going to do.

To torture myself further, I spin and lean against the glass, staring at the room, wondering how many of Riggs's other subs lived here. It oddly brings me comfort to think of myself as his sub instead of his wife. At the same time, it's a cruel stab to my already destroyed heart.

The jealous streak in me flares, and the regret of coming here begins to take hold. Thoughts of Aria here, kneeling for Riggs, re-sparks the hatred I had for him that night. And maybe that's why I came here. Perhaps I need to hold on to hatred so I don't run back to him, allowing him to manipulate me into thinking that what he did isn't a big deal. If I sweep what he's done under the rug, there'll be no limit to what he could do to me in the future.

No, Riggs can't get away with what he's done and not have any consequences. Yet, I'm still trying to determine what those consequences should be.

Am I really willing to divorce him?

To never be with him again?

To not let him love me?

The one question that's been nagging me reappears, igniting more queasiness I haven't escaped all day: *How could he have loved me and done what he did?*

I go into the bedroom, and all I can focus on is the last time I was in this room. I was mad at Riggs. He was just as angry with me. But still, I had him, and even in the mood I was in, I wanted him.

I assess the decor and then freeze, staring at a piece of paper on the pillow. I go over to it, and my pulse creeps up. I read it, and every word hurts. I can hear Riggs saying, "Pet" in his demanding and affectionate tone. It tears me up more, and I'd give anything to have the last twenty-four hours go away and hear him say it as if everything is normal between us.

The first statement of the letter shreds me. I knew he found the tests when Ears told me his threat about the "secret box." Yet the words on paper seem to make it real, and I can only imagine what's going through Riggs's mind.

Are you pregnant with my child?

I'm not pregnant. I took all the tests in the box to ensure that it wasn't a false negative. It doesn't explain my missed periods, but maybe the hormones he initially gave me to stop my period, the stress, or even a combination of the two messed up my cycle.

Riggs thinks I'm pregnant.

I once again feel relieved and disappointed all at once. And I curse myself. I'd be bringing a baby into a broken home like the one I was raised in. I vowed to never do that to my child. And the way things are between Riggs and me right now, that's what I'd be doing.

Yet as much as I know it's a good thing I'm not pregnant, I can't get the image of a little boy who looks like Riggs out of my mind. And if I can't have Riggs ever again, having a part of him wouldn't be so bad.

I squeeze my eyes shut, reprimanding myself for the thought.

I should call Riggs and tell him I'm not pregnant or text him at the very least. Maybe then he'd back off. Perhaps it's the only reason he's coming after me still. Would he even be chasing me now if he didn't think I was pregnant? He's destroyed my father, and all his cards are visible, so what else does he need from me?

That thought only deepens the wound I think may never heal. I don't want it to be true. I want his love to have been real. I want his demand that I come home to be because of it, not because he thinks I'm carrying his child. But he betrayed me so much, I don't know how it would even be possible to ever believe he loved me or still does.

I glance back down at the letter.

You and I are tied together forever. There's no escaping our love, and you know it.

My tears fall on the paper, blurring the words, creating a blue blob of ink. *Is it another lie?*

No. It's not. He does love me.

He used me. That's not love.

Is there some other purpose he needs to use me for?

I swipe at my tears, force myself to put the note in the nightstand drawer, and wonder what items other women have put in it. Then I curse myself again for coming here. I consider going to the L.A. apartment, and my stomach curls. So I finally leave the room, wander down the hall, and stop in the doorway of the red room.

Everything looks the same. Sex furniture is scattered across the room. I saw the same things at Club Indulgence and wonder how they're used. It's another reminder of how naive I am to everything Riggs has mastered. I gingerly step through the doorway and walk over to the wall displaying the toys, floggers, paddles, and many different restraints.

It looks untouched. My eyes lock on the black flogger that Aria chose.

He never used it on me, only her.

He only spanked me.

Why?

The thought plagues me. I pick up the flogger and run my finger over the leather tassels, unable to stop wondering why Riggs didn't use it on me. There are no answers. I finally put it back on the wall and turn, staring at the 14-ring steel St. Andrew's Cross, imagining the vision of my body restrained to it and all that Riggs did to me that night.

My core stirs. I wish we could return to that evening and my naivety. As much as there were things I hated, it awoke something in me. I loved every minute of being at Riggs's mercy and watching him dominate Aria, even though my jealousy flared.

I clutch the metal and close my eyes, fighting more tears.

How will I ever feel alive again the way Riggs knows how to light me up?

It doesn't matter. He only wanted me as a way to get revenge on my father.

THE VOW

He promised he'd always protect me and especially from my father. But he didn't. It was all lies.

I sniffle and then lock eyes on the bench that Aria laid on. Something snaps inside me. I walk over to it, then position my body the same way she did. Gripping the legs of the bench and staring at the cross, I wonder what it would feel like to have Riggs flogging me, belting out commands. I imagine staring at Aria, merciless and restrained on the cross, watching me the way Riggs made me watch her.

Why am I thinking about her?

He doesn't think I can handle what she can.

Ugh! I'm screwed up.

What does it even matter?

Because I saw the flame in his eyes. I saw the power he felt and the dominance he needed to display—the dominance I know he has to act on.

He had that look for her, not for me.

But he married me, not her.

My stomach somersaults again. No matter how much I try to remind myself he married me and not her, being in this room and reminiscing about that scene won't go away. And the truth doesn't blind me.

He only married me to get at my father, not because he really wanted me.

The emptiness I feel only grows. I squeeze my hands tighter around the metal legs, my vision blurry, sobbing hard against the bench. I'd do anything to have Riggs behind me and slapping the leather against my skin to distract me from the mental anguish that I can't escape.

A puddle of tears pools under the bench. I finally rise and force myself to leave the room. I go into the kitchen and open the fridge, surprised it's full but unsure why I'm shocked. It's a total Riggs move. He's always taken care of me and I've never wanted for anything.

Unless he had another sub here before I demanded this place.

What am I talking about?

Riggs has never cheated on me. Even when he brought Aria here, I know he only did it in order to train me.

How do I know anything I thought was true isn't a lie?

Maybe it all was part of Riggs's twisted game.

The rabbit hole I dive into only deepens as the night goes on. I keep my personal cell off and only have the burner phone on, torturing myself by reviewing the content again and again. Then the burner phone dies, and I realize I have no chargers for either of my phones.

I pace the apartment, and I finally can't handle it anymore. I turn on my cell, ignore the dozens of missed texts and voicemails from Riggs, and text him.

> Me: I need chargers for both phones.

He tries to call me. A photo of us together in Hawaii pops up, and the pain intensifies. I almost answer it, but I send it to voicemail on the fourth ring.

> Me: Text only.

Riggs: I'll bring it over.

Me: No, have them delivered. And I said both, not just mine, Riggs.

Riggs: Pet, no good can come from you continuing to review those messages.

Me: Not your decision. I want the chargers.

Riggs: We need to talk.

Me: I'm not ready.

Riggs: You're having my baby. We need to talk.

I freeze, and my pulse pounds.

Riggs: Pet, I'm sorry. Let's work through this. I'll be damned if we don't raise our baby together.

Me: I'm not pregnant.

A moment passes.

Riggs: Don't lie to me, pet. And I won't have you keep our child from me.

Me: I'm not pregnant. And I'm not the one who lies.

Riggs: Then why the tests? And you haven't gotten your period.

> Me: All three tests were negative. I had Rhonda get more today. I'm not pregnant. And I probably missed my period because of the hormones you shot me up with or all the stress I've been under.

There's silence as dots appear and then disappear. It happens several times.

> Riggs: Do you swear the tests were negative?

> Me: Yes. I wouldn't mislead you about a baby. Plus, I'm not the liar in this relationship.

Dots fill the screen and I quickly type another message.

> Me: Sorry, ex-relationship.

"Ugh! Why did I say that?" I mutter and bang my head against the back of the couch.

> Riggs: Don't say that.

> Me: It's true.

> Riggs: Why didn't you tell me you thought you were pregnant?

Anger flares within me.

> Me: You didn't tell me a lot of things, now, did you?

More minutes pass. And I can't control the rage circling throughout me, spinning and spinning like a tornado out of control.

> Me: You used me, Riggs.

Riggs: I used the situation to my advantage.

Me: So that makes it okay?

Our photo appears on the screen again. I send the call to voicemail.

Riggs: Nothing between us was a lie. I've always been honest about how I feel about you.

My tears drip off my chin as the message blurs. How can I ever believe that again?

Riggs: Pet, I love you. You know this.

His statement is a knife twisting deep into my heart. I can't think about if we were real or not anymore. The hurt spirals out of control, and I don't want to end my communication with him, but I can't keep discussing what he claims are his feelings for me. So I change the subject.

Me: Why didn't you use the flogger on me?

Riggs: When?

Me: When we were here.

Riggs: Why did you choose Apartment Thirteen?

Me: Don't change the subject.

Riggs: You should come to the L.A. apartment or return to the beach house. It's where you belong, not Apartment Thirteen.

> Me: Why? I'm not good enough to be here?

> Riggs: Why would you say that? You're too good to be there.

> Me: Answer my question. Why didn't you use it on me?

> Riggs: You didn't need it.

> Me: Answer me honestly, for God's sake.

> Riggs: I just did.

> Me: I don't believe you.

> Riggs: I'm coming over, pet.

My heart pounds so hard it makes me dizzy. I almost don't reply, wanting so badly to wait for him to show up at the door. But it's wrong. I know I'll regret it tomorrow if I let what he did slide.

> Me: No, you aren't coming over.

> Riggs: I'll be there in ten minutes.

My heart races faster.

> Me: You're not in Malibu? You're in L.A.?

> Riggs: Of course I'm in L.A. I'm not leaving the city until you're with me.

> Me: Go back to Malibu.

As soon as I send it, I cringe. Thinking about him at the beach house without me aches.

> Riggs: You're my wife. I'm not going anywhere when you're here.

His wife. I squeeze my eyes and tap my hand on my thigh, my heart swooning in the way Riggs always makes it while also reprimanding myself for reacting to his words.

Actions speak louder, I remind myself.

He can show up at any moment.

> Me: Do not come over here. Nothing has changed between us.

Please come over. Please come over. Please come over.

What am I wishing? He needs to stay away.

> Riggs: Pet, don't say that. We need to talk. I'm coming over.

I stare at the L.A. skyline. It's dark out now, and everything's blinking like a magnificent piece of artwork. I turn toward the direction of the apartment, hurting more than ever, wondering if he's staring out the window and looking toward me as well.

> Me: No, don't come over. I'm getting a divorce attorney if you don't respect my wishes.

The phone rings. I send it to voicemail, my heart pounding like a jackhammer.

> Me: I'm not talking to you right now.

> Riggs: Do not say you're divorcing me. That's not an option for us, and you know it. We're not meant to be apart, pet.

His statement only makes the pain expand. I don't want to divorce him. But why would he want to keep me? He married me to get at my father. I text him one final message.

> Me: Stay away. Or I will go get a divorce attorney. Goodnight.

I turn off my phone and go into the bedroom, slipping under the covers, trying to smell any remnant of Riggs from the last time we stayed here. But the sheets have been washed, adding to my fears. There's no trace of him anywhere. And I wonder if there will ever be a time when things are as they were between us.

As exhausted as I am, I can't sleep. I should close the shades, but there's comfort in the lights of the city.

It's another example of calm chaos.

More pain fills me. I wish the city could swallow me up and make me disappear, numbing the ache of reality I can't escape.

I toss and turn for hours, cry on and off, then finally curl into a ball, staring past the side of the bed he should be on and at the buildings.

Then the scent of woody spice laced with orange peels flares in my nostrils, and I think I'm imagining things. I inhale deeper, and a creep of electricity bursts throughout my skin.

I'm losing it.

"Pet," Riggs's voice demands.

A shiver runs down my spine. I clutch my thighs together and hold my breath, wondering if I'm going crazy or if he's really here.

"Pet, look at me," he commands.

My pulse skyrockets. I slowly turn, my insides quiver, and I open my mouth, but nothing comes out.

Riggs crouches next to the bed. Even in the darkness, I can tell his eyes are bloodshot, his hair wild. I've never seen him look so disheveled. It reminds me of how my father looked at the fundraiser.

Riggs slides his large palm over my cheek.

My tears fall freely, his scent and touch lighting me up and killing my soul, all in one powerful surge of torture. I hate that I still want him so much. I told him to stay away, yet deep down, there's comfort he's here.

He slides next to me, tugging me into his arms, and all I can do is sob. He repeatedly murmurs, "Shh" and "I'm sorry."

He holds me like he always does. Like I'm his, as if he owns me and nothing feels safer.

Yet I'm not protected. He's proven he can destroy me and not think twice about it. So I finally force myself to push at his chest and look up. I accuse, "How could you?"

He tightens his hold around me, answering, "It wasn't meant to hurt you. I would *never* hurt you."

His statement refuels all my anger. I blurt out, "You already did."

Guilty remorse crosses his expression. He nods. "I know. I didn't mean to. I promise you, I didn't mean to."

I stare at him, more tears falling, unsure where to go from here, struggling with wanting his body around mine and the fight to push him out of my life forever.

He holds the back of my head, presses his mouth to mine, and slips his tongue between my lips.

I cave, reacting to him with a need too great to ignore, then somehow finding the willpower to retreat. I break the kiss and barely get out, "No."

"Pet—"

"No, Riggs! You can't just come in here and use your body to seduce me back into your life," I declare.

"You *are* in my life. You will *always* be in my life," he asserts.

I shake my head. "You did this! You broke me! You broke *us*!"

He swallows hard, then replies, "I made a mistake. It will never happen again."

An emotion-filled laugh escapes me. "You'll never again use me to get at my father? Why? Because you've already destroyed him?"

Riggs clenches his jaw.

Tense silence fills the air. I can't stop crying, blinking as fast as I can, my lips trembling.

He claims, "Blakely, we have to get past this. I love you. You're the only thing in this world I love."

Every word cuts me deeper. I clasp his cheeks. "If that's true—"

"It is! Don't you dare doubt my love for you!" he exclaims.

I sniffle a few times, choking out, "That's the worst part about it, Riggs. I won't ever understand how you can claim to love me but still did what you've done."

Agony fills his expression. A desperation I've never seen on him blooms to life. His voice cracks, and he says, "We have to get past this."

As much as I want to forget about everything, I can't. I sit up in bed and find my strength, announcing, "You have to go. Do not come back unless I tell you to."

"Don't say—"

"Now!" I scream, unable to control all the rage and sadness I feel.

"Pet—"

"You've destroyed us! You don't get to do that and slide back into bed with me. Now, get out! And I swear to God, Riggs, if you don't respect my wishes and give me the time I need, I will get an attorney," I threaten, hating every part of it.

He pins his eyes on me, and the blood pounding between my ears grows louder. Time stands still with neither of us moving.

He finally rises, leans over me, and kisses my forehead. With his lips brushing against my skin, he murmurs, "I love you. No matter what I've done, do *not* question it." He slowly leaves the room, closing the door behind him.

It only takes a few seconds before I miss him. I hold myself back from running after him, more confused than ever about how to get past this or if I should even try. The only thing I'm clear about is even after what he's done, I still love Riggs.

What scares me the most is I'm unsure how I'll ever be able to stop.

4

Riggs
A Week Later

Blakely refuses to speak to me. Whenever I try to call or message her, she ignores my efforts. Sometimes she'll reply with, *"I'm not ready to talk to you."*

I know her schedule. My drivers inform me of her every move, and I watch her from afar. Her single hit number one, and I've never been so proud of anybody in my life.

I've sent her flowers. I've texted her and left her voice messages about how excited and how proud of her I am. But she hasn't responded.

Each day that passes tests my willpower to respect her wishes and not storm into Apartment Thirteen. And this morning, I woke up and saw on the internet that she's opening for Colton Linwood.

He's a well-established musician with several songs charting right now. She's flying to Detroit tomorrow night, yet no one told me, which means Noah removed me from receiving notifications on her schedule.

Nothing burns me more.

I drive to the studio and wait for Blakely to arrive. It takes everything I have to stay in my car. I've not gone near her except for that first night at Apartment Thirteen. Her threat of divorce is enough to hold me back. So I've only watched her from afar.

Noah arrives, and I curl my fists. I wait ten minutes, then text Ears.

> Me: I'm coming inside. We've got business matters to discuss regarding security for Blakely. And don't argue. You know I'm to approve all of it, and that's not changed, no matter what Noah's telling you.

A moment passes, and Ears steps out of the building. I exit my vehicle. He crosses his arms, his expression warning me there better not be any trouble, then nods for me to follow him inside.

He leads me past security, going directly to his office, then says as a reminder, "You better stay calm. I don't need a fistfight going down in my office. Understand?"

"There wouldn't be a fight. I'd tear that pussy's head off, and you know it."

His eyes turn to slits, and he barks, "That attitude isn't going to help Blakely. Is that what you want?"

I sigh and run my hands through my hair. "No, of course not."

"Then are we clear?"

I grunt. "I'm clear."

He assesses me momentarily, then asserts, "You stay here, and I'll go get Noah." He leaves the room.

I fight my demons not to break down the recording room door. I want to see my pet and pull her into my arms. The longer we're apart, the more distraught I'm getting, the more desperation grows, and I don't know how I'll ever fix this.

I thought by now she'd at least talk to me. Every moment of silence kills me a little more.

Ears finally returns with Noah in tow. He's got a cocky look on his face, as if he's won something over on me.

I snap. "I'm going to be put back on the notifications for Blakely's schedule, and all security still goes through me. This hasn't changed."

Noah laughs. It's arrogant and haughty, and I want to slap the shit out of him. He declares, "You have no control over her anymore. Go home, Riggs. You're not welcome here."

I attempt to keep my cool, but I seethe, "So Blakely told you to take me off everything?"

The look in his eyes tells me that she didn't. But he claims, "Yeah, she's aware. She wants nothing to do with you. Now get the hell out of my face."

My heart pounds harder. I clench my fists at my side and call his bluff. "Bullshit."

"She doesn't want anything to do with you, so deal with it." Noah smirks.

Fuck this.

I rush at him, and he steps back, flinching. I bypass him and tear down the hallway toward the recording studio.

Ears calls out, "Riggs! Get back here!"

I ignore him and bust through the door into the small recording box.

Blakely's eyes widen. She stops playing the piano and removes her headphones, rising off the piano bench. "Riggs. What are you doing here?"

I grab her around the waist and start leading her out of the room.

"Riggs," she protests, but it's not very strong.

Noah demands, "Get your hands off her!"

I tug Blakely closer, threatening, "Don't you dare get between my wife and me."

Noah glances at Blakely. "Tell him to release you. He doesn't have any power over you."

"Do not order my wife around," I threaten, stepping closer to her.

Noah's voice becomes sterner. He steps closer to me, keeps his gaze on her, and states, "Blakely, you don't have to let him manhandle you."

Every ounce of anger I have spins out of control. The feeling I have when I do severe damage to people cyclones through me. I push Blakely behind me to protect her, then shove Noah against the wall. I grasp him around the neck, squeezing so he can't breathe.

His eyes bulge. His arms begin to flail.

Blakely screams.

It only makes me tighten my hold on him. I lift up so he's on his toes, then growl out, "I've warned you to stay out of my wife's and my business."

"Riggs. Don't. You're going to kill him!" Blakely claims.

Ears demands, "That's enough, Riggs!" He grabs me by the shirt and tries to pull me back.

It's pointless. I have too much adrenaline moving through me. My grip on Noah's throat tightens, and the anger festering inside me won't allow me to release him.

I stay planted, scowling at him, squeezing him harder so his cheeks turn red, snarling, "You will not remove me from my wife's schedule. You will not take her security into your own hands. Do you understand me?"

Ears asserts, "Riggs, let him go!" He grabs my shoulder and yanks me back with enough force to make me release Noah.

He begins to sputter, grabbing his neck and clutching his stomach while bending over to find air.

"This has gone too far," Ears states angrily.

I try to lunge at Noah again, but Ears pulls me back. I threaten, "Are we clear who runs my wife's security?"

Noah straightens to his full height, getting another set of balls. He declares, "You aren't coming near her, nor are you involved any longer in her career. Now, get out."

More rage ignites inside me. I don't know who this guy thinks he is. Ears owns the studio, not him. And there's no way I'll ever allow him to make all the moves in Blakely's career, especially about her security.

THE VOW

I take a deep breath, trying to control my demons, wishing I wasn't shaking inside so hard. I turn to Blakely. "Did you tell Noah to remove me from your schedule?"

She opens her mouth, glancing between us, then stares at me.

I attempt to soften my tone, but it's useless. I push in a harsh tone, "Well?"

She shakes her head. Hope and relief grow inside me.

Thank God she didn't authorize Noah to remove me.

She still wants me to be part of her life. I know she does. She still loves me even if she's not talking to me right now. Surely, our love is strong enough to get through this.

I curse myself again for what I did, but I can't worry about that right now. I ask her, "And what about your security, pet? Did you tell him not to trust me regarding those details?"

She glances between us again, then softly answers, "No. I didn't give him any instructions about my security or your involvement."

I continue, "So you had no idea?"

She shakes her head. I release an anxious breath, then turn to Noah. I warn, "Do not ever make decisions for my wife again that aren't yours to make, or I *will* kill you."

I reach for Blakely's waist and lead her out of the room.

She once again protests, this time stronger than before. "Riggs!"

Ears shouts, "Riggs, get back here."

I ignore all of them. I guide her into Ears's office, then lock the door. I step in front of it so she can't leave, and assert, "You can be pissed at me for as long as you want, but no one will handle your security but me. Are we clear?"

She stares at me, her lips quivering, and I hate myself for the look on her face. I know I've hurt her beyond the point I ever thought I could. I can see the pain and fear. And time hasn't healed anything. She looks just as upset as she did a week ago when I saw her at Apartment Thirteen.

My heart thumps hard against my chest cavity. I want to clutch it, but I'm trying not to appear weak. I need her to know that I'm still the strong man she fell in love with and nothing has changed. I try to calm my voice. I declare, "Noah will never protect you the way I can. There's going to be a lot of people who want you. Your single's number one. Your career is just getting started. You have to have good security. No, scratch that. You have to have the best security. And I'm the one who can provide the best. You know this, pet."

She blinks hard, her eyes filling with water.

I step forward, sliding my palms on her cheeks, admitting, "I've never fucked up so badly. I know I hurt you, and I'm sorry. I promise you I'll never do anything like that again. I will *never* break your trust again."

A tear slides down her cheek, rolling between my fingers. Her lips quiver harder, her voice cracking when she says, "I don't know how I could ever trust you again, Riggs."

Everything inside me breaks into pieces. "Don't say that."

"It's true," she claims.

In a desperate voice, I beg, "I need you to forgive me, pet. Please."

More tears fall, and she shakes her head, whispering, "I can't right now. I want to, but I can't."

My core shatters. My heart hurts more than I ever thought it could. I add, "What do I need to do? I've stayed away. I've—"

"You call this staying away? You almost killed Noah," she cries out.

The sound of his name on her lips angers me further. "He's lucky I didn't kill him after what he's done."

"You can't just rush in here and do that," she claims.

I try to stay calm, but it's hard. I'm doing a horrible job at it. I grit my teeth, claiming, "He took me off your schedule. He eliminated me from your security. He did this without your permission. Why are you sticking up for him?" The thought that maybe something has happened between them goes through my mind, and my chest tightens.

She squeezes her eyes shut, taking long breaths.

"Tell me you're not with him." I bite out the words.

Her eyes fly open. "Why would you say that?"

Relief fills me. "I'm sorry. I just—"

"You don't have a right to accuse me of things after what you've done. I'm not the one who screwed us up," she reminds me.

I hold my hands in the air. "I know."

She turns away.

"Look at me," I demand.

She obeys, making the ache in me grow. It's a reminder of everything we have, everything I've lost, and everything I need again. Moments pass between us. I finally question, "What did you tell me you wanted for your career? When we went through all those negotiations, what did you tell me was most important?"

More silence fills the room.

"Pet, tell me the most important thing."

She sighs and replies, "Control over my music."

"Yes. And what did you tell me you wanted me, not Noah, to handle?" I push.

She lifts her chin.

"Answer me. What did you want me to handle?" I insist.

She swallows hard. "Security."

"And why?"

She tries to look away again.

I turn her chin so she can't escape me. "Pet, this is important. No matter what's happened between us. Tell me why you wanted me to handle your security."

She sniffles and takes a few shallow breaths, admitting, "Because you'll always protect me more than anyone."

"Has that changed?" I question, the fear in me rising again.

She scrunches her face as if in pain, confessing, "You didn't protect me against my father. You promised me you always would, and you didn't. You threw me in the lion's den."

So much disappointment in myself reignites. I hate myself for what I've done. But I reply, "Did I hand you over to him? Or at any time did I tell him where you were?"

She cries out, "That doesn't make it right, Riggs. What you did... How could you?"

I've asked myself over and over how I could have been so stupid to make the biggest mistake of my life. But I don't have any answers besides revenge. And nothing I can say will resolve my errors. So I answer, "No, it doesn't make it right. But somehow, I *will* make this up to you. I promise you I will."

She gives me a look like she doesn't believe me.

Focus on what's important at this moment.

"Do you think what I did means I would ever drop the ball on your security? That I would ever let anybody come near you to harm you?"

She closes her eyes for what feels like forever. I do my best to be patient, but I can't help myself and murmur, "Pet, it's Noah or me. Who do you believe will go to the ends of the earth to protect you?" But I'm afraid of what she might answer, and I've never felt so unsure about anything.

She slowly opens her eyes and admits, "You would protect me more."

Relief fills me. Still, I stay cautious, knowing I'm not out of the doghouse and have a long way to go. I reach for her cheek again, caressing it with my thumb. "That's right, pet. And are you okay with Noah eliminating me from your security or your schedule without discussing it with you?"

She takes another deep breath, then shakes her head. "No, I'm not okay with that."

More relief grows inside me. I continue, treading lightly. "Then give me your permission to continue playing the role you wanted me to—to ensure that you're safe at all times." More silence fills the air, and I begin to panic again. I blurt out, "Pet—"

"I'll allow it for now, Riggs," she interjects.

My pulse skyrockets. I bark, "For now? What does that mean?"

Tension explodes all around us. Her expression only gets firmer, more steadfast in whatever she's trying to express in this statement of hers.

She squares her shoulders and steps back, answering, "It means I hold the cards, not you. If I decide to change things in the future, you have to promise me that you'll respect it and go quietly."

Go quietly?

Every part of that statement, I hate. My insecurity gets the best of me. I blurt out, "We have to get past this, pet."

Pain fills her expression with agony twisting all around her beautiful features. Yet what scares me the most is her voice growing firmer. "Promise me you'll respect my wishes, Riggs. If you can't, I'll tell Ears to kick you out for good and ask Noah to take over."

It's a kick to my gut. The thought of her choosing Noah over me for anything makes me feel ill. And her expression screams that she's not bluffing. So I finally cave. "Okay. I promise."

Over my dead body.

She swallows hard and nods. "Thank you for agreeing."

I hesitate, then reach for her, tugging her back into me. I press my lips to hers before she can escape. She pushes on my chest, but it doesn't last long. After a few seconds, she slides her hands through my hair and returns my affection.

For a split second, everything feels right between us. I murmur, "I regret every moment of our time together when I wouldn't allow you to kiss me. And every moment that I wanted to kiss you but didn't."

She freezes, then retreats. "We shouldn't be doing this."

"Why? You're my wife," I remind her.

She pushes my chest. "This doesn't solve our issues, Riggs. You can be involved in my security, but that's it. I'm not going to promise you anything regarding the future."

It destroys the spark of hope that just ignited within me.

She continues staring at me, then demands, "Release me now."

"I can't. No matter what you think, I love you and always will. So I can't just release you."

To my surprise, a tiny smile plays on her lips. "If you don't release me, I can't tell Noah to add you back to my schedule and that you're in charge of my security and not him."

It's possibly the only thing she could say to make me contemplate releasing her. To my surprise, I chuckle, muttering, "And you claim I'm the evil one."

She bats her eyes, making my dick hard. I haven't seen her do that in over a week, and I've missed it. She declares, "I'm only giving you what you want."

"I want you back home with me," I proclaim.

Her face falls. She closes her eyes, whispering, "I can't. Don't make this harder for me."

I debate with myself, not wanting to let her go, but I finally remove my arms from around her. The emptiness resumes. I force myself to open the door and motion for her to step through.

She goes down the hall, and I follow her into the recording box. As soon as we step inside, the room turns silent. The musicians, tech people, Noah, and Ears turn toward us.

Noah rises, stepping toward Blakely. He grabs her hand. "Are you okay?"

I push him away. "Do not touch my wife."

Ears steps between us. "Riggs, settle down."

I step back and hold my hands in the air. "That's fine, for now. But he's not to touch my wife. Nothing has changed. Or I'll invoke the clause in his contract."

Blakely tilts her head. "What clause?"

I keep my gaze pinned on Noah, admitting, "The clause so you can get a new agent."

"Riggs, I don't need a new agent. Will you be able to control yourself in this situation, or do I have to make a different decision?"

I want to kill Noah and wipe the cocky look off his face. All it would take is one of my fists connecting with his haughty expression.

She asserts, "Look at me, Riggs."

I slowly obey.

She arches her eyebrows. "Well?"

I swallow my pride, then nod.

Blakely assesses me another moment, then in a firm voice, informs Noah, "You're to add Riggs back to my schedule."

His face drops. "Why? Why would you want him on your schedule?"

She lifts her chin higher. "And he'll remain in charge of my security until I say otherwise. Is that clear, Noah?"

His head jerks backward. "Blakely, you don't have to let him pressure you."

Anger festers in her voice, but so does confidence. Pride gushes within me. She adds, "Don't ever pull any crap like this again, Noah. If you're going to make major decisions for me, you have to talk to me. It's clear in my contract, and we've had multiple conversations about this."

He clenches his jaw, not saying anything.

"Well, answer her," I prod.

Blakely shakes her head at me in disappointment. My gut drops. She turns toward Ears. "Can you escort my husband out of the building, please? I have work to do, and I think we've held everyone up long enough."

5

Blakely
The Next Day

*E*ven though a lot's been happening that I'm sad about, excitement runs through me. Tonight's the concert in Detroit. It's a pretty big deal. I was shocked when Noah told me that I was going to be the opening act for Colton Linwood.

I'm almost to the airport when my phone rings. I glance down, and my heartbeat increases.

How did she get my number?

It's my mother's number. It rings and rings and rings, and I finally answer it. "Mom?"

She slurs, "Blakely, I'm so glad you answered."

"How did you get my number?" I ask, my insides quivering.

She ignores my question, her voice cracking and barely audible from whatever she's on when she says, "Come home, baby. I need you to come home."

I cringe. Nothing has changed. She's still an addict. I almost hang up, but then the memory of her and how she looked when I saw her at the charity event fills my mind. It's the worst I've ever seen her, and that's a hard statement to swallow.

She repeats, "Please, baby, come home."

I firmly state, "Mom, I'm not coming home."

"Don't say that," she demands.

I question, "Where are you?"

Please be somewhere safe.

Riggs destroyed my parents. He said there was nothing left. Is she still at my old house?

Her voice turns angry, and I cringe. This always happens when she's not sober. She displays every emotion possible and rotates between them. She snarls, "What did I ever do to you?"

Anger fills me. How would I even begin to answer that? She was never there for me. Her drugs and alcohol were always more important, along with her men, just like my father's business and ego were always more important to him. Yet she's still my mother. So I struggle with what to say.

Her tone flips to desperation. "Please, baby, I want to see you. Just say yes, and we can talk...just like the old times."

My hand taps against my leg, and I look down. Riggs used to hold it, and ever since he came into my life, I've become more conscious of how I do this when I'm nervous. Something about Riggs's hand over mine always calmed me, but right now, I stare at it, watching my fingers graze my thigh, the deep ache I've felt all my life resurfacing.

All I ever desired was to have a real mom instead of a selfish, addicted one. But I got what I got, and nothing will change my family dynamics.

She asserts, "Blakely, you owe it to me to see me."

"I owe you nothing," I say, then close my eyes, leaning against the headrest.

Don't let her guilt you.

She's a mess. I should help her get better.

There's no helping her. Don't get sucked in again.

"Please, baby!" she begs.

"I can't," I murmur.

Her voice softens, and more desperation fills it, igniting another wave of guilt. "Please, Blakely, I need to talk to you. There's so much going on. I'm going to completely lose it."

The thought of my mom losing it more than when I saw how skinny she was and how she already looked like she was on death's door only scares me further.

She's my mom, no matter what.

I cave. "Fine. We can meet for coffee. But, Mom, you have to be sober. If you're not sober, I'm leaving."

"I'm always—"

"Don't lie to me, Mom. I don't want to hear your lies about not drinking or taking more of your pills," I warn.

Silence fills the line. The car stops. I glance out the window at the big jet on the runway. My heart beats way too fast, and I put my hand over it, trying to stop the pain shooting through it. I finally tell my mother, "I have to go."

"Wait!" she cries out.

I freeze, taking deep breaths.

"Let's meet tonight," she suggests. "We can go to dinner at that place you love. You know, the one with the balloon animals."

I squeeze my eyes again. A mother should know that her grown daughter no longer cares about balloon animals. But it stings worse that she doesn't know her daughter's about to sing at a major concert. Then again, my parents don't know anything about my career. Even though my single just hit number one, and they should, they're clueless. And my mother is obviously still in her own world.

She coos, "Please, sweetie."

I admit, "I can't tonight, Mom."

"Then when?" she questions.

I go through my calendar in my head, then offer, "Saturday morning. We can meet for coffee. I'll text you later the time and place."

"But—"

"That's what I can do, Mom. Take it or leave it," I threaten.

She sniffles and then agrees. "Okay, great. Thank you."

"I mean it, Mom. I'm leaving if you aren't sober when you show up." I hang up the phone, fighting my tears before she can start arguing with me again, which my mother always does. She always claims she's sober, even when she can barely walk. And I

61

hope she'll figure out how to get clean for a few hours to meet me, but I'm not getting my hopes up.

It takes a while to feel calm, and I finally program my mom's name into the phone. Then I straighten my shoulders and knock on the window. It's another security feature that Riggs created for me. The driver will never open the door unless I knock on it, which gives them permission. I thought Riggs was being silly at first, but now I'm grateful for it.

The door opens, and my pulse skyrockets. The wind gusts, and the familiar woody spice laced with orange peels scent flows into the SUV. Riggs's big frame looms in the door's opening, and he looks as handsome as ever. His disheveled blond surfer hair and the smile on his lips make my blood heat.

He's not supposed to be here.

I curse myself for reacting to him and accuse, "What are you doing here?"

He cockily states, "I'm in charge of your security."

"But why are *you* here?" I question again.

Why did I ever think that he would stay away if he's in charge of my security?

Of course he's not going to let other people manage things.

He reaches for me, and I automatically take his hand. I hate that about myself. I obey him like a puppet, but my body doesn't want to fight him. He helps me out of the car and answers, "Because I'm in charge."

I declare, "You can't come to every gig. You have a business to run. You should trust the guys you hire."

He grunts. "I trust no one with you, and you should realize this by now. And don't worry about my work. I have everything under control."

"Of course you do. You're a control freak," I mumble.

He leans close to my ear. "The last time I checked, you appreciated the fact I was one. Especially when you're kneeling, waiting for my commands. And my bet is that you're missing it as much as I am."

I ignore the butterflies in my stomach. I can't deny the craving I have to fully submit to him. But I'm not telling him that, so I snap, "Don't make me regret allowing you to oversee this."

He slides his hand around my waist, and I want to sink into his body. I try not to, which only makes it awkward. He tugs me closer, and I give in, melting against him. He questions, "Why would you regret it? I'm doing my job."

I mutter, "No, you're inserting yourself into my life." I glance up at him.

Hurt fills his expression. He sniffs hard, pinning his gaze on mine, making me feel bad for my words. Then he insists, "I'm doing my job, pet."

"Are you?" I challenge.

Tense silence fills the cold air that whips between us. My eyes water from it.

He tugs my hair, then leans in so his mouth is an inch from my lips, pinning his blues on mine. I inhale sharply, squeezing my legs together. His eyes turn darker, and he claims, "I won't lie, pet. While it's true I'm doing my job, I'm not unhappy I get to spend time with you." He grasps my ass and presses me against him.

My insides turn to hot lava. His erection grows, and the reminder of what it's like to be his intensifies. My lips quiver, and everything seems to disappear.

Another cold burst of wind whips at my face. He pecks me on the lips and asserts, "We have to go so you aren't late. But we're celebrating tonight after your concert, pet."

I inhale sharply and start to shake my head, but he tightens his palm on the back of my head so I can't move. Everything inside me lights up, and I feel alive for the first time in days. I curse myself for not knowing how to eliminate my desire for him, especially when he touches me.

His lips twitch, and his eyes erupt in blue flames. His voice lowers. "If I have to remind you why you took a vow to be my wife, then I will."

I'm unsure if I should take his words as a threat or a gift, but a shiver runs down my spine.

He sees the effect he has on me, smirks, then spins, guiding me toward the plane.

I don't have any more energy to fight. I've been fighting my whole life with my parents and now Riggs. So I don't respond, climb the steps, then enter the plane.

The flight attendant, Chrissy, appears, beaming. "Hello, Mrs. Madden. Congratulations on your song hitting number one! I'm so happy for you. Can I get you something to drink?"

The sound of my married name makes my heart soar and hurt simultaneously. I want to resume the life Riggs and I had more than anything, yet I can't seem to get past his betrayal. I swallow the lump in my throat, force a smile, and reply, "Thank you. I'm okay right now." I walk past her and then freeze.

Noah rises from his seat. He motions to the spot next to him, ordering, "Sit, Blakely."

"My wife's sitting with me," Riggs's deep voice booms behind me.

I cringe.

Noah claims, "We have work to do."

"She needs to rest before tonight," Riggs counters.

Noah opens his mouth, and I hold up my hand, crying out, "Enough! You two argue without me." I go into the bedroom and shut the door, sick of the power play that always ensues whenever Riggs and Noah are in the same room.

My phone vibrates. I glance at the screen and wince. It's another text from my mother.

> Mom: I can't wait to see you.

The cell buzzes again, and I stare at the screen.

> Mom: What if we go to the country club for brunch? There are so many people there who'd love to see you! We could get you on the committee for the Christmas Ball.

> Mom: We could go shopping after. I'll buy you something new.

> Mom: I have someone I want you to meet. Don't tell your father.

> Mom: Should I book a spa day for us?

Her texts infuriate me. I should have known nothing would have changed. It's so typical of my mother. Get wasted, then send me messages about whatever new boyfriend she has, not listen to a word I say about what my boundaries are, and try to insert me into the life I never wanted to live.

I don't know why I agreed to meet with her. No matter what I say, she's always going to be intoxicated. I gave up years ago trying to save her, but the little girl in me still wishes I could.

Years ago, I attended Al-Anon meetings. The meetings are like Alcoholics Anonymous for family members of people who suffer from addiction. After the last time I ran away from my parents and cut off all contact with them, I stopped attending the meetings. But I remind myself of what I learned from years of weekly sessions.

I must set my boundaries, be clear about them, and stick with them.

I cannot enable my mother to manipulate me.

It's up to my mom to change. I cannot change her.

I send one text.

> Me: The only thing I agreed to is coffee on Saturday at the place I choose.

I turn off the phone to avoid further messages, knowing how my mother is once she gets an obsession in her head. In some ways, she's just as bad as Riggs. I'm sure I'll wake up to a hundred different text messages, and every one will annoy me.

Exhaustion suddenly hits me. I crawl under the covers, curling up into a ball. It doesn't take long before I fall asleep, but my dreams haunt me.

I'm back in my parents' home. I'm a little girl, maybe ten, and I'm shaking my mother and screaming for her to wake up. She finally sputters a few times, her eyelids opening and shutting.

My father's voice states in an annoyed tone, "It's just another one of her episodes where she took too many pills."

I'm hugging my mother and sobbing against her when I hear Riggs repeating, "Pet. Wake up."

His warm hand strokes my cheek. He murmurs, "It's time to get up." His lips graze my forehead.

I turn toward him, forgetting for a moment he hurt me and we're at odds.

He tightens his arms around me and quietly asks, "Pet, you okay?"

I take a moment, then remember things aren't okay between us. I slowly retreat.

He smiles, but concern tightens his features. It's the Riggs I know, the one I thought would never hurt me, the one I believed in more than life itself.

My pulse quickens.

Why did he have to do what he did?

I slowly sit up.

Pride fills his expression. He asks, "Are you ready for your big night?"

Nerves replace some of the sadness I feel. "What if I mess up?"

His face falls. He furrows his eyebrows, declaring, "You won't. They're going to love you. Hell, they already love you. You're number one."

I glance out the window and try to squash the growing anxiety, admitting, "This is big. I've never had such a big opportunity. Colton Linwood isn't just some singer. He's the real deal."

"So are you."

"Not like him."

"Bullshit," Riggs states.

I glance out the window at the runway. A black SUV is waiting, and snow lightly falls.

Riggs restates, "Pet, you're going to be amazing."

I force a smile and move toward the door, but he steps in front of me.

He tilts my chin and locks his eyes with mine. In a stern voice, he asserts, "I mean it. There's nothing to worry about. You're going to be amazing on that stage."

The storm inside me calms a bit. His no-nonsense confidence is everything I love about him. And at this moment, I'm grateful he's here.

Without thinking about the consequences, I admit, "I'm glad you're still in charge of things for me. I can't imagine doing this without you here." Then my cheeks heat, and I blink hard when tears threaten to spill down my cheeks.

Riggs's lips softly curve. He claims, "I would never miss your big night."

I can't blink hard enough to stop the tears from escaping my eyes. I ask, "Why did you do it?"

His face falls.

I take an emotion-filled breath, then question, "How could you send anyone, especially my father, those images and messages about me?"

His chest rises and falls slowly, and he never takes his sad gaze off mine.

His silence both pains and infuriates me. "Tell me!" I demand.

He finally answers. "I wanted to destroy him. I told you that I wanted to destroy him. What he did was unforgivable. He needed to be destroyed in all ways. But it was never my intention that you would find out."

Rage fills me. "So that would make it okay? If you sent all those messages and I never found out, that would make it okay?" I accuse.

"Why would it matter if you didn't know? Your father would be destroyed, and we'd still be happy," he declares.

My stomach pitches. I hold it and seethe, "You aren't sorry for anything. Are you?"

He wrinkles his forehead. "What are you talking about? Of course I'm sorry. I've told you a million times I'm sorry."

I push past him. "Stay away from me, Riggs." I storm through the plane, ignore Noah, and step in front of the doorway. The snowy, cold air hits my face.

Riggs barks, "She needs a coat, Noah!"

"Then why don't you give her one?" he replies.

I spin, tired of it all. "Shut up, both of you! Do your jobs and just shut up!" They freeze, leering at each other.

I climb down the stairs, go straight to the SUV without acknowledging the driver, and climb in. I stare out the window, unsure if I'm more pissed or sad that Riggs hasn't learned one thing.

He never will.

Why am I holding out hope?

Noah and Riggs get inside, but I don't speak, and neither do they. The drive to the arena feels like it takes forever. I keep my focus on the window, but a blanket of white snow is all I can see.

The others stay silent, doing nothing to cut the tension. The entire way, I try to convince myself that it's best to let Riggs go. I try to figure out how, but it's impossible. I know I need to, but I still don't know how.

6

Riggs

Twenty-five-year-old Colton Linwood, has everything that makes pop stars famous. His tall frame is slightly muscular but not too over the top. His thick, dark hair has a tiny wave, with locks curling on the sides close to his blue eyes. He's constantly pushing them back, but they always return. The white T-shirt he wears stretches in perfection across his chest, as do his designer jeans over his thighs. He's talking quietly to a few sound techs.

Blakely freezes, staring at him.

He spins and pins his gaze on her, his face lighting up. He gushes, "Well, if it isn't Blakely Fox in the flesh!"

His enthusiasm for my pet puts me on high alert. It doesn't help when he leaps across the room and gives her a hug so big that her feet come off the ground.

She laughs, and he puts her down and stares at her. She says, "Thanks for the warm welcome. It's nice to meet you."

"I'm a huge fan. In fact, I'm totally fangirling," he claims.

A flush fills her cheeks. "Really?"

He belts out a line to her number one song, "Invisibly Broken." *"If you loved me, you'd see what you're doing to me."*

Blakely gapes at him. "You aren't joking?"

He scoffs. "Hell no! You've got talent, girl!"

"Thank you! That's... That's huge coming from you. I'm a big fan of your music as well," she claims.

His grin grows. He leans closer to her, and I clench my fists. He suggests, "Enough that you want to mix it up and do one of your songs and one of my songs together tonight?"

She opens her mouth, then catches herself. "Seriously?"

He chuckles, then his expression turns serious. He holds his hand in the air, stating, "Scout's honor."

She nods. "Yes! Of course! That would be incredible!"

"Awesome. We've got a lot of work to do, then," he declares, then turns and says, "Noah. Good to see you. And you must be the famous entrepreneur husband?"

My stomach flips. I'm not a moron. I realize this will be huge exposure for Blakely, but the instant connection they seem to have made puts me on edge. I hold out my hand and firmly state, "Yes. I am. Riggs Madden."

He takes my hand, and I squeeze it firmer than normal. He winces, then looks back at Blakely. "Seems like your hubby doesn't understand some things."

I don't lighten my grip. I snap, "Yeah? What's that?"

He demands, "Don't break my hand. I play the guitar. Time to release me."

I wait another moment, and Blakely orders, "Riggs!"

I unclasp my hand and stare him down.

Amusement fills his features. He puts his hand on my back and invades my personal space. He licks his lips, and his eyes drift down my body, then relock on mine. His lips twitch as he declares, "Nothing to be jealous over, Daddy. You're more my type than your wife is. I only admire her musical talents." He glances behind him. "Sorry, doll. But your hubby is pretty sexy with his older-man vibes. I see why you snatched him up."

Blakely puts her hand over her mouth, stifling a laugh.

I know more about Colton than I let on. He's a regular at Club Indulgence, but he frequents area three, which is where anything goes. I assume he's bi-sexual, based on rumors within the club and what facts are public knowledge. So I question, "Aren't you dating Sarah Stenmore?"

Colton smirks. "Of course I am. It's better publicity than being a gay pop artist. Right, Noah?" Colton's expression turns sour.

Noah flinches but catches himself, pointing out, "You're still selling out stadiums, right?"

Colton scowls, keeping it aimed at Noah, and I realize he doesn't like Noah any more than I do. He claims, "I told you I'd be okay having a smaller fan base if it meant living my life freely."

Blakely gives me an uncomfortable look.

Noah shifts on his feet, proving further to me that he's a coward. He replies, "People say that, but they never mean it."

"All you care about is money," Colton accuses.

Noah groans. "Not this again. Do I have to remind you about the life of luxury you've grown accustomed to?"

More hatred fills Colton's expression. He tears his glare off Noah and turns to Blakely, asking, "He make you do anything you don't want to yet?"

Her eyes widen. "No."

Colton nods. "I hope it stays that way."

"Don't be so dramatic," Noah orders.

"Maybe you should get in the current century," Colton declares.

Noah scoffs. "You're lucky you have me to guide you. No way you'd be topping the charts if you didn't have the publicity you do."

Red fills Colton's cheeks. He snottily asks, "Should I thank you for allowing me to make music with Blakely?"

Noah's lips curve. He replies, "I don't know. Should I think about it for a while?"

Colton huffs and says, "Riggs, I'm stealing your wife. You're welcome to join us if you want."

I realize I have nothing to worry about with Colton and that I actually like him. It's clear to me he didn't negotiate some of the clauses I did for Blakely's contract. And I feel sorry for him. Being under Noah's thumb must be hard. Also, it's good for Blakely to have a friend in the business. I open my mouth, but before I can answer, she says, "No. He has stuff to do. Don't you,

Riggs?" She gives me a challenging stare, and something tells me not to fight her on this.

I step forward, kiss her on the forehead, and add, "Have fun." I turn to Colton and say, "If you ever want me to review your contract with Noah, let me know."

Noah seethes, "Shut up, Riggs."

I ignore him and add, "You never know. There might be some things you didn't understand that work in your favor."

Colton nods. "Thank you." He glances at Noah and states, "I might just do that."

Noah's eyes turn to slits.

I step back, relieved he won't be hitting on my wife. At least there's one person around here I don't have to worry about crossing the line.

Colton turns to Blakely, slides his arm through hers, and declares, "We've got six hours to figure this out. Let me show you to my dressing room."

They leave, and Noah snaps, "Don't ever talk to my clients again."

I spin, challenging, "Or what?"

Noah clenches his jaw.

I step closer, and he flinches. I stop an arm's length in front of him and assert, "I'm going to do my job. You go do yours." I push past him and walk over to the security team.

"Benny, do you have a full assessment of the place?" I question. He's been my go-to for years. He made a name for himself by handling some of L.A.'s biggest events with high-profile people. There's no one else I'd trust to protect Blakely in this situation.

He turns his large body away from his group of men and gives me an annoyed look, replying, "Don't insult me, Riggs."

"Good man," I say and slap hands with him.

He orders his men, "Double-check your areas and report back."

They scatter in different directions, and he points to the upper left corner of the arena, stating, "The biggest threat lies there."

"Why?" I question. The thought of anyone getting close to Blakely while on stage makes the hairs on my arms rise.

"Let's go over there and I can show you," he answers.

I follow him to the corner. It's not too far from the stage and has several exit doors. "What am I looking at?"

Benny states, "There are several blind spots with the video footage. Anyone who breaches this line of security can slip through those doors."

"Which lead where?" I ask, feeling uneasy.

He motions to the door on the left. "That one goes directly outside. The middle leads to the main lobby, and the right is another backstage entrance."

My skin crawls as I stare at the doors, then say, "There's no way someone's luring her offstage, so the true threat lies in someone getting backstage, correct?"

Benny nods. "Exactly. We'll have it roped off with a wall of my men so no one breaches it. But if there are any unexpected issues with the crowd, like if they all decide to push forward, I can't guarantee no one will cross over. It would be easy to dash to the door."

"Lock it," I order.

"We can't. According to the arena, it's a fire hazard."

"Fuck the rules," I declare.

He groans. "You can't go against the fire code, Riggs. The entire concert will get shut down."

My chest tightens at the thought of anyone coming close to Blakely while she's on stage. I scrub my face, then order, "Put more men on it."

He shakes his head. "The dimensions you sent over for the arena don't match. If I move anyone, it'll create another threat."

I jerk my head back. "What do you mean the dimensions are wrong?"

Benny crosses his arms. "I don't know where you got those plans, but they were from before the arena was renovated and doubled in size."

My gut drops, and anger sears through me. I mutter, "Fucking bastard."

"Sorry?" Benny asks.

I glance over at Noah, then shake my head. He sent me the floor plan. I tear my angry gaze off him and question, "So we don't have enough men?"

Benny responds, "You told me to double up, so we have enough, but it was based on the wrong measurements."

"Then you aren't doubled up?" I ask in frustration.

"No, but my guys got this. However, if someone breaches the line and gets backstage, there's no video footage for the first two hallways, where Blakely and Colton's dressing rooms are. We can't monitor it like the rest of the arena."

My pulse skyrockets. I seethe, "My wife is back there now with no security?"

He holds his hands in the air. "Calm down. Our guys are standing guard outside the door."

His answer does nothing to reduce my concern. I start moving toward the door that is the biggest threat.

Benny follows. "Riggs, she's fine."

"Get more surveillance up," I order.

"There's not enough time," he argues.

"Not enough time? You've got a little under six hours," I bark, flinging the door open.

"Everything has to be wired. The concrete is from the original structure. The internet signal isn't strong enough to support a wireless camera. We've already checked," he states.

"Then get it wired," I demand.

"The arena won't allow us. There are permits that have to be pulled and—"

"Fuck the permits," I interject, stopping in front of one of Benny's guys and demanding, "Is my wife in there?"

He nods. "Yes, sir."

I release an anxious breath, turn the doorknob, and open the door.

"Yo—" Blakely stops singing mid-word and arches her eyebrows. "Is something wrong?"

I step inside. "No. Just wanted to see if you or Colton needed anything."

He bats his eyelids at me. "Aww, isn't that sweet? Daddy, I like Blakely too much to steal you from her, but I'll take a clone of you."

"Enough with the Daddy," I order.

Blakely bites on her smile.

Colton smirks. "Sorry. Do you prefer, Sir?"

I scowl at him, not into his humor.

Blakely stifles a laugh, putting her hand over her mouth.

He glances at her, and his eyes light up. He gapes at me, then declares, "Oh, you *do* like to be called Sir." His head jerks back to Blakely. "Do you kneel too?"

A flush begins to crawl up her neck, and I bark, "That's enough, Colton. No more Daddy, Sir, or hitting on me. Got it?"

He holds his hands in the air. "Sorry. Just trying to have some fun."

"Find another way," I order.

"Yes... Sir," he replies, then winks.

I ignore him. "Blakely, do you need anything?"

Colton coos, "Aww. Such a sweet and doting husband."

Blakely's face turns stern. She replies, "No. I'm fine. If I need anything, I'll call you."

Shit. Now she's pissed at me again.

I stare at her for a few moments, and she doesn't flinch. The challenging expression I love and hate fills her features.

She asks, "Is there anything else? If not, Colton and I have a lot of work to do."

I walk over to her, kiss her on the forehead, then answer, "Nothing else. Have fun." I leave the room and return to going through security issues with Benny.

When we finish, I find Noah. He's flirting with one of the dancers, and I yank the back of his shirt.

"Whoa!" he cries out.

I spin him as the dancer's eyes widen. I inform her, "You're dismissed."

"Riggs, what the—"

"Did you even look at the arena plans you sent me?" I accuse.

He scrunches his forehead. "No. Why should I?"

I lean closer to his face. "You sent me old plans."

Confusion fills his face, as if he has no clue what I'm referring to or why I'm upset.

"They're from before they renovated," I bark.

"And?"

"And they're not accurate, dumbass!"

He furrows his eyebrows deeper. "We need to adjust, then. We have time."

Heat floods my blood. I clench my fist, accusing, "Are you a complete idiot? We're strapped thin on men and are missing surveillance equipment in certain areas. There's not enough time to solve those problems!"

"Calm down—"

"Don't you dare tell me to calm down! That's my wife on stage. And this is exactly why you aren't the right person to ever handle her security."

"Looks like you aren't either," he sneers.

I pull my arm back, but Benny grabs it and spins me, saying, "Whoa."

Noah retreats several feet away from me and out of my grasp. Not that I could get close to him since Benny's holding me back.

I seethe, "He's the one who sent the wrong arena plans."

Noah claims, "It was an honest mistake. I forwarded what the arena sent."

I glare at him. "You should have checked!"

"I should have? You're in charge of security," he points out.

My gut drops. He's right, but I snarl, "I'll never make the mistake of trusting you again."

"Riggs, let's go figure out our problem," Benny coaxes, steering me back to the corner of the arena.

"Should have let me hit him," I growl.

"So you get arrested and aren't here tonight? Sure. That would be a great idea." He shakes his head and points to the door. "This is what we have to focus on so your wife is safe."

He's right. I take several breaths and concentrate on the task, asking, "How are we securing this?"

Benny locks eyes with me. "The only way is to work with Colton's security team."

"You mean Noah's team? No way! You saw how he doesn't pay attention to detail!"

Benny nods. "Yeah, but it's the only way. It's too late to bring more of my guys in. Plus, I know the head of his team well. He runs a tight ship, just like I do."

"Who is it?"

"Kalim Voght."

"Never heard of him."

Benny shrugs. "So what? You know me, and I'm telling you, he's someone we can trust."

I stare at the door and try to figure out other options but nothing comes to my mind. I finally assert, "Then tell me about him."

"He's former military and Interpol. He's the best of the best. A few years ago, he parted ways with Interpol and returned stateside. His team members are all highly skilled and former military," Benny claims.

It sounds good, but I'm not trusting anyone until I meet them. My gut usually tells me everything. I ask, "Where is he?"

"Follow me," Benny replies and leads me to the back of the arena.

A well-built man with a shaved head gives orders to several other men. They all look at him respectfully, and it's clear he's in charge.

Benny introduces us. "Riggs Madden, Kalim Voght."

He tears his dark gaze off his men and pins it on me. He orders, "We'll finish this conversation later." He holds his hand out toward me.

I shake it, and his grip is as firm as mine, which I respect. He's a few inches taller than me, and everything about him gives me the impression he doesn't take anything lightly. It's another plus, in my opinion. I offer, "Nice to meet you."

He gets right to the point. "You too. I hear you have a few issues?"

"So I'm told. And my wife's going to be on that stage, so we need to eliminate them," I declare.

He nods. "Benny's filled me in. If we beef up security at the door and in front of the dressing rooms, it should take care of any breaches. I can also add a few monitoring devices."

My ears perk up. "How? Benny said the wireless signal is bad."

Kalim's eyes flicker with light. His lips twitch. "I have equipment that will work anywhere."

I arch my eyebrows. "Yeah? Where from?"

"That's classified," he replies and winks. He pulls a handful of devices, the size and shape of buttons, out of his pocket. "There's no problem with these. I've already tested them. We'll monitor the area and work together. And I can assure you my guys are equipped to handle anything that could occur."

Something about his confidence, demeanor, and ability to solve the issues Benny and I couldn't, calm me. My gut says to trust him, so I nod. "Then it's settled."

His eyes turn to slits. He adds, "There's only one thing."

My chest tightens. "What's that?"

He glances at Benny and then locks eyes with me. "I'm in charge. Both teams follow my lead at all times."

Benny stiffens next to me. I assess the situation and decide Kalim isn't one to back down. I turn to Benny. "Follow Kalim's orders."

Benny clenches his jaw, unhappy.

I don't care about his feelings or ego. Whatever it takes to keep my pet safe, I'm doing. To ensure he's on board, I ask, "You clear?"

He grinds his molars, then answers, "Yeah, Riggs. I'm clear."

"Good." I refocus on Kalim. "You take the lead, but if anything happens to my wife, it's your head on the platter." I leave before he can respond, feeling better about the situation but still not happy there even was one. I glance at Noah, vowing that one of these days, I'm taking him down.

He's put my wife's security at risk.

There are consequences and he's going to pay.

Blakely appears on stage with Colton, and they begin rehearsing one of his songs with the dancers.

The ache in my chest grows. It's been too long since I've had her. The need to see her kneel, waiting for my command, and listen to her begging me to let her come spirals within me.

I need to punish her for her recent defiance.

She's my wife. No matter what I've done, she made a promise to always be mine.

I pick up my phone and email my assistant.

> Connie,
> Make sure I have two adjacent suites. Have the hotel remove the doors between them. I don't care what it costs, but it's to be done immediately.
> Riggs

. . .

Tonight, I'm reminding my wife why she married me and who's in charge.

7

Blakely

Colton and I rehearse for an hour, then I go through my solo performance. After I finish, Noah claps and declares, "Nailed it!"

I admit, "I'm a bit nervous."

"Don't be. You're going to kill it," he praises.

I glance into the arena at the thousands of empty seats, imagining what it's like when it's full. My stomach flips again, and I put my hand over it.

Noah announces, "There's a few-hour window if you want to get some rest in your hotel room."

Before I can say anything, Riggs steers me out of the building and into an SUV. As soon as the door shuts, I accuse, "You could have let me decide to leave or stay."

He glances at his phone and swipes his finger over the screen. He replies, "You decided when you admitted you were nervous."

"What? That makes zero sense," I admit.

He leans over me and twirls a lock of hair around his finger. I inhale a lungful of his intoxicating aroma and try to stay annoyed, but it's hard. I clench my thighs together, and he slides his hand between them, cupping my pussy.

"Riggs," I warn, but my pulse races. It's been so long since he touched me.

He declares, "You seem to have forgotten I'm your husband."

"I'm fully aware," I state.

He grunts. The blues in his eyes remind me of the calm chaos of the waves and the yearning to return to the beach house and have everything be normal again resurfaces. He claims, "I don't think you are."

I tilt my head and glare at him.

He squeezes my pussy three times, and I inhale sharply. His voice lowers into the tone he uses when commanding me in bed, and everything inside me aches. He says, "It's been too long since you've submitted."

Heat fills my core. I pull at his hand, but he's got it firmly locked on me. "Remove your hand, Riggs."

"You know the safe word," he replies.

I tug at it again, squirming in the seat and hating how much I love the sensations filling my lower body.

He challenges again, "Say the safe word."

I've only said it once, and it wasn't during anything sexual. It was when I was leaving him the night I found out what he did. And maybe we're connected more than I want to admit because it's like he has ESP and knows I'm thinking about that moment.

"You said it before. Say it again," he half-seethes, half-smirks.

I blink hard, remembering how that night felt.

"Just say it, and I won't touch you ever again," Riggs calmly says, but it's a threat. He knows as much as I fight him to stay away, it's killing me.

I swallow hard, not taking my eyes off his, and wonder again how we got here.

The car stops, and the driver turns the engine off. Riggs slowly removes his hand, puts it under his nose, and inhales deeply. My heart races faster, and he leans into my ear, declaring, "My favorite memories include eating your pussy."

I close my eyes and try to maintain my breathing, but the needy ache I can't escape only intensifies.

To make things worse, Riggs adds, "I'm doing it tonight until you make that sound that I love."

I don't know what he means. He always says it, but I never know what he's referencing. Everything throbs at the thought of him bringing me to the place where I cry out whatever it is he wants me to, but I'm not ready to forgive him.

But I need to submit. It's killing me.

No, I don't.

Riggs studies me for a brief moment, then chuckles. He knocks on the window, and the door opens. A gust of wind blows snowflakes into the SUV, and he gets out and quickly escorts me into the hotel.

We go past the check-in desk, into the elevator, and to the level below the penthouse. When the doors open, I find my senses and say, "I'm not staying in your room."

Arrogance fills him. "I knew you'd say that. Don't worry, pet. You have your own space."

He guides me down the hall, pulls a key card out of his pocket, and unlocks the door.

"Where did you get that?" I ask.

Amusement fills his expression. "I have people. They brought it to the arena."

"Oh. Right."

He motions for me to go into the room.

I step inside the suite, then turn. "What room are you in?"

He shuts the door behind him and steers me around the room. "This is your suite. That's mine." He points to a doorway, but the doors have been removed.

I gape at him.

"You can have that one if you prefer," he states.

"Did you have the door removed?"

He smiles. "Do you have a problem with it?"

Anger sears through me. "Seriously, Riggs? What part about I'm not ready to forgive you do you not get?"

"I gave you tons of space," he claims.

"You removed the door!"

"So? You're my wife. Or have you forgotten?" he accuses.

I sarcastically laugh. "Like you would ever let me forget it."

He steps toward me, and I retreat until the backs of my knees hit the bed. I fall on my butt. He places his palms near my hips and seethes, "That's right. I won't. You took a vow for me, and I took one for you."

My pulse skyrockets, pounding hard between my ears. I shout, "I don't need this right now! I have a show, and I'm already nervous enough."

In a swooping move, he tugs me farther up the mattress and then cages his large frame over mine. He pins my wrists above my head, and our eyes lock. He claims, "Don't worry, I'll take care of it."

"Take care of what?"

He ignores my question and reminds me, "'Stop' is the safe word, in case you forgot."

Anger fills me. I hurl out, "Of course I didn't forget. But I'm not having sex with you, Riggs!"

"No, you aren't right now. You haven't earned my dick inside you. In fact, you've been nothing but disobedient lately," he replies.

I glare at him, then spout, "I'm not the one who fucked up our life!"

He grinds his molars, studying me, then challenges, "Say your safe word, pet." A wildfire bursts across his expression.

I open my mouth to speak but nothing comes out. I've always been a sucker for Riggs, especially when he gets that heated look on his face. And I curse myself for being so weak.

He slides his hand between our bodies, slipping his long fingers under my leggings, then between my panties. He slips through my slickness and positions his thumb on my clit. Two of his fingers enter me, and I whimper.

My breath turns ragged, my cheeks heating hotter with each second, yet I can't take my eyes off him. I can't use the safe word and tell him to stop.

He challenges again, "Say the safe word, pet." His determined, crazy expression explodes against his dark features.

It's everything I've missed that I can't shake, no matter how hard I try.

I dream about how he looks at me when he needs to take control of my body.

My spine buzzes with anticipation, knowing what he can do to me with very little effort.

His hot breath merges with mine, making my mouth water, desperate for his lips to crash into mine. Yet he keeps them an inch from me, fully aware he's torturing me. He pumps his fingers inside me, swiping and curling in all the right spots while seamlessly circling his thumb on my clit.

A moan fills the air, and it takes me a moment to register it's mine. I thrust my hips into his palm, needing more.

He freezes, demanding, "Did I permit you to grind your pussy on me?"

I swallow hard, barely breathing, staying quiet.

Say the safe word.

I can't. I need this.

I don't.

"I expect you to answer me," he warns.

I lick my lips, glancing at his mouth, dying to taste everything I've been craving. I take several inhales of his intoxicating scent and try to secretly push against him.

He catches me and repeats in his commanding tone, "Tell me if I granted you permission to grind your pussy on me. And address me appropriately."

Without thinking, I submit, blurting out, "No, Sir."

That same look passes in his expression, but it doesn't stay long enough for me to decipher it. I attempt not to fall prey to him again, weakly claiming, "Riggs. We shouldn't be doing this."

He manipulates my body, quickening his speed, and taunts, "If you believe that, then say your safe word, pet."

I can't, nor do I want to. It's been too long since he's touched me. Too many nights have passed since we've been together or I've felt the high he gives me. So instead, I whisper before I can stop myself, "Please!"

"That's not your safe word!" he growls, then leans into my ear and murmurs, "You didn't say, Sir. You just added to your punishment later tonight."

Adrenaline rushes faster through me. The mere thought of him punishing me almost makes me giddy.

He continues, "You've been a bad wife. It's time you remembered who your husband is and stop ignoring me. Now, tell me how much you want your punishment." He circles my clit so fast I get dizzy.

I cry out, "Pu-pun… Oh God! Please let me come, Sir!"

He barks, "No! You're not coming until after you've received your punishment."

"Rig...oh..."

He covers my mouth with his, sliding his tongue against mine and urgently flicking it.

There's no point in fighting him. I want it as much as he does. I've missed everything about how we were, and I've never been able to not return Riggs's kisses.

He swirls his thumb faster while mimicking the same move inside me, curling his finger from time to time.

Heat annihilates me and sweat pops out on my skin. His kisses become more intense, more needy. Or maybe that's my reaction to him.

He dips his mouth to the curve of my neck and slides his palm over my mouth. He sucks so hard that I'll have a mark, but I miss those too. The proof that he was consumed with my body and I was his to do with what he wanted.

I whimper underneath him, trying not to release, fully into submission without even thinking about it. But that's what Riggs does to me. He turns me into his obedient woman without me fighting it. And even though my body quivers, I'm not over the edge. So I continue holding back, but I don't know how much longer I can. We've fixed nothing between us, yet not one ounce of my body wants to disobey and disappoint him.

He removes his hand from my mouth. He kisses me again, then stops his fingers from manipulating me. He retreats an inch from my lips and states, "When you get home tonight, you'll put on the outfit on your bed. You'll kneel by the window in my room. And you'll wait for me to punish you."

Our heavy breathing is the only sound in the room. I blink a few times and finally realize what I'm doing.

"No. We shouldn't—" I start.

He covers my mouth with his hand again. "You're my wife. You'll obey me. Don't fight me on this."

He pulls his hand out of my pants, then shoves his fingers into his mouth and sucks on them while continuing to hold his palm over my lips.

My heart never slows. The throbbing between my legs doesn't lessen.

He leans into my ear and orders, "You're not allowed to touch your pussy and get off without my permission. Don't forget it."

My whisper cracks when I reply, "You're such an ass."

His lips curl in satisfaction. He adds, "If you need it now, then strip. Sit on the desk, press your heels on the edge of the wood, and play with yourself. I'll allow it."

I shoot him a dirty look but contemplate it, then reprimand myself.

Satisfaction flares in his face. He pecks me on the lips, rolls off me, and says nothing. He strolls into his suite.

I sit up and stare at my reflection in the mirror. I shouldn't be doing anything with him, and the more time that passes, the angrier I become. I march into the other room, declaring, "Nothing is happening tonight. You can't just act like everything is fine."

He grunts. "I'm fully aware we aren't fine. But I'm your husband. I know what is best for you, and continuing to stay away from me isn't happening."

"It's not your choice," I claim.

"Want to make a bet?" he retorts.

"And how selfish of you to do this on the night I'm about to take the stage for the first time!" I accuse.

He stands taller and smiles, making my gut sink.

"Why are you looking at me like that?"

He stays calm, but cockiness shines all over him. "You still feel nervous?"

"What?"

He arches his eyebrows. "Answer the question, pet. Do you still feel nervous about singing tonight?"

I open my mouth, then snap it shut. I can't claim I do. It's like it all disappeared.

More arrogance washes over him. He declares, "That's what I thought. And don't worry. If you show any sign of anxiety once we get back to the arena, I'll take care of you."

I gape at him, deciphering what he just admitted and hating how his arrogance isn't totally out of line. He did replace my anxiety.

He steps forward and strokes my cheek. "Like I said, I'm your husband, and I know what's best." He points to the window. "That's where you'll kneel. Tonight. And I'm not fighting anymore or repeating myself."

I'm too frustrated to argue with him anymore. "Ugh!" I mutter and go into my suite.

He calls after me, "You've got an hour before we have to leave."

I storm back into his suite, snarling, "You don't get to do this."

He crosses his arms. "Do what?"

"You know what."

"Make my wife submit to me?"

I glare at him.

He steps closer and grabs my chin. Butterflies erupt in my stomach, and I curse them. He leans down and states, "Don't tell me you haven't missed me. I know this life. I know what I trained you to do...who to be. And you don't just leave it. You saw firsthand, when Aria had her meltdown, what happens if you try to forget about your need to submit."

I huff, then try to deny it. "I'm not Aria. I don't have to take part in what you want."

"Then why did you just submit to me?" he prods.

"I didn't," I lie.

He leans into me, holding my head firmly against his chest and murmuring, "You begged me. You called me Sir. You wanted me to dominate you as much as I wanted it."

I almost slap him. Instead, I cry out in frustration, "Ugh! You don't know everything!"

"I know everything about what you need. So admit it felt good to submit to me a few minutes ago."

I spin and walk toward my suite. I declare, "I'm not playing your game, Riggs."

He follows me. "Answer me, Blakely."

"No."

He continues, "Why didn't you use the safe word? You could have told me to stop at any time, but you didn't."

I curse myself further. I throw my hands in the air and shout, "Just leave me alone, Riggs."

He stares at me for a few minutes as tension grows between us, then claims, "I will do whatever I have to do to make us whole. But you have to give me a chance."

Tears well in my eyes. "You broke my trust."

He shuts his eyes briefly, then pins them back on me. "I know. And I'll say for the hundredth time I'm sorry."

I laugh through my tears. "But you aren't. You don't even know what you should be sorry for."

Surprise fills his expression. "Is it not enough that I'm sorry I hurt you? That I know I harmed the only person in the world who's ever loved me, and I hate myself for it? Is it not enough to feel regret so deeply it makes it hard to breathe?"

I don't know how to answer him. I want to tell him it is and that everything can go back to normal. Instead, I reply, "Would you do it again?"

He freezes.

I add, "If you had to destroy my father all over again, would you do it?"

Silence fills the air.

More tears fall. "I guess I have my answer." I spin and go into the other room.

He follows me and grabs my wrist. "Blakely!"

I angrily turn. "Don't!"

"You told me it was okay to destroy your father. You never once told me to stop."

"You used me to do it! You told me you'd protect me and never turn me over to him!" I cry out.

"I didn't turn you over to him! I did protect you from him!" Riggs claims.

My insides quiver. "Do you really believe sending those text messages to my father was protecting me? Are you that big of a fool?"

He glances at the ceiling and takes a few deep breaths. He finally meets my gaze and in a calm tone, states, "I made a mistake, pet. I know what I did hurt you, and I'm sorry for it. But you have to let this go."

I swipe at my tears. "That's easy for you to say, Riggs. You weren't the one who was used. I have to get ready. Let me be." I push past him and go into the bathroom, locking the door behind me, unsure if I'm ever going to be able to get past what he did—especially if he can't fully understand why I'm so upset.

8

Riggs

The arena erupts in ear-shattering applause and screams. Kalim gave me noise-canceling earbuds, claiming they're the best on Earth, but they still can't drown out the enthusiastic spectators.

Blakely stands and bows, raises her arm in the air and waves, declaring, "Thank you so much! I'm Blakely Fox, and I hope to see you soon! Now, if you're ready, someone else is dying to come on stage!"

The crowd continues screaming, and Colton runs out, joining Blakely on stage. He hugs her and picks her up off her feet. She laughs, and when he sets her down, he steps back and asks, "What do you think about helping me with a few songs?"

"I don't know. What does our audience think?" Blakely teases, beaming at the fans.

The crowd gets louder, which I didn't think was possible. Pink and green lights flash, and the drummer pounds out a chop while Colton holds his hand to his ear. When the drummer finishes, Colton puts his finger over his lips.

It takes several minutes until the noise settles to barely anything.

The intro to Colton's song fills the arena, and he and Blakely belt out the words. When they finish, they move into one of Blakely's songs she released earlier in the week, and the fans eat it up.

Colton slings his arm around Blakely and declares, "Ladies and gentlemen, you saw her first with me! Give it up for my girl, Blakely Fox!"

The noise only grows.

Blakely takes another bow and runs toward me, glowing as she exits the stage.

I pick her up and hug her, yelling, "You were amazing!" I squeeze her tighter, and she returns my affection for a moment. It's like nothing's wrong between us and everything is how it used to be.

As soon as I set her down, Noah embraces her, and I have to hold myself back from tearing her away from him. He releases her and steers her away from the stage toward her dressing room before I can cut in.

I follow them, not happy with his hand on my wife's back. And I'm not blind when he tugs her closer to him as they round the corner. Nor do I enjoy realizing how comfortable she is with him. So I follow behind them, not next to my wife as I should be, and squeeze my fist inside my pocket to try and calm down.

A dozen VIP reporters wait in a line behind a red rope. A mix of Kalim's and Benny's guys are with them, making sure no one crosses the line. When we get closer, they clap and give Blakely their praise.

The three of us go into her dressing room and shut the door. Noah sits next to Blakely on the couch, puts his hand on her thigh, and claims, "I'd put money on both songs you just sang with Colton fly to the top of the charts."

She widens her eyes. "Do you really think so?"

He leans closer, glances at her lips, then answers, "No doubt."

"You have two seconds to get your hands off my wife," I threaten.

Blakely glances at his hand as if she didn't notice it, then turns her head toward me with a guilty expression.

He slowly follows, keeping his hand on my wife's leg. He replies, "Or what? You're going to ruin her big night?"

She slips out from under his grasp and rises. She claims, "He doesn't mean anything. It's just an innocent gesture, Riggs."

"Bullshit. He'd like nothing better than to sleep with you," I state, then scowl at Noah, warning, "I'll deal with you at a more appropriate time."

Blakely snaps, "That's enough, Riggs."

I glance at her, surprised she's continuing to stick up for Noah. I look back at his smirking face, and it takes everything I have not to hurt him. Instead, I refocus on my pet. "Are you ready to get these interviews over with?"

She lifts her chin and straightens her shoulders. "Yes."

I point to the oversized chair. "Sit there so Noah can keep his hands to himself."

She shoots me a defiant look, and I wince inside, thinking she might try to sit back down next to Noah. But she finally mutters, "Whatever," and sits in the chair.

I leer at Noah until he looks away, then go to the door and open it. I announce, "Blakely is ready for her interviews now."

For three hours, the reporters come in and out of the room. Pride sweeps through me as I listen to Blakely answer a handful of different questions. When the last reporter steps outside, Colton strolls into the room.

He questions, "Riggs, keeping things real back here?"

I grunt. As much as Colton can get on my nerves, he's starting to grow on me. Plus, anyone who has a beef with Noah is a friend in my book.

He pats me on the back and sits on the armrest of Blakely's chair. He states, "You riding with me?"

"Where's that?" I question.

They glance at me. Blakely answers, "To the after-party."

The hairs on my neck rise. I ask, "What after-party?"

Colton laughs, replying, "The after-party celebrating your wife and yours truly." He lowers his voice and bats his lashes. "That's me, in case you're wondering."

I ignore him and blurt out, "No one told me about a party."

Colton arches his eyebrows and then pins his gaze on Noah, shaking his head and dramatically voicing, "Tsk, tsk, tsk. It looks like you're at it again."

"At what?" I seethe.

Colton glares at Noah.

Noah points at him. "Stop trying to cause trouble."

Colton shakes his head and declares, "Noah has a thing about not informing spouses or significant others about parties. He likes to keep them in the dark so they get pissed and feel left out. Then when things get heated, he drives the wedge between them deeper. Isn't that right, Noah?"

"Stop telling lies and being dramatic, Colton," Noah scolds.

I cross my arms over my chest, growing angrier. I snarl, "I'm to know Blakely's schedule at all times."

He shrugs and takes a sip of his beer. Arrogance washes over him, burning brighter with every breath. He claims, "It's not a performance."

"Excuse me?" I challenge, clenching my fist at my sides.

"Maybe you should draw on clues."

"Meaning?" I seethe.

He glances at Blakely. "Want to tell Riggs why you didn't tell him about the party?"

She gapes at him, then quickly looks at me.

I lunge across the room and drag him off the couch.

Blakely shouts, "Riggs!"

Colton mutters, "Oh shit!"

I slide my hand over his throat, squeezing until he's gasping. Maroon fills his cheeks.

I snarl, "Don't you ever insinuate anything about what my wife thinks again."

"Riggs, let him go!" Blakely frets.

Kalim and Benny push between us, and I have no choice but to release Noah. Kalim backs me up against the wall and shouts, "Calm down!"

"Get off me!" I push back.

He spins me so fast that I lose my footing. His arm circles my neck, and he puts me in a headlock. My arms flail, and he snarls, "I said to calm down."

It takes a minute for me to get past my stubbornness and realize he might be one of the few people capable of killing me with his bare hands. While Benny acquired his skills on the streets, Kalim has specialized training I'm gathering not many people in the world have, which is a different level of muscle. So I finally stop fighting.

"Are you ready to stay calm?" he questions.

I hold my hands in front of me in surrender.

He warns, "I'm going to release you. But you better not try anything." He unhooks his arm from around my neck and steps back.

Blakely glares at me, her face red with anger, shaking her head in disapproval.

My gut sinks. But I refocus on Noah and state, "This is the last time I'm reminding you that I'm to know Blakely's schedule at all times."

My warning isn't strong enough, or maybe it's standing next to Benny that gives him courage to continue fighting me. He declares, "You're only to know her work gigs."

I take a step forward, but Kalim tugs me back, barking, "Easy."

I shake him off and point at Noah. "Your days are coming to an end soon."

"Enough!" Blakely scolds.

I lock eyes with her, and my chest tightens. She lifts her chin and puts her arm through Colton's, announcing, "We're going to the party. You aren't invited."

My pulse skyrockets higher. "Excuse me?"

She stands taller and declares, "You heard me."

"I'm your husband," I seethe.

"Then act like it instead of a petulant child!" she snaps.

I take several calculated breaths before ordering, "Everyone but my wife, please clear the room."

Blakely takes several steps toward me and then shakes her head. "No. I'm going, and you aren't."

"You don't mean—"

"This is my night! Not yours! Mine! Since you can't control yourself, that's my final decision. Do you understand me?" she interjects, her blues blazing in a sea of turbulent chaos.

I lower my voice, attempting to sound calm, but it comes out harsh. I repeat, "I need to speak with you."

She shakes her head and blinks hard. "No. I'm not going to listen to whatever you want to say to try and justify what you just did."

Bile crawls up my esophagus. I swallow it down and state, "You have security issues I need to take care of."

She locks eyes with Kalim. "Can you be my bodyguard for the evening?"

"That's—" I start.

"Don't, Riggs! It's clear you trust him since he's in charge," she states.

I widen my eyes.

She laughs. "What? You didn't think I noticed that Kalim took the lead and Benny stepped back?"

I stay quiet, not sure how to respond. But I am shocked she noticed, even though I shouldn't be. She's smart and has always observed things that surprise me.

Noah cockily states, "Guess this situation is handled. Are you ready to go?"

She spins and crosses her arms. "Noah, you aren't invited either."

He jerks his head backward. "Don't be silly."

Her voice turns sterner. "Don't talk to me like I'm beneath you. And stop doing things to rile Riggs up."

"I'm not—"

"Just stop!" she commands, putting her hand in the air. "You're constantly doing things to get under his skin. And let me make it known to everyone in the room. I am not attracted to you now, nor will I ever be. Is that crystal clear?"

Her statement is a sunny ray of light beaming through the dark. Noah flinches, a hint of red fills his cheeks, and he stares at her.

I demand, "Well? Answer her."

Blakely shoots darts at me with her glare. "You can't help yourself, can you?"

Fuck! Why did I say that?

Get control of this situation.

She's making me do stupid things by staying away from me for so long.

"Noah? Do you understand?" she questions.

"Yes," he finally mutters.

She stares him down a moment, then adds, "I don't want to have this discussion again." She spins back to Kalim. "Can you please be my bodyguard this evening so my husband doesn't worry?"

Kalim nods. "If that's what you wish."

"It is." Blakely turns to Colton. "Are you ready?"

He smirks. "Yep. Dying for a drink, superstar."

She takes a deep breath. "I'll meet you in the car. I've changed my mind. I want to speak with my husband alone for a moment, so if you all could leave the room, I'd appreciate it. Kalim, I'll be out in a quick minute."

Good! She's coming to her senses.

The room's other occupants slowly disperse until it's just the two of us. Kalim is the last to step out, and he shuts the door behind him.

"Pet—"

"Be quiet!" she orders.

I ball my fists, feeling like a kid in school who's in trouble with the teacher. Not one part of me likes the predicament I'm in, yet I don't know how to flip it.

Blakely steps forward and studies me for a moment. Then her face softens and she reaches up. Her warm palm cups my cheek, pummeling me with emotions.

I get a quick flashback of my mother doing the same thing to me. She had woken up after being beaten by the John who hit me so hard I flew across the wood floor. I was still sobbing and scared. She held me in her arms and kept her hand on my cheek for what felt like hours, trying to calm me down.

Blakely's voice tears me out of the flashback as she softly states, "We can't go on like this."

Alarm bells go off in every cell of my body. I open my mouth, but she puts her fingers over my lips.

She continues. "I love you. I do. And I want to believe that deep down, the love you claim to have for me is real."

"It is," I blurt out, not understanding how she could think otherwise.

She blinks hard. "If we stand any chance—"

"Don't say that," I scold.

She closes her eyes a moment, then slowly opens them. She begins again, "The only chance we have of surviving what we're going through is for you to learn to trust me."

"I do trust you. I trust you with my life," I declare, which is true. She's the only person who has my full faith.

Her lips turn into a sad smile. "But you really don't. You think you do, but you don't."

"That's not true.

"It is. If you did, you'd realize it doesn't matter what any other man tried. I'd never choose them over you. Even in this challenging position we're in, I'd never pick another over you," she claims.

I tug her into me. "I trust you. It's them I don't trust. And especially Noah."

She sighs. "If you trusted me, you wouldn't have to worry."

I scoff. "I know what sleazeballs like Noah do—"

"It doesn't matter! I'd never allow anything to happen!" she cries out.

I stay quiet, wishing she could see things how I do. Then again, a part of me wants to keep her naive about all the seedy things men will do to get a woman like her.

She adds, "I can't have you on Noah's ass all the time. He's my agent."

"He's overstepping," I claim.

"Then I'll handle it," she states.

"You shouldn't have to."

Her voice turns sterner. "Riggs, this is my career. I've worked tirelessly for years. You don't know what I've sacrificed to get here."

I tighten my arm around her. "I do. And I'm so proud of you and what you've done. You were amazing tonight."

She smiles. "Thank you. I know you are. But I can't have you and Noah at war all the time."

"Then he should keep his hands off you and his eyes where they belong," I insist.

She groans and scrubs her hands over her face.

I remove them and state, "You don't deserve that type of unprofessional treatment."

She swallows hard, then announces, "You can't be in charge of my security anymore."

My stomach flips faster. "You don't mean that. You're just upset with me right now."

She closes her eyes and shakes her head.

"Pet—"

"No, Riggs. I'm telling you that this isn't going to work. You and Noah just don't get along. You can't put your differences aside. And you promised me if I changed my mind, you'd respect it. So I need you to honor your word," she asserts.

My entire world collapses all around me. First, my marriage is on the rocks, and now, my wife just fired me. I try not to beg and say, "We'll get rid of Noah. There are clauses I can have my attorney make a case on."

Her face hardens. "No."

It's another bomb hitting me at full blast. "No? You're going to choose him over me?" I question.

"It's not like that, Riggs."

"Sure looks like it from where I'm standing."

"It's not."

"Then let's get rid of him. Problem solved."

Red flames fill her cheeks. She seethes, "He's my agent. I'm here, in Detroit, singing my songs for a sold-out crowd because of him."

I sternly retort, "No, you're here because of your talent and hard work."

She shakes her head. "We both know how this industry works. It's all who you know. And you wanted me to pick my agent. I chose Noah, and he's doing his job. So until he doesn't, I'm not looking to jump ship."

Rage, disappointment, and shame all swirl within me. I've never been fired, but it's not only that. My wife is choosing Noah over me. I tell her, "Your security is more important than your agent. You can't replace your life."

She reaches up and caresses the side of my head. "I know. But I'm pretty sure that any man you trust, who's ballsy enough to put you in a headlock, is capable of making sure I'm safe."

"There's more to it than that," I proclaim.

"I can't do it anymore, Riggs. I can't be in the same room as you and Noah while you go at each other's throats."

"Like I said, we'll get you a new agent."

She stares at me with sad yet confident eyes and softly says, "No. Respect my wishes. I'm going to ask Kalim to take Benny's place."

It makes me realize there's nothing I can do. But at least she's choosing who I believe is the stronger of the two. So I switch gears from trying to keep things as is to not get eliminated completely. "Then let's compromise."

She furrows her eyebrows.

"I'll work with Kalim on your security but stay away from Noah."

"I don't see how that can work."

"Someone has to coordinate things with Kalim. Let me do that," I push.

She stays quiet for a minute.

I'm reduced to begging. "Please. I can't handle it if I don't know you're safe. I'll stay away from Noah and work with Kalim behind the scenes."

Another tense moment passes. She finally answers, "Okay. But if you don't keep your word, we're done."

"Done?" I ask.

Pain crosses her features, along with determination. "Yes. You already lost part of my trust. If you disappoint me on this issue, we won't be able to repair us."

More sickness fills me. I tug her against my chest and murmur into her ear, "Don't give up on me, pet."

She tilts her head. "Then don't let me down."

"I won't. Now, please tell me you're letting me come to the party with you," I state.

She shakes her head. "No. I meant it. Neither you nor Noah are invited."

Disappointment and fear grow stronger. "There's going to be everything you hate there. Tons of booze, drugs, and people desperate to do whatever they can to befriend you. It'll be just like the L.A. parties you despise," I argue.

She takes a deep breath and retreats from me. "I'm not a child, Riggs. Go to the hotel. Get some rest. I'll see you tomorrow."

"Tomorrow?" I seethe.

She nods. "Yes. Tomorrow. Don't wait up for me. I'm not your child."

"I know. You're my wife," I grit between my teeth.

She exhales deeply, as if fed up with me. She lifts her chin and declares, "I'll see you in the morning. Have a nice evening."

I take a step to follow her, but she spins, threatening, "This is the point where you respect me enough to not fight me any further."

Something about her warning makes me freeze. She disappears out the door, and the hardest thing I've ever done is stand there and watch her leave without me.

9

Blakely

Kalim leads me through the arena. Three of his guys wait at the exit. He asks, "Ready?"

The hairs on my arms rise. "For what?"

He arches his eyebrows. "There's a crowd out there."

My nerves escalate. I blurt out, "Do I need to worry?"

He shakes his head. "No. We'll protect you. Just keep moving."

I lift my chin and nod. "Okay. Let's go."

His blond, twenty-something guy opens the door. Reporters and fans swarm the small alley, held back by a red rope. The three men form a barricade around me. Kalim and another guy are on either side. One is in front, and one steps behind us. They move in tandem, pushing past the screaming fans toward a black SUV.

Lightbulbs flash so brightly that I lower my head to protect my eyesight. We're almost to the vehicle when there's a breach over the rope. A crowd of people move toward us. Kalim shouts, "Get back," but no one listens.

The guy in front of me steps to the side, and the door to the SUV opens.

I slide inside next to Colton, relieved when the door shuts and the lock clicks in place.

"Welcome to the land of insanity," he chirps.

I glance out the window as the front door slams shut. The SUV nudges forward and people bang on the windows. It stops, then moves another inch. Then it stops again.

The banging becomes more intense, and fear fills me. I slide closer to Colton. He protectively puts his arm around me, and I question, "Is it always like this?"

He grins. "Yep. Better get used to it, superstar."

My stomach flips. Ears told me about this. Noah always dismissed him, claiming I could handle anything and saying that's why we have bodyguards. But I can hear Ears in my head warning me.

The SUV turns the corner, and the driver accelerates down the road. I exhale an anxious breath.

"Potential catastrophe over!" Colton announces.

"Is that normal?"

"Yep. But the real question is, are you okay? That was a bit intense back in the dressing room."

I groan. "Don't remind me." I momentarily forgot about the exchange between Riggs, Noah, and me.

He opens a bottle of whiskey, pours three fingers into a tumbler, and holds it in front of me. "Have a drink."

I wrinkle my nose. "Not a whiskey girl."

He chuckles. "Should have known, Beverly Hills." He grabs a bottle of champagne and pops the cork. The fizz overflows and drips down the bottle and onto the carpet.

Surprised, I ask, "How do you know I'm from there?"

He dramatically inhales. "Don't insult me. I said I was a fan. I researched you." He fills a flute and hands it to me.

I laugh, which feels good after the last hour. Still, I'm shocked that someone at Colton's level of success took the time to learn about my life. I take a sip and tease, "Do I have to worry about you stalking me?"

He grins. "Only if you're lucky. But honestly, I'd probably stalk your husband over you. Sorry, but I got needs."

The thought of Riggs with Colton amuses me. And since I'm so comfortable with Colton and already trust him, I blurt out, "I don't think you can handle what Riggs is into."

His face lights up. He leans closer and whispers, "Oh! Tell me more. Is it whips and chains? Does Daddy tie you up for hours and make you beg for days on end?"

Heat crawls up my cheeks. I elbow him. "Stop."

He jerks his head backward and declares, "He does, doesn't he? Are you a submissive?"

More embarrassment floods me. I don't answer him, not wanting to lie but unsure what to say.

He chuckles and touches my cheek. "No need to be ashamed. I'm down for kneeling for a few hours."

I nervously laugh. "Very funny."

His face turns serious. "Do I look like I'm joking?"

"You're a sub?"

He nods. "Yep. Bring me a Daddy like yours, and I'm at his service."

I stay quiet, stunned at his revelation.

He inquires, "Why do you look so shocked?"

"I... I don't know. You're such a strong force on stage. And you aren't afraid to tell Noah off. I... I can't see anyone ordering you around and you obeying," I admit.

He acts insulted, asking, "So you think I'm a shitty sub?"

"Umm...didn't say that."

His voice turns firm. "Listen, Mrs. Superstar. I'll have you know I'm not an amateur. In fact, I'm highly requested at my club, and that was before I became famous."

My ears perk up. "Club?"

He purses his lips and stares at me.

I push, "Why are you suddenly being shy?"

A few more moments pass, and he finally confesses, "The club is a secret."

My pulse increases. I didn't see any gay men at Club Indulgence, so I'm sure his club is different, but I want to know more. I question, "Is it in L.A.?"

He licks his lips, then confesses, "Yes."

"Do they have auctions for Doms to buy subs?"

His eyes narrow. "Yes."

I continue, "And there are contracts between actioned subs and Doms?"

"Duh. Why are you asking me this?" he demands.

I shrug. "I'm curious about your club. I'm part of one too."

He returns to his antics, slapping my hand. "Well, do tell! What's the name of yours?"

I smirk. "It's a secret too."

He crosses his arms. "You're no fun."

I try to play cool. "If you're not willing to trust me with the name of yours, then I can't tell you mine."

Silence fills the air. Several moments pass while we stare at each other.

He snaps his fingers. "What if we both say the name at the same time?"

Feigning insult, I accuse, "You don't trust me?"

His lips twitch. "Sure. But let's just do it at the same time on three."

I roll my eyes. "Fine. But you can't tell Riggs I told you. He'll have a fit. Promise me you'll never tell anyone I revealed the name."

He scoffs. "Of course. The same goes for what I tell you. We can pinky promise." He holds his pinky finger in the air.

I laugh and curl mine around his, vowing, "I promise not to tell."

"I won't breathe a syllable to anyone," he declares. Then he says, "One. Two. Three."

At the same time, we both state, "Club Indulgence."

I gape at him.

He chuckles. "Want to know another secret?"

"What?"

He grins. "I already knew you were a sub and member of Club Indulgence."

Confused, I ask, "How?"

He knocks back his whiskey, then answers, "Your husband has a reputation."

I let his statement sink in, then I clear my throat, asking, "How is that possible?"

"What do you mean?" he asks.

"How are you part of the club? You're gay."

"So?"

"I've never seen any gay men there."

"You've never seen a male Dom and male sub?"

I shake my head, then stop. "There was one incident on stage where there was a male Dom with three subs. Two were men, but they focused on the woman."

"Then they're bi," he claims.

"How do you know?" I ask.

He reveals, "Male Doms only take male subs if all parties are into each other. Trust me on this. And I assume you've seen the lesbians?" he questions.

"No. Well, I saw some activities, but they were subs. Their Doms made them."

He chuckles. "Is that what you really believe?"

"What do you mean?"

He smirks. "Honey, if subs are doing things with others of the same sex, they're either gay or bi-sexual. Did you forget that the subs agree to everything?"

I ponder his statement, then point out, "My contract said it was at Riggs's discretion if he decided to bring someone else into our activities."

Colton waves his hand in front of me. "They all say that. You have a safe word. It's meant to be utilized if you aren't okay with anything. Or do you not understand what it means?"

"Of course I understand," I claim.

"If a sub isn't comfortable with same-sex activities, they'll say their safe word." He leans closer. "Would you use the safe word if Riggs wanted you to get with a woman?"

I don't hesitate. "Yes. No judgment, but I'm not into females."

"There's your answer," he claims, then clinks my flute with his tumbler.

I take another sip of champagne, then question, "But why haven't I seen any gay men? I assume you aren't the only one."

He squints, assessing me.

"What?"

"You haven't seen the entire club, have you?"

I shrug. "I guess not. I've only been there a few times."

He reveals, "There are three areas. One for heterosexual activities only. Those are the real prudes. Then there's the section for the Dom's who are okay with women on women. The third area, well, that's where the magic happens."

I question, "Why is that?"

He winks. "Anything happens there. My people can live it up."

"Oh." I let it sink in, then say, "It sounds like segregation and unfair."

He groans, then takes a large mouthful of whiskey, grimacing. "It's not. It's rich people paying for what they want. No point having those who aren't into what I'm into around my sex scene."

I think about what he's stating. Then ask, "How did I see the Dom with the three subs on stage if I wasn't in area three?"

"Easy. He agreed to keep the focus on the woman." Colton downs his drink, refills it, then spins in my direction, exclaiming, "Wait! Why did you ask about the auctions?"

More heat fills my face. I admit, "Riggs bought me in one."

His jaw drops.

I slap the back of my hand on his chest. "Don't look at me like that."

"Sorry. I've been out of the loop, but I wouldn't have known. I'm not privy to activities that happen in area two," he admits.

"You're not?"

He shakes his head. "No. The confidentiality clause is a real thing, even from one area to the next."

"Oh."

The SUV comes to a full stop. Kalim opens my door. I make a mental note to inform him he needs to wait for me to knock on the window, then get out.

Colton follows, slips his arm through mine, then leads me inside a large stone mansion.

"Where are we?" I ask, glancing around the grand marble foyer.

He assesses the room, then replies, "Who knows. I don't think we're in Detroit anymore though."

"West Bloomfield," a server with a tray of champagne informs us.

Colton takes two, hands me one, then asks, "Where's the bar?"

The server points at the door. "Through there."

Colton downs his champagne and leads me into another room. He says niceties to random people approaching us until we get to the bar. He says to the bartender, "Whisky, three fingers, neat."

I tease, "Don't get specific or anything."

He smirks, and the bartender hands him the drink.

I add, "Riggs doesn't think alcohol should be more than two fingers."

Colton's face fills with a smug expression. "Does he now?"

"Yep."

"I'll keep that in mind when I see Daddy next." He grabs my arm and escorts me around the mansion, introducing me to people who display way too much enthusiasm over us.

It doesn't take long for me to realize that Riggs was right. There are people half-naked and even having sex in different areas of the house for all to witness. And I saw a lot when I was a server at Cheeks and with Riggs at Club Indulgence, but I didn't expect this at a party.

Colton introduces me to many people, downing three glasses of whiskey to my one flute of champagne.

Whenever I turn around, Kalim's looming in the background. He stays far enough away but close enough to attack someone if needed.

The third glass of champagne begins to go to my head, and I grab Colton's arm.

He teases, "Whoa! You okay, superstar?"

"Can we sit down?" I ask.

"Sure." He leads me into an empty room. It's small, and there's a fireplace, a few pieces of furniture, and soft lighting. He says to Kalim, "You stay outside," then shuts the door.

We sit on a love seat in front of the fire. Colton props his feet on the ottoman and I do the same. He slings his arm around me and inquires, "You aren't having fun, are you?"

"Why do you say that?"

He stares at me. "This isn't your scene." He takes a big sip of his drink.

"Has it always been your scene?" I ask.

He shrugs. "Not sure if I'd say that, but you get used to things."

Something in me doubts that. "Do you?"

He peers at me closer. "Are you referring to Noah running your life or all the strangers who want a piece of you?"

I grimace, muttering, "You make it sound so amazing."

He stares at the fire, takes several sips, and then reveals, "There are things about this business that will make you feel on top of the world. Then there are others..."

I blurt out, "Do you hate Noah?"

He sniffs hard, swirling the whiskey in his tumbler. His eyes turn darker.

I soften my tone, adding, "You don't have to answer my question."

He shakes his head and turns so he's facing me. He props his knee on the couch, then states, "No one has ever point-blank asked me that. But yes. I think I do hate him."

"Why do you stay with him?"

Colton glances at the ceiling, then answers, "He's one of the best. But it doesn't matter. I'm in a contract. And once you sign with Noah Kingsley, you're in it for life. There's no escaping." He finishes the rest of his drink.

My stomach flips, and the air turns stale in my lungs. The thought of not having a choice to work with Noah or not suffocates me.

Riggs made sure I could get out if I wanted.

What if it doesn't hold up?

Why am I thinking this? My career is just getting started, and Noah's doing his job.

Riggs negotiated. He made sure I was protected.

My heart beats faster thinking about how Riggs diligently went through every word of the numerous contracts the agents presented. He spent hours with them and his attorney to ensure I had the deal I wanted.

Colton tilts his head. "I can see a million thoughts spinning in your mind."

I blurt out, "You should have Riggs look at your contract if you want out. He's really smart. He negotiated mine and swears I have several get-out clauses."

Colton licks his lips. A fire burns in his eyes, but then he frowns.

I ask, "What's wrong?"

He goes to the built-in bar and picks up a decanter. He pours the liquid into his tumbler and spins. He leans against the wall and mutters, "You don't live if you leave Noah."

Goose bumps break out on my skin. "What do you mean?"

He sarcastically chuckles, then drinks half his whiskey. He stares at me with a sad expression. "You're way too innocent, superstar."

The hole in my gut widens. "Meaning?"

He shakes his head. "If you leave Noah, no one in the industry will touch you."

"But I had a dozen agents after me," I argue.

He sniffs hard. "And you didn't choose them. You're dead to them. Noah will blackball you faster than you can contact any of them."

I put my hand over my churning stomach. "Riggs wouldn't let that happen to me."

Colton sits down and grabs my hand. "Listen closely, Blakely. Riggs doesn't run this industry."

I furrow my eyebrows, not liking what Colton is insinuating. Did I choose the incorrect agent? Is Noah really that powerful?

He sighs, confessing, "I'm going to have to end my career to have a life or stay in the closet forever."

"I don't think that's true. Really. You should talk to Riggs," I insist.

He downs the rest of his whiskey, and his phone buzzes. He pulls it out of his pocket, glances at it, and stares at me.

"What is it?" I question.

He hesitates.

"Go on. Tell me whatever you want to say," I encourage.

He winces, then answers, "How bad would it be if I asked you to leave the room?"

"Why?" I question.

"I need to let off some steam." He arches his eyebrows.

It dawns on me what he's insinuating. "Sorry. Duh. Who's the lucky guy?"

He shrugs. "Does it matter?"

I don't hesitate. "Yes."

He scoffs. "Says the married woman. Then again, if I had Riggs to go home and kneel to, I wouldn't be here."

I open my mouth to object but nothing comes out. I snap it shut, and the throbbing sensation in my core that rose when Riggs warned me he was going to punish me tonight takes hold.

"Is he as good as I think he is?" Colton inquires.

I can't lie. My face burns hot, and I look away. Tingles race down my spine thinking about Riggs.

Colton groans. "I thought so. Well, lucky you."

I try to rise, but I'm wobbly on my feet. I curse myself for drinking too many glasses of champagne.

He grabs me. "You okay, superstar?"

I take a deep breath. "Yep."

He bites on his lip, waits a minute, then states, "I'll probably be an hour. Is it okay if I text you when I'm done?"

The thought of being at this party without Colton next to me doesn't excite me. And I realize there's only one thing I want to be doing. I lift my chin and shake my head. "No. I think I'm done with this scene. I'm going to have Kalim take me home."

Colton's lips twitch. He teases, "Going to surprise Daddy and beg him for a punishment?"

My butterflies flutter so hard that I become queasy. I step out of Colton's grasp and reply, "Have fun. Call me tomorrow and let me know how the rest of your night went."

He grunts. "Sure thing. But if I kiss and tell, you're going to as well. I'll be waiting to hear all about what techniques Daddy uses."

"Sorry," I chirp. I pretend to zip my lips, then toss the key away.

He moans. "Don't be a prude."

"Not a prude," I declare.

He chuckles. "Says you. Regardless, I'll still call you tomorrow."

I hug him, leave the room, and have Kalim escort me out of the mansion. I spend the ride home debating whether I should give in to my desire to have Riggs punish me.

The nagging voice in my head telling me I need to go home, get into bed, and not let Riggs touch me, never shuts up. It reminds me that we're not okay. There are too many issues in front of us that need to be resolved, and I wonder if they will be.

Yet the burning in my core only grows hotter. The need for me to forget our problems and allow Riggs and me to do what we do best screams just as loudly.

When the SUV pulls up to the hotel, I'm still trying to figure out what route to take. The closer I get to our suites, the more intense my needs become until I can no longer think and only feel.

10

Riggs

Nothing will cool me down. I pace the hotel room, drinking scotch, and staring into the thick blanket of snow.

How did I get into this position? I'm in a Detroit hotel room while my wife is partying with strangers, including men who I'm confident all want her.

Men who will do anything to get her.

The thought that Noah isn't there only gives me a little relief. I know thousands of men in this world would do anything to get with my wife, and the more famous she gets, the worse it'll become.

Images of Blakely drunk, mobbed, or hit on by sleazy pieces of shit fill my mind. It all makes my stomach churn. No matter how much liquor I drink, nothing makes it disappear.

A gust of wind blows, turning the atmosphere whiter with such a thick blanket that I can't see through it. I mutter, "Why the hell did I agree to let her go out without me?"

A cold shiver runs through me, as bitter as the terrain outside. I add, "She fired me. How did I ever let that happen?"

I close my eyes, clueless about how I can change the situation that just seems to keep getting worse. I've lost all control. There's nothing between her and me anymore that I'm in charge of.

The defiant Blakely I knew before I even got with her is stronger than ever. This new woman she's become, I never anticipated. And I don't know how to handle it.

I down the rest of my scotch, walk over to the bar, and pour another two fingers. Then I sit on the oversized armchair and turn on the T.V., flipping through the channels.

My gut drops. The pounding of my pulse beats harder between my ears, making me dizzy. I lean forward in my chair.

A bald man and a brunette sit behind a news desk. A photo of Blakely leaving with Kalim, then one with Colton in the backseat of an SUV, appears. People are swarming the vehicle, which only increases my anxiety and anger.

The woman chirps, "Well, Chuck, it's an interesting night in Detroit. Megastar Colton Linwood left his concert in Detroit with newcomer Blakely Fox, and it looks like things will get hot, hot, hot."

The man chimes in, "There's more juice! Both Colton's girlfriend, actress Sarah Stenmore, and Blakely's much older billionaire husband, Riggs Madden, are nowhere to be seen."

"Much older," I mutter and grip my tumbler so tight I might break the crystal.

The woman leans closer to the bald guy and lowers her voice. "Should we take a bet on where this is going?"

He chuckles. "Well, last time I won, but then you claimed you did and never paid me."

"Well, let's just get this on record in front of everyone, then," she taunts.

He smiles at the camera. "I give it a month before full facts are revealed between these two people."

"Always an optimist, aren't you?" she teases.

I down another large mouthful of scotch, but rage burns hotter than any alcohol ever could.

He asks, "What are you betting? Say it on the record this time. And when I win, you'll have to pay up, so don't spend all your money this weekend."

I groan, rising. I'm unable to tear my gaze off the T.V. I clench my fist, to the point it hurts.

She asks, "Well, should we up the ante?"

He grins. "Sure. Let's say a thousand instead of five hundred this time."

She turns back to the cameras. "You're all my witnesses. A thousand dollars and these two are too hot to not go up in flames! No way it'll be a month. I give it two weeks before this new love match sizzles so bright that Sarah and Riggs are out of the picture."

"I'd hate to be them," Chuck states.

"Motherfuckers," I bark out, then turn off the T.V. and toss the remote at it. It hits the glass, and a spiderweb appears on the screen. I plop back into the chair.

"You know Colton and I are only friends, right?" Blakely's soft voice hits my ears, and her hands slide over my shoulders to my chest.

Relief and anger swirl inside me. Her sea salt and driftwood scent flares in my nostrils. It hits me how it's ironic that we're in Detroit in the middle of a blizzard and she still smells like all my favorite things, even though there's no ocean here.

I tilt my head up at her, intoxicated with her calm chaos, remembering the first time I told her what it meant. Her long, soft blonde hair falls over my shoulders.

She giggles. "You're always so serious." She kisses the top of my head. "You should try to relax more often."

I turn in my chair, slide my hand through her locks, and palm the side of her head. I curl my fingers, gripping her strands so they're taut. The flush in her cheeks that always appears whenever I fist her hair blooms across her skin. Her plump lips part and her breath quickens.

It all makes my blue balls hurt more. Ever since I played with her this afternoon, it's been driving me nuts. And I'm fully aware that my wife isn't close to being mine like she used to be.

I remind myself, *I have no control over anything anymore.*

The knowledge that I've lost all control whips through me like a tornado. This isn't who I am. I'm the one who calls the shots, but she's calling all of them, and it's like I'm her fricking puppet.

She licks her lips, and the neediness in her eyes erupts like a volcano overflowing with lava. I debate whether I should bend her over and fuck her or punish her for doing this to me.

She declares, "Colton's gay, in case you didn't get the memo."

I stay quiet, unsure of what move to make and hating how I suddenly don't know how to make my wife happy or take control of all the things that are falling apart between us.

Why did I do what I did?

How could I be so careless and stupid to think that she wouldn't find out?

Maybe I just shouldn't have done it.

Did I really need to do it? I could have destroyed her father without it. Sure, it was more fun. But, God, it's like I'm the one who lost everything now.

"Riggs, say something," she says.

I snap, "Yeah, I got the memo, but that doesn't make it right. You think it's okay for the world to think you're with him?"

She tilts her head. "Do you really care what other people think?"

"It's not about that, Blakely. You're my wife," I seethe.

"So you constantly remind me."

"Don't do that," I say.

Her face falls. She accuses, "Are you ever going to trust me?"

"Me, trust you?" I laugh.

Her eyes turn to slits. "Yeah. You don't trust me at all, Riggs."

"And we're back to this," I mumble and down another mouthful of scotch.

She studies me, then steps back and says, "If you want to be my husband, then be it."

"And how do you want me to do that?" I question, feeling more defeated than ever before.

She arches her eyebrows, looking more beautiful than ever. Then she steps back. She slowly strips, removing her jacket and dropping it to the floor.

I watch her like a hawk, not able to tear my eyes off her, feeling the throb in my cock grow. Her short little skirt falls to the floor, and I reprimand her. "You shouldn't be going to a party in that, especially without me."

She softly laughs. "Why? What would you have done if you were with me and I wore it?"

I groan inside. Everything I say is just playing right into her game.

What the fuck is happening here?

She slowly removes her glittery mock-neck top. The thickest of her gold collars shines against the darkness of the room.

I inhale sharply, asking, "When did you put that on?"

She smirks. "Oh, I have my secrets, darling."

Blood pounds faster and hotter in my veins. It's my favorite collar. She knows it's my favorite. I can restrain her to anything in that collar.

She stands, and my eyes drift down her body, taking in her gold bra, which shows the hint of her nipples. Her delicate thong is a bit darker, and the craziness inside me grows.

She's already wet.

That's my good little pet.

Her lips twitch. She slides her fingers over her pussy and taunts, "Should I call you Daddy tonight?" She giggles.

My chest tightens and I warn, "Don't fuck with me, pet."

She smirks. "Why? What are you going to do about it?"

I state, "I'm not into your games, Blakely."

She leans over my chair. Her scent drifts in my nostrils again, and I'm on the border of exploding from the insanity I can't seem to escape. She puts her hands on the armrests and her face right in front of mine.

I grip the chair's seat.

She states, "Oops. I broke rule two. Sorry, Sir." She bats her lashes.

I refrain from touching the one thing I want to feel more than anything—the one thing I need but am scared I'll never have again.

She pouts. "So you don't want to play? You've lost interest in me?"

Regain control.

I take calculated breaths, trying to calm the adrenaline that's building within me, but I can't, and she only makes it worse.

She takes her fingertip and traces the bone around my eyebrow, down my cheek, and over my lips, taunting, "Oops, I seem to have broken rule seven too."

I peer closer at her. Her eyes are a tad bloodshot. "You're drunk," I accuse.

She shakes her head, her long hair flowing, her expression innocent. "No, not drunk, Sir." She leans closer and whispers, "But I might have broken rule thirteen and had one too many glasses of champagne."

"Then you're drunk," I assert.

Giggling, she shakes her head again and glances at the minibar. Then she grabs my tumbler out of my hand and holds it in the air. She tilts her head and declares, "But it looks like you might have had too many as well."

I cringe inside. I never wanted her to see me anywhere near intoxicated after the last time I lost control.

She murmurs, "At least I don't have to take your keys away."

I wince, remembering that night and wishing I could take it back.

In a seductive tone, she suggests, "Why don't we give ourselves a pass and forget that either of us has had drinks tonight?"

It's a rule I never break. I never engage with anyone if I've been drinking heavily, nor if they have.

She rises, removes her bra, then slowly shimmies out of her panties. She steps her long legs out of them, then tosses the flimsy lace on my lap, questioning, "Do you remember when you got these for me?"

I glance down, hold myself back from sniffing them, and answer, "Yeah, I was living in the L.A. apartment and you were at the beach house."

"Eyes up here, Riggs," she orders.

Like the loser I've become, I obey.

She smiles and slides her hand over her pussy, dragging it up over her belly button and to her breast. She keeps her blues on me, accusing me in a sad tone, "You left me at the beach house to suffer on my own."

"It was so you could work on your music," I remind her.

"You did it to punish me."

I firmly insist, "No. I did it so you could get ahead in your career like I promised you."

She tilts her head and sadness expands everywhere. She softly asks, "Is that really the truth?"

I furrow my eyebrows and jerk my head backward. "Of course it is. Do you think I've ever wanted to be anywhere except with you? Do you think I stayed away for any other reason? I did that for you. Only you. Not me. And that was one of the hardest things I've ever done. But it was all for you."

She doesn't answer me, and I feel like I've lost everything.

How can she think these thoughts? All I've done except for those damn text messages and video I sent to her father has been for her well-being.

The longer she stares at me, the more anxious I become. I blurt out, "You're the one who's choosing to stay away and push me out of your life. That's on you, not me."

She bites on her lip, then blinks a few times. She takes a deep inhale, then picks up my crystal tumbler. She asks, "Is that what you wanted to talk about tonight? What you did to me? How you humiliated me and used me?"

The same knife that has sliced my heart since she found out what I did takes another vicious stab. I didn't think it had any more life left in it, but apparently, it does. And the pain shoots through me worse than before.

But I'm also angry, and I seethe, "I'm done apologizing, pet. I'm not perfect, and you knew it before you ever touched me, before you signed the contract and decided to stay in my life, before you took the vow you willingly took to be my wife forever."

Her glare stabs into me and she snaps, "So that means you can do whatever you want to me, and I'm supposed to be okay with it? I should just look the other way and not hold you accountable for anything?"

I think for a minute, trying to calm down, then answer, "No. You're supposed to find a way to forgive me and return to loving me."

"I do love you," she claims.

"Really? You have a funny way of showing it," I state.

"Once again, you're Riggs Madden and can do whatever you want. I'm only the wife who's supposed to put up with everything," she fumes.

I rebut, "No, you're supposed to remember who we are together."

Deep disgust fills her expression. She studies me for a moment so intensely, I feel an inch tall. She asks, "And who are we, Riggs?"

My heart beats harder. I stay quiet, remembering how good we were together and how it felt. Nothing came close to being as good, nor has it ever felt as bad as it does now. I loathe not having her by my side. It kills me how she hates me, and the worst is knowing she's right here but I can't have her.

She prods, "You can't answer me?"

I swallow, trying to lubricate my throat, which seems to have gone dry.

She coos, "Aw, does my husband need a reminder of who we are?"

"Don't play with me," I warn again.

She lifts her chin, spins, and slowly strolls across the room to the bar.

I assess all of it.

Her blonde locks sway over her spine, hitting the curve of her waist. I stare at her heart-shaped ass, remembering how it felt to make it mine, yearning to see my handprint on her cheeks and be inside her once again. Then I stare at her legs, perfect thighs, the back of her knees, calves, and right down to her goddamned heels. I love all of it. All of it is mine, or it's supposed to be, I remind myself.

She picks up the scotch decanter, pours two fingers just like I taught her, and spins. She slides her fingers over her cleavage.

I grip my armchair tighter, and she walks toward me, holding the tumbler in front of my face. She lowers her voice into her seductive tone and bats her eyes. "Sir, your scotch."

Everything in me feels like it's about to explode. I've never felt such chaos. Even when surfing and fighting the waves, I have more control than in this situation.

I don't know how to flip it, but I need to. I'm supposed to be the one in control, and she the one who submits to me. Right now, our roles are reversed and I don't like it one bit.

I slowly take the scotch, hating that she's holding the cards and I'm unsure what hand to play. Nothing I do feels right. Everything seems wrong. So the only thing I can do is threaten, "You're asking for a punishment, pet."

At this moment, I realize what a vixen my wife truly is because she purses her lips, studies me for a moment, then leans into my ear. She whispers, "I've been a very bad wife. All night I thought about putting on this collar and kneeling at that window." She points to it, then glances back at me. "Now, what are you going to do about it, dear hubby?"

My mouth waters and the blood boils in my veins.

She rises, struts over to the window, and kneels, just like I spent the day imagining her doing when I first laid eyes on this room. She keeps her head bowed to the floor, spine straight, ass on her calves, and hands in her lap. Making it more torturous is the snow. It silhouettes her through the window, and she becomes a perfect display of artwork.

My wife, the majestic creature I no longer know how to dominate.

I debate whether to give in to her, which I fear will make me lose even more control.

But maybe it's what I need.

What we both desperately need.

11

Blakely

Silence fills the room. I don't dare look anywhere but at the floor. A touch of the bitter cold from outside permeates the glass. Goose bumps pop out on my skin, but I wonder if it's from the chill or the anticipation of what I can't escape needing.

A long time passes, which doesn't surprise me. While my body becomes tired of the position I don't dare break, I'm grateful for the time lapse. It's familiar. Whenever Riggs makes me wait, I'm unsure if he's debating what to do to me or just watching me, seeing if I'll dare to defy him and rule number one.

At first, I hated kneeling for him. I assumed it was degrading, but now, I crave it. Something about showing Riggs I can do all the things in his contract won't ever seem to go away. Now, more than ever, it seems important.

He's slipping away from me.

No, we're going through issues.

Why am I doing this when I haven't forgiven him?

Maybe I have.

No, I haven't.

The debate continues and spirals faster until electricity sizzles in the air and I realize Riggs is standing behind me. More excruciating minutes pass until he trails his finger down my spine.

I shudder, unable to stop my reaction.

He murmurs, "Do you remember what I added to my vow on our wedding day?"

My heart swoons the same way it does whenever I think about that moment. I answer, "Yes, Sir."

He moves my hair over my right shoulder, then kisses the curve of my neck. I inhale deeply, fighting to stay in my position, as he questions, "What did I promise you, pet?"

"You said, 'I vow to prove you wrong and work on my faults,'" I tell him.

He adds, "The first day you recorded in the studio, you sang about how we weren't forever and that I was okay with it. Well, news flash. I'm not okay with it. I've never been okay with it and never will be."

I blink hard, willing myself not to cry. I'm tired of the tears. There've been too many, and I promised myself I wouldn't spend tonight with wet cheeks surrounded by tissues.

He circles me and lifts my chin, pinning his dark leer on me. His controlling tone ignites an inextinguishable fire in my core as he demands, "Tell me what you added to your vows."

I don't want to answer him. I know my husband well. It's too painful to admit, and there's no doubt he'll use it against me.

Riggs knows I don't want to obey. His lips curl into a tight curve, and he firmly reminds me, "Who's in charge, pet?"

My butterflies take off. I try to lift my chin, but he's holding it firmly. I answer, "You are, Sir."

The darkness grows in his expression, and my insides throb. "Your vows, Blakely. Admit what you decided to declare in your vows to me, your husband, who you chose without any hesitation," he orders.

It's another truth I can't deny. And I still don't want to speak the words out loud, but I know I have to. So I take several deep breaths to control my emotions, hating and loving how Riggs flipped me into submission and made me lose all control to disobey him.

He adds, "Say it exactly as you stated it to me on our wedding day."

A tear drips down my cheek. I confess, "I vow to always accept all of you, your faults and all."

A flicker of the look he gave me when I said it on the beach in Maui appears on his expression, then quickly fades back into the darker one he wears whenever he's in his Dom role. He picks up my hand with my wedding ring and positions it over my collar so I'm gripping it. He stares at the diamond and then locks eyes with me. "It seems you aren't keeping your promise to me, are you?"

"Are you?" I hurl, pissed he's accusing me of breaking my vows while not upholding his.

His eyes turn to slits. He rises, yanks me off the floor, and pins me against the cold glass, fisting my hair so I'm facing the ceiling. I inhale sharply, squeezing my thighs together as he hovers his face above mine. He hisses, "You forgot the Sir."

The bratty side of me appears. Riggs can't stand it when it comes out, and I know it. There's a split second where I can squash her, but I let her fly, smirking. "Sorry, Sir. Are you upholding your vow?"

Red crawls up his neck and into his cheeks. I rarely see it, and I've barely pushed him, so I'm surprised it appears so easily. But the look he gives me when he's like this only causes the adrenaline to rush through me faster. He declares, "I try every day to be better for you."

"Do you, Sir?" I push, grinding my thigh into his erection.

He glances down, then slowly drags his gaze back to mine.

Before he can say anything, I add, "Oops. Rule seven. Sorry."

I know I'm going too far. I'm weaving in and out of my role, which I haven't done since the beginning of my training. A mix of rage, confusion, and desire spins over his sharp features.

I'm on a slippery slope. I don't know how Riggs is going to deal with my insubordination. I'm not a naive sub in training anymore. The rules are clear, and I'm choosing to break them.

To further rile him up, I reach up and slide my hand up his chest and around his neck, gripping his hair the same way he grips mine. I whisper, "What you did wasn't doing better."

"'Accept all of you. Faults and all,'" he snarls. Then he challenges, "Or was that a convenient lie at the moment?"

I snap, "Of course it wasn't!"

"Then tell me how you're upholding your vow," he challenges.

I can't form any words to answer. We stare at each other in the soft darkness. The sound of the wind whipping against the window gets louder, making the glass colder, a stark contrast to the warmth of my husband's body.

His face changes, and the control I usually see in it returns. The deep-seated need to be his, to obey his commands and submit to him without thinking about any of our issues, festers. He leans into my ear and murmurs, "Tell me you love me, pet."

I don't hesitate, claiming, "I do love you."

His lips graze my neck as he states, "Tell me you accept me, faults and all."

My insides quiver. I had forgotten my vow to Riggs. I knew he was twisted and capable of anything when I married him. And while I meant it, I'm struggling to let what he did slide. I admit, "I didn't know you'd use me."

He freezes, his hot breath creating tingles under my skin, his heart beating against my shoulder.

I release his hair and slide my hands over his cheeks. He lets go of my locks, and I move my face in front of his. I stroke his lips with my thumbs, blinking a new river of tears that slide down my face at record speed. I confess, "More than anything, I want to forget about what you did."

"Then do it," he orders, with a desperation I've never heard in his voice.

"It's not that easy."

He glances at the ceiling, then sniffs hard. Moments pass, then he relocks his blues on me. Fear fills his tone as he questions, "So you didn't mean your vow? It was only acceptance of what you chose?"

I've never felt so horrible in my life. I want to tell him no, that I meant what I promised him. Yet instead of answering, I accuse, "Did you think my vow meant you could do whatever you wanted without consequences?"

"You went around my question," he seethes.

I close my eyes, unable to see the suffering on his face any longer.

"Look at me," he orders.

I obey, finding the courage to stand tall under his angry gaze.

He surprises me. I think he'll release me, but instead, he slides his hands on my cheeks and kisses me. His tongue tastes like scotch. It slides past my lips and urgently flicks in my mouth.

There's nothing I can do but submit, grasping his head and holding him as tight as possible, displaying the same desire to be his as he has to be mine. I reach for his pants and tug on his belt.

He retreats, stepping back and breathing hard. I step toward him, and he slings his arm around my waist and maneuvers me in front of the full-length mirror. He holds me tight to his frame, pinning his eyes on my reflection. He quizzes, "What do you see, pet?"

"You. Me."

Disappointment fills his voice. He claims, "Wrong answer. Try again."

More tears escape. I confess, "Two people who love each other but can't figure out how to move forward."

"Still wrong," he barks.

I jump slightly, then shake my head, crying out, "I don't know what you want me to say, Riggs."

He tightens his hold around me. His erection digs into my back, and his hand cups my pussy. He demands in my ear, "Think."

I say the only thing that comes to my mind that I think he wants to hear. "A Dom and his sub."

Riggs's eyes widen. His agony intensifies, and I instantly regret my words. He releases me and steps back. He speaks so quietly that I barely hear him. He asks, "Is that what you see?"

I spin, admitting, "I don't know what you want me to say, so whatever this is, I can't win."

His jaw twitches. He declares, "Why don't you ask me what I see."

I soften my tone. "Tell me what you see."

He stares at me with a sad expression, still full of hurt, and it scares me. He admits, "I see a husband who would do anything for his wife. And he wants his wife back, no matter what. But the wife only wants her husband when it's convenient for her."

"What? Riggs, no! That's not—"

"Don't give me more of your excuses, Blakely! I've apologized until I'm blue in the face. I took the blame for what I did. I don't know what else to do. But you... Fuck, pet. Congratulations. You fooled me."

"Fooled you?"

His lips tremble and he nods. The anger reignites in his eyes, and he continues, "I believed everything you ever uttered to me. When I made my vow to you, I meant it. You, on the other hand... You didn't mean a goddamn word."

My voice cracks. "That's not true!"

"You just admitted it!"

"No, I didn't. I-I..."

He crosses his arms, seething, "You can't even argue I'm wrong because you know it's true."

"You aren't being fair," I claim.

"I'm not being fair? Me? I'm not the one who lied on our wedding day!" he barks, his eyes wild with rage and hurt.

I gape at him, unsure what to say or how to make things better. All I can do is repeat, "I didn't lie. I meant my vow. I do love you."

My statement only makes him angrier. He prods, "Then why haven't you accepted me and all my faults, Blakely? Hmm?"

I need time to think. I never saw things the way Riggs does, and I need some time to decipher it.

He takes my silence the wrong way. He walks to the table and picks up his phone and wallet. He slides them into his pocket, then heads to the closet.

Fear fills me. I follow him and grab his arm. "Riggs, what are you doing?"

He removes his coat from the closet, then shrugs out of my grasp, firmly stating, "I need some air."

"It's freezing outside," I blurt out, then reach for him.

He grabs my hands, lowers his voice, and warns, "Don't touch me right now, pet."

"Riggs, don't go! Stay here and—"

"And what, Blakely? We'll do what?" he barks.

I freeze, quivering inside, unsure what to say to get him to stay.

He steps backward, then adds, "I'm not touching you again, pet. You need to decide if you want me or not."

"I do want you. It's not about that!" I insist.

He squeezes his eyes shut and takes a few breaths. He opens his eyes and pins them on me and states, "Figure out if you're capable of keeping your vow. If you're not, I'll let you go."

"Riggs, that's not—"

He opens the door and steps out into the hallway. He firmly shuts it, and by the time I finally react and open the door, he's gone.

I wait up all night. When the sun begins to rise, I call him, but it goes to his voicemail. I text him.

> Me: Riggs, where are you?

An hour passes. I finally get a response.

> Riggs: Kalim will get you at eight for the flight home.

The hairs on my neck rise.

> Me: Where are you?

> Riggs: On my way to L.A.

I gape at the screen for a moment, then call him again.

He sends me to voicemail.

> Me: What are you talking about?

> Riggs: I meant what I said, pet. I love you, but the ball's in your court.

I stare at his message, feeling sicker.

How did we get here?

Tell him you forgive him.

As much as I tell myself to let it go, something stops me. I reread our brief exchange, and all I can do is cry, wondering why this is so hard. But I also wonder why I forgot the vow I made to him. As angry as I am about what he did, part of me can't argue with his reasoning.

I made the vow. He didn't force me to say it. I put those words together and made that promise all on my own.

Then why am I having such a hard time upholding it?

Has so much changed that I can no longer keep my promise of unconditional love to him?

The answer never comes. When it turns seven, I shower, dry my hair, and wait for Kalim. I continue deciphering all that happened between us and whether I'm willing to forgive Riggs and accept all of him—faults and all.

There's a knock on the door, and I get a sliver of hope that Riggs has returned. I open the door, and my heart drops.

Kalim holds out a cup of coffee. "Good morning, Mrs. Madden. Riggs said you'd want this. Are you ready?"

Mrs. Madden.

My heart sinks. It seems cruel to hear those words after everything that transpired between Riggs and me. And it's just like Riggs to still make sure I'm taken care of even though we may be at the end.

The thought of us no longer being together makes my stomach flip.

I realize Kalim is waiting for an answer, so I take the coffee and reply, "Thank you. I'm ready."

But nothing has ever been further from the truth. I have no idea what lies in front of me, and the wedge between Riggs and me has grown. I didn't know how to make things right before we left for Detroit. And I sure don't know how now.

And the fact Riggs is willing to walk away hurts. Knowing how he sees things, I can't blame him. The easy thing to do would be to tell him what he wants to hear and move past this issue. Yet I can't seem to do it.

12

Riggs
One Month Later

With everything going on between Blakely and me, I forgot about her father. He's stayed away from the office since after the charity event. There was only one time he approached the building, and I had already revoked his access.

I've watched the video footage over and over. Seeing him arguing with the security to the point they had to remove him physically gives me great satisfaction. But since then, he's not attempted to come close.

We've exchanged a few heated texts, but I no longer get a high like I used to. I still don't have my wife with me, and anything that used to give me joy no longer does.

A few weeks ago, I had my assistant put Hugh's personal items into boxes. Not that I should give him anything after what he did, but I don't want the shit. Plus, he'll remember how he lost it all every time he looks at it. And to further humiliate him, I'll let him carry it out of the office in front of the staff and security.

But today is the day to close the book on him. So I get back to the L.A. apartment from surfing at the public beach and text him.

> Me: Time's up, meet me at the office at nine.

> Hugh: You don't order me around me.

> Me: I think you need to understand the situation you've put yourself in.

> Hugh: That's funny coming from you. From what I see on the news, you're nowhere near my daughter anymore.

Rage ignites deep in my soul, quickly flaring all around me. I pound out on the screen another text.

> Me: It's this or a jail cell. Take your pick.

He doesn't respond, but my gut says he'll show up.

I shower, hating how I can only rinse off on the beach. I go into the closet and stare at the few items Blakely has here. As she requested, I sent her things to Apartment Thirteen, but not all of them. And she said nothing about the few items here, so I kept them.

I reach for the shirt she wore the day she got changed for the charity event. I've not allowed the cleaners to wash it. Every morning I come in here and I inhale her scent. Today's no different.

I put the material close to my nose, taking as deep a breath as possible and leaning against the door while closing my eyes. My insides quiver. I fight the urge to tell her not to worry about her vow and just come home.

The phone vibrates, and I glance at the screen.

> Kalim: Blakely's interviews got canceled. We're going to fly back to L.A. later this afternoon. We'll land around 3:30.

My blood heats. I reread the text, contemplating if I should meet Blakely at the airport and try to convince her to come with me or not. It's the same conversation I have every time Kalim texts me that she's going to be landing. But, like always, I force myself not to do what I am dying to do.

One part of me wishes Blakely would get over our issues. The other part wonders if it's me who has to get past it. Maybe I just shouldn't worry about it. At least she'd be back with me. Yet something about her coming home, not forgiving me, and not accepting me for who I am and all of my faults the way she told me she would just seems wrong.

So I decide against it. If she's not going to hold up her vow, I'll always have it in the back of my mind that she really doesn't love me, and I'm not living like that.

I squeeze my eyes shut, trying to fill my lungs with fresh air, but it's just stale. I inhale another whiff of her scent on the top, and her beaming smile fills my mind.

The recurring debate plagues me.

Will she ever look at me like that again?

How can she claim to love me but not forgive me?

Were her feelings for me superficial? Have I been kidding myself all these months that she was the only woman on Earth who would never hold my faults against me?

She promised me. I didn't tell her to say those words. She said them of her own free will.

She didn't mean them.

Yes, she did. She's just being stubborn.

More heartache fills me, and it's more intense than I recall. They say time heals all wounds, but for me, time's not doing anything but making things worse. And I'm wondering how much more I can take.

Stop being a pussy.

I force myself to hang up the shirt, get dressed, and go to the office. I arrive an hour before Hugh and try to get lost in my work.

It's pointless.

I don't consider myself a nervous man. Today, I am though. Maybe it's the fact that my last encounter with Hugh was at the charity event when my whole life unraveled before me. Perhaps it's because he stole my happiness with Blakely and he knows it. There's nothing I can say to even try to deny it.

Then again, I thought I would be elated, knowing I've taken him down. But with my wife not by my side, it just doesn't feel how I thought it would. It feels hollow.

The more time that passes with me not seeing Blakely, the harder it's gotten to stay away from her. And I know I'm only a few steps away from breaking.

Since Detroit, our communication's been limited to text messages, and they're strained. Every conversation ends with me asking her if she's ready to live up to the vow she gave me on our wedding day. But she always goes around the question, telling me she loves me and misses me, but she never answers affirmatively.

And whenever I'm in contact with Kalim over her security, I want to order him to bring her to my place as soon as the plane lands. But I never do.

And I force myself to not get on a plane and to go to her concerts. Every night that she's not in L.A., my struggles haunt me. I imagine her on stage with all the fans and all the different scenarios of things that could happen to her. I'm not naive. I know the majority of the population will want a piece of her now that she's famous. Hell, they wanted a piece of her before she was, and it's surely only gotten worse.

And my love-hate relationship with Colton is another complicated battle.

He went behind Noah's back. Soon after their first concert, he announced on his social media that Blakely was taking the spot for the former musician who opened his concerts. The fans went crazy, and so did Noah.

Part of me is satisfied that Colton got one over on him. The other is angry. I don't want my pet out of L.A. all the time, even though it's good for her career. If she would invite me to go with her again, I'd be happy. Yet every time I schedule her security with Kalim and have to stay in L.A., it cuts me deeper.

So I'm trying not to be bitter about it because I want her to succeed. I know how hard she's worked, and she deserves it. Yet the selfish part of me wants her as close to me as possible.

THE VOW

I can't deny I love seeing Noah pissed. He couldn't fight it after the fans applauded Colton's announcement so loudly. He warned Colton to never go behind his back again but couldn't do much more about it. The few concerts that had yet to release tickets sold out faster than ever. So Noah had to shut up and drop it.

Besides the constant updates that I make Kalim give me and the media posts I see about her, I'm out of the picture. Nothing ever felt so lonely or miserable.

Yet until she tells me that she meant the vow she made to me, I can't do anything about it. I've given strict instructions to Kalim not to leave Blakely in a room with Noah by herself. And he's assured me he won't. But I hate that Noah's with her and I'm not. He got to stay in her life, but I got pushed out, not by him but by my wife. So it stings.

I've tried to throw myself into my work like I have in the past when things were off in my personal life. No matter how hard I try, it's not working.

Today I've got to focus on work. I need to transfer Hugh's shares over to me. I should have done it a month ago, but the issues with Blakely have me off my game.

All the money he stole from the client accounts has now been returned. It includes the deficit from what he spent over the years. That came out of my pocket. I took the hit on it and made everything whole.

Our clients nor the SEC know anything about this situation, which is what I wanted. But it doesn't give me the satisfaction I thought it would when I took him down.

So the days are long, stretching out as if they'll never end. And I miss everything about being with Blakely. I can't even go to the beach house. I tried once. I went there, and I could only stay ten minutes. I kept looking at the Heintzman & Co crystal piano, feeling like my heart would explode. It was all too much.

Visions of Blakely playing for hours, singing while her fingers seamlessly worked the keys, or me fucking her on top of it never left my mind. Her pleading cries echoed throughout the house, haunting me, reminding me of everything I'd lost and everything we were. Then I began to question how maybe none of it was even real. How could it be if she couldn't hold up her vow?

So I left almost as soon as I arrived, unable to stand it, struggling more than before.

To add to my woes, the L.A. apartment's closing in on me. I miss surfing on my beach, getting glimpses of my pet on the sand with her blonde hair blowing in the breeze, or on the deck, sipping her coffee and watching me fight the waves. The public beach I now attend is crowded, and there's no image of Blakely anywhere.

Before she came into my life, all the activities I used to do to stay entertained while in L.A. involved playtime. I'd frequent Club Indulgence or go to Apartment Thirteen to break in a new sub. Neither of those things are options anymore, but the need to dominate hasn't gone away. If anything, it's festering, dancing on the surface of all my thoughts, and making my skin crawl with renewed craziness.

It would be easy to go into Club Indulgence and pick a sub, but none would be Blakely. And my wife's the only person I'm craving to submit to me.

When Blakely's gone touring, I often find myself in Apartment Thirteen, staring at the St. Andrew's Cross. All I remember is how my pet's curves gleamed while restrained to it and how her face morphed between innocence, determination, and anger. A few times, I stayed the night, sleeping on her side of the bed, breathing in her scent that lingered on the pillow. So while every moment in Apartment Thirteen tortures me, I can't stop myself from going.

Connie knocks on my office door, tearing me out of my thoughts. She calls out, "Riggs?"

I glance up. Anxiety riddles her expression. "Hugh's in the conference room with your attorney," she informs me.

"Is Benny there watching him?"

She nods. "Yes."

"Good," I state, knowing it'll anger him further to know he doesn't have any reign over our office.

She hesitates a moment, then leaves. I wait a half hour longer to piss him off more, even though my attorney's on the clock. I stare out the window and into the chaotic city, wondering what my pet's thinking. And I can't stop myself and pull out my phone and text her.

> Me: How's your morning going?

She replies straightaway.

> Blakely: Okay. How's yours?

> Me: Same.

> Blakely: Busy day?

I take a deep breath, tapping my thigh, contemplating whether I should tell her.

Secrets got me into this mess, I remind myself and decide it's best if I fess up.

> Me: I'm about to go into the conference room. Your father is here to sign his shares over to me.

Minutes of silence pass, and my chest grows tighter until I can't breathe.

Maybe I shouldn't have said anything?

I text her again.

> Me: I didn't want to keep it from you.

Another few excruciating moments pass.

> Blakely: Thank you for telling me.

I stare at the people below the building, rushing to wherever they're going on the sidewalk, wondering how everybody can go on with life so easily while I'm in hell and can't seem to escape.

> Me: Are you angry with me for finishing this?

So much time passes, I panic again. She finally responds.

> Blakely: Anger isn't the right emotion.

> Me: What is?

> Blakely: Maybe sadness.

I contemplate her response. I know it's her father. As much as I hated the situations my mom put me in, she was still my mother. However, Blakely agreed that it was okay for me to take him down.

Maybe now, after everything I've done and all the things she found out about, perhaps her opinion on this situation is different.

> Me: But you aren't mad at me?

> Blakely: No, just sad about it all.

I don't know what else to say.

> Me: I don't want you to be sad.

> Blakely: I know.

Because I can't help myself, I torture myself further.

> Me: Are you ready to keep your vow to me and come home?

Dots appear, then disappear, then appear again. She sends me the same message she always does.

> Blakely: I love you. I'm trying to get there.

My gut spins and spins until I feel nauseous. All the anger and regret I feel boil within me, and I decide to take my rage out on Hugh. He deserves it anyway.

I storm out of the office and into the conference room past Benny. I sit next to my attorney, Peter.

Hugh scowls across the table, his eyes beady, with less hair than I remember.

I slide the paperwork in front of him, ordering, "Sign it."

He defiantly lifts his chin, reminding me of Blakely, and the ache sears deeper inside me.

He claims, "You're not paying me enough."

"That's all you're getting. And you're only getting anything because I have to show something. So take it, or you'll get nothing but a concrete cell," I seethe.

He gives me a look I would've been intimidated by years ago before he took me under his wing. Now, it's just pathetic.

He slowly picks up the pen, signs, and stands. I lean back in my chair, announcing, "Benny will walk you out. Your boxes are near the elevator."

He scowls harder at me, then snarls, "I made you. You're only here because I made you."

It's the same claim he's always held over my head. I used to believe his lie, yet now, I no longer do. I scoff, declaring, "The company is in the position it's in because of my work—my ability to get clients and do things that you couldn't. So you might have started this with me, but we both know that the last decade has been based on the work I've done. All the while, you've sat here and done barely anything."

He starts to object, and I nod at Benny. "Get him out of here."

Benny grabs his arm, and Hugh tries to shake out of his hold.

He threatens, "I'll get you, Riggs. This isn't over."

"Yeah, sure you will," I state, then rise and step toward them.

Benny steers Hugh out of the room, and I follow them, not looking away until they turn the corner.

I go back to my office and stare out the window.

It's over.

I've finally taken Hugh Gallow down.

I should be celebrating, yet all I can see is my pet's face. It's filled with the pain I caused her, and I hate how I can't deny it's my fault. And I'd do anything to see her laugh and gaze at me how she used to, yet I'll never see it again.

My pulse races faster as I stare at the building across the way. For the first time, I wonder if taking Hugh down was even worth it.

13

Blakely

When the plane lands, I hurry off it, get into the SUV, and text Riggs.

> Me: Is it over?

Minutes pass. I stare at the screen, and more sadness washes over me. I'm so conflicted about what Riggs has done. I know my father's a horrible man. After stealing from Riggs and their clients, he deserves to lose it all, but seeing my parents look so broken at the charity event made me feel sorry for them. It's the first time I actually felt anything but anger and hatred toward them in a long time. And the vision of how horrible they appeared haunts me.

My father's a thief.

> Riggs: Yes. I need you to come to the office and sign some forms when you land.

My pulse skyrockets.

> Me: What forms?

> Riggs: I'll explain when you get here.

There's only one explanation I can think of, and a new fear takes root.

> Me: Are you divorcing me?

> Riggs: Is that what you want?

My stomach pitches. I close my eyes, trying to stop the pain shooting through my chest before replying.

> Me: No.

> Riggs: Good. Neither do I. I'll explain everything you need to know about the forms when you arrive.

I almost tell the driver to go to Riggs's office, but I hesitate. I don't know if I can control myself around him. The last time I knelt for him, he denied me. Ever since that night, I'm fully aware of the growing desperation that plagues me at all hours of the day and night.

It's no longer a craving. It's become a full-on need to submit to Riggs. The throbbing inside me reignited when I saw his name, just like every time he texts me.

I'm scared about what will happen if I don't find a way to quench it. As hard as I try to get past everything that's happened between us, I still can't tell him that I'm ready to uphold the vow I gave him so willingly. And I curse myself for giving it to him without ever thinking about the dark, twisted part of him. I should have never assumed he wouldn't bring me into his vengeance with my father.

Still, as much as I know what he did was wrong, I can't help continuing to love him. It would be much easier if I could hate him, yet I don't.

My phone vibrates, pulling me out of my worries. I assume it'll be Riggs, but it's not.

> Mom: I need to see you.

New anger forms deep in my soul. I forget my promise to myself not to engage with her, and I fire back a response.

> Me: You weren't there the last two times I showed up.

> Mom: I told you I was sorry. I need to see you today. It's really important.

> Me: So I'm just supposed to drop whatever I'm doing, go wherever you tell me to go, and maybe you're there and maybe you're not?

> Mom: I promise I'll be there.

She sends me a photo of her at the cafe where we agreed to meet the last few times.

> Mom: I'm here. I promise I won't leave until I see you.

I debate whether I should go, but I know my mom won't stop bugging me until she gets what she wants. And while I could block her, I know deep down that somehow she'll probably find a way to find me.

Now that she knows I'm married to Riggs, she has too many connections to him. I don't put it past any of her country club friends to somehow get my phone number, even if I change it 5,000 times.

I cave and reply back.

> Me: Are you drinking?

> Mom: No. I promise.

I don't know whether I should believe her or not. I've heard her lies too many times, and she was super intoxicated the last time I saw her. I've never seen her so bad, except when I was a child and found her on the floor in her room. I thought she was dead and screamed for the nanny to help revive her.

After lots of pondering, I decide I'll go and get it over with. If she's not sober, I'll leave immediately. I glance out the window and ask the driver how far away we are from Riggs's office.

He replies, "Only about two minutes. Is that where you want to go?"

The debate continues, but I decide if I go to Riggs, I'll have to leave to meet my mom. I can find out what he needs me to sign and if it is divorce papers. I cringe at the thought but realize it's better to know. I can meet up with my mom directly after, so there won't be any chance of me taking things with Riggs somewhere that we shouldn't.

I reply to the driver, "Yes, please." Then I respond to my mom.

> Me: I'm going to be about 30 to 60 minutes.

Mom: I'll wait.

> Me: I swear to God, Mom, if you're not there this time when I show up, this will be it. I'll stop taking your calls and block you.

Mom: Don't worry. I'll be here.

> Me: Fine. I'll text when I'm on my way.

It doesn't take that long to get to Riggs's office. I easily get through security and travel to the top floor with Kalim in tow.

He steps out of the elevator after I do and states, "I'll wait here."

"Thank you," I reply, my stomach flipping. It's a strange feeling being in this building. I've been here to visit my father numerous times while growing up. Now it feels foreign.

The secretary at the front desk looks up. I've never met her before. She beams, "Hello, Miss Fox."

"Madden," I correct her. My insides quivering as I lift my chin higher. For some reason, I want her to know I belong to Riggs. "*Mrs.* Madden," I emphasize.

Her face turns red. "Yes, Mrs. Madden. I'm sorry." She swallows hard, then asks, "Are you here to see your husband?"

I soften my tone. "Yes. He's expecting me."

She picks up the phone. "Connie, Mrs. Madden is here." A moment passes, and she nods. She puts the phone down and motions. "He's in his office. Connie said you can go through."

"Thank you," I say curtly and head down the hallway. I get in front of my father's office and freeze.

It's empty. There's nothing but his mahogany desk and oversized executive chair. Everything about it feels cold. Even the paintings have disappeared. I wonder where they went. I know they cost a lot of money. Did Riggs toss them or give them to my father?

It doesn't matter.

My stomach churns, and I put my hand on the glass, blinking hard. How could he have been so greedy? I finally tear my eyes off the sad sight, unable to take it anymore, and continue down the hall.

I stop in front of Connie's desk. She looks up and smiles. "Mrs. Madden, it's good to see you again."

I return her smile, happy and relieved to see a friendly, familiar face. But I state, "Connie, you've always called me Blakely. Please don't stop."

She beams brighter. "Okay, Blakely. Riggs told me earlier to send you in when you arrived."

"Thank you," I say and walk past her. I open the door, step inside, then shut the door.

Riggs stands in front of the window with his arms crossed, lost in thought.

I stare at the back of my husband's body.

God, I miss him.

Ink flows over his forearms, blocked by the cuffs of his rolled sleeves. He's always hidden his tattoos for work, based on some deal he made with my father, who didn't approve of them.

The fact that Riggs is no longer hiding them makes me happy. It's also a display of how much things have changed.

The taut fabric stretches across his back, over his muscular surfer shoulders, and I ache to see him fighting the waves at our beach house. His perfectly tailored pants hang over his ass in just the right way, and I have to tear my eyes off it.

I assume he didn't hear me come in. He looks lost, and I can sympathize. It's exactly how I spend most of my day.

How can two people feel so horrible apart and want to be together yet can't figure out their issues?

I clear my throat, suddenly nervous. I've not seen my husband since the hotel room in Detroit when he left me. I fought going to the L.A. apartment or coming here, and even though we're in contact daily via text, it's not the same.

I've missed everything about him. The electricity a room has when he's in it, even if he believes he's all alone, always amazes me. And how his unruly hair can be disheveled while still sexy, is something most men can't pull off. But just being in his presence makes me feel alive, even if we're not sure where we stand with the other.

He spins, and his face lights up. It's not as much as it usually is when he sees me, but I still notice it. Yet there's also a sadness in his expression, and I don't miss that either.

He hesitates, which is unlike him, then walks over to me and tugs me into his arms. His spicy, woody scent with that hint of orange peels flares in my nostrils, turning the heat in my core hotter.

I don't think. My body naturally responds to his, and I wrap my arms around him, melting into him, not wanting to let him go. For the first time in a month, I feel safe again.

He kisses the top of my head and murmurs, "I missed you, pet."

I force myself to look at him, honestly replying, "I've missed you too. So much."

He opens his mouth and snaps it shut, inhaling deeply through his nose, never taking his eyes off me.

I fret, "What's wrong?"

Sadness expands on his face. He kisses my head again. Then retreats. My body instantly regrets the loss of his warmth and the safety he always provides. I've been craving it and didn't realize how much.

He orders, "Come sit down," and points to his desk.

Still unsure what forms he's referring to or what's about to unfold, I nervously obey.

He slides a folder across the desk and sits next to me. I question, "What is this?"

He assesses me, then announces, "It's the company shares your father signed over to me. Also, all the things I took out of his safe are in my office. It's the one at the beach house. Everything is yours."

My stomach flips, and I gape at him. *What is he talking about?*

He carefully watches me for a few minutes, then opens the folder. He asserts, "You need to sign for the shares."

I glance at the forms and jerk my head back toward him, declaring, "I don't want any of this."

In a neutral tone, he answers, "This belongs to you. Although I am taking over the ability to make the final call on any business deal. Your father held that power, and it's the one thing I need to run the company."

The hairs on my arms rise. My mouth turns dry, and I try to process what he's offering me, but it's all too much.

He picks up a pen, then takes my hand and positions my fingers over the barrel, gently declaring, "I need your signature, pet."

I put my hand over my stomach, blurting out, "I don't want the shares. I know nothing about this company and haven't done anything to earn it. This is your thing, not mine."

His jaw twitches. He calmly claims, "No, pet. I'm not asking you to run it. That's my job. But this is your inheritance. This isn't mine to keep."

"It is. It's all yours," I argue.

He sighs. "Of course it isn't."

"I don't want it," I seethe.

Confusion fills his expression. He lowers his voice. "Why are you mad at me over this?'

It takes me a moment to gather my thoughts. I finally admit, "When I left my father's house, I left everything behind. That included his money. And I don't want anything that he built."

"Well, I built most of it," Riggs mutters.

"I-I believe you, which is another reason I can't take this."

Riggs furrows his brows. "Don't be foolish, pet. There is over a billion dollars-worth of stock and millions per year in revenue."

The sound of that makes me queasy. I rise. "No, I don't want this. I'll earn my own money."

He stands and cups my cheeks, holding me so I can't avoid his blues. He asks, "Why wouldn't you want what is yours?"

I assert, "It's not mine. It's my father's."

"*Was* your father's," Riggs states.

I continue, "Like I said, I know nothing about managing a company or stock."

Amusement fills his face. "It's okay. I told you I'll run things. You don't have to worry. All you have to do is sit back and collect your money in your bank account."

"It's not my money! It's yours!" I cry.

He firmly declares, "You're my wife. Whatever I have is yours."

My heart beats so hard I think it'll explode out of my chest. I question, "Then why are you making me sign for this?"

He gives me no answer other than firmly restating, "It's yours."

My fears take hold. I blurt out the biggest one I have, accusing, "You're going to divorce me, aren't you?"

He slowly shakes his head. "No. Stop saying that. This has nothing to do with our issues."

My voice cracks when I say, "I don't believe you."

Red crawls into his cheeks. He proclaims, "This is only about giving you what's rightfully yours." He picks up the pen and, in his most controlling voice, orders, "Now sit down and sign, pet."

His tone makes my blood race faster. I squeeze my thighs together and almost do it just from hearing him give me a command, but I fight it and step back.

"I'm sorry. I can't," I cry out and run out of the room.

He follows me and grabs my arm when I get to the elevator. "Pet."

"I'm not doing it, Riggs. It's yours. Do whatever you want with it, but I'm not taking it from you."

"Blakely, it's not mine to keep," he firmly repeats.

The elevator doors open and I step inside. He takes a step forward, and I push on his chest. "Do not follow me. I'm not changing my mind, and I need to go."

Kalim steps between us. He calmly states, "You heard her, Riggs. Another time."

Riggs doesn't move, asking, "Blakely, where do you need to go? What's so important that we can't discuss this further?"

I admit, "I'm meeting my mom."

His eyes widen. He lowers his voice and asks, "Why would you do that?"

Kalim repeats, "Step back, Riggs. We've discussed this." He turns his warning glare on him.

Riggs hesitates, then eyes Kalim. He scowls but steps back, demanding, "At least answer my question. Why are you meeting with Madelyn?"

Tears well in my eyes, "I don't know. If you want the truth, I have no idea why I'm doing anything anymore."

Sympathy and frustration erupt on his expression as the doors to the elevator close. Kalim hits the button and it moves down.

I wipe my face. I avoid looking at him or anyone else and allow him to lead me to the SUV. I pull myself together and text my mother.

> Me: On my way. Are you still there?

I silently plead for her to tell me she left or for her to not answer me. Then I wouldn't have to deal with her today, but my plea goes unanswered.

Mom: Yes. I'm waiting.

She sends me another selfie as proof.

I groan, then tell the driver where to go. Within ten minutes, he pulls up to the cafe. Kalim escorts me inside, and I slide into the booth across from my mother.

Her face is bright red. She chirps, "Don't I get a hug?"

"You've been drinking," I snap.

She leans forward, and the hint of vodka hits me. Most people claim you can't smell it, and that's why it's an alcoholic's choice, but I always can. I grew up with her smelling like a fifth. She squeezes my hand and disregards my comments stating, "You've got to give me money, baby girl."

I hold my breath again, shocked. I shouldn't be. I should have seen this coming. I don't know what I expected, but we'll never have the relationship I've always wanted. I figured this out years ago in Al-Anon meetings. All our relationship has ever consisted of is what I can give her.

She slurs, "Help your mama out. I can't live like this. Your father got caught."

My heart races faster. I lean closer, wishing I hadn't heard the last part.

Please, God, tell me she didn't know.

She adds, "I told him not to be careless, but he didn't cover his tracks well enough." She blinks several times, as if she might pass out.

I yank my hand away from hers. My voice shakes as I whisper, "You knew?"

She blinks harder and closes her eyes, saying, "Money, Blakely. I need your money, baby girl. Don't leave me like this."

The vision of my mother turns fuzzy. I swipe at my cheek, grab all the cash I have in my purse, and slap it down on the table. I rise and declare, "That's all you're getting. Don't ever contact me again."

I glance at Kalim and realize the entire cafe's taking photos and whispering. No doubt it's about my mother and me and her drunken state. Embarrassment fills me, and I can't get out of there quick enough.

Kalim quickly leads me out to the vehicle. I sit back in the SUV, exhausted from the day and the entire state of my life.

My stomach churns, knowing my mother knew my father was stealing.

How much worse can my family situation be?

They aren't my family anymore. Riggs is.

For how long? What if he wants a divorce?

I need to get him back.

Why can't I tell him what he needs to hear?

I don't know why I'm surprised about my mother knowing. I shouldn't be. Her morals mirror my father's. But it's just another blow to my heart.

Then the thought of Riggs trying to give me the shares of his company tears at it further. I can't get the notion out of my head that he's doing it to try to divorce me. I can imagine it being his way to ensure I'm financially stable on my own.

Why else would he want to give them to me if what's his is mine?

When I finally get inside Apartment Thirteen and slide into bed, I sob hard. I've never felt so out of control, and all I can think about is calling Riggs and having him help me get back in control.

Then my phone rings. I glance at the screen and answer, "Riggs, my answer's the same. I don't want any of it."

Concern fills his voice. He admits, "I saw the photos. Are you okay, pet?"

I sit up in alarm. "Photos? What do you mean?"

"There are a lot of photos of you and your mom on social media."

More tears escape me. I sniffle. *Of course there are.*

He states, "I'm coming over."

I blurt out, "No, don't. I mean it. I need to be by myself right now."

The moment I say it, I regret it, but as much as I want him, I can't seem to tell him to come over.

Minutes of silence pass. He finally concedes. "Okay, but I'm here if you need me."

Need him.

My heart hurts more than anything about how much I need him. But instead of telling him how much, I repeat, "Don't come. I'll be fine." I hang up.

I sob until I fall asleep for a few hours. When I wake up, it's late in the evening and dark out. My phone vibrates. I glance at the screen.

> Colton: Get dressed in your sexiest attire, superstar.

> Me: I don't feel like going anywhere. I'm in for the night.

> Colton: I know what you need, so get ready. I'm not taking no for an answer. Those photos were pretty harsh.

I squeeze my eyes shut, just imagining what's out there. I start to type an objection, then freeze.

Another message pops up.

> Colton: We're going to Club Indulgence.

My pulse skyrockets. Nothing has ever felt more right than submitting to Riggs right now, but he's not going to be there.

> Me: I can't. Riggs would kill me, and I'm not interested in anyone else.

> Colton: I didn't say anything about you doing anything with anyone else. Come with me. I'll show you the entire club. It'll make you feel better.

My heart pounds harder as I debate about what to do.

> Colton: I'll be there in an hour. And I'm not taking no for an answer.

I decide there's no point in fighting him and take a shower. I debate about what to wear, then put on the collar Riggs gave me for our wedding night, a silver thong, slip dress, and matching stilettos. I wrap a trench coat around me to be safe.

When Colton arrives, I give myself a final glance. I pick my phone up, ready to cave, but stop before I text Riggs to meet me at the club.

I decided that maybe Colton is right and being in the atmosphere of Club Indulgence will help my mood.

I hesitate once more about texting Riggs, then decide it's best to leave my phone at home.

There's no way I'll be able to be there and not beg him to come find me.

14

Riggs

Frustration engulfs me at an all-time high.

Why wouldn't she sign the forms?

How could I have let her leave my office without making things right between us?

I clench my fists, staring into the L.A. nighttime horizon, not focusing on anything in particular. Since I saw Blakely and pulled her into my arms, my unsettled cravings spiked like an out-of-control fever.

I need my wife back.

I drop my head, inhaling the faint smell of her still left on my shirt. Muted sea salt and driftwood notes barely register, and my yearnings dig into me deeper.

She wore her pink collar.

It has to mean something if she's wearing her collars, not just with me but in public.

I go to my desk and tap the return key on my laptop. Images of my pet fill the screen from the search I did earlier today. I scan ten pages of results before I lean back, even more frustrated, tugging on my hair. And the carnal urges burning inside me plague me.

She has a collar on in every photo.

Since I became a Dom, I've never gone this long without making a woman submit. Normally, I can go to the club, pick a submissive or a switch who likes to play both roles, then demand they kneel before me. After I finish with them, if the itch isn't scratched out of me, I can find someone else and keep going, even if I'm there for days.

Not once have I been in a situation where I've committed to a sub and I haven't been able to have them whenever and wherever I wanted. So this entire ordeal tests every ounce of restraint I possess.

I'm pretty sure I'm losing the battle. Blakely's no closer to coming home than before she walked into my office today. If anything, I've pushed her farther away.

Reality makes my skin crawl with desires I can't act upon. I curse myself further.

Why didn't I make her submit in Detroit? I could have gotten some of this out of my system.

I shouldn't have let her leave my office.

I return to pacing the room, practically tearing my hair out, wishing my nerves weren't so frazzled. All our interactions since the charity event replay in my mind. They're on a movie reel that won't shut off, highlighting all the curves my pet displayed in the Detroit hotel room while she knelt by the window. It flashes against the smile she gave me when I held her earlier today, which all drives me to the point of insanity.

My phone jars me out of the nightmare, and my gut churns as I read the text.

> Kalim: I dropped Blakely and Colton off at a private club. She slipped past the bouncer and went inside. He's not letting me in.

My chest tightens. I grind my molars, feeling sick.

> Me: What club?

> Kalim: There's no sign. The bouncer seemed to recognize her, and she seemed to know him.

He sends me a photo of the head bouncer at Club Indulgence.

My stomach flips faster. I grab my keys and get to my Porsche at record speed.

For the first time ever, I curse myself for having such strong security measures, and wait for the lift to position my vehicle on the ground floor.

I tap on the wheel in the darkness and call Blakely. It rings four times, then goes into voicemail.

"Fuck!" I shout.

I text her.

> Me: Call me immediately. This isn't a request.

The message says delivered and I wait for it to say read, but it never does.

The lift doors open, and I peel out of the parking garage and into the L.A. streets, weaving in and out of traffic at a dangerous pace, continuing to call her but always getting voicemail. I run every stoplight, pull into my space inside the club's parking garage, and continue lecturing myself for my stupidity on the way inside.

I streak through the dark hallway, unsure where I'm going, and glance at the windows of the viewing rooms as I pass.

Where is she?

She's with Colton.

Club Indulgence is huge, with three sections. It hits me that if she's with Colton, she'll be in the section where everything goes.

What's he getting her involved in?

Anger and fear catapult inside me. It's no secret at the club that Colton is a member. I don't see him since I don't wander into his section. My motto is *to each their own*. I don't care what he does, but it doesn't do anything for me. So I've never met nor seen him until Detroit. Yet I should have considered that if he and Blakely became friends, he might try to bring her here.

I turn another corner and run into one of the managers, Maureen.

"Whoa! Where's the fire?" she teases.

My delivery is harsher than I mean for it to come out, but my blood is boiling too hot to control it. I bark, "Where's my wife?"

Her eyes widen. "Blakely is here?"

I exhale through my nose. "So I've heard. With Colton Linwood."

Maureen's eyebrows arch higher. "Oh. Ummm..." She swallows hard. "I'm... I'm sorry. I didn't anticipate that. I assumed that they're into different things."

"She's not into him," I seethe, running my hand through my hair, and demanding, "Maureen, find out where she's at!"

"Oh. Right. Sorry," Maureen states, then removes her phone from her pocket. She swipes at the screen, types something in, then waits half a minute. Her phone buzzes. She reads the message, then declares, "They're in area three. Room forty-five."

"Inside or outside?" I question.

She glances at her phone again, then relays, "It says in."

I'm not familiar with the rooms in area three. My gut drops further. I mutter, "Thanks," then shove past Maureen.

I continue down the dark hallway, not replying to anyone who offers me a greeting, and open the door for area three. Not once have I been in this section. I never had a reason to come here. There are some Doms and subs I recognize who move between my area and this one, but I ignore them too.

Every step I take creates a bigger stirring of worry. I don't know if there's a viewing space inside room forty-five or if it's participation only.

Please let there be a viewing space.

I'm going to kill Colton for bringing my pet here. Kalim's on my list too, even though I know that unless you're a member, there's no getting past the club's security.

I follow the signs, keeping my focus in front of me, borderline sweating by the time I see the number forty-five hanging outside the room.

There's no glass, which could mean anything. The red light is on, indicating a session is taking place and no one is to enter.

For the first time ever, I break the rules, not caring or even considering the consequences. It's a dangerous thing to do at Club Indulgence. Every area and room have different repercussions, including losing your membership for extreme defiance.

I fling the door open, and a buzzer rings. It's quick and soft but enough to stop the Dom, who's in a session with four subs. Two are women, and two are men. To my relief, the room's packed with several dozen viewers.

All eyes turn on me, including the Dom.

Even though I don't frequent this area, he's highly regarded in the club. No one knows his name, as he prefers to be called Papi, a Latin term for Daddy. However, he never enters other areas and always chooses to play with multiple bi-sexual subs. I've met him a few times when we had round table sessions for Doms.

He narrows his gaze on me, which may intimidate others, but I give him an equal stare down, then nod in an apology. I scan the spectators until Blakely comes into view. My adrenaline buzzes through my veins like a lightning bolt.

She's wearing the platinum and diamond collar I gave her for our wedding night.

How could she come here without me and wear it?

Her eyes widen, and her lips part in surprise, slightly trembling. I glance at her breasts. Even with the short distance, her hardened nipples make my mouth water.

How long has it been since I've had my lips on them?

I need to get her out of here.

I squeeze my fists tighter, beeline over to her, then reach for her, demanding, "Let's go."

"Sit and stay awhile," Colton interjects, smirking at me.

I scowl at him, vowing to deal with him later. I'm in a touchy position and need to get my pet out of here. I refocus on her, firmly ordering, "Now."

Blakely slowly takes my hand. It's shaking, and she rises.

I tug her close to me and move about ten feet.

Papi booms, "Riggs, you interrupted my session."

I take a deep breath and turn. "Yes. I apologize. My wife and I are just leaving." I take several more steps.

He grunts, then asserts, "I don't think so."

The bouncer moves in front of the door, and my chest tightens. I tighten my hold on Blakely's waist and spin us.

Papi claims, "You broke the rules."

I silently beg him to show me some mercy, locking eyes with him and repeating, "I extend my biggest apologies. As I said, my wife and I are leaving."

His lips curl. He shakes his head and states again, "I don't think so."

"Papi—"

"You broke the rules, Riggs. Consequences are in order," he declares and arches his eyebrows.

Blakely's body stiffens next to me. My pulse skyrockets. I clutch her tight to my side. I want to argue with him, but a Dom cannot allow anyone to break the rules without dishing out a punishment of some sort. It demonstrates to members that it's not okay to disregard protocol.

Papi gives me a moment, continuing to give me his challenging stare, and I realize there's no getting out of this.

I swallow hard, then ask, "What are the consequences of this room?"

Satisfaction fills his expression. He states, "I think I'll use my authority to override them."

Relief fills me. I nod. "Thank you." I move Blakely a few steps.

He shouts, "Wait!"

My gut sinks again. I look at him in question.

Papi announces, "I didn't say there will be no consequences."

Blakely's hand grips my thigh. I inhale her driftwood and sea salt scent and grit my teeth, seething, "Then get on with it."

A dark expression fills his face. I've seen it with Doms and am sure I possess it too. It sends a chill down my spine. He focuses on Blakely and questions, "Why did you come without your husband?"

"It's none of your business," I snarl.

Papi scoffs. "Are you going to break more rules, Riggs?"

I almost protest, then snap my mouth shut. He has all the authority now. I'm in his room, interrupting his session. I don't need to dig the hole I'm in any deeper.

He turns back to my pet, pushing, "Well?"

She trembles harder, her forehead creasing with anxiety.

He leaps off the stage, lunges toward us, and slides his hands on her cheeks, inquiring, "Tell me. Why did you come into my session without your husband?"

"Take your hands off my wife," I warn.

He locks eyes with me, waits a moment, then slowly obeys, taunting, "Rather possessive, aren't we?"

"Don't push me," I threaten.

Even though he's at least six inches shorter than me, he never flinches. The tense silence grows with all eyes on us.

He finally asserts, "So the media reports have some truth to them."

I stay silent.

He continues, "It seems you two have some issues to work out."

The air tastes stale. I try to calm the growing riptide in my stomach. No matter what has happened between Blakely and me, one thing I don't want is for anyone, even members who are contracted to secrecy, to know our business.

He refocuses on Blakely. In a powerful tone, he inquires, "When was the last time you had a session with your husband?"

She blinks hard, her eyes watering.

He softens his tone. "Ah. I see." He studies her for a moment, and my skin crawls.

A dozen scenarios about what he might require her to do to atone for my sin enter my mind. In a low tone, I warn, "No one touches my wife but me."

He states, "She came here with Colton."

Colton blurts out, "We're only friends. No one touches her but Riggs, Papi."

Papi jerks his head toward Colton, and I go back on team Colton for a minute, even though I'm still pissed he brought my wife here.

Colton tears his eyes off him and tells Blakely, "You have your safe word. No one can make you do anything."

Papi's eyes turn to slits. He returns to assessing us and then announces, "We will use this as a learning moment."

"Meaning?" I ask.

His lips twitch. He points to people in the front seating area, ordering, "Find a different spot."

The spectators get up and relocate, the Doms shooting him daggers. It's a coveted spot they would have paid a pretty penny for, but like me, they're at the mercy of Papi.

He calls out to his subs, "Clear the stage and go to the couches. Strip when you get there."

The four of them scramble, obeying him and undressing the moment they step in front of the couch.

Papi goes over to them, directs one of the men and one of the women to sit and spread their knees, then unlatches the restraints on the back of the sofa. He secures their wrists. Then he orders the other two, "Kneel with your face in position."

The standing man obeys and puts his mouth next to the other guy's dick, and the woman does the same to the restrained woman's pussy.

Papi turns back to Blakely and me. He asserts, "You will go on stage and demonstrate your skills. You will find out why your wife came into this room."

I try again to get out of this, claiming, "We're in the wrong area. My apologies. As you know, we stay in area two."

His lips turn into a tight smile. "Yes, and your wife came in here. I authorize you to utilize any sub or switch in this room unless they state their safe word."

My heart almost pounds out of my chest. I repeat, seething, "No one touches my wife except me."

"What does she want?" Papi arrogantly asks.

My insides quiver, and my mouth turns dry. I turn toward Blakely, not wanting to believe she would want anyone to touch her but me. She was clear when she signed our contract she didn't want anyone else involved in our relationship.

That was before our issues.

I'm suddenly unable to know for sure, so Papi is right. She did come in here. What if what I've been giving her isn't what she wants?

She gapes at Papi, her chest rising and falling faster.

"Well? What do you want, Mrs. Madden? The sky is the limit in here. Whatever you want, your husband will have to give it to you tonight."

My stomach spins so fast bile flies up my throat. I barely swallow it down.

She lifts her chin and squares her shoulders. Her lips quiver as she states, "Only my husband has the authority to touch me."

Amusement and disappointment swirl in his expression. His eyes turn to slits as he studies her.

"You heard her. I'm sorry again that we interrupted your session," I restate and move Blakely toward the door.

"Stop, Riggs," Papi demands.

I freeze, close my eyes for a brief moment, then lift my chin. I spin us toward him again.

He questions, "Where are you going?"

"This isn't our area."

"It is tonight."

I run my thumb on the back of Blakely's waist, trying to calm her. She's shaking harder against me, and I don't know if it's pure fear or something else.

Either way, I need more time to figure it out, and I don't have it. Papi issues a threat, stepping forward and lowering his voice. "There are only two options here, Riggs."

I scowl, stating, "No, there aren't."

"Yes, there are You interrupted my session, and I get to decide the punishment. Option one is you go on stage and find out why your wife agreed to come to this club without you and into my area. Or, your membership will be terminated for repeated disobedience," he warns.

Not only did I never think I would break a rule, but I suddenly don't care about my membership. All I want is to be with my wife, and I'll be damned if I put her through this. I snarl, "Then cancel my membership."

The room gasps.

Papi's head jerks backward. He blurts out, "You don't mean that."

"I'm not—"

"We'll do it," Blakely interjects, her voice cracking.

I turn toward her, sliding my hands over her cheeks, declaring, "No. I don't care about this place anymore. All I care about is you. We'll go home and talk about this, but not here."

Her defiant expression erupts on her face, making my cock hard. I hate myself for it. She challenges, "No. We aren't getting kicked out."

"You don't have to do this. We'll talk at home," I repeat.

She swallows hard, claiming, "I'm not going home with you, Riggs."

More gasps fill the air. Anger, hurt, and disappointment whip through me, mercilessly beating me with new force. "You don't know what you're saying."

She blinks harder. "I do."

"No. You don't."

She closes her eyes, then retreats from my grasp. She goes to the stage, climbs the stairs, and removes her slip dress, revealing her bare breasts. She kneels in only her silver thong and stilettos, her spine straight and her perfect round ass on her calves. She locks eyes with me, her blues I've always loved with extra heat swirling amongst the chaos.

The craziness I feel whenever I step into my Dom role ignites, torching every part of my body.

She tears her gaze off mine, lowers her head toward the floor, and waits.

Papi mutters, "It's your show now. Time to find out why your wife is here without you." He walks away, sits between his subs, and caresses the heads of those kneeling.

Electricity fills me as I stare at my wife, kneeling perfectly, waiting for me the exact way I envisioned her when I first fell for her over a decade ago.

There's no more arguing. No matter what my thoughts were, they no longer matter. The power I feel whenever she submits to me becomes a blanket, wrapping tighter around me until I can barely breathe.

I assess the stage, taking in all the sex furniture, the restraints, the St. Andrew's Cross, and the wall of toys. Everything spins in front of me. The time away from her only makes me think about all the things I've wanted to do with her and couldn't.

The only debate now is what route to take at this moment.

Whatever it is, I'm not stopping until I find out everything I need to about my wife and how to get her to come home to me.

15

Blakely

The tension crackles around me as goose bumps break out on my skin. No one in the room speaks, and I can feel their eyes studying me. I count seconds, trying to calm my quivering insides, but lose track of how many minutes pass.

Why did I say I would do this?

Everyone can see me almost bare.

I should stop this now.

An intense throbbing within me gains power, pumping blood in my lower body to areas I can never satisfy, no matter what I do to quench the cravings. Only Riggs knows how and it's been too long since he gave me what I need.

My skin heats as more adrenaline ignites in my system. He's behind me, not touching me, but I know he's there. Then, he drags his thumb down my spine, taunting me, creating a shiver so violently that my entire body shakes.

I focus on the floor, doing my best to regain control of the positions, but it takes more time than it has in the past.

Riggs's hot breath hits my ear. He whispers so no one can hear, "You're going home with me tonight."

Butterflies break out in my belly, fluttering at full force, making me dizzy. I want nothing more than to be at the beach house, waking up with Riggs next to me or going outside to watch him in the surf.

I can't. There are too many unresolved issues between us.

Don't let him leave you like he did in Detroit.

I squeeze my eyes shut, attempting to regulate my breathing, asking myself again why I agreed to put myself in this position.

"You're my wife. *Mine*," Riggs murmurs, his lips hitting my ear, answering the question that doesn't need an explanation.

My husband's powerful. His strength and dominance sear through me, singeing all of my atoms, curling my toes, igniting a tremor inside me I can't stop. It's everything I've missed and yearned to feel again but didn't know how to retrieve.

He adds, "Forever, pet."

I blink hard, reminding myself there's a room full of people who want to see me break. And as much as I want Riggs to do what he's an expert at, the defiant part of me accepts the challenge.

If he shatters me into millions of pieces here, will it be the same as when we're alone? Or will I feel different, somehow too exposed?

He steps around me, his shiny brown loafers an inch from my knees. He crouches, lifting my chin and pinning his dark gaze on me.

My soul awakens further. I haven't seen that expression on Riggs since Detroit when he left me on my own, dying for him to return. And a cyclone of memories spin, flashing our past encounters in my mind—from the first night when he restrained me to the towel rack, to the way he left me desperate for him on the piano. Then there's our trip to Maui when he demonstrated his different skills every day. It all flares like a siren, turning me hotter as he continues to assess me.

His face hardens. More time passes until my chin quivers against his palm. Then arrogant satisfaction erupts on his sharp features. In a haunting voice, he states, "You don't belong in this club without me." His eyes drop to my collar. Anger and hurt fill his expression, and he lifts his blues, locking them on mine.

Anticipation flares, and I inhale sharply.

He reaches for the platinum choker and slides his fingers under the metal, gripping it so it's tight against my neck. He tries to keep his voice steady, but I hear the emotion as he accuses, "Did you plan on allowing someone else to play with you, pet?"

"No!" I blurt out.

Daggers fly from his eyes.

I correct myself, saying, "No, Sir."

He purses his lips together, tugging on the choker, positioning my face in front of his. The scent of woody spice laced with orange peels assaults me, escalating the throbbing I can't stop. He speaks louder, "Who do you belong to?"

"You, Sir," I reply.

He grits his teeth. "Then why did you wear this to come here without me?"

I stay quiet, pondering how to answer him.

Rage grows on him, swirling with the pain I seemed to have caused him. It adds to the tiny hint of fear I always feel. It's comforting and disturbing all at the same time.

I reiterate, "I only belong to you, Sir."

My answer doesn't seem to appease him. He snarls, "Yet you wore this here without me."

"I-I..." I exhale an anxious breath, trying to come up with the words to express my thoughts.

He doesn't give me time to figure it out. He jumps to his feet, slides his hands under my armpits, and pulls me off the ground. He fists my hair, tugs my head back, and leans over my face.

Heat spikes in my veins. My heart pounds frantically. I squeeze my thighs together and hold my breath.

He seethes, "Your actions speak louder than words, pet."

I open my mouth to reply, yet nothing comes out.

He declares, "Punishments exist for pets who wander off."

"I haven't ever—"

He puts his hand over my lips. He continues staring at me, calling out, "Permission to record the session, Papi."

My stomach flips. All the recordings of me he sent my father blaze in my mind. Will Riggs send more footage to further destroy him, and thus me?

"Permission granted," Papi answers.

"Riggs—" I try to speak from behind his palm.

He leans into my ear and states, "Rule six, pet. Either use your safe word or walk over to the X on the floor, face the crowd, and wait for me." He points to the middle of the stage and gives me a challenging stare.

A million thoughts race in my mind about what he could do with the video. All of them hurt me. The longer I look at my husband, the more our reality shines.

He releases me and taunts, "Say the safe word, pet."

I lift my chin, scared of what he might do but unable to say it.

"What's the safe word? Assure me you remember it," he demands.

"It's stop," I answer.

His lips curve into a tight smile. "Good. Now say it and this will be over."

I can't. No matter how much my brain screams at me to say stop, I can't.

With his eyes pinned to mine, he shouts, "Permission for the microphone, not just video footage."

My stomach churns. I glare at Riggs.

Papi replies, "Granted."

Riggs once again orders, "Say the safe word."

I blink hard, trying not to cry, yet unable to end what's about to happen.

Riggs traces my collarbone and continues, "Permission to use the footage however I want, outside the club."

My insides quiver. My breathing turns shallow, and the stale air never leaves my lungs.

Papi repeats, "Permission granted."

Riggs crosses his arms, commanding, "Say the safe word or assume the position for your punishment."

My mouth turns dry, and I open it, but once again, nothing comes out.

He purses his lips, arching his eyebrows, daring me to say it.

I swallow hard. My throat feels like it'll crack from the lack of moisture, and I square my shoulders. I cross the stage, stand on the X, and focus on the back wall so I avoid the eyes of the other members.

The lights dim further, or maybe it's my eyesight from staring for so long as my pulse pounds between my ears. Then the grinding of metal agitates my senses further as a pewter contraption lowers from the ceiling and a bench rises from the floor.

Riggs steps behind me, slides his palm over my hip, and tugs my hair so my head rests on his shoulder. His lips graze my ear, and new tingles shoot through my spine. He asks again, "Why did you wear your collar and come here without me?" He moves his thumb to the front of my thigh, caressing my skin until I shudder and close my eyes.

"Answer me, pet," he gently prods.

I stare at the ceiling, the high of having his body against mine rushing through me, wanting to tell him how I can't stand the thought of not wearing a collar because it keeps me as his. Yet I can't find the words, nor do I want to admit this to a roomful of strangers.

He softly chuckles in my ear, stating, "There's my defiant little pet."

I shift my gaze to try to glance at him, but he holds me firmly.

He asks, "Remember when Aria stared at you, taking her punishment?"

The anger I feel toward his close relationship with her flares. I hate her name on his lips, yet my cells also buzz with excitement. Still, I stay quiet.

"Answer me," he orders.

"Yes, I remember, Sir."

He takes a deep breath and kisses the curve of my neck. He declares, "Punishment time." He traces my slit, then orders, "Lie on the bench." He pushes my thong over my hips and it falls at my feet. He releases me, steps back, and the cold air hits my back.

I obey his command, lying down and grabbing the legs as Aria did.

He crouches in front of me and shakes his head. "No, pet. It's not going to happen like this."

"I-I don't understand, Sir," I reply, confused.

He rises, reaches for something, then yanks a chain from the ceiling.

My heart pounds against the bench, unsure of what's happening.

He unlatches a double cuff, then secures my wrists in them. He locks eyes with me, strokes my cheek, and says, "There's a reason you entered this area."

I shake my head, protesting. "No."

He snarls, "Don't lie to me, pet."

I'm only here because Colton wanted to come, and I'm suddenly fearful of what Riggs might allow. My voice cracks as I whisper, "Only you, Sir. Please. Only you."

His face never flinches. He declares, "You'll keep your eyes on Papi and his subs at all times. Just like Aria studied you, you'll watch them. Understand?"

I scrunch my face, still hating how he refers to her with such ease. And I don't understand why he's making me focus on them.

He adds, "You want to be here, so you'll take it all in."

"I don't—"

He puts his finger over my lips, claiming, "There's no negotiation. I'm enforcing all the rules, understand?"

I take a deep breath, nodding. "Yes, Sir."

"What's rule three?" he questions.

I answer verbatim, "The sub will only come when permitted by the Dom, Sir."

"And rule four?" His lips curve into a tight smile.

I shift my hips into the bench, reciting, "The sub will allow the Dom to engage with her in any sexual positions he desires, at any time he desires, and at any place he desires. Penetration will include vaginal, oral, and anal, sometimes simultaneously, Sir."

He drags his hand over my spine, quizzing, "Rule six?"

The anger I can't seem to escape rears its head again. I glare at him.

"Don't make me ask again," he warns.

I fight the defiance and answer, "Toys, restraints, and other accessories will be utilized when the Dom wishes. Video and/or audio recordings are at the Dom's discretion, Sir." I blink hard, wondering again how he'll use the footage. Will he hurt me with it, making me relive my nightmare again?

As if he knows my fears, he continues focusing on me, and calls out, "Papi, remind my wife who has total control over the recording."

My butterflies flutter while my stomach flips. It shocks me. I realize a part of me wants to be recorded. I'm excited at the thought of Riggs watching me after tonight. I can't deny it, even though I'm also pissed he asked for it after all he's done to me.

Papi shouts, "You have complete control, Riggs."

I clench my jaw.

Riggs rises, slides his hand over my ass, then fingers me, slipping easily inside my pussy. He arrogantly declares, "Won't be long until there's a pool of your fluids on the leather."

Heat flies to my cheeks. I close my eyes, inhaling his scent, hating how he always knows how my body will react to anything he does. Yet I also love it. There's never a time when he touches me and I don't crave more.

He demands, "Tell me about rule nine."

For all the things Riggs and I have done, we've never used rule nine. I kind of forgot about it. I answer, "The sub agrees to all forms of hot or cold play, Sir."

Riggs continues, "What is the last part of rule eleven? After the testing information."

My stomach flips. Guilt hits me, even though I have no desire to do anything with anyone besides my husband. I quietly state, "The sub will not engage in any play with anyone besides the Dom unless the Dom determines it's in her best interest. At any time, the Dom can allow an audience, Sir."

"Say it louder," he demands.

I bite my lip, unsure how to make him understand I'm not here to find another Dom or play with anyone.

"Say it," he seethes.

"Sir, the sub will not engage in any play with anyone besides the Dom unless the Dom determines it's in her best interest. At any time, the Dom can allow an audience," I repeat.

He sniffs hard. "Did I determine it's in your best interest to engage with others?"

"I didn't come here to do anything with anyone," I protest.

He narrows his eyes. "Let me remind you about rule number two."

I quickly add, "Sir."

He assesses me, then moves behind me. He widens my legs, restrains my ankles to cuffs on the floor, then rubs his hand over my ass, asserting, "I think it's time you understood all the ways I can punish you."

Without thinking, I buck my hips toward his hand.

He slaps me hard, and I gasp. "I didn't tell you to move!"

I grit my teeth, closing my eyes, attempting to find the strength I have whenever I'm at Riggs's mercy.

He reaches under the bench. He steps aside, and the chains creak, pulling my arms straight in front of me until they're as straight as possible, and Riggs presses something underneath me.

Anxiety fills me. I've never been in this position. I stare at my hands, suspended in the air.

The sound of another chain fills my ears, increasing my pulse. Riggs crouches in front of me again, his expression on the border of being out of control, which normally doesn't happen until we're well into a session.

It intensifies all my conflicting emotions. I swallow hard, wondering what else he'll do with whatever just lowered from the ceiling.

He whispers in my ear, "You're my wife. You took a vow. There's no undoing it."

I squeeze my eyes shut, knowing I'm hurting him, still in pain myself. And I wish I could move on and return to how things were. Yet even in this position, at his mercy, I can't.

He moves my hair to the side, attaches something to my collar, then pushes another button under the bench.

The loud whirring makes my stomach flip. My head lifts until my chin is off the bench and I'm looking straight at Papi and his subs. They're still in the same positions he instructed, only he's rubbing the heads of the two who are kneeling.

Riggs murmurs in my ear in a commanding tone, "You came into this area for a reason, so now you'll see it. Don't you dare take your eyes off them." He takes several lungfuls of air, his hot breath teasing my skin, then adds, "Show our guests how good of a pet you are. No coming until I say." He rises and steps away.

Several minutes pass, and my heart pounds harder as I wonder if I'll survive his punishment. The entire time, I obey Riggs, not that there's any ability to move anywhere. But I never take my eyes off Papi and his subs.

Riggs returns, drips something on my spine, and massages it all over my back, ass cheeks, and thighs. It feels nice, which calms me a bit but not much. Knowing everyone in the room is staring at me adds another layer of anxiety I can't shake.

Papi curls his hands in the hair of his subs, holding them in position. The restrained subs and Papi stare at me while he commands, "Start."

On cue, the man and woman begin licking the restrained subs' privates. The muscles in their arms tense, but they can't move them due to the cuffs. Heat creeps into their faces, and their chests rise and fall faster as they stare at me.

Papi leans over to the woman, whispers something in her ear, then bites her neck.

A soft moan comes out of her mouth, and she shifts her hips closer to the woman's face.

Papi catches her as if he knew it would happen. He tugs the kneeling woman's head back a bit so her tongue barely grazes the woman's pussy, then commands, "Faster."

The woman's tongue turns into a snake, flicking yet barely touching the other woman's glistening clit, causing her to loudly whimper.

Riggs states, "Don't move, pet," tearing my thoughts back to the realization I'm on stage, naked, suspended and restrained, at my husband's mercy.

Something hot drips on my back, initially making me feel like my skin's burning. I flinch, lifting my ass the few inches I can.

A sharp sting hits my ass cheek, and I cry out.

Riggs barks, "I said don't move!"

I breathe through my teeth, blinking back tears as the heat begins to cool.

Papi unlatches the restraints on the woman's wrists. He pushes the kneeling man's head over the restrained man's cock. Papi barks, "Don't you dare come." He begins forcefully moving the head of the kneeling sub so he's working the other man's cock while gagging.

The restrained man clenches his jaw, never removing his eyes from me, breathing through his nose.

Riggs drips more heat on me, drizzling it on the back of my thighs. I flinch again, and several stings flare widely on my ass. I realize it's a flogger and not his hand. He shouts, "Why did you come here without me?"

I lock eyes with Papi, trying to avoid what's happening next to him. The darkness in them reminds me of Riggs, which is almost comforting.

"Tell me!" Riggs demands, pouring the hot liquid on my arms.

I cry out, "I didn't want to, Sir!"

"Then why did you?" he barks, flogging me harder.

I glance at my arms, realizing it's wax. I blurt out, "Colton wanted me to come!"

"Don't blame him," Riggs accuses as he rubs his hand over the sting, then pours the hot liquid over my cheek, creating a feel-good yet painful sensation. He slides his fingers inside me until it feels like his entire fist is twisting inside my body.

New heat races through my veins and sweat pops out on my skin. Incoherent sounds fly out of my mouth and my body throbs against Riggs's hand.

He snarls, "Don't you come or look away from Papi and his subs!"

The wax begins to tighten over my skin, and I relock my gaze with Papi's, determined to follow Riggs's orders and not let my body do what it's dying to do.

"Oh yes!" the restrained sub cries out, and my eyes drift to her.

Papi's dark eyes glow hotter. He pushes her head to his cock and orders, "Start."

She begins licking him just like the man licked the other.

Papi reaches for the woman on the floor and pushes her face into the other woman's pussy, holding it there, barking, "Eat."

The woman sucking Papi's cock reaches for the gagging man's head. She laces her fingers through Papi's and matches the pace of the other subs.

Riggs leans over my back, grabs hold of the corner of the bench, and enters me, taking me by surprise, pushing into me until his pelvis hits my ass.

I cry out, "Oh God!"

Papi growls, "Come, Kitty Kat."

The woman giving him a blowjob continues while her body erupts in convulsions.

Riggs positions his face next to mine, demanding, "Is this what you wanted? To see this?" He locks his arm so it cradles my head and then slows his thrusts, torturing me.

I try to look at him.

He warns, "Don't you dare take your eyes off them. You wanted to come here. You're going to take it all in."

"Riggs, please, I—"

He slides his hand under my body and pinches my nipple.

I yelp as my insides begin to spasm, trying to grasp his cock.

He threatens, "You'll address me as Sir. And don't you dare come on me until I permit you to. You may have forgotten your vow, but you will not disobey me."

A new fear takes hold. It's not that I had forgotten who my husband was, what he was capable of, or all the ways he could control me.

I had forgotten how high he makes me feel in these moments. How any taboo act, whether between us or others, he can turn into something exciting—something that spikes my adrenaline to the point I can't see straight.

He snarls, "You will come home with me. This ends tonight."

The biggest thing I forgot about Riggs is he always gets his way. And I'm the fool for assuming I'm capable of fighting him. All I want to do right now is give in.

I almost agree. Then I see the green blinking light from the corner of my eye. It's a reminder that he's recording me and can do whatever he wants with the footage.

And that little light is the new thorn in our marriage.

16

Riggs

I thought she'd use the safe word when I asked Papi for permission to record our session. No matter what I said, though, she wouldn't cave.

And now, I'm past the point of feeling like I'm in control. It's been too long since I got to dominate my wife. Her determination to defy me is still there, but she's different than before.

The naivety is gone. She's gotten into my world deeper than I ever thought she would go. She's curious about more things. She claims she didn't come here to find another Dom, but I don't believe her.

So I'll remind her exactly why she married me, even if it requires me torturing myself, like right now. The ache my body's felt for too many weeks is finally getting some relief. Yet I can't give in and allow myself my pleasure.

Not yet.

I'm not coming until I get her home tonight. Once she's in my bed, begging me, that's when I'll freely release inside her. Then I'm going to wake her up and do it again in the morning. But until then, I have to be careful. It would be easy to forget my discipline and give myself instant gratification.

My pet's body grips me like a vise, and I grit my teeth, thrusting faster, watching her reaction, then slowing down to stop myself from passing the point of no return.

Her body's trembling, and it's everything I've been craving. Nothing haunted me more than how she is when she's doing everything in her power not to give in to the high she wants.

The moaning in the room grows louder. I don't look at anyone except my wife, yet I know the activities taking place. There isn't a Dom or sub not involved in some perverse action right now, and it all adds to the heightened atmosphere.

Blakely's eyes open and close quickly. Her lips part, her breath hitches, and the flush in her face is more beautiful than I remember. She keeps her eyes on Papi and his subs and whimpers, "Please, Sir. Please!"

I murmur in her ear, "Please, what?"

Her voice cracks, "Let me come!"

"No. Not permitted," I answer, then glance at Papi's female subs. I ask, "Is that what you want? Someone else to eat your pussy?"

She scrunches her face, her lips trembling.

"Answer me," I order and tear the wax off her arms.

"Oh," she whimpers, blinking quickly.

"Tell me. Who do you want to eat your pussy?" I repeat.

"You. Only you!" she states.

"I don't believe you," I admit.

She tries to turn her head toward me.

I put my cheek next to hers, keeping her focus on the scene in front of us. I stop thrusting but keep my dick inside her. I mutter, "Rule eleven."

She swallows hard, furrowing her eyebrows.

I state, "The sub will not engage in any play with anyone besides the Dom unless the Dom determines it's in her best interest."

"I don't want anyone else, Sir," she claims.

"Liar," I accuse, then reiterate, "Unless the Dom determines it's in her best interest." My stomach flips at the thought of anyone else touching her, but there's a reason she's here.

"I'm not—"

I cover her mouth with my palm, then reach forward with my other hand and unlatch the double cuff. I murmur, "You'll submit how I see fit."

She blinks hard, and a tear falls down her cheek.

I swipe my finger over it, taunting, "Don't cry, pet. You didn't marry just any man. You married me. And there's nothing I won't give you. But make no mistake. You're coming home with me tonight."

More tears fall over my hand.

I add, "Don't move until instructed." I slowly pull out of her. Her tiny moan vibrates against my palm. My cock aches but so do my heart and ego. I never believed she could look for anyone else. Yet she came here wearing her collar.

I rise, then unlatch the ankle cuffs. I tear the rest of the wax off her, and she cries out. I lean down, kiss her ass cheek, and she shudders.

"Not yet," Papi calls out.

I ignore him and the other lewd sounds, then help Blakely to her feet, holding her firmly so she can catch her footing.

She stares at my chest, like the good sub she is, until I tilt her head. Her flushed cheeks and blue eyes make my balls ache again. I fight the inner demons that want to keep her all to myself and put my hand on her cheeks. My chest tightens, and I have to swallow down rising bile. I ask, "Do you want a male or female?"

She scrunches her face again, then slowly shakes her head. "You aren't listening, Sir."

"You don't have to pretend. Now answer my question, or I'll pick for you," I order.

Her lips tremble harder. Her breath shallows, and more tears fall.

For what feels like the hundredth time, I repeat, "You came here for a reason without me. You wore your collar."

"I don't want anyone else," she states.

Every time she says it, my heart soars. But she's lying. And I won't have any more lies between us. So I spin her into me and move her across the stage. I pick her up and set her on a medical examination table. I order, "Lie down."

She stays frozen.

In my most commanding tone, I repeat, "I said, lie down."

She gives me a painful look, then finally lowers her body onto the metal table. I've never seen her look so scared, even when I've done some pretty insane things to her.

My stomach flips, and I extend the stirrups, positioning her feet in them and then latching the ankle cuffs. I slide my hands over her thighs, then grab her wrists. I position them above her head and restrain them to more cuffs.

"R-Riggs," she whispers.

"Who am I?" I demand.

She swallows hard. "Sir." More tears fall down her cheeks.

I lean over her, trying to put on my more confident expression. "Don't cry over me. I'm giving you what you need. Then we're going home."

Confusion fills her face. "I-I don't—"

I put my fingers over her lips. "No more denying the obvious." I open the drawer under the table and pull out a gel mask. I place it over her eyes and lean into her ear, murmuring, "I love you. Now, last chance. Who do you want to eat your pussy? A man or woman?"

She shakes her head. "I only want you, Sir."

I squeeze my eyes shut. It's everything I want to hear, but she's only saying it to appease me. So I reply, "You wore your collar. Here. Without me. Not just any collar, but the one I gave you as our wedding gift. So I hear you loud and clear, pet. Now tell me which one."

Her forehead wrinkles deeper. She cries out, "Neither!"

I drag my fingers down her cleavage, and she shudders. I declare, "Since you came to this area, I assume you want a woman."

"No! I—"

I put my hand over her mouth, asserting, "Enjoy yourself. Papi's sub is now mine to utilize for you. But you still don't come until I permit you. And no talking, moaning, or making any sounds until I say. I'm still your husband. I'm still in charge."

A wet spot grows on the mask. My gut flips further. I know she doesn't want to hurt me, but I won't deny her what she craves. So I walk away from her, keeping my eyes locked on Papi, struggling with the debate in my head.

What am I doing?

This is what she wants.

I point at his two female subs, asking, "Which one of them deserves to eat out my wife?"

Papi's lips curl. My pulse skyrockets and my stomach pitches. Both his female subs look at him, hoping to get chosen. It all makes me feel sicker.

I've allowed others to play with my subs before. It was always something they spoke to me about and wanted to explore. And I never really cared.

Everything about this situation, I hate. I wish I could feel how I normally do, but I don't. All I can think is that my wife is supposed to be mine and mine alone. But I'd rather keep her than lose her. If this is what she needs, I'll give it to her.

Papi shakes his head. "Neither."

I jerk my head backward, accusing, "You said I had access to any of them."

He grins and rises, turning. He dramatically lifts his arm in the air and snaps.

A light turns on, illuminating a cage on a round wheeled platform. A brunette's inside, with chains draped around her naked body. Her wrists are secured to a dual cuff above her head. It has a chain about twelve inches long, allowing her to touch the bars in front of her.

Papi declares, "Tell Riggs and his pet how long you've been inside your cage, Princess."

She clears her throat. In a meek tone, she replies, "A month."

The room gasps.

"Louder," Papi orders.

She takes a deep breath, and her voice rings through the room. "A month."

"That's right. I allow you outside of it for less than three hours a day to eat, shower, and go to the bathroom. And you watch every session that takes place on this stage, or at my house, without being able to participate in anything. So tell everyone why I've kept you in the cage for a month," Papi commands.

She bites her lip for a moment, then squeezes the bars. She replies, "I disobeyed you."

"How?" he prods.

Her face turns red. "You ordered me to stop eating Angel's pussy."

Papi pushes, "Why didn't you stop?"

"I-I couldn't. I..." She swallows hard, and admits, "I love it too much."

Papi motions to a redhead standing next to the cage. He asks, "Did you finger yourself, then let Princess sniff your hand tonight?"

"Yes, Papi. I obeyed you," the woman answers.

Papi's twisted expression intensifies. He questions, "Did you drag the vibrator up and down her thighs as I ordered?"

"Yes, Papi."

He nods. "Good girl." He refocuses on Princess. "If I come over there, will I see a pool of your juices on the cage floor?"

"Yes, Papi," she breathlessly answers.

He reaches for his male sub on the floor and puts his hand on his shoulder, asking, "Why is it so wet?"

Princess doesn't hesitate. "I couldn't stop imagining what it would be like to eat his pet."

A loud moan fills the room, and more bile rises in my throat. I ignore searching for where it came from, then glance back at my pet. She's spread out on the exam table, her pussy glistening in the soft light, and all I want to do is end all of this.

Papi asks, "If I let you out of the cage, have you learned your lesson?"

She declares, "Yes, Papi."

"You're able to stop and start as Riggs commands you?" he questions.

"Yes. I promise, Papi," she claims in a desperate voice.

He announces, "Even if I allow Riggs to flog you while you do it?"

My heart pounds harder. I would have been into this before Blakely. But having her on the receiving end of another person's mouth is killing me.

"Please," Princess begs.

"I need a better answer than that," Papi states.

She licks her lips, replying, "I'll behave. I promise, Papi."

He stares at her a moment, then warns, "If you can't, then you'll be back in the cage. Only this time, I'll keep your pussy and ass full of devices I control. I'll deny you orgasms all day and night. It'll make the puddle under your feet look like a raindrop. Understand?"

Fear fills her expression. She takes a deep breath, nods, then answers, "Yes, Papi."

He snaps. "Release her."

The redhead steps in front of the cage. She unlocks the cuffs, then opens the door.

Princess carefully steps out. She stretches her arms, then walks up to Papi.

He reaches for her, tugs her into his arms, then fists her hair. He grabs a handful of her ass, whispers in her ear, and she grips his thigh, as if to steady herself.

The sickness I feel grows. I grind my molars, stare at my pet, and hate how she's trembling.

It's from her anticipation.

She wants this.

I can't do this.

Don't be a selfish bastard.

Cringing inside, I go to the toy wall, pick up a black leather flogger, and return to my pet. I lean into her ear, "I love you, and that's why I'm allowing this. You will come home with me when this is over."

"I don't—"

I press my lips to hers, sliding my tongue into her mouth and urgently flicking against hers.

She whimpers, returning my affection, and the world around us disappears for a moment.

"Assume your position," Papi calls out, pulling me back into reality.

I force myself to retreat, put my hand on my pet's cheek, and remind her, "No coming until I say." I step away before I change my mind and wince inside.

Princess kneels in front of the table. She presses a button, and the table lowers until my pet's pussy is in front of her face.

My stomach dives, and the worst feeling I've ever had fills me.

I need to stop this.

It's what she wants.

I stand taller and ask Princess, "What's your safe word?"

She glances at me, answering, "Crown."

I almost groan. I've never understood safe words that are anything besides stop. I reply, "Understood. When I order you to stop, you release my wife. You move a foot away from her body. Do I make myself clear?"

"Yes, Sir," she claims.

I instruct, "You can only use your tongue and lips to please my wife. Your fingers don't enter or touch her. Is that clear?"

She nods. "Yes, Sir."

"You will not bite my wife's clit. Understand?" I add, knowing how some of these subs can get carried away and I don't know what she's fully into. The last thing I need is her drawing blood.

Disappointment fills Princess's expression.

Alarm bells scream in my head. I turn to Papi. "If she can't fully obey this rule, we aren't doing this."

He holds his hand up. "Princess, tell Riggs you understand his pet's clit is not to be bitten."

She bats her eyelids. "Aww, Papi."

I bark, "Papi—"

"She'll obey. Stop being a brat, Princess," he orders.

Her face turns serious. "Sorry, Papi."

Papi crosses his arms. "Apologize to Riggs and assure him you understand the rules."

She turns to me. "I'm sorry, Sir. I won't bite your wife's clit."

I leer at her.

Her eyes widen. She holds up her hand. "I promise, Sir."

"She'll obey. She's good at following most rules. She has a problem with stopping, but hopefully, she learned her lesson," Papi assures me.

I take several deep breaths, still wanting to unlatch Blakely and run out of this room.

Don't be a selfish bastard.

It's the only way to keep her and save us.

The eyes of the entire room are on me. I finally point to my pet and order Princess, "Assume the position to begin."

"Riggs!" Blakely's shaky voice cries out.

"Relax, pet," I order in my most confident voice, feeling like a total sham. I announce, "Princess, you will not touch my wife until I give an order, understand?"

"Yes, Sir."

She stays on her knees in front of the table. She presses her palms against the metal, directly underneath my pet's pussy. Her face is a foot away, and I cringe inside, freezing.

Tense silence fills the room. I'm still determining how much time passes before Papi calls out, "Thank you for your respect. You may begin, Riggs."

It pulls me out of my trance, reminding me I'm a Dom on the stage. There are expectations. Part of me is relieved Papi thought I was being courteous to him. The rest of me just continues to feel ill.

I pull my arm back, then move it forward, aiming the flogger at Princess's back. The leather straps hit her, creating a loud slap, and she gasps. She arches her back so her shoulders stick out.

I hit her several times until she yelps. The audience begins to grow louder, no doubt getting turned on by the scene. Blood drains down my face, pushing me to the point of dizziness. I can't stall anymore. I know this and would if I could. But I can't.

I muster the words, barking, "You have permission to lick my wife."

Princess moves forward, and I pull my arm back. Her tongue is almost on my pet's pussy when Blakely screams, "Stop! Stop! Stop!"

Princess freezes, and my heart continues beating against my chest cavity.

"Stop! Stop! Stop! Riggs, please! Stop!" Blakely shrieks.

"Get back," Papi orders.

Princess obeys, and I rush over to my pet, releasing the ankle and wrist cuffs. I rip her tear-soaked blindfold off.

There's only fearful chaos in her blues. In a hysterical tone, she repeats, "Stop! Stop! Stop!"

I pick her up and tug her into my arms.

She sobs, pushing against my chest. She cries out, "I only wanted you. Why can't you listen?"

I tighten my arms around her, my insides shaking so hard I don't know how I'll move to get out of here. I murmur, "Shh."

She sobs harder.

I turn my head and demand, "Blanket. Now!"

Someone brings me one, and I wrap it around my pet. I pick her up, and she hides her head in my chest, still crying.

I don't look at anyone, carrying her out of the room and going directly toward the parking garage.

I get to the exit, walk barefoot on the concrete, and open the door to my Porsche. I help Blakely in and put my hand on her cheek. "Pet—"

"Riggs," Papi calls out.

I spin, barking, "Not now."

He hands me my clothes. "You need to put these on. You know the rules."

"Fuck the rules," I seethe as I grab the clothes and shut the passenger door. I race around the front of the car, slide into the driver's seat, and turn on the engine.

The tires squeal as I pull out of the garage. Neither of us says anything, and all I hear the entire drive is my pet's sniffles. I glance at her occasionally, but she never takes her eyes off the window.

It's only when I reverse into the beach house driveway and turn off the engine that she looks at me. So much pain is on her expression that I can barely breathe. And my gut dives when she asks, "Why did you bring me here?"

17

Blakely

*R*iggs doesn't answer my question about why he brought me here. I stare at the closing driveway gate, my insides quivering. I've wanted to come home to the beach house for so long. Yet I thought we would have our problems worked out when I finally did. But all we have after tonight are more issues.

My stomach dives, thinking about lying on the metal table, with my legs in stirrups, blindfolded while Riggs negotiated with Papi.

I assumed Riggs was doing it to prove a point to me. I kept waiting for his possessive side to come out and declare that no one besides him touches me. Instead, I was prey for that woman and all the people in attendance.

Riggs gave me up as if in offering. It confuses me more than anything else he's done. How could he have willingly done that if he claims to love me and doesn't want anyone else to have me?

Is it any different than him using me to take my father down?

The question blazes in my mind, making me queasy.

Riggs retains his silence, gets out of the car, and walks around the Porsche. He yanks open my door, holds his hand out, then orders, "Let's go, pet."

I cross my arms over my chest, letting the anger and pain soar through me. I announce, "I'm not going anywhere."

He reaches in, puts his hands under my armpits, and pulls me out of the car.

I cry out, "Don't touch me!"

He booms, "We aren't doing this out here!" He maneuvers me into the house, which only makes my heart bleed. The first thing I see is the crystal piano. Everything we've lost flares in front of me, crushing my soul deeper than I thought possible. All the hours I spent on the piano, how Riggs surprised me with it, and the things we've done on it all seem like a cruel reminder of our damaged relationship.

My shoulders shake from my sobs. I put my hands over my face, unable to cope with everything that's happened this evening, along with all the past traumas.

He tugs me into him, securing his strong arms around me like a security blanket. I hate that he makes me feel safe, but he does, and it only highlights the ache.

"Shh," he coos repeatedly, stroking my hair.

I finally gain control, sniffling like in the car.

He quietly asks, "Pet, are you okay?"

A new rage builds within me, flaring through every cell of my body. I push him away, pleading, "How could you do that to me?"

He arches his eyebrows, claiming, "I thought that's what you wanted."

He throws in my face again, "You wore the collar I gave you on our wedding night. Then you went to the club without me. Thanks to the media, everybody knows that you're my wife and we're having problems. So even if you weren't trying to find another Dom, what kind of message do you think they get when you do that?"

Air turns stale in my lungs. I never thought about it, but he has a point. Still, I reach for the platinum, grip it, and lift my chin higher. I state, "I always wear my collars."

"Because you want to find another Dom!" he accuses again.

"You're such an idiot!"

His eyes grow darker. "How am I an idiot?"

"You can't see what's in front of you," I declare, then start to cry again.

His eyes turn to raging flames. He barks, "What's in front of me? I'll tell you what's in front of me. *My wife.* The only person in the entire world who means everything to me yet won't have anything to do with me! But she doesn't just stand here, rejecting me. No! My wife wears the collar I gave her on our wedding night. A gift I had designed for her and only her! And she doesn't just wear it without me. She goes to the club in it!"

My emotions are too out of control. I shriek, "That's right! I'm wearing the collar *you* gave me!"

Devastation flares in his expression. Riggs pins a hateful scowl on me. He accuses, "You're wearing it because you wanted to notify all the Doms that you're looking for a new one!"

I shake my hands in front of me. I'm tired of tears, but more fall out, streaming down my cheeks. I admit, "I wear my collars because it's all I have left of you. It's the only thing that makes me still feel like I'm yours!" Heat burns in my cheeks, and I turn away from him, embarrassed by my admissions. I shouldn't be, but I am. And I wish things weren't so complicated between us but that's our reality. Right now, I'm unsure how they're ever not going to be.

More sadness hits me. I used to be able to tell Riggs all my thoughts, yet everything is so strained between us, it feels like we're foreigners speaking different languages.

His arms wrap around me tighter, and he holds me to his body. The woody-spice-laced-with-orange-peel scent hits me, torturing me again, making the pain of everything we've lost much more intense. It's a knife cutting through me to the point I'm gushing blood. And I just want this ache to go away, but it seems like it never will.

We're further apart than before. Making it worse is that the safety I always feel in his arms fights against the reality of how messed up we are.

He murmurs in my ear, "You have all of me, pet, and you'll always be mine. I'm never letting you go. Haven't I made that clear?"

I wish I could stop the rage filling me, but I can't. I spin into him, jabbing my finger into his chest until it hurts, accusing,

"You were going to have someone else—*some woman*—touch me. How could you do that?"

His eyes narrow into dark storms of blue. It's a look I normally crave to see. And my loins burn while the confusion and anger tornados through me.

His silence only hurts more.

I whisper, seething, "How could you?"

"I thought it's what you wanted," he claims again.

I sarcastically laugh. "What I wanted? What did I tell you when I signed the contract regarding other people?"

He remains silent.

I add, "What did I reinforce to you when you had Aria in Apartment Thirteen, claiming she was there to train me?"

His face darkens, and he spouts, "I didn't want the club to enforce rule fourteen. You know why I had Aria come that night. Stop trying to make it something it isn't. I did it for you."

I grit my teeth. I've always gone back and forth fighting the facts that I know Riggs did it for me. I know he didn't want the club to enforce rule fourteen and he thought Aria could help, but I still hate that he did it.

So I ignore his statement and push, "What did I make clear, Riggs? From the get-go, what have I always told you about inserting other people into our relationship?"

Regret bursts onto his face. His confusion, sadness, and frustration mimic my own feelings.

But I can't give him a pass. I still assert, "*No one else*. All I've ever said is no one else. Yet you put me on that table, restraining me for some stranger—someone who wasn't you! How could you do that to me?"

He keeps his voice low, asserting, "I told you I have never had any desire to share you."

"Then why would you do what you did tonight?" I shriek, unable to control my temper anymore.

He glances at the ceiling, his chest rising and falling as he takes deep breaths. When he finally locks his gaze back on mine, he asks, "Why were you there if you didn't want to engage with others?"

I step farther away from him and cross my arms. "I was there with Colton. Stop creating a scenario that isn't real."

"You should never have gone with him!" Riggs spouts, red flaring in his cheeks.

"My friend Colton, who's gay," I add.

"That means nothing," he declares.

More fury snowballs inside me. It gets bigger and bigger, and I remind him, "I'm only friends with him. You know this."

"I wasn't worried about Colton," he admits.

I freeze, staring at him. I try to calm myself and lower my voice. I remind him, "I told you any chance I got that I only wanted you, and you wouldn't listen to me."

He accuses, "You have no idea what thoughts were going through my mind. And you were so engaged in what was happening that you didn't even read my text message or answer my calls!"

I seethe, "I didn't bring my phone."

"I'm sure that was Colton's idea," he says snidely.

I put my hand on my hip, confessing, "I didn't take my phone because I knew I'd break down and call you."

"And why would you do that?" he shouts, his eyes blazing with fury.

"Because I knew I'd beg you to come be with me," I admit.

"And that would be horrible, now, wouldn't it?" Riggs snarls.

I shout, "Well, we both know what happened the last time I begged you to be with me."

He freezes, silent tension crackles in the air between us, and once again, embarrassment washes all over me.

I look away, unable to stand his painful gaze and thinking about how I begged him to be with me in Detroit.

He says in a calmer tone, "It wasn't because I didn't want you."

Hurt flares through me as fresh as that evening. "You didn't just deny me. You left me, never came back, and made me wonder where you were all night. I even started thinking I would never see you again." I try to control the new wave of emotions that assaults me and put my hand over my eyes.

He steps forward and turns my chin, removing my hands, muttering, "Pet."

My flutters take off. All I want to do is melt against him and forget everything that's happened.

He swipes his fingers over my cheek, wiping away the tears, and stares at me. Unspoken words spiral around us, with too many distraught emotions lighting up his normal confident expression. He opens his mouth but then snaps it shut.

My voice shakes as I say, "You don't want me, but you do. And I'm over the mixed messages."

"That's not true," he declares.

"It is," I insist.

In a firm tone, he asserts, "No, it's not. But I can say the same about you."

More tension fills the air, buzzing between us. I do everything in my power not to flinch under his dark gaze. I believe he's going to retreat, but instead, he takes me by surprise. He slides his hands into my hair, pressing his lips against mine. His tongue flickers in my mouth—hot, greedy, and exactly how all of our kisses are, as if nothing wrong has happened between us.

Every second lights me up, and the fight within me lessens. Within seconds, he has me pressed against the wall, his naked body against mine, and the anger between us begins dissipating.

His palms stretch against my ass, lifting me up until my legs wrap around his body seamlessly. He kisses me harder, groaning while his body glides into mine, filling me to the point I finally feel whole again. He drops his mouth to my neck, sucking on the curve and teasing me with slow thrusts.

I lose all of my resistance, unable to deny myself what I don't only crave but what I need. Then my eyes flutter open, and the green light blinking in the corner of the ceiling appears in my peripheral vision.

He's recording me.

Even in our home, he's always been recording me.

Of course he is. That's how he got all the footage of me.

The sharp sting of what he's done and how he asked for Papi's permission to record me at the club assault me into a new tornado of horror.

I freeze and push at his chest, needing to stop the new nightmare spinning around me.

He mummers in my ear, "What's wrong, pet?"

It's all too much. We have too many problems. There are too many things I don't understand and too many fears that I need him to squash. But I can't fathom how he'll ever be able to.

As the green light blinks, the trust I yearn to have for him again doesn't seem like it can ever be repaired. So for the second time tonight, I use the safe word and order, "Stop."

His body tenses. He stares at me with fresh hurt in his expression. He furrows his brows, questioning, "Why? What's wrong?"

I reply with the only thing I can come up with. I recite, "I utilized the safe word. According to your rules, our play is suspended for the next seventy-two hours."

He blurts out, "I'm not playing, pet. This isn't a session."

My face hardens until I feel it may somehow break.

He reiterates in a firm voice, "We aren't playing. You're my wife. I love you. The last thing I'm going to do is play right now. Do you understand?" Desperation is laced in his affirmation and his expression.

It pains me so much, and I wonder how much more I can take. I lift my chin, blinking fast, claiming, "I can't do this right now. Please obey the rules that you created. I'll stay in the guest bedroom." I push past him, moving toward the hallway.

"Blakely, stop," he orders.

It's one of the few times in my life that I don't obey Riggs. I step into the guest room and lock the door, more unsure about what's happening between us than ever before.

I ignore his pounding on the door. I shower, and all is quiet when I exit the bathroom. My heart bleeds as I slide under the covers, pulling the silky sheets around me and staring at the door.

I have no more tears. A few times, I get out of bed and pace the room, holding myself back from going into our suite and climbing into bed with him.

But I never do. Riggs crossed too many lines. The walls between us only got thicker tonight. I try to see where he's coming from, but his actions are like bees stinging me at full force.

I finally fall asleep and dream I'm in Maui. Riggs and I are on the beach in our wedding attire. He keeps promising, "I vow to prove you wrong and work on my faults."

Each time he says it, I state, "I vow to always accept all of you, your faults and all."

I sit up in bed, covered in sweat. It's still dark outside, and I go into the bathroom and splash cold water on my face. I stare at the mirror, hearing Riggs's voice say his vow.

And after the events at the club, I wonder if he thinks he's working on his faults.

Then I feel guilty. Am I any better than Riggs when I promised to accept his faults and am struggling to do so?

There are no answers. And when the sun rises, I get out of bed and stare out the window.

My heart beats faster. Riggs is on his surfboard, riding a wave until it breaks near the shore. His wet, dirty-blonde hair falls over his eyes in thick sections. His wetsuit displays his muscles.

He approaches the shore, tosses his board, and unzips the top of his wetsuit, displaying his tattoos.

I take a deep breath, holding myself back from running outside and tossing my arms around him.

I decide that life is cruel when I can want someone so much yet can't figure out how to have them. Especially when he's right in front of me.

18

Riggs
A Few Hours Earlier

The morning light tries to break through the darkness. I sit against the wall, staring at the guest bedroom's door, unable to reduce the frustration flowing through my veins.

All night, I've beaten myself up, replaying the events at the club. I've always gotten it right before. I've always known what my subs needed, so how could I have been so misguided about what my own wife needed?

The thought of Princess's face near my pet's body makes my stomach flip. All I want is my wife back, but I'm now further from her than I was before I stepped into the club.

Pink hues streak across the sky. I rise and walk to the window, staring at the ocean. The itch to reclaim something intensifies, even if it's my beachfront hobby and not Blakely.

I glance at the door a final time, then leave the hallway. It feels like I haven't surfed on this beach forever, and it's the first thing I've looked forward to in a long time. I step past the kitchen and then freeze.

My keys are on the table.

She can't leave.

How am I going to keep her here?

Agitation continues to burn in my soul, and I finally decide to lock up the phones, car keys, and laptops in the safe. My pet won't be able to drive away or call anyone to pick her up. I can surf without the added worry of her leaving me again.

I take everything to the office and put them inside, right next to all the items I took from her father's safe. It bugs me how Blakely seemed upset with me for telling her what is hers. And it's another issue she'll have to get past. There's no way I'm keeping her father's stuff. It belongs to her. She's owed what I took from him, but that'll have to be a fight for another day.

I leave the house, step into my wetsuit, and grab my board. It takes a few minutes to get to the water, and I paddle as far out as possible, past the break of the waves.

For hours, I surf. Adrenaline fills me, and I finally feel alive again, inhaling the salt water and pushing my body to its limit. I catch a final wave and ride it to shore.

I look up at the house and catch Blakely staring out the window. I wave, but she doesn't return it. She spins and disappears.

The feeling of being alive deflates like a balloon. I return to the house, strip out of my wetsuit, and turn on the shower. I stand under the water, staring at the wall, remembering the first time I took my pet and truly made her mine. I do everything in my power to relive what it was like to be inside her then, with her body gripping mine and our tongues in a heated battle.

I had finally allowed myself to kiss her. And I curse myself again for being such a fool. I should have taken every kiss she ever wanted to give me.

The unsettled desire to have my wife only worsens the more I think about that moment. It tortures me until the water turns cold.

I turn it off and reach for a towel. I dry myself off, then wrap it around my body. I go into the kitchen to make breakfast but realize there's nothing here. The fridge is empty besides condiments, and it's another slap in the face that we've been living apart and not here where we both belong.

After some debate, I wander down the hall and stop in front of the guest room. I hesitate to knock. I can't believe she's in this room again and not in our bedroom suite.

Blakely reciting the seventy-two-hour rule pops up in my head, making me wince. I curse myself further for creating that damn rule. I have it in there to ensure that my subs are emotionally stable after they use their safe word.

It's a big deal to use it. It means I've pushed them too far. I've done something they're not comfortable with, beyond their boundaries and limits.

Blakely has never used it with me during any session or when we have had sex. And she used it twice on me last night. The only other time I heard her use that word was the night she left me, but we weren't intimate then. Now that she has, I feel like I fucked up even bigger.

How could I have gotten last night so wrong?

Maybe it was because I chose a woman? Would she have still used the safe word if I'd chosen a man?

I reprimand myself for the thoughts. My pet sounded adamant that she didn't want another Dom or anyone else. Still, the nagging feeling won't stop.

After everything we've been through and the fact that she can't even stay in our own bedroom when we're in the same house, is it still true that she doesn't want anyone else?

I detest that I'm questioning my wife's intentions, especially on something so important. All the times Blakely told me last night she didn't want anyone besides me, haunt me.

Why didn't I listen?

Nothing has changed about how she feels. When she signed the contract and when I brought Aria to Apartment Thirteen, Blakely warned me there should be no one besides us in our relationship. And I never had any intentions of letting anyone else touch her. Yet, I truly thought it was what she needed—what she wanted.

How did our trust in each other get so broken?

My stomach dives with the truth. It's because of me. I fucked everything up. I took the only good thing in my life and destroyed it, and now I don't know how to get it back. But even with us at odds, I know we're still meant to be together. What we have isn't dead.

The door opens, startling me. Blakely's eyes widen, and they dart between my bare chest and face before she asks, "Riggs, why are you standing out here?"

My chest tightens. My wife looks so damn beautiful without makeup, her hair slept on, hanging in loose curls and her pink lips slightly parted. Fuck, I love everything about how she looks right now. It only makes me ache more, reiterating that I need to figure out how to make things right between us.

And I'm not stupid. The longer this goes on, the worse our situation will get. The more chance there is that she's going to leave me. My fear that she'll get a divorce attorney and serve me papers only grows. It's been a constant on my mind that won't go away.

I softly reply, "Morning, pet. We don't have any food here. I thought we could go to breakfast."

She bites her lip, studying me.

The uncertainty about whether she should even spend time eating a meal with me makes me feel sicker. I ask myself again how we got here before I blurt out, "We can go to that little cafe. You know, the one overlooking the cliff? You can have your favorite lemon ricotta pancakes." Nerves dance in my belly, and I can't believe I'm nervous asking my own wife to go to breakfast with me.

Her lips twitch, but she stays quiet.

I add, "Afterward, we can go downtown and walk around the farmer's market."

She arches her eyebrows, declaring, "You hate the market."

"I never said that," I state.

She tilts her head, and amusement overpowers her expression.

A burst of happiness pops inside me just from seeing her smile.

"Don't deny it, Riggs. I know you don't like it."

I shake my head, declaring, "No, it's not that I don't like it. I mean, there are other things out there that sometimes I prefer to do, but you love it, and I'd really like to take you there today."

Tense silence builds between us. She is correct. I don't love the market, but I do love the way her expression lights up as she walks around the little booths, picking up crafts and other silly things that sometimes have no purpose. Her ability to see beauty in those things always surprises me. And it's something I admire in her. So I'll give anything to put that expression on her face today.

Her continued silence only deepens my fears. I'm afraid she's going to say no, so I try to sweeten the deal by adding, "The puppies will be there. You can get one if you want."

She jerks her head backward.

"What's wrong?" I ask.

She tilts her head and narrows her eyebrows. She replies, "I thought you didn't want the responsibility of a dog. Remember the big lecture you gave me?"

I groan inside and then shrug, asking, "Do you still want one? If you do, we can get one."

Her face falls. "You weren't wrong. I'm touring a lot. It's probably not the best time to get a pet."

My stomach spins. I hate how she's touring and I'm not with her. Plus, it still burns me that she fired me.

I question why everything feels so hard now when it used to be so easy between us. Yet no answers come.

She states, "I'm not sure how hungry I am."

I'm normally not a quitter, but right now, I don't know if I should push her to come with me or not. I finally decide it's best not to, so I step back and announce, "Okay, I'll just go order groceries so we have some food when you are hungry."

I take a few steps toward the kitchen, and she grabs my arm, calling out, "Riggs."

My heart beats harder, pounding against my chest cavity. Tingles burst under her hand, rushing straight to my cock. I freeze, take a deep breath, and turn. I softly ask, "Yeah?"

She hesitates, then inquires, "Can you give me a half hour so I can get ready?"

Excitement fills me. I mentally give myself a high five and try to remain calm. I nod. "Sure, take as much time as you need."

"I'll be out soon," she says, then goes back inside the room.

I hustle down the hallway into our bedroom and go into my closet. I put on a pair of khaki shorts and a white designer T-shirt, then slide into my sandals. Then I go into the office and open the safe.

I remove my keys and phone. I make an online reservation for breakfast at the cafe, and a notification pops up. My pulse skyrockets as I read it.

> Club Indulgence: Your video is on the cloud.

I stare at the message for too many minutes, but I can't stop myself. It's too much temptation. I click on the link provided in the notification, and videos pop up.

Multiple screens show Blakely kneeling on stage last night in her silver thong and stilettos. Her platinum collar gleams from around her neck, and each screen shows a different angle of my precious pet.

I'm like a kid in a candy store, unable to decide which shot I like best, so I continue surveying all of them until it comes to the moment when she's lying on the bench. Once her arms are restrained as far out in front of her as possible, I choose the screen position directly on her so I'm staring at her face.

"Ready?" Blakely chirps, bouncing into the room.

I tear my eyes off the video. "Yeah." I shut the footage down, then slide my phone into my pocket.

She scrunches her face, "Is something wrong?"

I step toward her and assure her, "No."

"Are you sure? You look... I don't know. I think disturbed isn't the right word... Maybe frazzled?" she questions.

I shake my head. "Nothing, just something with work. It's not a big deal."

She gives me a look like she's not sure if she believes me.

I lean down and kiss her head, stating, "You look gorgeous."

She smiles and gazes down at her pink sundress, answering, "Thanks."

I slide my hand into hers and state, "Let's go eat pancakes." I lead her out to the car.

We get inside the Porsche and don't say a lot on the way to the cafe. I pull up at the valet, step out of the car, and hand him my keys. He gives me a ticket, and I meet Blakely on the sidewalk.

I tug her into me, still hard from viewing the video footage, and reprimand myself for looking at it. I should have known better. I had no business looking at that before we left the house, especially while I'm on this seventy-two-hour hiatus.

I need to figure out how to break it.

I lead my pet inside, and the hostess greets us. She bats her eyes and says in a flirty tone, "Welcome. I'm Candy. You're Mr. Madden, correct? I recognize you from your company website." She drags her eyes over my body, then relocks them on mine.

Blakely stiffens next to me.

Her admission that she's looked at my website irks me. I don't need this little tart screwing more things up between my wife and me. Plus, I know how Blakely gets when other women hit on me, so I tighten my grip around her. I use my coldest tone to make it clear I'm not into the hostess's attention, and answer, "Yes. We have a reservation."

Candy's eyes brighten, and she dares to toss Blakely a dismissive glance. She lowers her voice and leans closer, stating, "Mr. Madden, I selected our best table for you. Is a private balcony okay?" She gives me a seductive smile.

I use the same voice and narrow my eyes on her. "That will be fine. Please show my wife and me to our table."

She glances dismissively at Blakely again, then smirks at me. "Sure. Right this way." She spins and saunters across the restaurant, swinging her ass as she walks.

I keep Blakely tight to my side and don't miss her glaring at Candy. I kiss her on the head to try and reassure her that I have no interest in this little gold-digging slut in front of me.

We get on the balcony, which is built into the cliff. The deep-blue water sparkles below, stretching as far as the eye can see. Sea salt flares in my nostrils, and it starts to calm me. I pull the chair out and motion for my pet to sit.

Candy puts her hand on my arm, and my chest tightens. She chirps, "Is there anything else I can get for you, Mr. Madden?"

I grab her wrist, tighten my fist around it, and hold it near her shoulder. I snarl, "Don't ever touch me again. And tell my wife you're sorry for disrespecting her."

Candy gapes at me, her cheeks flaming.

"I'm waiting," I seethe through gritted teeth.

Candy finally turns and clears her throat. "I'm sorry, Blakely. I like your newest song, by the way."

I ignore her compliment and add, "Try again. It's Mrs. Madden to you."

Nerves fill her features. She straightens her shoulders, quickly asserting, "I apologize if I was disrespectful, Mrs. Madden."

"There's no doubt about it, you were," I declare, release Candy's wrist, and sit down next to Blakely.

Candy shuffles away.

Blakely turns toward me and bites her lip in amusement. I wait for her to speak, and she finally says, "Tad harsh, don't you think?"

"No," I insist, sliding my arm around her shoulders and leaning into her ear, claiming, "You're mine, and I'm yours, pet. No matter how fucked-up things are between us, that's never going to change."

Her lips curve into a tiny but unsure smile. She admits, "I want to believe that more than anything. And I wish we could go back to how we were."

It's her first admission that gives me a sign of hope. And I've not had any hope in a long time, so I'll take it.

I give her a chaste kiss and declare, "I promise you we're going to get back there."

19

Blakely

The server fills our coffee mugs, asking, "What can I get you?"

Riggs orders, "My wife will have an order of lemon ricotta pancakes, and I'd like a Denver omelet, please."

The server smiles and chirps, "Great. Would you like white, rye, or wheat toast with your omelet?"

"Rye," Riggs answers.

She nods. "Coming right up," she says, then disappears.

Riggs sits back in his seat and drinks a mouthful of black coffee.

I add sugar and cream to mine, stir it, and take a sip, gazing at the horizon. The waves are high and crash on the shore into white foam.

Riggs blurts out, "We need to talk, pet."

My chest tightens. I don't want to talk anymore. I know we have to, but every time we talk, things only get worse. Yet, I realize we have to discuss these things or nothing will ever change. I ask, "Where do you want to start?"

"We should start with last night," he states.

The anger resurfaces. I take another sip and turn toward him, tapping my fingers on the hot cup.

Deep down, I know Riggs would never intentionally hurt me. But I still can't believe he did what he did. So I admit, "I'm still lost, Riggs. Last night was..." My stomach pitches. I continue, "I don't know why you would do what you did."

His face hardens. He narrows his blues, accusing, "Why did you kneel? We could have gotten out of there. I told you I didn't care about their rules anymore, but you went on stage and kneeled."

My gut drops. I turn back to the ocean, blinking hard. He's right. I didn't have to kneel. We could have left. So why did I?

Because I needed to submit.

He turns my chin back toward him. "Just answer my question. I need to know why you kneeled instead of leaving with me."

I kick myself for not leaving and decide lies aren't going to get us anywhere. I ask, "Was it not obvious?"

He arches his eyebrows. "What do you mean?"

I shut my eyes, not wanting to admit things but knowing I need to. I blurt out, "I can't stop the cravings."

"For what?" he questions.

I lock eyes with him. My voice shakes, and I answer, "For you."

The spark in his blues lights. He picks up my hand and kisses it. "You should have just come home with me, then."

I accuse, "So you could deny me again like you did in Detroit?"

Pain fills his expression. He shakes his head. "Things are messed up between us, pet. I don't want it this way. Every minute of the day, I think about you. Jesus, you're everywhere, consuming all my thoughts. I couldn't even stop it when I took my shower outside. All I could think about was the first time we were out there together, how it felt to be inside you like that. So this isn't just hard for you."

Tingles race through my veins. I can almost feel him pinning me to the outside wall and taking me. It all adds to my longing to be with him.

Riggs suggests, "When we go home today, let's return to being us. Let's forget about everything that's happened and end this. We're both miserable without each other. Can't you see that?"

His solution sounds so simple, yet it can't be. The messages he sent my father and the green blinking light from last night fill my mind. They stop me from agreeing. I reply, "We're under the seventy-two-hour rule."

"I'm not playing, pet," he firmly states, just like he did the other night.

Butterflies go crazy in my stomach. Still, I don't give in to them. I remind him, "It's your rule."

Frustration fills his expression. He claims, "Then I should be allowed to break it."

I take a sip of coffee, still tapping my fingers on the mug, wanting to agree but unable to. There are too many questions I still have and just as many explanations I need. And I don't know if I'll ever get answers that will make things right for me—make things right between us. So I question, "Why do you have the rule?"

He takes a deep breath and slides his hand over my cheek, tracing his thumb over my lips and assessing me with his darkening expression. He answers, "It's to make sure that subs are okay. If you use your safe word, I've gone too far. So it's a cooling-off period for my sub and me."

"So other people need it, but I don't?" I question.

He opens his mouth and snaps it shut. He shakes his head. "I don't mean it like that."

"But you mean I don't need it, and other people do," I repeat.

He releases his hand from my cheek and says, "You aren't like anybody else, pet. Don't you know that?"

I don't answer, wanting to believe that's a good thing but fighting with my self-confidence. It always pops up whenever I think about Riggs with any of his previous subs.

He adds, "I don't think I'm like anybody else either. It's probably why we fit so well together. So maybe these rules I created for others aren't for you. Maybe we need to make new rules."

"Why would we do that?" I ask, afraid of what that means. I like the rules. They're not guidelines. They're boundaries for Riggs and me. And something tells me that we need them.

He answers, "I don't feel like you need the seventy-two-hour rule, nor do I. Not in this situation."

"Well, that's convenient," I say, upset that he wants to get rid of the rules.

He crosses his arms, questioning, "Why did you snap at me?"

I scrub my hand over my forehead, keeping it on the top of my head, and confess, "All I've ever wanted to be is good enough for you—no, better than everybody else. If we don't have rules, what does that make me? Does it mean you think I can't handle them?"

He furrows his eyebrows. "No, not at all. I'm saying you aren't like the others, and I don't want the others. Don't you know that by now? I married you, not any of them."

I blink hard, revealing, "I don't know, Riggs. I still don't know if you married me because of me—because you really did love me—or if it was to get back at my father."

Disappointment fills his features. He scowls. "You don't think I love you?"

"I want to believe you do. But every day, I think about what you did, and I wonder how everything we had could have been real."

Regret bursts into his eyes. He swallows hard and lowers his voice. "I'm sorry I did what I did. It was a mistake."

I point out, "But you didn't have any issues putting the recording on last night. Are you going to send that to my father too?"

His eyes widen. "Is that what you think?"

I hurl, "What am I supposed to think?"

"I thought it would make you say the safe word so we could go home. I didn't want to be in that room. All I wanted was to bring you home, where we could be alone," he reveals.

I stay quiet, pondering his statement, trying to make sense of this entire nightmare.

He grinds his molars, staring at me, making me more confused than ever. Then he pulls out his phone.

"What are you doing?" I question.

He holds up a finger. "Just give me a minute." He swipes on the screen and glances around us even though we're in a secluded area. He scoots his chair even closer, slides his arm around me, and says, "Watch."

Nerves fill me. My pulse beats hard between my ears. Last night appears on his phone. I'm facing the camera on the bench, and he's behind me.

I glance at him. "What—"

He puts his finger over my lips, ordering, "Just watch it."

I turn back and obey. I watch him pouring wax on my body, flogging me, and then he's on top of me.

He leans into my ear. "I also recorded this to watch you. I miss you. There's nothing better than watching you when you're at my mercy." He turns on the volume and my moans fill the air.

I squeeze my thighs tighter, and he slides my hands between them, saying, "I made this for us. For you and me to watch. And I see what this does to you. It does the same thing to me, pet. But I can assure you that this is staying between you and me. Do you understand?"

"How can I trust you on that?" I blurt out.

Agony rips through his features.

I hate that I've asked him that. I detest that I've created that look.

He replies, "Because I will never do anything to hurt you again. I will always protect you to a degree I failed to do so with your father. And I need you to return to trusting me. Please."

A tear falls down my cheek. I swipe at it, confessing, "I want that to be true, Riggs."

"It is," he claims and turns the video off. He tosses his phone on the table.

I turn back toward the ocean, looking far past the break of the waves and into the calm chaos. Can it really be this easy? Can I just trust him again?

The server comes onto the balcony. She sets my pancakes and his omelet on the table and chirps, "Is there anything else I can get for you?"

"Pet?" Riggs asks.

I shake my head and force a smile. "No. Thank you so much."

She looks at Riggs.

He answers, "All set. Thank you."

She leaves, and more silence fills the air, creating tension between us.

Riggs quietly orders, "Eat before your food gets cold."

I obey, barely tasting the lemon ricotta pancakes since I'm so lost in thought.

The silence continues, and I'm unsure if we're farther apart or closer together.

Did he really create the video for only us?

Can I trust he won't do anything with it?

We finish our breakfast, not saying anything else about last night. Riggs pays the check. He leads me out of the restaurant. We walk down the street to the market.

He normally looks ready to leave at any given moment, but today, he's engaged. He appears genuinely happy to be there with me.

I love it, but it also hurts my heart. I normally bounce through the booths, but I'm a little more cautious today, barely looking at the items. There's just too much on my mind.

Riggs tugs me into him and says, "Pet."

I arch my eyebrows. "Yeah?"

He takes both hands and places them on my face. He kisses me and says, "I want you to enjoy today." His lips turn into a small smile.

"I am," I claim.

He smirks. "You look really uptight. No offense."

I softly laugh. "That sounds like an insult."

He grins. "It's not meant to be. But relax, pet. Do your thing."

I take a deep breath and nod. He's right. I am acting differently. So I step into the next booth and begin sorting through clothes. Then I take in some sculptures and handmade jewelry.

Riggs keeps asking me what I want, but nothing catches my eye. Then we get to the pet booth.

A dozen cute puppies are in a little pen. A white furball Maltese runs toward me, barking.

"Aw," I coo. I bend over and pick him up over the small wire fence.

He's only a few pounds and licks my face.

I laugh and hold him in the air, beaming. "Look at you." I put him next to my chest, and he curls into me. I pet his soft fur and say, "Aw, he's so cute."

Riggs pets the back of his head. He states, "He's really tiny."

"Only four pounds," the owner informs us.

"How big will he get?" Riggs questions.

The owner answers, "Malteses get about twelve inches tall. They normally stay under seven pounds."

"Seven pounds. That's nothing," Riggs comments.

"Yeah, people like them. They're easy for traveling, going shopping, basically taking them anywhere you want to go," the owner states.

"Easy for traveling, that's good," Riggs claims, wiggling his eyebrows.

I kiss the dog and then put him back down into the pen. It pains me, but Riggs was right the last time we were here. It wouldn't be responsible for me to get a dog. He'd have to take care of it if I'm not there, or I'd have to hire someone to come with me. There are already enough people on tour with me. I don't need one more thing to worry about.

The owner adds, "They don't take up a lot of room in the bed either."

Riggs grunts. "We won't be sleeping with him."

I pretend to pout. "You're mean. I guess it's not meant to be, then." I glance back at the puppy.

The puppy stays near the fence, barking, jumping up, and trying to escape.

I crouch down, feeling guilty. "Aw, I'm sorry, buddy. I'd take you home with us, but there's just too much going on in our lives. I'm sure you'll find a good home."

The puppy barks louder and whines, making me feel worse.

Riggs whips out cash and asserts, "We'll take him."

I jerk my head toward him in shock. "What? We talked about this."

The look he always has, the one that says he's in total control and knows exactly what's right, appears. It also screams not to question him. It's the same expression that makes my insides throb.

He replies, "It'll be okay, pet."

I meekly say, "We do have a lot going on."

Riggs picks up the puppy. The fluffball stops, tilts his head, and stares at Riggs in the face. Riggs laughs, saying to the puppy, "Just don't think that you're in charge, buddy."

The dog barks, then tries to lick him.

My heart skips a beat. Riggs talking to the puppy might be the cutest thing I've ever seen.

Riggs asks the owner, "Is he old enough to come home with us today?"

The owner nods. "Yeah, I have his papers and everything. He's had his first set of shots."

"Great." Riggs turns to me. "Don't worry. We'll hire someone to care for the dog while you work."

I shake my head. "I don't want to take him with me."

Riggs arches his eyebrows. "Why wouldn't you want to?"

"It's a lot. You know I have enough things to worry about when I'm on tour. And besides, I don't want it to be my dog. If we get a dog, I want it to be ours. And you don't want him around when I'm not there, so we shouldn't get him," I say, trying to be responsible, even though I want the puppy.

Riggs stares at me.

The puppy whines.

Riggs glances at him, then me. He claims, "We'll figure all this out, don't worry about it. It will be our dog."

I put my hand on my hip. "That's a big statement for you to make. How will you take care of him when I'm gone?"

An exasperated look fills his features. "You know there are people who take care of dogs. They walk them and come feed them when you can't."

I continue to assess him, wondering if this is the right thing for us to do when we have so many issues we haven't resolved.

Riggs asserts, "You might change your mind too. You're going to miss him when you're gone. Maybe you'll decide you do want him on tour."

I gaze at the puppy, then reach for him. I pull him toward my chest, and he licks my chin. It's the final straw. I can't fight Riggs anymore, and I cave. "Okay, let's get him."

Riggs grins at the owner, declaring, "Let me see the paperwork."

I continue to rub my new puppy's head, and he licks me again. I'm already in love with him. He's perfect.

The owner tells us what food the dog eats and reminds us to always have water for him. He says, "I'm putting the vet's business card in the envelope with the rest of your paperwork. Just in case you need one."

"Perfect, thank you," Riggs says, then folds the envelope and puts it in his pocket. He points to the table and asks me, "Do you want to pick out a collar and leash?"

I glance through the options and choose a black one.

Riggs pays for it and secures the collar around the dog's neck. He clasps the leash and hands it to me. He asks, "Ready?"

I'm still a bit in shock. I ask him again, "You really are serious about this?"

He slides his hand around my back and starts leading me down the street, answering, "Yeah."

We take a few steps, but the puppy isn't used to the leash. He keeps jumping on me.

Riggs states, "He really likes you."

Happiness fills me. I glance at my new puppy and bend down, stroking its fur. He jumps up, and I laugh again. It's been a long time since I laughed as much as I have today, and it feels good.

"What are you going to name him?" Riggs questions.

"Let me think. I didn't exactly expect to come out to breakfast and leave with a dog," I admit, and ponder the question while we continue walking down the street.

It only takes about half a block for the puppy to catch on to how to walk next to us.

Another dog approaches us, roughly barking at my puppy. Instead of cowering, he growls back, lifting his chin in the air and standing taller.

Riggs chuckles. "Looks like he takes after you."

The other dog owner nods and passes by us, keeping her pet away from ours.

I inquire, "Oh? How does he take after me?"

Riggs grins. "He doesn't back down."

I squint. "And you like that about me?"

His face turns serious. He slides his palm on my cheek. Kindness and love fill his expression, making me yearn to be back to normal more than ever. He softly replies, "Of course I do. Don't you know that?"

I confess, "I didn't, but I guess I do now."

He steps closer and gives me a chaste kiss.

The puppy jumps up at us, barking.

I glance down. "Someone's jealous."

Riggs looks sternly at the dog and asserts, "We're going to have to work on this."

The dog barks back at him.

Riggs chuckles and continues to lead me down the street. He stops outside a pet shop. "Let's go inside and buy some food."

We step inside, and I snap my fingers. "I know what I want to name him."

"Oh?" Riggs asks.

My lips twitch. "King Madden."

Riggs glances at the dog and then leans into my ear. In his demanding tone that always makes my adrenaline perk up, he states, "That's fine, pet. But just so we're clear, there's only one ruler in our house."

Butterflies take off inside me. There's so much between us that I still don't know how to solve. But I've never wanted him to take control and return to issuing me commands as much as I do right now.

20

Riggs

lakely and I spend the rest of the day playing with King Madden on the beach and in the house. He's full of energy, and the way my pet's face beams makes me happier than I've been in a long time.

King Madden is super protective of her. I playfully slapped her ass earlier, and he growled and snipped at me. She's definitely the one he's choosing to be his favorite, but I'm okay with it.

For dinner, we grilled steaks and ate on the deck. King Madden never left her lap. Now, the sun's setting and the daylight's fading. I sip my beer and stare at my precious wife, who's smiling at her puppy, looking more beautiful than ever.

She glances at me and tilts her head. "Why are you staring at me?"

My heart pounds harder. I debate about bringing it up. We've had a great day, but there's still so much more we need to talk about. And I want to get past our issues once and for all.

Her voice turns more serious. "What is it, Riggs?"

I decide not to be a coward. If we're putting everything out on the table, then I need to know something that's been bothering me. I tread carefully, asking, "Why didn't you tell me you thought you were pregnant?"

She freezes, her hand on King Madden's back. "Why are you asking me this?"

I take her hand and slide my thumb over the back of it. I attempt to not sound like I'm accusing her of anything and inquire, "If you were pregnant, would you have told me?"

She scrunches her forehead, answering, "Of course I would've told you. Besides, I couldn't have hidden it from you. You know a baby grows in your belly and gets big, right?"

I know she's trying to make a joke, but it's not a matter I find funny. So I stay quiet, clenching my jaw, trying to push down more of my past I thought I had forgotten about, yet only feeling the sting.

Her eyes widen, and she jerks her head back. Her face falls as she asks, "You think I would've gotten rid of our baby?"

My mouth turns dry. I try to inhale some fresh air into my lungs, but it's not working. I feel suffocated, yet I know there can't be lies between us anymore. So I answer her, "I don't know. Would you have?"

Horror fills her expression. In an insulted tone, she seethes, "Why would you ever think I would do that?"

I cringe. I'm making more mistakes and should have avoided bringing this up. It's been nagging me ever since I found that box under the cabinet, but I should have shut my mouth. I don't know what I was thinking. Yet now I'm in this conversation, so I state, "I would hope not."

She stares at me with anger growing on her face. Then she snaps, "Why would you think I'd make a decision like that and not even talk to you about it? And how could that even cross your mind?"

I curse myself again for bringing this up.

"Riggs, don't you dare go silent on me right now," she demands.

My stomach flips again. I release a tense breath and decide to fess up. Choosing the right words isn't easy, but I admit, "I'm sorry. When I was eighteen, my girlfriend got pregnant."

Blakely's eyes widen. She asks, "You have a child?"

I shake my head. More nerves fill my belly. "My ex told me she was pregnant, and it freaked me out." My mouth turns dry, and I can't continue. I stare at my beer bottle, tapping it like Blakely taps her fingers when she's nervous. I curse myself again for picking up her bad habit. I lock eyes with her.

My pet swallows hard. Compassion fills her expression, and she squeezes my hand, softly asking, "You told her to get an abortion?"

"No, not at all." I take a large mouthful of my beer, trying again to find the words. I wonder why this has to feel so bad and why so many emotions have to hit me all at once.

"Riggs, it's okay if you did. Just tell me. I won't judge you."

I lock eyes with her, firmly stating, "No. When my girlfriend told me, I admit I didn't know what to do. I was poor. Hell, we both were poor. I was still in high school, and all I wanted to do was get out of Compton as soon as I could. I saw a big future for myself, and I didn't know how that could happen if we had a baby."

Blakely gently states, "That's probably a normal thought. You were young."

I release a stress-filled breath, admitting the thing that still haunts me, saying, "I didn't say the right things when she told me that she was pregnant." Shame fills me, and I think back to that moment, cringing.

Blakely questions, "What did you say?"

My chest pounds harder against my chest cavity.

"I told her that our lives were over," I quietly confess.

Tension fills the air. The waves crash against the shore, and it sounds louder. Disgust fills me, and it's like reliving that moment all over again.

Blakely keeps her tone non-accusing, continuing to interrogate me with the same question she already asked. "So you asked her to get an abortion?"

I shake my head. "No, I already told you I didn't. But she did get one. She went to the clinic, and a few days later, she came to my house. She told me what she did, and I was in shock. I didn't think she would have done that without talking to me. She just went and did it."

Blakely gapes at me.

I quickly add, "But it's my fault. She wouldn't have done it if I had acted like a man and not been so freaked out. We would've talked. We would've figured it out...something. But she did it and was all alone, and I just... It was because of what I said."

"Riggs, that's a lot to blame yourself for," Blakely declares.

The self-hatred I have for how I acted in that situation continues to pummel me. I insist, "It's true though. It is my fault."

Blakely disputes my claim. "How do you know? She might have done it even if you were happy about the baby. Eighteen is really young to be pregnant. I'm sure she was scared, and who knows what went through her mind?"

I take another mouthful of beer, barely tasting it. It slides down my throat and into my churning stomach.

I claim, "No, I knew her. She wouldn't have gotten one. She did it because of what I said."

More silence fills the air. It's not often I think about what happened, but it's been on my mind ever since I found those pregnancy tests. I've even had nightmares about it. And I've always wondered if the baby was a boy or a girl and what they'd be like. It'd be an adult by now.

I can't argue my life would've turned out very differently, and who knows if I would have gotten out of Compton. But I still regret what I said to make my ex do that without even talking to me first.

I finish my beer, and Blakely rises. She puts the puppy on the chair and sits on my lap.

King Madden jumps on the chair and barks.

She reaches for him and sets him between us, and he curls into her. My heart soars. Something about Blakely with her dog just makes me feel good.

I tighten my arm around her waist and pat King Madden with my other hand.

She slides her arms around my shoulders, lacing her fingers around my neck. She claims, "It's not your fault, Riggs. She made her own decision."

"I shouldn't have reacted how I did," I repeat.

Blakely stares at me for a moment, then asks, "Did you really think I would do the same thing she did?"

I admit, "You thought you were pregnant, and you didn't say anything to me. You had pregnancy tests and hid them. I didn't know what to think."

"I didn't hide them. They were in the cabinet," she says.

"There's a reason you had them. And you didn't say anything to me," I restate.

Nerves fill her blues. She slowly confesses, "I won't lie to you, Riggs. I wasn't sure if I was, and if I was, I wasn't sure how you'd take it."

More of my past haunts me. I declare, "Because you assumed I wouldn't want our baby." My chest tightens, turning the air in my lungs stale.

She cries out, "No, I didn't say that."

I stay quiet, wishing I could escape my demons and detesting how they never really disappear.

She softens her tone and says, "You were very clear in the contract we both signed that you didn't want a baby."

"You're my wife," I state in a firm tone.

She scrunches her face. "So? That doesn't negate what's in the contract. It was so important to you that you put it in writing."

I've always loved having a contract with my subs. It keeps the arrangement clear. Now that same contract only seems to have made my life more complex. I reply, "Since we're being honest, I won't lie to you either, pet. I didn't want a baby with a woman who wasn't my future. When we signed that contract, all I knew was that I wanted you, but I didn't think we'd end up here."

A bit of hurt fills her face.

I quickly ask, "Did you think we'd end up here? Married? Together forever?"

She slowly shakes her head and lowers her voice, "No, I didn't think you'd want me that long."

Her admission astonishes me. It also hurts. I insist, "It wasn't ever about not wanting you."

She blinks hard, looking at the ocean.

"Pet," I say.

She turns back to me. "You had an expiration date for me. It was very clear in the contract how long we were supposed to be together."

I sigh, confessing, "It's just what I used to do. Don't be mad at me. I never expected you to walk onto that stage."

She closes her eyes and takes a deep breath. When she opens them, they're glistening. Her voice shakes as she accuses, "You wanted to use me to avenge my father. You had those plans when I signed that contract, didn't you?"

My stomach dives. I wince, admitting, "If I could take it all back, I would."

Her face hardens. She pushes, "Why?"

I don't understand why she's asking me this, so I question, "Why what?"

Her lip slightly trembles, and I hate that we're discussing this same issue again for what feels like the hundredth time. And we still aren't closer to the forgiveness I need her to give me.

Pain fills her tone. She questions, "You got exactly what you wanted, Riggs, so why would you take it all back?"

There's no hesitation. I reply, "It's not what I want. I see how much it hurt you, and nothing, not even destroying your father in all ways, was worth the consequences."

"You didn't think twice about hurting me," she claims.

"That's not true! I never thought you'd find out, and not once did I consider it would hurt you."

A tear falls down her cheek. She adds, "You hid it from me. You had to know it would hurt me."

I ponder her statement, feeling worse. I slide my hand over her cheek, replying, "I was so caught up in revenge, it's all I saw. But you have to believe me. It wasn't my intention to hurt you. And if I could go back and fix this, I would."

She stays quiet.

More anxiety plagues me. It's a panic that I can't seem to escape. I fear I've lost her and she's never coming back. I tug her closer to me, pressing my forehead to her shoulder, feeling so damn desperate. More loathing fills me, but I have no shame left anymore to worry about. I close my eyes and beg, "Please, forgive me. This is killing me, pet."

King Madden whines, and it matches the constant pain in my soul. He rises and licks my cheek.

She softly laughs.

I lift my head away from her. She holds King Madden next to her, glances at him, then at me. She cautiously claims, "It looks like King Madden wants me to forgive you."

An ounce of hope fills me. I slide my hand over her back, palming her spine. "I admit I've never felt regret in my life, pet. And I've done a lot of bad things, but I've never regretted them. It won't surprise you that I've hurt people, but the only one I've ever regretted hurting is you."

She takes a deep breath and blinks hard. My heart pounds harder, and she finally caves, stating, "Okay."

Hope springs bigger in my chest, but I've felt it before when we've discussed this issue. I don't want to assume anything anymore. So I ask, "What does okay mean?"

She leans an inch from my lips, locking her calm chaos with mine. My cock grows harder. She replies, "I don't know if I'll ever be able to forget it. But as of this second, I forgive you."

It's not a perfect answer, but it's a start. I open my mouth to speak, but she puts a finger over my lips.

She adds, "I'm going to try and trust you again, Riggs, but I'm not fully there yet. Honestly, I don't know when I will be or if it's even possible."

My gut sinks. Forever is a long time, and I want her to trust me again. I need us to go back to how we were. Still, this is progress. So I nod, replying, "Okay, pet, but I promise you I won't ever do anything to break your trust again. I am going to earn it fully back."

Her expression is hopeful yet cautious. I detest that it's my fault we're still not back to where we were.

She replies, "I want to. I do. And I hope you never do anything again like what you did. Because, Riggs, I will leave you. I can't go through it again. I mean it."

I loathe the thought of her leaving me. I firmly repeat, "I won't," then slide my hand to her hair and fist it.

She gasps, her lips part, and she shifts on my lap.

King Madden barks, but I ignore him.

I tug her head back, lean closer, and state, "I think we need a new contract."

Her eyes widen. She breathes out an "Oh?"

I peck her on the lips and assess her until she squirms in my lap again. I hold in my groan, knowing she's wet. She always is when she does that. I want my body back in hers where it belongs. Fuck, I need my body back in hers. I confess, "There's something I should have said long ago."

She arches her eyebrows.

"You're my wife, pet. I married you because you're the only person I've ever loved on this entire planet. All I want is you, and I want everything with you. Do you understand me?" I assert.

The crash of the waves against the beach gets more intense.

She licks her lips and hesitates before asking, "What does 'everything' mean?"

I glance at the puppy, then study her. I'm nervous but need to be clear about things I never thought I would want and suddenly realize I do.

I have no doubts about the life I see with her. So I confess, "Everything means you, with me and King Madden. It includes a house full of babies and you in my bed every night."

A tiny flush fills her cheeks. My dick grows so hard it hurts. That ache in my body intensifies, and I question how much longer I can go without having my wife.

She glances at my lips, then questions, "You want a house full of babies?" as if she doesn't believe me.

I shake my head. "No."

Confusion fills her face. "I don't understand. Did you just say that, or did I mishear you?"

I answer, "I want *this* house full of *your* babies. *Our* babies. Do you understand?"

A tiny smile forms on her lips.

I add, "Do you see the difference?"

Her smile grows. She softly answers, "I don't know if we're ready for that yet."

Disappointment fills me, surprising me once again. I wonder how I could want things I always thought I didn't. I try to hide the disappointment but assure her, "It's okay, pet. There's no rush. But I do need you back in our bed. Starting tonight."

21

Blakely

King Madden's asleep on my lap and yawns. I still can't believe Riggs insisted we get him. I've never had a puppy and always wanted one. And King Madden's the most adorable dog I've ever seen, like a little white furball.

Riggs reaches over and pets him, saying, "Wake up, buddy."

King Madden looks up and sleepily tilts his head. Riggs chuckles and rises. "Time to go to the bathroom." He picks him up off my lap, sets him on the ground, and secures the leash to his collar. He takes him outside, and King Madden does his thing.

I toss Riggs's beer bottle into the recycle bin and unload the dishwasher.

Riggs steps inside, ordering, "Say goodnight to King Madden." He removes his leash.

King Madden runs over to me, jumping up. I pick him up and kiss his head. I ask, "Can't he sleep with us?"

Riggs shakes his head and taps the cage. "Nope. We've been over this."

"He's going to be so lonely," I state, feeling guilty.

Riggs groans, proclaiming, "He's a dog. He'll be fine. Besides, it's his house. You'll see."

I pout and then try to cuddle King Madden, but he gets a burst of energy, licking my face. I giggle and coo, "Aw, I love you too."

King Madden finally settles down and relaxes back into my arms. I take another look at the cage, then claim, "He won't take up a lot of room in the bed."

Riggs points to the cage and replies, "It's not negotiable. Now, are you putting him in, or do you need me to?"

I wince, adding, "It seems like a jail cell."

Riggs scoffs, muttering, "A jail with a big, fluffy bed and blanket. It might as well be a spa."

I continue assessing the cage. We did our best to pick the best bed with the thickest cushion. The blanket goes over the top only halfway so King Madden can slide under it easily. But even though it's the best, I'm still leery.

Riggs takes the puppy from me and holds him in front of my face. He commands, "King Madden, say goodnight to your mommy."

King Madden gives me more kisses, then Riggs whisks him away. He sets him inside the cage and orders in a firm tone, "Lie down and go to sleep."

King Madden barks. Riggs gently pushes him down under the blanket. He holds his palm on his back for a moment, saying, "Stay down."

King Madden curls into the bed and Riggs shuts the cage door. He rises and says, "See, I told you. Look how comfortable he is."

King Madden rises, escapes the blanket, and begins to whine.

"He's scared," I fret.

"He just needs to get used to it. He'll quiet in a little bit. You'll see," Riggs disagrees.

It's a hard statement for me to accept, especially when King Madden's whines get louder. I crouch in front of the cage, put my fingers through the bars, and pet him. He licks my fingers, then tilts his head and continues whining.

More guilt fills me.

Riggs holds his hand toward me and states, "Come on, let him get settled."

I pout some more but cave, saying, "Goodnight, King Madden."

I take Riggs's hand and let him pull me up. He leads me through the family room, turns off the light, then guides me to the bedroom. I freeze outside the door.

Riggs's face hardens. He asserts, "Let's not move backward."

My nerves escalate. I told him I forgave him, and I did. I had to. I had no other choice. I love Riggs. And no matter what, I can't deny how much. And I had to admit that it hurt to be away from him more than what he did to me. So I can't keep going around and around about it and holding it over his head.

Yet something about staying in our room again makes me hesitate. Things are better after our day together, but they still aren't a hundred percent, and I don't want to move too fast based on everything that happened.

King Madden's whine fills the air. I glance back, and Riggs tugs me into the bedroom, stating, "He'll be fine." He shuts the door and spins me against it, tilting my head and pinning his blues on me.

Electricity bursts between us, sizzling over my skin. His familiar scent flares in the air, stirring my core to the point I feel weak in the knees.

The dark expression Riggs always gets begins to form. I squeeze my thighs together, and he twirls a lock of my hair around his finger, declaring, "We have a lot of lost time to make up for, don't you think, pet?"

King Madden's whine turns into a loud bark, pulling me out of my trance. Guilt replaces all the tingles in my body. I declare again, "He's scared. He's too young to be in a cage by himself."

Riggs clenches his jaw.

King Madden's barks become louder, mixing with his whine, and it sounds like he's in pain.

It makes me freak out more. I cringe. "Please, we have to do something. I can't handle it."

Riggs releases my hair and puts his forearms on the door around my head. He claims, "I'll turn on some music so you won't hear him. Eventually, he'll stop and go to sleep. You have to trust the process."

A sharp bark fills the air.

Trust the process, my ass.

I duck and slip under Riggs's arms and reach for the doorknob. I admit, "I can't leave him like that. It's just not in me."

"He has to get used to it," Riggs claims again.

"I'm not mean like you."

Riggs sighs.

I open the door, rush through the hallway, and coo, "It's okay, King Madden. We're here."

"Pet..." Riggs reprimands.

I crouch down in front of the cage. I unlatch the lock, and King Madden rushes out, jumping into my arms. He gives me dozens of kisses.

I pick him up and hug him, murmuring, "It's okay, sweetie." Then I feel his racing heartbeat. "His heart feels like it's going to burst through his chest. I told you he was scared."

Riggs rubs his hands over his face, frustrated. He restates, "He's fine. Once he gets used to it, he'll want to be there. Trust me. Cages for dogs are like their homes. It's his own safe space."

I look at the cage once more, still not convinced. I rise with King Madden. I suggest, "Let's put him in our room."

Riggs gives me a disapproving look. I already know how he feels about that. We had several long conversations today any time I mentioned it.

Still, I can't leave King Madden on his own. I pet his fluffy hair again and say, "Okay, I guess I'm sleeping on the floor out here."

"Seriously?" Riggs asks, crossing his arms.

"Or I can go to the guest room with him," I toss out, knowing there's no way Riggs will let that happen. He's made it clear all day that I will be back in his bed tonight.

He shakes his head. "You aren't sleeping in the guest room any longer. We've gone over this. We're not moving backward, pet."

I warn, "If you don't want us in the guest room, and you won't let King Madden in our room, then I'm going to sleep here. Let me get my pillow and a blanket. I'm not going to leave him out here while he's scared."

Riggs groans, claiming, "It's part of the process. He has to learn. Even the people at the pet store talked to us about this. It'll only be a few nights where he doesn't like it."

"Maybe our dog is different," I assert.

"He's not."

"How do you know?"

Hurt fills Riggs's expression. He asks, "Is this your way of not sleeping with me?"

My chest tightens. He's right. We can't go backward, but I'm also not leaving King Madden out here crying. So I step close to Riggs, slide my palm on his chest, then bat my eyes. I suggest, "If you bring the cage into our bedroom, I'll put a nice outfit on for you."

He narrows his eyes, assessing me for several minutes. Then he declares, "You're trying to manipulate me. When did you become the manipulator in this relationship?"

I softly laugh, then feign innocence and stroke King Madden's head. I tease, "You don't want me to put something nice on? I think it's something that you'd enjoy."

His nostrils flare wider. I step closer as his erection pushes against my stomach. I crawl my fingers up his chest, adding, "I bought something special for you before I moved out. It's still here, but if you don't—"

"Fine," he snaps. "You win." He picks up the cage and shakes his finger at King Madden. Then he reprimands, "You've got your mama wrapped around your paw already. But I'm the boss of this house, not you."

King Madden tilts his head at Riggs and barks.

Laughing, I stand on my tiptoes and kiss Riggs on the cheek. I beam. "Thank you, Sir." Then I bounce into the bedroom with King Madden before Riggs can change his mind.

He follows me and sets the cage in the corner of the bedroom. He holds out his hands, ordering, "Give me King Madden, and you go change. You're making good on your promise."

My butterflies take off. I kiss King Madden's head, tell him goodnight again, then hand him to Riggs. I go into the closet and sort through my lingerie drawer.

The fishnets and mesh black teddy with white ruffles are still in there. It resembles a maid's outfit, which Riggs joked about once. I got it a couple weeks before I moved out.

I open the drawer with all the collars Riggs has bought me. I select a white one I've only worn once. I put it on along with everything else and slide into black stilettos. Then I grab the feather duster I hid in the drawer and saunter out into the bedroom.

Riggs is on the phone, talking quietly and staring out the window. His back muscles tense.

I watch him, wondering if everything's okay, but I set the duster on the bedside table, then step toward the corner to kneel and wait.

King Madden starts barking. I fall out of my role and go to his cage, sticking my fingers between the bars and stroking his fur again. "It's okay, sweetie. Lie down and go to sleep. We're going to be right in this room with you." I push him into the position the same way Riggs did, and he curls into the bed and then quiets.

I coo, "Good boy. See, it's nice. Just like Riggs said. It's your own space."

I rise and turn toward Riggs. He holds up his finger and leaves the room, saying into the phone, "Tell those morons we're on Pacific time. If they don't get their shit together, I'm getting a different team on this."

Relieved it's a work issue, I go to the opposite corner, hoping Riggs will return soon. I assume my position with my back straight, my ass on my calves, and my hands folded in my lap. I look down at them.

King Madden whines. It starts off low and grows louder.

My heart races and I'm so guilty I break my position, glancing at him.

He barks three times, returns to his whine, then barks again.

I can't help it, and I break my kneeling position. I rise, quickly go to him, and reprimand, "It's time to sleep." I try to get him to lie down, but he doesn't want to.

He keeps whining and barking. And I finally get him to quiet, surprised that Riggs still isn't back into the room. I return to the corner, but as soon as I kneel, King Madden returns to barking.

I get back up, go over to him, and finally take him out of the cage. I put him on the bed and get eye level with him. I order, "Go to sleep."

Riggs isn't going to like it. He told me earlier, *"There's no way King Madden's coming into our bed."* But I don't see any other option, so we'll have to avoid that section of the mattress.

Satisfied King Madden looks happy, I resume kneeling and stare at my hands.

King Madden barks, and I stay in position but scold him in a hushed tone, "Shush!"

The room quiets. I give myself a high five for solving the problem, even if Riggs won't approve of it, but I'm sure my maid outfit will help him forgive me. Or maybe he'll decide to punish me, which I won't mind either.

Maybe he'll put me over his knee and spank me.

He could chain me to the headboard and edge me for hours, not letting me come.

He could flog me.

The longer that time passes, the more I become obsessed with Riggs punishing me. I'm unsure how long Riggs is gone before I hear the door open.

Goose bumps pop out on my skin, but then Riggs's voice booms, "You've got to be kidding me."

22

Riggs

Blakely's body stiffens. She stays in her position, but her shoulders flex from my outburst. Her round ass is in full view, minus a little ruffle around the hip area.

I groan inside, thinking about how much I've missed everything about my pet. And there are several things I want to do to those cheeks.

King Madden kneels behind my wife, with his butt on the ground and his back arched. His white fur sticks up, and his ears perk toward the ceiling, but his eyes stay focused on Blakely.

I'm never getting laid again.

I crouch in front of Blakely and tilt her chin up. I inquire, "Why is the dog out of his cage?"

Her eyes widen, making my dick ache more. She puts on a sweet voice and answers, "Sorry, Sir. He was upset and wouldn't stop barking. So I put him on the bed. I figured we could avoid that space so he doesn't bark."

"You figured?" I question, peering into her blues.

She bats her eyes. "Yes, Sir. I assumed you wanted me fully focused on dusting the furniture. Or maybe changing the sheets? Or perhaps you have some other needs I could give my attention to?" She drags her eyes down my body, focusing on my cock, and licks her lips. Then she swallows hard and slowly lifts them, pinning her innocent, questioning gaze on me.

The blood heats in my veins, racing through my body, rushing straight to my balls. She's playing this little maid part perfectly, even with King Madden being a nuisance.

So I work hard to keep my face stern, fighting the smile playing on my lips.

And I suppose King Madden fell in love with Blakely as quickly as she did with him. As much as I'm dying to reunite with my wife, I can't blame the puppy for wanting to be near her.

Still, we're going to have to figure this out. I point behind her, declaring, "Your dog isn't on the bed. It seems he has a disobedience problem as much as you do."

Confusion fills her expression. She turns, and King Madden stays planted but cocks his head and whines.

My pet puts her hand over her mouth, giggling, then tries to contain it. She winces, chirping, "Sorry. Do you..." She glances at my pelvis again and continues, "Do you think I deserve a punishment, Sir?"

King Madden scoots next to her and resumes his kneeling position, but it isn't submissive. It's protective.

She glances at him, then asks, "Permission to pet our puppy, Sir?"

"Not permitted," I reply.

She traces the edge of the top of her dress, grazes her breasts, and bites her lip. Then she pouts, firing more adrenaline straight to my core.

I resist the urge to pin her on the ground and start fucking her. I state, "We've got a problem."

She grimaces, glances at King Madden, and replies, "I know...but he wants to be with us. I can't blame him. Can you?"

I ask, "Did I tell you to take your eyes off me?"

Her cheeks flush. She shakes her head. "No, Sir."

"Then why did you?" I question.

She lifts her chin. "I apologize, Sir. Is there something I can do for you to make up for my mistake?"

"Your puppy is cock blocking me," I state.

"Our puppy, Sir," she corrects me.

I glance at the dog. He stares at Blakely, wags his tail, and begins to whine.

I pick him up and tell him, "This is my castle, not yours. Understand?"

He narrows his eyes, barks at me, and it's clear I'm fucked. This dog isn't going to make it easy for me. But I'm not resting until I get what I want tonight. And what I've wanted for too damn long is my wife back in my bed.

Blakely asks, "Sir, permission to hold our puppy?"

I consider it.

She adds, "To help him get settled."

King Madden barks at me again, so I sternly order, "Don't bark at me, or you're not going back to your mama."

He quiets, then looks at Blakely and whines.

I cave and hand him to my pet.

She pets his head, then kisses him, declaring, "What are we going to do about you?"

He barks and wags his tail.

I mutter, "Put him in a doghouse outside."

Shock fills Blakely's face. She hugs him and says, "No! He's not an outdoor dog."

"He could be," I claim, even though I know it's not an option.

She tilts her head, reprimanding, "Don't say that!"

"Keep talking to me like that, and your punishment will increase," I threaten.

She smirks.

Every ounce of desire I have for her intensifies. I need to solve this dog issue and fast.

He needs a distraction.

I assert, "King Madden goes inside the cage. Put him in, and I'll be back."

"Where are you going, Sir?" she questions.

"You'll see," I reply and leave the room. I go into the kitchen and take out a bone. I find the chew toy he gravitated toward earlier in the day and take both of them into the bedroom.

Blakely kneels on the floor in front of King Madden's cage. She gently pushes him into a lying position under the blanket. She whispers, "It's time to go to sleep. Daddy is getting upset."

I stare at her bare ass for a few moments, deciding it's been too long. I'm not stopping tonight until I've had every part of my wife. It's time she gets a full reminder of what she's been missing out on.

King Madden doesn't want to stay down. He tries to push his way out of the cage.

Her voice turns sterner when she says to him, "Go to sleep."

I crouch next to her and put the chew toy into the cage. King Madden's tail wags, and he barks. I hold the bone out, and his mouth waters. He lunges for it, but I hold him back, keeping the bone a few inches from his mouth.

He whines, and I instruct, "No more interrupting us. Do you understand?"

He tilts his head to the side, whining louder.

I give it to him, and he lies down and chews on it. Satisfied, I shut the cage and lock it. I rise and reach for my pet, figuring I have thirty minutes maximum before he starts bothering us again. It's not what I wanted for this evening. I wanted to savor my wife for hours, but I'll have to adjust my plans.

She takes my hand, and I tug her into me. She parts her lips, a soft breath escaping them.

I tell her, "You've been disobedient."

Maroon grows on her cheeks. She answers, "Yes, Sir. I have."

I assess her, trying to calm the raging chaos in my body, fighting the part of me that isn't patient. We might be limited on time, but I'm going to utilize every second. I take three deep breaths, observing her pulse beating in her neck. I trace my finger over it and palm her ass with my other hand, sliding my pointer under the thin lace strip and over the hard ridge of her forbidden zone.

She inhales sharply. Desire sweeps across her expression. Her eyes flutter a few times.

I demand, "Go dust the table."

Her lips twitch. She lifts her chin and strolls over to the table, swaying her hips. She picks up the duster, glances over her shoulder, and says, "I think I'll start with the headboard first." She runs it along the top of the wood.

I turn on music, move behind her, and reprimand, "I said table, pet."

She defiantly meets my eyes and replies, "I think it's better my way."

"Did you forget Rule Two?" I question.

She smirks. "Maybe I need a reminder?"

The throbbing in my balls quickens. I warn, "Disobedient pets get punishments."

She sticks her ass into my thigh, replying, "What would my punishment be...Sir?" She purses her lips.

My patience is gone. I push her onto the mattress and yank on her thong.

She shrieks, and King Madden yelps.

I glance at the cage and, in a stern voice, order, "Be quiet!"

He whines.

I keep my eyes pinned on him, and he finally quiets down. He returns to chewing his bone. I turn my head toward Blakely, and she's staring at King Madden with worry all over her face.

It's clear my time is limited, not only for King Madden to behave but my pet to not focus on him. And she needs to stay quieter so he doesn't start growling. So I open my dresser drawer, pull out a ball gag, and shove it in her mouth.

Her eyes widen, and she blinks hard.

I've never gagged her before. We've talked about it, but I always imagined taking her by surprise, so this scenario is perfect. I secure the strap, lean close to her ear, and snarl, "Breathe through your nose. Now stretch your arms forward. Your head faces the window."

She hesitates, her eyes darting between King Madden and me.

I slap her bare ass cheek harder than I normally do. She flinches, whimpering, then arches her ass higher.

I groan inside, then rub my hand over her cheek, taunting, "You greedy girl. You don't get more until you obey."

She gives me a defiant glare, taking deep breaths from her nose.

I thrust two fingers inside her pussy fast, and her eyes flutter. I fist her hair, tugging her head back and claiming, "From what I remember, you like it best when I'm inside you, slapping those cheeks."

She whimpers, clenching against my fingers.

"Fuck, you're wet. You never disappoint me, pet," I announce, twisting my hand.

She moans, pushing her body into me.

I freeze, keeping my fingers inside her. I threaten, "Last warning. Hands and face forward, or I'll chain you to the dining room table all night. I'll leave you there to think about your disobedience."

She slides her hands forward until she's gripping the edge of the mattress. Her head faces the window.

"That's a good pet," I praise, curl my fingers until she's shaking, then remind her, "There's no coming until I say."

She whimpers louder, squeezing her eyes shut.

A song plays. Rumor has it that the artist recorded it during a real orgy in a BDSM dungeon. There are instruments and no words, only the sounds of moaning ecstasy.

I take my other hand and slap the same ass cheek as before.

She arches off the bed with muffled, incoherent sounds flying out of her, mirroring the voices in the song.

King Madden whines, but I ignore him.

I slide my cock inside her, hitting my pelvis against her, groaning from the tiny amount of release it gives me. I'm far from what I need, but it's a bit of instant gratification.

She grips the bed harder, moaning louder.

I thrust fast, coating my cock in her wet heat, sliding my fingers past her hardened ridge. Her body quivers harder, and I growl, "No coming."

Her whimpers fill the room, mixing with King Madden's and the intensifying cries from the song.

Something about the sounds heighten my senses. I pull out of her, slap her ass a few times, then sit on the edge of the mattress. I straddle her over me, remove the gag, and slide my tongue into her mouth.

She urgently flicks against mine, grinding her pussy over my erection, taking all of me in once more.

King Madden's whines turn into barks, but the music is louder, almost drowning it out.

I lift Blakely's hips, shove her toward me, then position my cock over her forbidden zone. I don't hesitate, sliding into her, and her body convulses. She cries out against my lips, "Riggs!"

"It's Sir," I remind her through gritted teeth and hold her still, letting her body get used to mine, feeling a relief I never thought would come.

She tightens her arms around my shoulders, burying her face in the crook of my neck, her lips creating fresh tingles on my skin.

I tug her hair so she can't avoid me, commanding, "Ride me, pet. Ride me and show me how much you've missed this."

Her eyes flutter a few times, her chest rising and falling faster. Sweat glistens on her skin. She slowly obeys, digging her knees deeper into the mattress, working my cock like a prized possession, and whimpering louder.

I study her, proud of how she always keeps eye contact with me, knowing most women can't, no matter how much I train them. But not my pet. She stays focused, almost challenging me right back. And I try my best not to release too soon into her, even though she's working my shaft to the point I'm ready to explode.

The music escalates, the sound of multiple people's orgasms, and the instruments turn bolder. King Madden barks louder.

She starts to turn her head, but I hold her firmly, ordering, "You focus on me. It's only you and me, pet."

She nods, her face flushing redder. Her hot breath hits my lips.

The room disappears. Only my body and hers exist. It's been too long, and everything is more than I anticipated. I kiss the curve of her neck, grip her hip, and move her faster on me.

Her voice cracks, and she begs, "Please, Sir. I-I-I need...please!"

"Not yet," I reply, determined to come with her simultaneously. To torture her further, I slip my hand between us and play with her clit.

"Oh...oh...Riggs!"

"Who am I?" I growl, needing to return to our roles, almost as if to prove it's still us.

"Sir! Please!" she cries out.

I create a pattern on her clit, rotating between rubbing and pinching until tears fall down her cheeks.

"I...I...oh...I can't..."

"Now!" I order, no longer able to hold back, staring into her blues. I pump into her like I never have before. It's violent, lasting longer than usual, and my groan silences every other sound.

Her eyes roll, and she shatters in my arms, savagely convulsing on me, crying out, "Oh God!" and then taking bated breaths.

I push my forehead against hers. My high continues until it finally simmers into nothing and we're left full of sweat, heaving for air.

The song flips to a new one, not as intense. King Madden's barks get louder and angrier.

I kiss my pet, my heart still racing, and slowly move her off me. She whimpers, and I pick her up, take her to the bathroom, and set her on her feet. I turn on the shower and ask, "You good to stand?"

She smiles and nods. "Yeah."

I kiss her and say, "I'll be back in a minute." I squeeze her ass and go into the bedroom. I let King Madden out.

He sprints past me and dashes into the bathroom, barking.

"Oh! There you are," Blakely coos, taking a step out of the shower. She leans down and pets him.

He wags his tail and jumps up.

I point to the mat and order, "Sit."

He narrows his eyes at me and barks, then returns to trying to jump on Blakely.

I push him to the mat and repeat, "Sit."

It takes a minute until he relaxes, but he finally does.

"Good boy," I praise, then step into the shower next to Blakely.

She glances at him. "Aww. He's pouting."

He's curled into a ball with his paws under his chin.

"Looks like you," I tease.

She bites her smile.

I slide my hands on her cheeks and stare at her for a moment.

"Why are you looking at me like that?" she questions.

Nerves dance in my belly. I admit, "I thought I might never get you back. All I wanted was to return to how things were between us. I'm glad we're finally back to normal."

She pins her eyebrows together, and my gut drops.

More anxiety fills me. "You don't want to be back to normal?"

She steps closer and runs her hands through my hair. She answers, "No. It's not that."

"Then what is it?" I ask, fretting.

She opens her mouth, then shuts it.

My stomach lurches. I demand, "Tell me."

The line on her forehead deepens. She carefully states, "I just think we should take it slow."

"What does that mean?"

"Don't get upset."

"Upset? How am I not supposed to get upset at that statement?"

She turns her head.

With gritted teeth and my pulse skyrocketing, I inquire, "Pet, what does slow mean?"

She hesitates again, then answers, "I don't want to rush into anything."

"Rush into anything? We're married," I remind her.

"Yes, I'm fully aware."

Anger fills me. I demand, "You don't sound as if you're fully aware."

"That's not fair," she claims and steps out of the shower. She grabs a towel, and King Madden jumps at her feet.

I follow, tugging the other towel off the rack. I admit, "This conversation is confusing me."

She dries off and secures the towel around her. She picks up King Madden and says, "Let's talk about this in bed."

I attempt to stop the quivering in my gut and tightening in my chest, but it's pointless.

She goes into the other room.

I stay frozen, attempting to stay calm and giving myself a pep talk not to lose my shit. I finally go into the bedroom.

She's in bed with King Madden curled next to her. She's petting him, and he's licking her arm.

I pull back the covers, slide next to her, and turn on my side. I put my elbow on the mattress and my head in my palm. "Want to explain?"

She stares at King Madden, continuing to pet him.

"Blakely, I need to know," I press.

She locks eyes with me, confessing, "I don't want everything to return to how it was."

My heart drops. I accuse, "You don't want to be with me?"

"No! I'm not saying that!"

"Then I don't understand."

She glances at the ceiling, then closes her eyes.

I lower my voice, trying to stay in control. I state, "I can't do what you want if you aren't honest with me."

She blinks hard, then turns toward me, revealing, "I don't want to be blind or have you doing everything for me."

"Blind?"

She nods. "Yeah."

"I need more clarification."

"Okay. Before things happened, you controlled everything. Our house. My career—"

"You wanted me involved. I pushed you to choose your agent, remember?" I remind her.

She holds her hand in the air. "Yes. Let me finish."

I force myself to stay quiet, yet my blood pounds between my ears.

She continues, "House, career, relationships. You controlled it all."

"You make it sound like I held you here as a prisoner," I argue.

She tilts her head, glaring at me. "Don't put words in my mouth."

I scowl.

She puts King Madden on the other side of her and scoots closer to me. She slides her hand through my hair, asserting, "Since we've been apart, I've had to do things for myself again. I don't want to lose my independence a third time."

"Third time?"

"Yes. First my parents. Then you. Now I have it back. I don't want to lose it once more."

Fear fills me. I take her admission personally. I seethe, "You're grouping me together with your parents?"

"You're taking this the wrong way," she claims.

"Kind of hard not to," I grumble.

She sighs then adds, "And we broke our contract."

Confusion mixes with fear. I ask, "We already went over this. The seventy-two-hour rule didn't apply to our situation."

She replies, "So things can't return to how they were."

"What do you mean? Technically, the contract ended once we got married and we decided to stay together past the finish date," I point out.

She caresses my head, then states, "I'm trying to put my cards on the table."

Her statement only freaks me out more. I blurt out, "Cards on the table?"

"Calm down," she orders.

I seethe, "All this sounds like to me is that you don't want what we had."

She cries out, "That's not it."

"Then how is it?" I question.

She pauses for a moment, then gives me a chaste kiss. It feels like a consolation prize. She retreats, then states, "I'm your wife. I'm back in your bed."

"Our bed," I correct her.

She smiles and slides her thumb over my jaw. "You're right—our bed. And I'm telling you I only want you."

"But you don't want me as I was…as we were," I point out.

She sighs, repeating, "You're taking this personally."

"How am I supposed to take it? You just said you didn't like our old life," I snarl.

In a stern voice, she declares, "No. I didn't."

"Sounds to me like you did," I say.

She glares at me, then flips and reaches for the lamp. She turns off the light and hugs her pillow. King Madden curls into her, and she asserts, "I'm tired. I don't want to fight. We'll talk about this tomorrow when you've calmed down."

I clench my fist, unsure how things turned so quickly. I stare at her for hours, watching her sleep, listening to King Madden breathe next to her, and growing more fearful of the future.

If she doesn't want our past, what does that mean for our future?

23

Blakely

Riggs's side of the bed is empty when I wake up. I rise, go to the window, and catch a glimpse of him in the surf. Is he still mad at me?

Of course he's still mad, I reprimand myself. Riggs isn't the type of man who will let this go.

I cringe inside, knowing I hurt him last night, but I'm unwilling to return to the same situation. How will we ever survive forever if I'm not his equal? It's something I never thought about before I married him. Now, the nagging voice inside my head screams that it'll never work unless we're true, equal partners.

If only I knew what equal meant.

I want everything we had back, and it would be easy to let Riggs take over again. It's the type of man he is and a huge reason why

I love him. But if I rely on him to solve all my problems and make all the decisions, what value do I bring to our marriage?

And I want this to last a lifetime, but we must be on the same footing, or I'm no different than his other subs. So as much as I prefer him to take over, I have to figure out how to balance this out.

I turn from the window and go into the closet. I put on shorts and a tube top, not bothering to add a bra or underwear. Our beach is private, so I don't have to worry about anyone seeing me.

King Madden barks at my feet. He sniffs the floor around my body.

I coo, "Sorry, buddy. You probably have to go potty, don't you?"

He races toward the door. I follow him, attach the leash to his collar, and then open the slider door. He tugs me outside toward the spot Riggs designated for him.

"Good boy! You're so smart already knowing where to go," I praise.

He squats and does his thing. When he finishes, I move toward the ocean's edge.

Riggs is far out past the break and paddles fast to catch a wave. It swells behind him, and he jumps on the board, riding it until it tosses him off.

He falls into the water, and his board flies in the air. I hold my breath like I always do whenever he goes under. Riggs could surf professionally. He's that talented. Yet whenever the waves pull him under, my nerves skyrocket.

He finally pops out of the water, and I deeply exhale. He gets his board, slides onto it, then paddles farther away from shore.

I sit down on the sand, and King Madden jumps on me. I unlock his leash from his collar. He flies off my lap, running in circles around me. Sand flies in the air, and I laugh. I pat that spot next to me. "Come here, sweetie."

He yelps and then rushes down the beach, igniting my anxiety. He ran a lot on the beach yesterday, and he only went so far before turning around, and I don't want him to go any farther. Yet he passes the spot where he went the previous day.

I jump up, clap, and shout, "King Madden, get back here!" I hold myself back from running after him. Yesterday, Riggs and I learned quickly that if we run after him, he keeps moving forward.

It's exactly what's happening now. So I yell, "King Madden!" in a sterner voice.

He turns, positions himself in the sand, and barks at me, wagging his tail.

"Come get me," I yell in a playful voice, then jog the opposite way down the beach, worried my reverse psychology might not work.

To my relief, it does. King Madden comes barreling down the sand and pops in front of me, then throws his body on it, rolling around.

I crouch down and rub his belly, softly reprimanding, "Aw, you went a little too far this time."

He sticks his tongue out, and I scratch behind his ears. I laugh, "You're too cute."

He jumps up and barks at me.

I pick him up and kiss his head, admitting, "You're getting a little too brave for me. Next time don't go so far."

He nuzzles his head against me, and my heart swoons. How can I fall in love with a puppy so fast? It's not even been twenty-four hours, and I know I'd be lost without him.

How am I going to ever tour without him?

My stomach dives. I push the thought away. I'm going to have to. There are too many responsibilities to deal with when I'm away, and I don't want to shirk any of them. Nor do I want to let Colton down when he added me to his tour.

I wince, thinking about Colton and the other night at the club. He blew up my phone calling and texting all day yesterday, but I didn't want to talk to him when Riggs was around. I told him I was okay through text and said I would talk to him later. But he continued sending me one message after another. I finally told him I was turning my phone off, and I did.

I don't even want to turn it back on today to see how many more messages he left me. One thing I've learned about Colton is he pushes to get what he wants. In some ways, he's a lot like my husband.

Riggs booms, "Penny for your thoughts, pet?"

I snap out of my trance, turning to him. My pulse quickens. His unzipped wet suit hangs off his hips. Tattoos glisten over his arms, pecs, and torso. His tousled dirty-blonde hair has drops of salt water on the ends.

My husband's the sexiest man alive.

I need to keep him.

Equals. We need to become equals.

King Madden barks, wags his tail, and tries to escape my arms.

I blurt out, "Whoa!"

Riggs chuckles and takes him from me. King Madden licks the salt water drops on his chest. Riggs steps closer and kisses me on the lips with a quick peck. He declares, "You're up early, pet."

I shrug. "Looks rough out there today."

He glances at the waves. "It's perfect for surfing."

I add, "Still looks dangerous."

He chuckles again. "You worry too much."

King Madden squirms, and Riggs sets him down. He takes off down the beach in the same direction he went when we first got here.

I fret, "He's going too far."

Riggs whistles, and King Madden freezes. Riggs calls out, "That's far enough, King Madden."

He turns to face us, then lifts his head as if in a challenge, pinning his gaze on Riggs.

My husband grunts, muttering, "Is that how you want to play this?"

I laugh. "I think you've met your match."

Riggs whistles again, and the shrill sound flies through the air. King Madden races toward us.

I declare, "I need to learn to whistle."

"You just have to be stern," Riggs asserts, then he sits on the beach and pats the sand next to him.

"You're the one who gives the commands in this house," I tease, winking, my stomach filling with butterflies at the thought.

I sit on the sand next to him, and King Madden jumps onto my lap. Riggs gives me a tight smile, and my gut flips. I've seen that look before, and it comes out when he's upset.

He states, "We need to talk about last night."

My chest tightens and my pulse increases. I take his hand in mine, trying to reassure him.

I try to find the right words, but they feel off even as they come out. I declare, "It's nothing against you. I don't want to be reliant on anyone, including you. It's not fair."

"It's my job to take care of you. I'm your husband," he insists.

I quickly tell him, "You do take care of me, and I'm not asking you to not take care of me, but I want my independence. There's a difference."

He admits, "That doesn't make any sense to me."

I stare at the waves crashing against the shoreline, pondering how to explain this so that it makes sense. Yet I barely understand why I'm fighting him on this. I stroke King Madden's soft fur and state, "I want to be your equal."

"You are my equal," he declares.

I shake my head and sigh. "No, I'm not. At least, not how it was before everything went south between us."

Silence fills the air with tension growing between us. He turns to me, crisscrossing his legs.

King Madden jumps off my lap and lies between them.

"Traitor," I mutter.

Riggs grunts and then pets the puppy. His long fingers fill almost the entire back of King Madden.

He asks, "How are we not equals? Explain this to me, pet."

My stomach flips. I tilt my head, confessing, "You held all the power. I had none."

"That's not true," he claims.

I softly laugh, mostly because of my nerves, insisting, "Yes, you did."

He grinds his molars, his chest rises and falls faster, and he studies me. More tension swirls around us, and goose bumps pop out on my skin.

He states, "Give me an example, because I'm not following you."

I hesitate, trying to figure out how to make him understand what I'm trying to say when I don't even understand it on some levels.

"Tell me," he pushes.

I finally answer. "Okay, my career is only because of you."

He jerks his head backward. "That's not true. You have your career because you have a special talent. You've earned it."

I shake my head. "No, I'm only where I am because you made it happen with Ears."

"Bullshit," Riggs barks out.

"Riggs—"

"So you're upset I introduced you to Ears. Seriously? I'm being punished because I introduced you to my good friend, who happens to be the number one person in the industry. Wow. This makes a ton of sense, Blakely."

I cover my face in frustration, groaning. "No, it's just... Ugh. This is all coming out wrong."

"Then how is it supposed to come out?" he sneers.

I stay quiet.

Riggs adds, "People get where they are in life based on who they know. And for your information, I wouldn't have ever talked to Ears about you if you didn't have the level of talent he requires."

I confess, "I'm not wording things correctly."

He studies me, clenching his jaw. Hurt covers his expression. "Well, maybe you should figure it out."

I attempt to explain again, asserting, "Riggs, I'm grateful for all you do for me. Really, I am. But I relied on you. If you see an issue, you fix it for me."

"Yeah, I do. I'm your husband. So why is that bad?" he seethes.

I put my hand on his knee. "I'm not saying it's bad. I just..." I release a stress-filled breath. I can't blame Riggs for being frustrated with me. I wish the words would form so we could move past this topic.

He demands, "Just what?"

I blurt out, "If you're always making things happen for me, solving all my problems, I'll never be your equal. This will always be a marriage where you are at a higher level than me."

He puts his hand over mine, softening his tone, asking, "Do you think for one minute I would've married you if I didn't think you were my equal?"

The question about why he married me rears its ugly head again. I try to push it down. I told myself yesterday I'd let it go, so why can't I?

He groans. "You're still questioning why I married you."

I squeeze a handful of sand, focusing on it.

"You told me you forgave me," he accuses.

I lock eyes with him and declare, "I do forgive you."

His nostrils flare. He glances at the sky, muttering, "But you aren't ever going to forget it, are you? You're just going to hold it over my head for the rest of our lives."

My chest tightens, and the air in my lungs turns stale to the point I no longer smell the salt. I struggle to breathe and take in tiny breaths.

He drops my hand. Disappointment and pain fill his sharp features. He places King Madden on my lap and rises. He looks down and asserts, "I'm a man who gets shit done. If I believe in something or someone, I'll go to the ends of the earth to help facilitate whatever it is that needs to happen. So I'm not going to apologize for helping you make the right connections for your career. And I'll only tell you this one more time, pet. I never would've married anyone I didn't think was my equal. But this is who I am. So decide if you want me or not."

He storms away from me. Bile rises in my stomach. I swallow it down, feeling nauseous. I watch him put his board in the closet and disappear behind the outdoor shower.

King Madden leaps off my lap and races toward the house. He jumps up on each step and onto the deck.

Everything Riggs says repeats in my mind. I can't blame him for getting angry. I probably sound like an ungrateful brat in his eyes.

I rise off the sand and go up to the house. King Madden lies on the bed we bought for the outdoor area. He's chewing one of his toys and doesn't even look up when I come on the deck.

I step over to the shower. Riggs rinses the shampoo out of his blond locks. Suds drip over his hard frame, cascading down his spine, over his ass, and onto his thighs.

The water turns clear, and I step behind him, circling my arms around his waist and hugging him. Tingles shoot through my breasts, surprising me. It's only happened when Riggs has played for a long time with them.

He freezes, his back muscles tightening. They graze my nipples quickly, and I gasp, surprised again by the sensations.

His hand covers mine, and his dark voice states, "I'm not in the mood to play right now, pet."

I blurt out, "I'm sorry. I don't know how to describe what I'm feeling. The only thing I'm certain of is how much I want you. So don't ever question that."

He stays frozen, which only gives me more anxiety. My fear pummels me. I step between him and the wall faucets and reach for his hardening face. I claim, "I'm trying to figure things out. More than anything, I just want things to be good between us."

"Things are good between us. At least they were," he declares. His eyes turn to slits. He accuses, "But apparently, you don't think they were."

I briefly close my eyes. "That's not it, Riggs."

He sniffs hard. "Seems like you're trying to figure out if you want to be in this marriage or not."

I cry out, "No, that's not true."

Water soaks my back. The darkness in his eyes grows, stirring my core. He says nothing, pinning his leer on me. I step closer to him and stand on my tiptoes, tugging his mouth to mine.

He fights me, not returning my kiss, continuing to scowl. Then he moves his head to the side.

My regret for what I said turns to anger. I get a burst of energy and push him against the wall. I cry out, "Do not ignore me."

His eyes turn to slits. "Ignore you? You're one to talk. You ignored me for over a month. You acted as if I didn't even exist—as if you didn't care about us."

I point at him. "Don't you dare hold that over my head! You deserved that!"

He tosses his hands in the air, declaring, "I made a mistake."

"A fucking big mistake," I shout.

Rage bursts on his face, lighting up his entire expression. He questions, "Then why are you here, pet? If I messed up so bad, then why the fuck are you here?"

I toss my hands in the air. I take two steps toward the exit, declaring, "Fine, I'll leave."

He grabs me, spins me into the wall, and cages his body against me. His chest pushes into mine, pressing into my nipples, and I whimper from the adrenaline shooting up my core. His large hand grasps my throat, and he tilts my head. He swallows hard, glaring at me with his jaw twitching.

I squeeze my thighs together and open my mouth, but nothing comes out.

His erection presses against my stomach, growing harder and harder by the minute. He grits through his teeth, demanding again, "Tell me why you're here, pet."

My butterflies go crazy to the point I feel dizzy. The heat from the shower, his warm frame, and the tension around us make my entire body flush.

He tightens his hand around my throat. I can still breathe, but any tighter, I won't be able to. And it lights up my core further.

He drags his other hand up the curve of my waist and palms my breast. Zings shoot through my lower body. I quiver, and he sees it. His lips form into a tight line. He pinches my breasts until I'm whimpering, studying me, then accusing, "You're giving me mixed messages, pet. This is who I am. So decide if you want your husband or not."

24

Riggs

My pet gives me her challenging stare, heating my blood to the boiling point. I lean in an inch from her lips, staring at them, assessing her. Then I meet her blue flames, ordering, "Tell me what you want."

Another moment goes by with only the sound of the water hitting the tile. It echoes, and the tension builds.

I keep my hand locked on her throat, grazing my thumb over her ear and pinching her nipple.

She whimpers, her eyes fluttering, her face flushing pinker. And it makes everything inside me only heat further. Her hot pussy presses against my thigh, grinding into me. I seethe, "I didn't take you for a woman who was looking to change her man." I lower my hand from her breast, sliding it to her shorts and cupping her ass.

God, I love her curvy ass.

Hell, I love everything about her body.

She whispers, "I'm not looking to change you."

But she is. I know she is. Everything she said on the beach confirms that's exactly what she wants.

I warn, "You have three seconds to tell me the truth, pet."

She glares at me.

I start, "Three…two…"

"You," she cries out in a muffled tone.

My heart pounds harder against my chest cavity. Fire erupts in my balls. My erection strains to the point it hurts, and I'm so tired of my body aching when my wife is right in front of me. And last night didn't quench my hunger for her. If anything, it only made everything worse. I step closer, ordering, "Say it again."

Defiance fills her expression, mixing with the growing desire that simmers on the surface. I know that look. *I created that expression.* And I crave to see it on her face every second of the day. I lean into her ear, brushing my lips against it. I threaten, "You have a choice, pet. Me as I am, or no me. I'm a man who takes care of what's his, and I'm not going to change. So you want all of me or none of me. Decide."

She whimpers, quivering against me, grinding her lower body in small circles against my thigh. And I fight the urges as best as I can, but the demons within me wake up. They stir the craziness inside me to the point I feel out of control. And it's the danger zone where I'm capable of doing things I regret.

So I continue staring at her, waiting until I regain my sense of control again. Then I murmur, "Let me remind you of who you chose to marry." I lick behind her ear, sliding my fingers over the slit of her ass, running them over the hard ridge I owned the night before. Her breath hitches and her skin turns hotter against mine.

"Oh God, oh God," she whimpers.

I push the band of her shorts over her hips, then tug her tube top until it drops over her shorts. My skin presses into hers, and a tiny moan fills my ear. I grip the back of her thighs and pick her up, caging her between the wall and my frame. I nibble on the curve of her neck while squeezing, backing off, then squeezing it harder, then backing off again.

Her limbs circle my body, tugging me closer. She whimpers louder, lifting her hips and sliding her body over my cock in one quick motion. I groan, lifting my face in front of hers, breathing through my nose, and releasing her neck.

She digs her fingertips into my skull, lifting her upper body and pushing my face to her chest. It's not something she ever really does, but I don't hesitate. I suck on her breast, gently biting her tit while thrusting slowly inside her.

Her incoherent sounds louden, and she holds my head firm. Still, I retreat, but she pushes me to the other breast.

Her walls fight to grip my body, throbbing against my erection. A storm of fire rushes so fast in my veins, I push my elbow to the wall to steady myself. I suck on her other nipple, then tug her hair, forcing her to focus on me. Thrusting harder, I snarl, "This is who I am. *This is who we are.* Me taking control of your body. Me knowing exactly what you need. Me making decisions for us when you don't want to or can't."

She blinks hard. Her mouth forms an O. Her whimpers fill the air around us. She whispers, "Please, please."

"No," I growl, knowing she wants to come. I add, "You submit to me. You do it because you need to. You do it because you want to. No one forces you to do it."

"Riggs, please," she cries out, her eyes begging me as much as her mouth.

I thrust harder, watching her struggle, knowing her body as well as my own.

"Riggs," she says again.

"No," I reply, thrusting even harder, to the point that I struggle to stay in control.

"Please," she murmurs again, her body quivering harder and harder against me.

I grit my teeth, snarling, "No. And don't you dare disobey me." I slide my tongue into her mouth. She moans, flicking her own tongue against mine, digging her fingers harder into my skull, shaking even more violently.

But I know she's not there yet. She's not over the edge, and she has more in her.

More than ever, I need her to keep submitting to my dominance—to reiterate that this is who we are and how we thrive. And to prove to her that we need each other equally. Neither of us can function without the other in the roles we've chosen.

So I retreat, demanding against her lips, "Decide what you want, pet."

"You," she claims again, with no hesitation.

I wish I could believe her. I'd pay my entire fortune to quash the fear brewing since she left.

There was a point last night I thought it was gone. I assumed it would never come back. But then she revealed her inner thoughts, things I had no idea about—things I didn't understand how to take. Things that still make me question if she loves me. And it's a pain I can't control. It swirls around me, pummeling me at all hours of the day.

Desperation to keep my wife and get back what we had consumes me, and I order, "This is us. Say you want us." I force myself to slow down my thrusts, aware I'm going too fast and about to lose all control.

"Us," she whispers.

My balls tighten. I pull out of her. I'm unsure if she's telling the truth or saying it because I'm pleasuring her. But I need a break, or I'll go over the edge. I'll get the high that I crave, and then it'll all be over.

I force her onto her feet, keeping her pressed against the wall. I kneel and tuck her thighs over my shoulders. I lean my face into her pussy, enthusiastically flicking my tongue over her clit, on a mission to show her I'm the only one who knows how to give her what she craves.

"Riggs," she cries out. I glance up, not taking my mouth off her, locking my eyes on hers, sucking on her until she screams.

Then I spout, "The only thing I better hear out of your mouth is the word us. You need to choose us."

The chaos in her eyes swirls faster. She pushes my head back to her body, shoving her hips up. I keep my gaze pinned on her, reaching my palm over her breasts and tweaking her nipple while my mouth tornadoes through her pussy.

She cries out, "Us," so many times her voice turns hoarse. The only other word I hear from time to time is, "Please."

It's the begging that haunts my dreams. It's another thing that never leaves my mind. But hearing it in person only accelerates all my adrenaline.

I take her past the point of her self-control. I know where it's at. No matter how long we've been apart, I still know when she can no longer control her orgasms or obey my demands. I normally permit her to release the instant before it happens, but right now, I don't.

I can't. I suck her pussy so hard, her body convulses and her knees turn weak. But I don't let up. I've craved it for too long. And sometimes she needs to think she's disobeyed me.

This is one of those moments. I'm in charge of her body and I want her to see there's no use fighting me—fighting us. No matter how hard she tries to take the reins of control, she can't. It's my job to take care of her, and I'll die before stepping away or not protecting her.

She falls over my back, and I don't let up. Her nails scratch my skin so hard it stings. She shrieks, "I'm sorry. I can't, oh God! Riggs!"

Another violent round of adrenaline fills her. Her stomach quivers against my head. When the earthquake slows, I carry her to the outdoor mattress on the deck. I lay her down and cage my body over hers. I reenter her trembling body, no longer worried about containing myself. I move her hands to the umbrella pole and position her fingers around it, ordering, "Don't you dare let go."

She grips it. Her knuckles turn white. Her hips roll toward me, matching my thrusts. Her blues flare, wild, echoing my inner demons.

It's exactly how I love to see her—out of control, dependent on me, knowing I put her in this state.

How can she not see what we are?

How can she ever want anything different than what we had?

I bury my face into her neck. Muttering, "This is us, pet. Us."

She barely manages the word, "Us," loud enough for me to hear.

But I do. It registers in my brain, and it gives me a spike of hope. But it's just a small glimmer. The rest of my fears are too strong. I declare, "I don't believe you."

She argues in a hoarse tone, "No, Riggs. Us! Oh…God…us. Oh, oh!"

But the thought I'll wake up one day and she'll be gone never stops terrorizing me. Once upon a time, I knew she was mine. Now everything is in question.

I won't survive if she leaves me.

I'll die. There won't be a point of going on.

Fuck, what am I thinking?

It's the truth.

I lift my head and hold her face. Gritting out, "I need you to want us."

"I-I, oh God," she cries out, her eyes rolling as another wave of convulsions attacks her body.

It finishes me off. I grit through my teeth, muttering, "Fuuuuck!" as adrenaline erupts like fireworks, making my vision blurry. I pump everything I have into her, thrusting faster as her body squeezes my shaft.

All I want is for her to remember how we are together. How we're beyond good sex or two people with chemistry.

Does she not realize what we have isn't something you forget about or toss away? That you don't go looking to change it?

She begins moaning so loud King Madden barks.

I barely hear him.

A sound I've never heard before flies past her lips. Vicious convulsions hit her at a new level. Liquid pools between us, soaking the mattress, as I continue pumping into her. When I can't fill her anymore, and our bodies slow, I stare at her, hating the anxiety building in my chest.

She's made me vulnerable. I loathe her putting me through this. I detest I've allowed myself to get to this point, but I don't know what to do about it.

Neither of us moves. Our gazes continue being pinned on the other.

King Madden jumps on the lounger, whining, but we ignore him, locked in a challenging stare.

He curls against her hip, and the chaos turns to calm in her blues. Yet it does nothing to reassure me. The overwhelming sensation she'll leave me is a knife slicing my heart. And it's already too damaged. I've become a weak man, and I'm unsure how to strengthen him.

My mouth turns dry, and the waves crash on the shoreline, getting louder as I return to reality. I roll off my wife and rise, admitting more things I never thought I'd say. "You need to decide what you want. Only one person is holding the cards in this relationship. And I can assure you, it's not me. It's you."

She gapes at me.

My heart continues slamming into my chest. My gut dives further and further.

She declares, "Riggs, stop. This... You're not—"

"I'm only going to be played with for so long, pet," I state, turn off the shower, and go inside.

I'd do anything to quiet the fear inside me. I knew she was too good for me the moment I first noticed her. She was only eighteen, a mere child. But I knew it then, and I know it now.

Blakely's in full control of what happens between us. For the first time in my life, I have no power over my relationship. And as much as I've tried to resume my authority, I can't seem to.

Normally I'd manipulate the situation to get what I want. She would be mine. She would always be mine. But as hard as it is, my gut's stopping me. It won't allow me to go to the extreme lengths I normally would to ensure that everything in my life happens as I desire.

Deep down, the truth screams too loud to shut off. If she doesn't want me, then I'm going to have to accept it.

The hardest thing I'll ever do is figure out how to walk away.

25

Blakely

*R*iggs disappears through the door, and my stomach flips. I've hurt him, made him question my love, and the crazy part is I don't even know why I'm fighting him.

Is Riggs right? Am I really the one holding the cards?

King Madden scoots closer to me, whining.

I sit up, tug him into my arms, and he nuzzles his head on my neck. The pit in my stomach grows, and I kiss him.

I have to let whatever my hang-up is go.

I rise, carrying King Madden into the house.

Riggs turns the corner, wearing shorts and a T-shirt. He tosses several items on the kitchen counter. He crosses his arms over his chest and says in a hardened tone, "I won't try to keep you here anymore."

I glance at the pile. His two sets of keys, our cells, a few burner phones, and our laptops are in it. My stomach dives like I'm on a roller coaster. I step closer, stroking King Madden's fur, and question, "What are you talking about?"

His body stiffens. He stares out the window for several minutes, then finally meets my eye. He admits, "I put this in the safe so you couldn't leave while I surfed."

I gape at him, unsure why I'm surprised. It's a total Riggs move.

More hurt lights up his expression. He declares, "Yin and yang work because neither is the same, yet they can't exist without the other. Their opposition creates an interconnected force of oneness, giving them infinite potential."

I tease, "I didn't know you were so into spirituality."

His nostrils flare, his eyes darkening into storm clouds.

Crap. Why did I say that?

In a stern voice, Riggs adds, "Yin and yang are equal forces. And that's you and me. It's *always* been you and me. But you have to decide if this is what you want."

"Riggs—"

"No, pet." He holds his hand in the air.

My pulse skyrockets, and I hug King Madden tighter. I wait for him to speak as my mouth turns dry.

He lowers his voice, declaring, "I've made mistakes. I can't say I won't make more down the road. I'm more flawed than the average human. I'm fully aware of it."

Tears well in my eyes. I try again, "Riggs—"

"I love you. You're the only person I've ever loved. But I can't change who I am to keep you," he interjects.

I blurt out, "I don't want you to change."

He inhales deeply.

"I love you," I add, my insides quivering.

He glances at the ceiling, then swallows hard. He points to the contents on the counter. "You're my wife, but if you don't want to be here..."

"I never said that," I claim, stepping forward and placing my hand on his bicep.

His expression scares me. He slides his hand through my hair, palms my skull, leans down, and kisses my forehead. He murmurs, "I need to clear my head, pet." He retreats.

I set King Madden on the floor and then reach for Riggs's cheeks. "Don't run from me."

"I'm not," he claims.

"But you're leaving?"

"Yes." He takes a step backward, out of my reach.

"Then you're running from me," I accuse.

He squeezes his eyes shut, shakes his head, then stares at me. He confesses, "There's a part of me I don't ever want you to see. It's a demon out of control, and when he wakes up, it's not pretty. So I need to go for a few hours. It's for your protection."

Goose bumps break out on my skin. "My protection? What does that even mean?"

His face hardens. He glances out the window at the crashing waves. His chest rises and falls faster. He clears his voice, grabs his keys, and turns toward me. He announces, "I'll be home later tonight or tomorrow."

"Tomorrow? Riggs, I'm sorry. I—"

He puts his fingers over my lips. "I love you. I'm always going to love you. But I want you to be happy. So I want you to think about whatever it is you need from me and how to voice it. When I return, you tell me what it is, and I'll be honest with you about whether or not I can give it to you."

An earthquake of fear hits my stomach. I blink harder, fighting the tears.

He spins and leaves the house with King Madden barking at his heels.

I go to the window and watch him pull out of the driveway. The gate shuts, and my gut sinks further.

King Madden jumps at my feet. I pick him up and pace the house, thinking about everything Riggs said, wishing I could do over last night and this morning, and worrying about his demon confession.

The more I pace, the more I realize he's right. We are yin and yang, each bringing to the table what the other lacks. And why was I trying to stop him from doing things I don't want to do when he thrives at them? And it's not like he ever did anything with my career I didn't authorize, except for introducing me to Ears.

I should only express my gratitude toward him for believing in my talent. Deep down, I know he's telling the truth. Riggs wouldn't have set me up with Ears if he thought I wasn't good enough.

And I don't want him to change. I love his take-charge attitude and how he handles everything I want to avoid.

I sit on the couch, and King Madden jumps up. He rolls over, and I scratch his belly, muttering, "Ugh, I'm a moron."

He whines and rolls over. He jumps off the couch and sniffs the ground.

I go to the kitchen, pick up his leash and my cell. I take him outside to his bathroom spot and turn on my phone. As expected, there are dozens of messages from Colton.

I don't read them and try to call Riggs. It goes to this voicemail. I hang up and text him.

> Me: You aren't the only one who makes mistakes. Please come home. I love you.

I stare at the screen, but he doesn't reply.

King Madden finishes, and I go back into the house. My phone rings, and I get excited, but it's not Riggs. I send it to voicemail, and Noah texts.

> Noah: Where are you? Scratch is in town. He wants to discuss collaborating on his next album with you.

I gape at the screen. Even with everything going on between Riggs and me, a twinge of excitement fills me. Scratch is a hip-hop rapper. His fan base is different from Colton's but just as huge.

I text back.

> Me: Seriously?

Noah: Yes. Where are you?

Me: Home. At the beach house.

Noah: I'm in Malibu. I'll be there in five minutes.

I glance around the house and then at King Madden. Riggs said he won't be home until tonight or tomorrow, but something doesn't feel right about leaving.

Me: Can we meet tomorrow?

Noah: He's leaving tonight. You'll only get one chance with him.

I glance at the piano, debating.

King Madden barks, pulling me out of my trance.

Noah calls.

I answer, "Hey."

"One shot, Blakely," he states.

King Madden jumps at my feet, barking.

I pick him up and reply, "Is it okay if I bring King Madden?"

Noah asks, "Who?"

I walk to my room, realizing I'm still wearing a towel and need to get dressed. "Sorry. My puppy I just got. He hasn't stayed by himself before. Would it be super unprofessional if I bring him?"

Noah chuckles. "Nah. It's L.A."

I sigh. "Okay. I need ten minutes though. I just got out of the shower."

"Fine, but hurry. He's more interested in seeing how your voice mixes with his than your looks," Noah teases.

"Then stop talking to me," I rebuke.

"Done. See you soon," Noah says and hangs up.

I hurry and get ready, then I text Riggs.

> Me: Noah called. He's picking King Madden and me up to meet with Scratch. He wants to collaborate on his next album! I'll be home later. I hope you will be too. Love you!

I put my hair in a messy bun, toss on some makeup, and tell King Madden, "This is going to have to do!"

He barks and wags his tail.

I carry him to the kitchen and my phone buzzes.

> Noah: I'm here.

I toss my phone on the counter. I grab the puppy purse we bought at the pet store and put King Madden in it. I coo, "Aww. Look at how cute you are!"

He whines.

I sling the bag over my shoulder, run out of the house, and go through the gate door. I slide into Noah's car.

"Hey, gorgeous," he says.

King Madden growls.

I ignore his remark. He does it sometimes when Riggs isn't around. I normally reprimand him, but King Madden's growls don't allow me.

"Easy, boy," Noah instructs, pushes his mirrored sunglasses higher on his nose, and reaches toward us.

King Madden snaps at him, growling.

Noah jerks his hand back. "What the fuck!"

"Hey! It's okay, sweetie. This is Noah," I say, repositioning King Madden farther from Noah and petting him until he quiets.

"Jesus, don't let him act like that to Scratch," Noah states, then accelerates down the road.

"He's really sweet. He's just protective of me," I claim.

Noah grunts and then flies through a red light, barely missing a car.

"Whoa!" I cry out. I'm used to Riggs's crazy driving, but he's never been this aggressive.

"Sorry, on a time crunch," he declares and turns up the music.

I secure my seat belt.

Noah taps the steering wheel, runs another red light, and I glance at the odometer.

"Can you slow down a tad?" I ask.

He pushes the pedal, and the odometer increases by another ten miles per hour.

"Noah!" I reprimand.

He ignores me and turns the music higher.

King Madden angrily barks and growls, his head turned toward Noah.

I try to calm him, but Noah's driving continues to scare me. He gets on the expressway, weaves in and out of the heavy L.A. traffic, then goes on the shoulder and races down the lane.

"What are you doing?" I cry out.

"Calm down. Scratch is waiting," he orders.

"You're scaring me!" I admit.

"Don't be," he replies as he remains on the shoulder and races past traffic.

My stomach spins. I slide my hand into my purse to see if Riggs has responded to my texts. Plus, I want him to pick me up from wherever Noah takes me. I'm never getting in a car with him again.

But I can't. My phone is nowhere, and I squeeze my eyes shut, cringing. I must have left it on the counter when I put King Madden into the pet purse.

He barks louder at Noah, and I tug him toward me, trying to calm him, but nothing works. His barks intensify.

Noah veers off the expressway, races through town, and pulls into a parking garage. He turns the engine off.

I slap his shoulder.

"Ouch!" he shouts.

"You're an asshole. You could have killed us!" I accuse.

He grins. "But I didn't, did I?"

I glare at him.

"Jeez, Blakely. I've seen Riggs drive. Don't be such a hypocrite," he taunts.

"Riggs would never put my life at risk like you just did!" I declare.

He grunts and asks, "You want to bitch all day or go meet Scratch? I'll warn you, he doesn't like divas."

"I'm not a diva."

"You're acting like one now."

King Madden barks.

"That dog was a bad idea," Noah claims, then gets out of the car.

I take a deep breath, mutter, "It's okay, sweetie," and open the door. I follow Noah to the elevator.

We get in, he punches a code, and his voice turns sweeter. "Let's make nice. This is a big day for you."

I decide he's right. I nod. "Okay."

We stay quiet, and the elevator stops at the penthouse. The doors open, and the L.A. skyline is visible through the windows. White leather furniture fills the living space. The corner of the room has a piano, several guitars on stands, and a drum set.

"Wow. Scratch has an awesome setup," I state.

"It's not his place. It's mine," Noah informs me.

Confusion fills me. "Did you move?"

He shakes his head. "No. I only bring special people here."

His statement makes my chest tighten. Blood pounds between my ears. I set the puppy purse on the table and unzip it. I pull King Madden out of it and hold him to my chest. His heart is beating as fast as mine.

I coo, "It's okay, sweetie." I lift my chin, asking Noah, "Where's Scratch?"

"He'll be here—"

The elevator opens, and my mouth turns dry. My parents step off it and into the room.

Alarm fills me. I turn my head toward Noah. "What are they doing here?"

"Baby! There you are!" my mother announces and runs toward me.

King Madden growls at her, snipping like he did at Noah.

She jumps back. The smell of vodka flares in my nostrils. Her bloodshot eyes widen. She replies, "Oh! What do we have here!"

"Why are they here?" I ask Noah again.

My father steps forward. "To get my money back as well as your husband's."

Of course. It's always about money with them.

I seethe, "Over my dead body!" I glare at Noah. "Why would you bring us here?"

Noah's lips turn into a tight smile. He stays quiet, angering and scaring me further.

"Well?" I demand.

My mother's drunk laugh makes me cringe. She pats the back of my head and slurs, "Oh, honey. You can't let us stay poor."

King Madden wiggles so violently that he slips through my hands. He nips at her ankles, tearing the bottom of her pants.

"Get off me," she cries out and kicks him, and he flies across the room.

A pang shoots through my heart. I rush toward him, but he cowers, shaking.

I crouch down, cautiously petting him. "Are you okay?"

He whines, wincing.

"Stupid mutt," my mother says.

"Shut up!" I warn, then try to assess King Madden. I gently feel his ribs and he gets up and steps toward me. Relieved he seems to be okay, I pick him up and spin toward my mother. I threaten, "Don't you ever touch him again!"

She slurs, "That damn dog ripped my pants."

I hold King Madden tighter and murmur, "It's okay, sweetie. We're getting out of here." I go to the table and put King Madden in the bag. The zipper gets stuck, so I leave it open.

"You aren't going anywhere," Noah declares.

The hairs on my arms rise. I snarl, "Watch me."

My mother declares, "Baby, you just have to listen to your father. He has a really easy plan and—"

"Shut up!" I reprimand. My insides quiver, and I move toward the elevator.

My father steps in front of me. His bloodshot eyes drill into mine. He claims, "You aren't going anywhere."

King Madden barks loudly.

I pull my shoulder back so he's out of my father's reach, not sure what he will do. I reply, "Move!"

"Don't fight us, baby. You can't leave us poor," my mother repeats.

"Shut her up," my father orders, pointing.

A pop and then a thud fills the air.

A shiver runs down my spine. I spin, and bile rises in my throat. My mother's limp body lies on the floor with blood pooling around her head. Noah has a gun pointed at me. I put my mouth into my elbow, trying to keep the contents in my stomach down.

My father's voice is the same one that always haunts me. He used it when he kidnapped me and wanted me to choose which one of his men to marry. He threatens, "You'll be joining your mother at some point. But for now, I suggest you make it easier on yourself and do what we require."

26

Riggs

The waves crash against the shoreline, and three kids on boogie boards ride the latest surge.

For hours, I've stared at the ocean, attempting to ignore the people on the public beach. I never come here, preferring my privacy, but I couldn't stay home. I rarely get this agitated, but I am.

There's no way I'm subjecting Blakely to it. I don't trust what I'll do right now. The voice inside my head screams to lock her up and hold her hostage so she can't ever leave me. But the rational part of me knows it's not an option.

Yet I'm tempted and don't trust what might happen when I get like this. The anger and fear swirl so fast that I can barely see straight.

The sun blazes at full force to the point it's getting uncomfortable. I pull out my phone to see what time it is and realize it's off. I turn it on. Dozens of missed messages pop up. The only ones I'm interested in are from Blakely. I open the chain, and nausea pummels me.

I try to call her, but it goes to voicemail. I text her.

> Me: Where are you?

I jump off the sand, head toward the car, and call Noah, but he doesn't answer. So I text.

> Me: Where did you take my wife?

He doesn't reply. I call again, get sent to voicemail, and anger fills me. I send another message.

> Me: Where are you?

That text goes unanswered too. My gut drops, and I trot across the sand. I call Kalim.

He answers, "Riggs."

I reprimand, "I told you not to let Noah be alone with her."

"What are you talking about? They don't have anything going on today," he replies.

"She texted me he was picking her up to meet with Scratch," I inform him and open my car door. I slide inside and turn on the engine.

His voice lowers. "Riggs, I don't know anything about this."

"Then you better find out," I order.

"On it." He hangs up.

I call Jones and head toward the city, unsure where I'm going but trusting my gut.

"Riggs," he answers.

"I need you to tap into Blakely's phone. That bastard Noah took her somewhere, and I don't trust him," I admit.

"Okay, give me a minute," he says.

I wait, accelerate, and cut off a truck. The driver blares the horn. I run the red light and weave through more traffic, driving in the opposite lane.

"Her phone's at the beach house," Jones announces.

My chest tightens. I say, "She isn't there."

"You're there?" he asks.

"She sent the message thirty minutes ago that Noah was picking her up," I inform him.

"You got a number for this jackass?" he asks.

I find Noah's cell and send it to him.

He says, "Got it. I'll work on it, but it'll probably take an hour or two to hack it since he doesn't have a tracer on it like Blakely's phone."

"I don't have that much time," I declare.

"Riggs, calm down. She's probably fine," Jones suggests.

"My gut says she's not," I seethe.

"You're also a jealous guy."

"Just get the location for me," I order and hang up. I veer onto the expressway and continue driving recklessly.

Kalim calls.

I answer, "Where is he?"

"I don't know. My guy lives down the block and went to his place. He's not there. He isn't at the studio either. But I'll meet you at Colton's," he states.

"Why Colton's?" I question.

"He's been with him a long time and doesn't like him. Let's see if he knows where he might have his meeting at."

"Call him. It'll save time," I command.

Kalim declares, "I tried. He's not answering. He had a late night, and I bet he's sleeping. But don't worry. My guy says he's been there the entire time."

"So have him wake him up," I demand.

"He's positioned outside his penthouse."

"So tell him to go in."

"He doesn't have a key. We're going to have to be a bit creative," Kalim informs.

I groan. "Fine. Send me the address." I hang up.

Kalim sends it, along with a code to park in the garage. It takes fifteen minutes. I pull into a space and get out.

Kalim's standing next to the elevator. He slides a card into the slot and the doors open. We get up to the penthouse, and he nods to his guy. He asks, "No movement?"

His guy shakes his head. "Nothing. I've been pounding on the door and calling."

I slam my fist on the door, ignore the shooting pain surging through my arm, and shout, "Colton!"

"Riggs, relax," Kalim orders, then holds up a keycard.

"Why do you have the key and not your guy?" I ask.

"It's not his key. It's a universal one for these types of locks," he declares and slides it into the slot.

"He's got company," Kalim's guy announces.

"I don't care," I bark as the door opens and I push past, muttering to Kalim, "I need one of those keys."

"Sorry. Chances are slim. I stole it from Interpol," Kalim confesses.

"Colton!" I shout, moving through the large penthouse.

"Bedrooms all the way to the back," Kalim states.

I rush down the hallway, bursting through the French doors. "Colton!" I roar.

A naked man, maybe in his fifties, is on top of Colton, kissing him. He retreats, turns his head, then scowls, "Who the fuck are you?"

"None of your business. Get out," I growl.

Colton gives me a sleepy grin, adding, "You can join us if you want, Riggs."

Anger flies through me. I don't have time for Colton's games. "Noah has Blakely. Where would he take her?"

The color drains from Colton's face. He pushes the man off him, stating, "Take a breather, Daddy."

The man gives me another pissed look, caressing Colton's hair and challenging, "Maybe I should stay, sugarplum."

Colton's voice turns firm. "No. Go grab some food."

The man reluctantly gets up. He walks naked across the room and glances back. "I'll be only a shout away."

Colton motions with his fingers toward the door. "It's fine."

The man steps out.

Kalim tosses Colton a pair of boxers.

"Where would he take her?" I push.

Colton gets out of bed and slides on the boxers. His guilty eyes dart between Kalim and me.

My gut churns faster. I step closer, snarling, "What do you know, Colton?"

He squeezes his eyes shut briefly, then admits, "Noah has a place he takes the 'special ones.'" He makes quotes with his fingers.

Rage explodes inside me. I grab his shoulders and seethe, "What does that mean?"

Kalim pushes me off Colton, declaring, "Relax. He's not the enemy."

"Colton, you better start talking!" I warn.

He asks, "How do you know he has her?"

"She texted him about a meeting with Scratch," Kalim answers.

His face turns green. He puts his hand on his stomach, and his eyes fill with tears. He turns toward the window, and his hands tremble.

"My wife is with him. Start talking," I bark.

Colton's voice cracks. "He..." He clears his throat, then glances at the ceiling, admitting, "Noah has a penthouse about ten minutes from here. He lures you there to collaborate with a more successful musician than you, then..."

My blood flows hotter. I snarl, "Then what?"

Colton wipes his cheek and spins to face us but several tears flow from his eyes. He shakes his head, claiming, "He drugs you, records you, then blackmails you. He destroys your relationship with anyone he doesn't want in your life. And it ties you to him for life. Then he makes you sign even more of your royalties to him, keeping you in a decent lifestyle but not the one you've earned."

I clench my fists at my sides. "And you said nothing to warn Blakely?"

Shame erupts on Colton's expression. He chokes out, "I'm sorry."

"Where is it?" Kalim asks.

Colton grabs his phone off the desk then types on it.

My cell rings. I glance at the screen, and an address pops up. I order Kalim, "Let's go."

We rush through the penthouse.

Colton calls out, "Let me know she's okay. Please!"

I ignore him and push the button for the elevator. The doors open, and Kalim and I ride it to the garage.

He announces, "I'll drive," and hops into a black SUV parked near the elevator.

I get into the passenger side.

He turns on the engine, holds his phone to his ear, and states, "I sent an address. I need janitorial services." He hangs up.

"What's that?" I question.

He states, "How we're getting in unseen." He accelerates toward the exit.

"We don't need that. I have a guy who can tap into the security."

"So do I. But we still don't need witnesses stating we're there for whatever reason," Kalim claims.

I ask, "You have an extra gun?"

His jaw twitches. He glances at me without turning his head and presses a button on the roof.

The gate lifts, and he drives past the security stand.

I mutter, "Let me guess. More Interpol?"

He doesn't answer and turns right.

"Gun situation?" I push.

He weaves past a semi, takes a sharp turn, and asks, "Assume you've shot one before?"

I grunt. "Grew up in Compton. This isn't my first rodeo. Where's it stored?" I open the glove box, but it only has papers.

He states, "I don't carry an extra."

"Why not?"

"Don't need it."

"Looks like you do now."

He shakes his head. "Better I stay in control of the firearms. We don't know what's going on, and Blakely doesn't need to see a bloodbath. That shit will haunt anyone, but especially her."

My pulse creeps higher. He's speaking rationally, but I still want a gun. I order, "Give me yours if you don't have a spare."

He scoffs. "You can go fuck yourself before I give you mine."

"It's my wife," I seethe.

He runs a red light and locks eyes with me. "And if he's done anything inappropriate, I'll be the first to shoot."

I study him.

He refocuses on the road. The tires squeal as he takes another sharp turn. He passes a dump truck and then cuts in front of it. A horn blares.

I tap my hand on my thigh, trying to push the bile down my throat. After what Colton admitted, there's no question I was right not to trust Noah. I curse myself for not choosing her agent and letting her pick him.

A few more minutes go by, and Kalim turns onto a side road. He veers to the curb, parks, and turns off the vehicle.

"Why did you stop here?" I ask.

He turns in his seat. "We don't know what's going to happen in there."

"What's your point?" I hurl, pissed he's wasting time.

He motions to a black van with no windows in front of us. "That's our entrance."

My phone rings. I answer, "Jones. Tell me what you found."

He declares, "He's in the city. I just sent the address."

I glance at my screen, then respond, "Thanks." More anger flares. I hang up and lock eyes with Kalim. "He has her there."

He opens his door. "Time to go."

We get into the back of the van. There are two guys inside. I don't ask their names, nor does Kalim.

I restate, "I want a gun."

He shakes his head. "That's not changing, Riggs."

My rage overpowers me. I reach for his throat, and he grabs my arm and twists it behind my back.

In a calm voice, he states, "Let's get something straight. I'm on your side, but I'm in charge of this mission. Understand?"

"It's my wife," I seethe.

He nods and pins his dark gaze on mine. In a cold voice, he claims, "My only goal is to get her out of there unharmed. If anyone's getting shot, it's coming from my hand. Understand?"

I don't like it. I prefer to be the one in control. So I continue scowling at him, ignoring the pain that begins to crawl through my arm.

"I need your cooperation on this, or I'm not letting you go in," he declares.

The sharp sensation gets worse. I grit my teeth.

He questions, "What's it going to be, Riggs? Do I drop you off somewhere else, or are you capable of following orders?"

More tension fills the air.

He lowers his voice. "I think your wife might need you in there."

I swallow my pride. For once, I'm going to have to submit and allow someone else to take the lead. It's not my choice, but Kalim's proven to be nothing but a force. He always does what he says, and I have to admit that he's more skilled than I am. So I finally relent. "Understood."

He releases my arm and nods. "If you rub it, the sting will go away faster."

I grit my teeth again but don't touch my arm, preferring to feel the pain to help mask what Noah might be doing with my wife.

He grunts. "You're a stubborn bastard."

I snarl, "Just get me my wife back."

27

Blakely

"Sit," Noah demands, pointing at the couch.

My mother's body lies in front of it. The pool of blood widens around her, soaking her clothes and hair.

I can't control the bile and crouch down. I toss my cookies onto the wood floor while holding King Madden close to my chest. He whines and tries to escape, but I clutch him tighter, afraid of what my father or Noah might do to him.

"Jesus. Just like when you were a child," my father states.

I glance at my mother's bloody face. I can't hold it in and begin to cry. My mother wasn't a great person, but she was the only mom I knew. I choke out, "Why did you kill her?"

My father steps in front of me. His expression turns darker than I've ever seen it. His voice stays calm yet powerful, like the in-control man I've always known him to be until recently. He answers, "She was a loose cannon. We don't need dead weight hanging around. And you're not an exception."

My insides quiver harder. I squeeze my eyes shut, wishing all this to be a nightmare. My stomach spasms again, and I find a way to keep the bile down. I open my eyes and whisper through tears, "I'm your daughter. You're going to kill me too?"

"Not until we both get what we want," Noah interjects, running his hand down my spine.

King Madden growls as I jump away from his reach, ordering, "Do *not* touch me!"

He grins. "Always playing hard to get, aren't you?"

My vision blurs. I blurt out, "Riggs was right about you!"

His face falls. Anger lights it up, and he snarls, "Your precious Riggs won't save you now."

Chest pains shoot through me. Dizziness hits me, and I struggle to stay on my feet.

My father booms, "No, he sure won't. You'll be long gone by the time he sees you again."

I cry out, "I'm your flesh and blood!"

He scoffs, announcing, "You never were my daughter."

"Just because I left doesn't mean—"

"You're a bastard! Your mother finally admitted it to me," he shouts, waving his hands in the air.

Shock fills me as I attempt to register what he's claiming. I gape at him, shaking my head, declaring, "You're lying!"

"No. I'm not. Your whore of a mother slept with someone else. Imagine that," he sarcastically states. He turns to Noah. "Where's the scotch?"

"I'll get you one and let you attend to this family matter," he gloats, then strolls over to the bar.

My father points to the couch, repeating, "Sit."

I lift my chin, challenging, "How do you know she wasn't lying? You know how she gets when she's drunk or high."

His lips turn into a tight smile. He assesses me, his hate-filled eyes in slits. "*Got*. You know how she *got*, not how she gets. She's dead, so use the past tense."

I always knew my father was cruel. This is a new low, even for him. I look back at my mother, cringing from how her face looks, void of any life, paling in the drying blood.

King Madden whines again, his heart racing against my chest. I glance at him and coo, "Shh. It's okay, sweetie."

Noah hands my father a tumbler of scotch. He takes a mouthful of his own drink and scowls. "That dog's next on the list."

King Madden growls, baring his teeth.

I turn my upper body away, shielding King Madden, afraid of what he might do to him. I glare at Noah, snapping, "Don't you dare hurt him!"

My father booms, "I'm not telling you again to sit down!"

I jump, startled by his outburst. It gives me a flashback of the last time I was in his house, and I shudder. I quickly move to the couch and sit on the corner cushion, trying to hold King Madden, who's still growling and fighting to get out of my hold. I pet his fur and repeat, "Shh. It's okay."

"Damn dog," my father spits, then takes a swig of scotch. Then he adds, "You're just like her."

I glance at my mother again, trying to comprehend that I'm not his daughter, wondering if it's true. In some ways, I believe it. My mother was promiscuous. And I've always felt like an outsider with him. Yet it wasn't only my father who gave me that feeling.

"You don't know if she's telling the truth," I state.

He steps closer, seething, "Dumb woman. I tested it."

"How?" I ask.

"You left everything when you ran away," he admits.

"Everything?"

He downs the remaining alcohol, slams the crystal on the table, and shakes his head, answering, "Your toothbrush. Your hairbrush. Hell, it's not that hard to get a DNA test. I should have done it when you were born and kicked that drunk bitch to the curb." His gaze shifts to my mother, and more hate blazes over him.

I knew they had issues, but I didn't realize it was to this level.

He killed her.

Noah did.

But my father's okay with it.

He wants to kill me.

A lump grows in my throat. I swallow it, murmuring, "Shh," to King Madden.

He won't stop growling, baring his teeth, fighting to escape my grasp.

My father pins his eyes on him, shaking his head. "I'm two steps from shooting him."

More fear fills me. With the sternest voice I can manage, I command, "Quiet!"

King Madden's body relaxes a tad. He turns his head toward me. Confusion fills his face, and he softly whines.

Keep them talking.

I turn toward Noah and ask, "How could you kill her?"

He shrugs. "She's just another piece of ass. Last I heard, she wasn't mother of the year. So after everything she put you through, I'd think you wouldn't care."

"Well, I do," I insist.

Satisfaction fills his features. He replies, "Too late now, sunshine."

"We're wasting time," my father interjects.

Noah waves the gun in front of me, adding, "Agreed."

More dread washes over me. I blurt out, "How does killing me help you? I'm your client!"

A wild expression lights up his face. He answers, "You chose him over your family. Then you chose him over me. I give you opportunities, yet all you ever do is choose him. So now, it's time for me to cash in."

My voice cracks. "Cash in?"

He grins, making my stomach flip faster. He steps forward and announces, "A dead singer is sometimes worth more than a live one."

"That's not true!" I claim.

He sits next to me, and I move closer to the armrest.

He grabs my chin, digs his fingers into my skin, and forces me to face him. He studies me, and tears rush down my cheeks.

King Madden returns to growling and baring his teeth, but I have him positioned so he can barely move. If I release him, I'm sure he'll attack Noah, which will only worsen this situation.

Noah finally states, "With your fucked-up story, I think the movie will gross more than Selena's did."

My gut dives to the floor. I swallow hard.

Noah adds, "Your album sales will skyrocket. Any merchandise I can get out there will sell out. Yeah, I'll be able to milk your tragic life all the way to the bank."

"Speaking of the bank, it's time for you to do your job," my father claims.

Goose bumps break out on my skin. I'm unsure who I'm more afraid of, him or Noah. My gaze darts between them.

My father asks, "Noah, where's your laptop?"

"In the office."

"Well, don't sit on your ass. Go get it," my father orders.

Noah obeys, leaving the room.

My father goes to the bar and refills his scotch. He takes a large mouthful before spinning toward me. He points to my mother, declaring, "She's always been a worthless pain in my ass."

"You won't get away with this," I seethe.

He drinks more, then replies, "You're still naive."

"No, I'm not!" I claim, unsure why I'm bothering to fight with him.

He smirks. "Then tell me, dear bastard daughter of mine, who's going to know?"

My mother's dead eyes stare at me. A wave of grief and guilt rolls through me. I didn't do anything to save her. Not that I knew what Noah would do or how I could have stopped it, but it's just like the guilt I harbored all these years over not being able to help her get clean. And she might have been an addict, but she didn't deserve this. No matter what she did or how she hurt my father or me, it didn't justify this.

Noah returns to the room, carrying a laptop. He sets it on the four-top table and opens it. His fingers move over the keys, and he nods to my father. "All set."

My father demands, "What's the password to your and Riggs's accounts?"

I answer, "How would I know?"

He crosses his arms, pinning his disgust on me, accusing me, "Don't play dumb. You married him for his money, just like your mother married me for mine."

King Madden barks, then growls.

"Shh," I order, then reply, "That's not true!"

"Stop lying! Now, what's the password?" he demands.

I shake my head. "I don't know. I don't get involved with the finances."

Rage flares on his cheeks. He grabs the gun from Noah and points it at me. He threatens, "You have ten seconds to tell me the password."

King Madden's aggression gets louder.

My mouth turns dry, and my pulse skyrockets. I hug him tighter, unable to take my eyes off the gun barrel.

"Time's up," my father states.

Noah pushes the gun, and it drops to the floor. A loud bang erupts. A bullet flies through the air, tearing through the lower wall. He barks, "This isn't what we discussed! Don't be stupid! Until we have the money, she's valuable."

Red grows hotter on my father's cheeks. He seethes, "I want my money!"

"Calm down," Noah orders. "You'll get it. But don't make a mistake. We stick to the plan."

More fear hits me. I don't know what the plan is, nor do I want to find out. Without debating, I jump off the couch and run toward the elevator.

"Grab her!" my father orders.

I reach for the button, and pain shoots into my left butt cheek. I scream, "Ow!"

"Dumb bitch," Noah mutters.

I try to reach for the button, but everything starts to spin. King Madden falls from my arms, growling. My knees turn to mush, and I collapse to the floor.

Everything turns blurry. I try to move but I can't. King Madden jumps around me, then curls beside my face, whining.

The sound of their voices changes, as if they're in a tunnel.

My father states, "Send Riggs the message."

"It's too soon," Noah declares.

"It's not," my father insists.

Noah says, "It is. And I've not had my fun yet."

My father asserts, "You can do whatever you want with her after I get my money. Now send the fucking text!"

Noah's voice turns muffled, growing quieter until I hear nothing except King Madden's whine. Then I'm pulled to the couch, unable to stop them from moving me.

Someone lifts me. I think it's Noah, but I can't be sure. A white furball jumps on me, and King Madden snuggles between the couch and my limp body. Drool slides out of my mouth, slipping down my chin.

So much time passes that I wonder if I'm dead. Then the muffled noises come back, and the blurriness fades.

My mother's lifeless eyes stare at me. The dark-red blood around her is no longer fresh. The few spots of her untainted skin have no color left.

King Madden licks my cheek, and I realize my tears are still flowing. I try to reach for him, but I'm paralyzed.

The only words I can process are when they mention Riggs. And I wish he'd come to find me, but I know it's not happening. Noah knew what he was doing when he took me, and my fate is clear. I'm going to end up just like my mother.

28

Riggs

Kalim's driver utilizes the universal remote to get through the security at the parking garage. He finds a space on the fourth level near the elevator and turns off the engine.

I call Jones.

"Hey," he answers.

I ask, "Did you tap into it? Are we all set?"

He replies, "I just got in. You're good to go."

"Are you sure?" I question. My rage is so hot, I know I'm not leaving that building until I take care of Noah. If I have to pull the gun from Kalim, I will. And I don't need any evidence of being here.

Jones grunts. "Am I ever not sure?"

"Good. Stay tuned," I order. I slide my phone into my pocket and turn to Kalim. "He's cut the security footage. We're good to go."

Kalim pauses. "Are you sure your guy's good?"

I cross my arms. "Are you seriously questioning me about this?"

He puts his hands in the air. "I'm just asking. We can't afford to make any mistakes. I know my guys and their abilities. No offense, but I don't know anything about your contact."

"He's a genius. You have nothing to worry about," I assure him.

He studies me for a moment.

"You don't," I insist.

He adds, "I need you to keep your cool up there."

Seething rage boils in my belly. I scowl, stating, "Noah's going to get what's coming to him."

He frowns, declaring, "It's better if you let me handle him and keep Blakely's best interest in mind."

"I always have my wife's best interest in mind," I assure him.

He crosses his arms over his chest, challenging me with his stare.

I point out, "We're wasting time."

He gives me a final lecture, "I mean it, Riggs. Keep your cool."

I say nothing.

He mutters, "Why do I feel like I'm going to regret this?"

"Time to go," I insist.

He releases a deep breath, shaking his head. He orders his guys, "Have the SUV wait on the top level. You guys stay here in case I need you." Kalim gets out of the van, and so do I.

We step into the elevator and Kalim inserts a key and hits the penthouse button.

I comment, "I should have worked for Interpol."

He chuckles. "It comes in handy sometimes, but you have to take the things before you leave." He gives me a wink, then his face falls. He pulls his gun out and unlocks the safety. He holds it in front of him.

My blood pounds harder through my veins. I squeeze my fist to my side, trying to stay calm, knowing I need to use my head in this situation but not trusting I will.

The elevator rises, moving slowly through all thirty stories. My pulse skyrockets with every floor. The elevator nears the penthouse, and Kalim steps in front of me, stating, "I'm going out first."

I grind my molars but don't fight him. He's the one with the gun.

The doors open, and Kalim steps out, barking, "Don't move!"

I exit the elevator and freeze. Madelyn's lifeless body lies in a pool of dried red blood with a bullet in her skull.

Noah stands next to Blakely. She's sprawled on the couch with her eyes open, and my worst nightmare comes true. King Madden's curled against her, whining and licking her cheek.

The faint rise of her chest is the only thing that assures me she isn't dead. I snarl, "What did you drug her with?"

King Madden rises between her and the couch, pinning his gaze on me for a brief moment. Then his whines turn to barks. He jumps on the armrest and bares his teeth at Noah, growling.

Noah's eyes widen, darting between Kalim and me.

"Get your hands in the air," Kalim orders.

He slowly obeys. His voice falters as he threatens, "There's video footage everywhere. You should leave before my security arrives." King Madden gets louder, and Noah nervously glances at him.

I seethe, "Fuck you." I step toward him, but a door opening catches the corner of my eye.

Hugh walks out of another room, a tumbler of scotch in his hand.

"What the fuck is he doing here?" I ask.

"Well, well, well. Just who I wanted to see," Hugh snarls, not noticing Kalim or the gun.

"Don't move," Kalim orders, aiming the Glock at him.

The color in Hugh's face drains. He puts his hands in the air. "Who the fuck are you?"

"You're on my payroll," Noah reminds him.

Kalim ignores Noah. He commands, "Put the alcohol down."

Hugh slowly puts it on the table.

Kalim demands, "Take five steps back and then stop. Keep your hands in the air."

Hugh obeys.

Noah shifts, his eyes on the floor. I glance over and lunge toward a gun, and so does he.

"Freeze," Kalim shouts, but neither of us listen.

I tackle him, and we both reach for the gun, gripping it at the same time.

Hugh shouts out, "You're going to kill us!"

"Don't move," Kalim warns him.

Noah and I roll around on the floor, each struggling to gain control, then I finally seize the gun out of Noah's hands. I slide it farther down the floor toward Kalim.

I tumble over Noah, pinning him to the wood floor near Madelyn's corpse. I curl my fingers around his throat, squeezing, seething, "What did you give her?"

His face turns red. He sputters, his body flailing under mine, attempting to escape my hold, but it's pointless.

All the rage and hate I've felt for him escalates to a new high. The uncontrollable demons inside me take over.

I move one hand off his neck and grasp his hair. I slam his head on the floor over and over and over. There's a loud crack, and his skull finally breaks. Blood pools around us, merging into Madelyn's.

Kalim shouts, "He's dead. Let it go, Riggs."

I can't. The demons won't allow me. I slam Noah several more times.

Kalim orders, "Enough! He's dead. Blakely needs you!"

Breathing hard, I turn toward her.

King Madden returns to whining. He jumps off the couch, stays beside it, and barks at me.

Hugh claims, "It was Noah. I didn't want any part of this."

"Bullshit, you fucking bastard." I rush over to the couch.

King Madden jumps at my feet. I reach for him, but Kalim says, "Riggs, go wash your hands before you touch anyone."

I stare down at the blood dripping on them.

I killed him.

A surreal feeling bubbles against my rage.

"Riggs. Now," Kalim demands.

I turn toward him.

He keeps his focus on Hugh, his gun still pointed at him.

He calms his voice. "I'll watch her. Go clean up."

My rational side takes over. I go into the bathroom, scrub my hands until I can't see any more blood, then rush back to Blakely.

King Madden jumps up on my leg, and I pet him for a quick second, praising, "It's okay, buddy. Good boy." I pull Blakely into my arms. I put my fingers on her pulse, needing reassurance she's still alive. When I find a pulse, a bit of relief shoots through me.

I turn my attention back on Hugh, snarling, "What did you give her?"

A sinister smile forms on his face. He claims, "Nothing that she didn't deserve."

I reprimand, "She's your daughter, you motherfucker."

He grunts. "No, she's not."

"God, you're a bastard," I say.

He adds, "Actually, she's the bastard, seeing that Madelyn couldn't keep her legs together."

I glance down at the dead corpse in front of me, then back at Hugh, realizing what he's saying. I question, "Blakely's not yours?"

His face hardens.

I tug her tighter to my chest, demanding, "What did you give her?"

He stays quiet.

Kalim says, in a non-emotional voice, "Looks like he's not going to tell us, but there's a syringe over there. Should I get rid of the trash, Riggs?"

There's no hesitation. I reply, "Don't ask me stupid questions."

Without flinching, Kalim shoots Hugh between the eyes.

He drops to the ground, his body creating a loud thud. More blood pools on the wood floor.

I pick up my pet and rise. King Madden stays on my heels. I glance at Hugh's dead body, then nod to the pet purse on the table. I order Kalim, "Put King Madden in that."

He takes the bag and crouches to the ground. "Come here, buddy."

But King Madden won't leave me. He's jumping up, his tail wagging.

Kalim finally grabs him and puts him in the bag. He zips him in, and I take the bag from him. I go to the elevator, declaring, "We've got to clean this mess up. I'll call my guy."

Kalim claims, "No, Riggs. My guys are downstairs. I've got this." He stares at Blakely, stating, "My private medical team's on standby. Any equipment needed, they have at their disposal. The hospital isn't the best place considering the circumstances."

I glance back at all the blood and nod. The hospital means questions. And Blakely's too famous for those to be asked. I question, "Are they in the city?"

"Yes. Go to the top level. An SUV is waiting for you," he informs me.

"Thanks," I say and step onto the elevator.

Kalim bends down and picks the syringe off the floor. He states, "I assume this is the date rape drug. Give this to the doctor. I'll stop by as soon as I'm done here." He slides it into the pocket of King Madden's bag and zips it.

I nod, staying silent, hugging my wife closer to me. I kiss her head as the doors shut, and I hit the button for the parking garage. The elevator moves, and I murmur in her ear, "I'm sorry, pet. I love you. Everything is going to be okay, I promise." Yet the fear inside me is at an all-time high.

29

Blakely

"Come on, pet," Riggs murmurs. He brushes his lips against the back of my hand.

"Mmm," I moan, try to speak, and wince. My throat's dry, my head's pounding, and I try to see him but everything's black.

He slides his warm hand over my cheek. The scent of woody spice laced with orange peels flares in my nostrils. In a worried tone, he orders, "Wake up, pet."

King Madden's whine fills my ears. His tongue slides across my arm. His tail slaps my hip.

"Easy, boy," Riggs gently states. He kisses my forehead and repeats, "Wake up."

I move my hand across King Madden's fur. His tail hits me harder, and a shrill bark fills the room. I struggle to open my eyes but manage to blink a few times, cringing from the brightness.

"There you go. Come on, pet," Riggs encourages.

I fight the sleepiness and pounding against my skull until he comes into full view.

Concern fills his sharp features. He kisses me on the lips and caresses my chin with his thumb. He admits, "You had me worried."

I open my mouth, but a muffled noise comes out and my throat cracks. I squeeze my eyes from the pain.

Riggs places a glass near my lips, ordering, "Take a sip."

I obey, taking several until my throat no longer hurts. A beeping noise registers, and I glance at a machine near the bed. I push the glass away and ask, "Where am I?"

Riggs's face hardens. He informs, "At a private clinic. They drugged you."

"Who—" My stomach churns. Images of my dead mother's bloody corpse, my father scowling at me with hatred, and Noah's sinister expression all flood me at once. I stare at Riggs, unable to stop tears from flowing down my cheeks.

He swipes at them, and King Madden whines, then tries to get closer to my face, but Riggs pushes him away, ordering, "Stay, boy."

I force myself to sit up.

"Easy," Riggs says.

I reach down and tug King Madden into my arms. I ask, "Are you okay, sweetie?"

His tail wags, and he nuzzles into my chest.

More images fill my mind. I blurt out, "My mother kicked him. Before...before she..." I can't get the words out.

Riggs pulls me into his arms, holding my head. I bury my face into the curve of his neck and sob. "They...they...they killed her!"

"Shhh, I know. I know," he murmurs.

My body shakes, and he tightens his arms around me. King Madden licks my neck. I cry, "I'm going to squish him."

Riggs loosens his hold, but King Madden doesn't move.

"They didn't have to kill her," I claim.

Riggs retreats, holding my face. He says, "I'm sorry, pet. Did..." He swallows hard. Anger and fear swirl into his expression. He continues, "Did that bastard do anything to you? Besides drug you?"

I shake my head, but things are so fuzzy I can't be sure. I admit, "I don't think so."

Riggs takes calculated breaths, his lungs straining against his shirt.

So he won't obsess over what happened, I sternly state, "Nothing else happened."

His expression doesn't change.

I retreat farther and keep King Madden tucked into me. I ask, "How did I get here?"

He hesitates.

"Riggs, don't you dare keep this from me," I warn.

He glances at the ceiling, shifts on the bed, then answers, "I traced Noah's phone. But Colton is the one who told Kalim and me where he took you."

Shock fills me. "Colton?"

Riggs nods. "Yes. He's been to the penthouse before."

Goose bumps break out on my skin. I ask, "Why did Noah take him there?"

"That's a story for another day, pet," Riggs asserts.

His tone tells me not to push it. I study him and ask, "How did you get me out of there?"

Darkness overpowers his expression. He says nothing, pinning his blues on mine.

A chill runs through my body. I demand, "I want to know what happened."

He slowly licks his lips, staying quiet.

"Riggs, tell me," I insist.

He glances behind him at the closed door, then takes a deep breath. "This can never be repeated."

"Of course not," I assure him, my gut diving. Whatever he's going to tell me, I'm sure it's bad.

He keeps his voice low, stating, "They're dead."

Shock fills me, yet it shouldn't. The only way I got out of there alive was by their deaths. There's no way I could have escaped. So I take a minute to process his statement, then question, "You killed them, or did Kalim?"

He sniffs hard, stares at me, and stays quiet.

"You did?" I push.

His jaw twitches. He answers, "I'm not going to discuss the details. All you need to know is that the situation's been taken care of and no one will ever know what happened."

My chest tightens. I gaze out the window and then ask, "Is that why I'm here instead of a hospital?"

"Yes."

"And what did they drug me with?" I inquire.

More anger flares in his voice. He answers, "The date rape drug. The doctor said you'll be fine, but it's important we get a lot of water and electrolytes in you. And you need rest. Lots of rest."

"Is that why I have a headache?"

He nods. "Yes. It should go away in a day or so."

Tears well in my eyes again. I choke out, "Thank you for finding me." I sob, and tears fall onto King Madden's fur.

Riggs tugs me into his arms. He admits, "I can't ever lose you, pet."

"I shouldn't have gone with him. It's my fault," I claim.

"Shhh. No, it's not!"

"You warned me about him!"

"Even I didn't know how Noah was," Riggs confesses. He kisses my head.

There's a knock on the door, and someone clears their throat.

King Madden jumps out of my arms and onto the floor.

"Hey, buddy," Kalim says, crouching down and petting him.

King Madden barks.

Kalim chuckles. "You're a brave boy."

King Madden rolls on his back.

Kalim rubs his belly and looks up. "How you feeling, Blakely?"

Riggs shifts on the bed and slides his arm around my shoulder.

I grab the top of his hand and reply, "I'm going to live. Thanks to you both."

Kalim rises, and his face turns stern. "I'm just glad you're okay."

"Are we good?" Riggs asks.

The two men exchange a knowing look. Kalim nods. "All set."

"Thank you. For everything," Riggs acknowledges.

There's a lot Riggs isn't telling me, but everything hurts too much to push for more details. So I don't.

King Madden flies back across the room and jumps, barking and trying to get on the bed.

Riggs lowers and picks him up. He hands him to me and states, "I need a minute with Kalim." He rises, and they leave the room.

King Madden licks my face and softly barks, then tilts his head with his tail wagging.

"Well, I'm happy to see you too, sweetie," I coo, petting his head. "I'm sorry I took you around those bad people."

King Madden runs in circles on the bed.

I laugh.

Riggs walks back into the room with the doctor. He announces, "This is Dr. Phillips. He needs to give you another quick exam, then we can go home."

The doctor asks, "How are you feeling, Mrs. Madden?"

I smile. "My head's a little sore, but other than that, I think I'm okay."

"Let me check a few vitals," he states and takes out a light. "I'm going to shine this in your eyes. Just follow my directions, okay?"

"Sure," I say, but I wince when the light hits my eyes.

He spends fifteen minutes assessing me, then announces, "You'll feel better in a few days. In the meantime, drink lots of water, get plenty of rest, and let me know if any symptoms worsen."

"Thank you," I reply.

He grins. "I'm going to be shameless now." He pulls a pen and a small notepad out of his pocket. "You're my granddaughter's favorite singer. Would you mind giving me an autograph for her?"

I reach for the paper and pen, answering, "Sure. What's her name?"

"Nicky with a y."

I sign it and then hand it to him. "There you go."

"Thanks. Take care." He winks, pats Riggs on the shoulder, and leaves the room.

I slide my feet off the mattress, and a wave of dizziness hits me.

"Whoa!" Riggs exclaims, racing toward me. "Take it slow." He helps me onto my feet.

When I have my balance, I slide my arms around his shoulders and hug him.

He squeezes me back, declaring, "I'll take a million more of these."

I retreat, pinning my gaze into his, vowing, "Then that's what you'll get."

30

Riggs
The Next Day

"Blakely! Girl, I'm so sorry! I should have done more to warn you about Noah!" Colton claims, rushing past me and into the L.A. apartment.

I shut the door and grumble, "Done more? You did nothing."

"Riggs," Blakely reprimands. When Colton texted he wanted to come over, she warned me to be nice, but I can't help pointing out his faults.

Shame fills his boyish features. He winces, admitting, "I know." He pins his puppy-dog eyes on me. "I'm sorry. It's not easy for me to talk about what happened."

"And you don't have to. I'm happy you're okay," she says, pulling him into a big hug.

He returns her affection, lifting her off her feet.

King Madden wakes up, jumps off the couch, and jumps at Colton's feet.

"Easy. She's still recovering," I scold.

Colton sets her down and crouches on the floor. He picks up King Madden and coos, "Aren't you just the cutest thing!"

I step forward and point toward the office. "We need to talk."

Colton freezes.

"Let him say hi first," Blakely chastises.

"He already did," I state.

She tilts her head. "Riggs—"

"It's fine, love. Get some rest, and we'll talk after I face the music with Daddy," he interjects, handing King Madden to her.

I ignore his Daddy comment, motion to the office, and agree, "Good decision."

"Be nice," my pet warns.

I grunt, then nod for Colton to follow me.

We step inside, and Kalim spins. He crosses his arms, "Colton."

Colton freezes. "Didn't know you were here."

Kalim points to the chair, ordering, "Sit."

Colton's eyes drift between us. He sits, tapping his fingertips together. He asks, "Why do I feel like I'm in school and in trouble?"

I sit behind the desk, and Kalim takes the chair next to Colton. I assert, "There's some sensitive information we need to discuss, but it has to stay here."

Colton's face turns white. He puts his hand over his mouth. "He did something to Blakely she didn't tell me about?"

My stomach churns, thinking about how close she came to something much worse happening to her.

Kalim clears his throat. "No. However, there are things we've decided to talk to you about, and you're never to discuss them outside of this room. Understand?"

He arches his eyebrows. "Okay."

I toss a yellow envelope at him.

"What's this?" he questions.

I sit back in my chair, answering, "The footage Noah had on you. And all the digital footprints have been erased."

Colton gapes, then asks, "How—"

"Don't ask," Kalim answers.

Colton grips the envelope, staring at it.

I add, "There's going to be a lot of discussion about the whereabouts of Noah and Blakely's father, Hugh. You're going to do your part."

Colton squints. He tilts his head, questioning, "And what would that be?"

"You're going to call Noah daily for a month. Then, you're going to create a media stink about not having access to your agent," I inform him.

"And why would I do that?"

"Because you aren't ever going to hear from him again."

Shock fills Colton's expression. Goose bumps break out on his arms. He leans closer, asking, "Are you saying—"

"We're saying that you're going to express your disappointment in the lack of effort by your agent and file a lawsuit that he's in breach of his contract."

Colton sits back and presses his fingertips together again, inquiring, "What is the point of doing this?"

"So Blakely isn't the only one," I relay.

Colton runs his hand through his hair. "And why are we doing this? What am I missing?"

I rise and go around the desk. I sit on it and cross my arms. "So you can switch agents and it looks legit."

Colton stays quiet.

I continue, "This is what's going to happen. I will work with Ears to find an agent I approve of to represent you and Blakely. I'll handle the contracts and negotiate a fair deal. I'll also sue Noah's company for the rights to your backlist of songs, and since there won't be anyone to fight it, you're going to win."

Colton swallows hard. He slowly asks, "So I'll have ownership of them?"

"If my attorneys have their way in court, yes."

"And if not?"

I shrug. "Then nothing will financially change for you, but I'm confident you'll have full ownership."

His eyes turn to slits. "Why would you do this for me?"

"I shouldn't since you didn't protect my wife," I seethe.

Guilt fills his face. He holds up his hands, stating, "I'll always regret not warning her."

I stare at him until he squirms.

"Riggs," Kalim interjects.

I rise off the desk and assert, "From now on, you do everything in your power to protect my wife when she's with you. That means no clubs. No putting her in dangerous situations. And if you know something about someone, you fucking tell her and me. Understand?"

He nods. "Okay. I get it."

I release an angry breath and put our differences aside. I saw the footage Noah had on Colton. It'll haunt me for a long time. So as upset as I am that he didn't warn Blakely, I can't blame him for wanting to forget it happened and not tell anyone.

And Colton knows a lot of people in the industry. I'm counting on him to have learned his lesson and fill my wife and me in if there are issues with anyone.

I point toward the door. "You can go talk to Blakely now."

He rises and gets to the door, then spins. "You don't need to talk to Ears."

"Oh? Why is that?" I question.

He takes his phone out of his pocket and swipes at the screen.

My phone buzzes.

Colton states, "Laurie Fisher. Call her. She's an up-and-coming agent, and although she's not as seasoned as Noah, she knows what she's doing. I would have switched to her a long time ago if possible. Interview her. Let me know if you have any red flags, but all the musicians she represents seem to love her."

"How low on the chain is she?" I question.

He softly laughs. "You're ruthless."

"It's my wife's career."

"And mine." He pins his challenging stare on me.

"I'll interview her first and let you know."

"Good." He opens the door and leaves.

Kalim rises. "I'll make sure things go as planned and watch him over the next month."

"Thanks." I extend my hand.

He shakes it and leaves.

I stay in the office and open the safe. I remove an envelope, take out a thin sheet of paper, and then sit back in my chair.

I stare at the black-and-white photo in awe. When I brought Blakely to the private clinic yesterday, the doctor told me she was pregnant. I assume she wasn't lying and doesn't have a clue.

He took an ultrasound while she was asleep. I heard the heartbeat, and he asked if I wanted to know if it was a boy or a girl.

I told him no. As much as I wanted to know, I didn't want to find out without her awake. But she was still foggy when she woke up, and there was so much she was processing I didn't want to overwhelm her.

The doctor made me promise to tell her today. I've already made an appointment with her gynecologist for Monday and had her pregnancy vitamins delivered to the apartment. It was easier to stay in L.A. yesterday than subject her to the long drive back to Malibu.

I put the photograph back into the envelope and take it to the main room. I set it on the table and sit next to Blakely. She curls into me, and King Madden readjusts himself on her lap.

Colton stays a few hours. They talk about a lot of work stuff that is out of my element, but I'm okay with it. My pet has a happy glow on her face, and that brings me peace.

Colton finally leaves, and I walk him to the door.

Blakely announces, "I need to tell you something."

My stomach flips. *Maybe she does know she's pregnant and hid it from me?*

"Sit," she says, patting the cushion next to her.

I obey, and she turns to me.

Minutes pass, creating tension, making my chest tighten. I finally ask, "What's going on, pet?"

She takes a deep breath, her eyes turn glassy, and she announces, "I vow to always accept all of you, your faults and all."

I freeze, my pulse skyrocketing. It's all I've wanted to hear since she discovered what I did to her.

She adds, "And I love you. I want you to know how much I love you." A tear rolls down her cheek.

I reach for it, swiping it off her skin, then rise. I go to the table and pick up the envelope. I hold it out to her.

"What is that?" Blakely asks.

"Something the doctor gave me," I answer. My butterflies turn frantic. I sit down and order, "Open it."

She scrunches her face. "Is something wrong?"

I shake my head, trying to contain my smile. "No, pet. Nothing is wrong."

She hesitates, then opens the envelope. She pulls out the paper and freezes. Her eyes widen, and she turns her calm chaos on me.

My heart pounds harder. She made it clear the other day that she wasn't ready for babies. We didn't plan this, but I hope she's as excited as I am.

She opens her mouth, then snaps it shut. She glances back at the photo and then locks eyes with me. She asks, "Is this a baby?"

I pick up her hand and kiss it. "Yes."

Her bottom lip quivers. Her eyes water as she questions, "Our baby?"

I nod, softly answering, "Yes."

She stares at it, then traces the outline of its body, asking, "How...?" She jerks her head up, meeting my eye. "I didn't lie, Riggs. I took tests. Several. How is this possible?"

I scoot closer to her, reassuring, "The doctor said some women don't register they're pregnant with at-home tests until later in their pregnancy. He did an ultrasound while you were still sleeping."

"Why didn't you tell me?"

"I didn't want to overwhelm you. There was a lot for you to process yesterday, and you were still foggy," I admit.

Anxiety explodes on her expression. She puts her hand on her belly, stating, "The drugs...did they...?" Her face falls.

I slide my hand on her cheek. "No, pet. The doctor assured me everything was fine with you and the baby. He ran several tests.

We have an appointment with your gynecologist on Monday too."

A tiny bit of relief appears in her expression but not enough.

I tug her into me. "Everything is fine."

She tilts her head. "You're sure?"

"Yes. And I want you to know something."

She arches her eyebrows.

I take a deep breath, repledging, "I vow to prove you wrong and work on my faults. Not just for you but for our family."

A full stream of tears falls down her face. "You already have."

"I love you more than anything. And I'm going to do better," I promise, then tug her into me.

She nods, embraces me tight, then retreats. She stares at the photo for a while, then asks, "Is it a boy or a girl?"

I confess, "I don't know. I wanted to wait until you were awake."

She studies it longer, then turns toward me with a huge smile. "So we're having a baby?"

Excitement flares within me. I almost feel giddy. "Yes. It looks like we are."

She sets King Madden next to her and straddles me. She slides her arms over my shoulders and her hands through my hair. "Do you know what this means?"

I arch my eyebrows. "No. What?"

Her lips twitch. "You're going to get cock blocked a lot more."

Amused, I jerk my head back. "Why would you think that?"

She softly laughs. "If you think King Madden is hard to deal with, just wait until the baby comes."

"Babies, you mean," I tease.

She bites her lip, arching her eyebrow.

I tug her closer and firmly state, "I'm not joking, pet."

She smiles, her calm chaos lighting me up just like the first day I noticed her. She bats her eyelashes and suggests, "Then maybe we should practice some more."

EPILOGUE

Blakely
Seven Years Later

"Mommy!" Christie shrieks, flying across the living room with King Madden on her heels.

I crouch down, pulling her into me for a hug. King Madden barks, wagging his tail, and I pet him, laughing. "I take it you missed me."

Her eyes widen into a serious expression. She replies, "I did, Mommy!"

I hug her again, stating, "Well, I missed you more!"

King Madden barks again.

"Shh! You aren't supposed to bark," Christie scolds.

I kiss her on the head and pick up King Madden so his face is in front of mine, asking, "Were you a good boy too?"

He tilts his head and barks.

I kiss him and set him down.

"Thank God you're back," Riggs booms, carrying our three-year-old twins, Conrad and Clark, on each hip. He bends down and kisses me on the cheek.

I kiss each of the boys and reach for them.

"They're dirty," Riggs states in a semi-annoyed, semi-amused voice.

I glance at their clothes, then take them from him, declaring, "I take it they had another food fight?" I ignore the food that's going to get all over my clothes and kiss each one on the head.

Christie informs me, "It got everywhere! Daddy and I were cleaning up."

Riggs tugs her close to him—she's a total Daddy's girl—and she beams up at him. He praises, "That's right. You've been a big help while Mommy was away."

I gaze over at the kitchen. Orange, green, and yellow smears cover the booster seats, table, and floor. I wince, trying not to laugh.

While we have a dependable nanny, Riggs takes more time off work to be with the kids while I'm on tour. Neither of us wants the children to be raised by someone else. Yet like most things, Riggs takes it to the extreme sometimes.

I reiterate, "You really should ask Lucy to help out more when I'm gone."

He glances at the kitchen and then crouches down in front of Christie. He asks, "Do you think we need more help when Mommy is gone?"

She shakes her head. "Nope." She turns toward me and relays, "Daddy and I have this under control."

I can't help but laugh. She's as stubborn as Riggs and sometimes too serious for a child of six years old. I blame that on him too. Every night they sit down and he teaches her ten new vocabulary words. I don't know how it started, but it's their thing, and she gets upset if I interrupt.

King Madden barks and runs in circles.

"Someone wants to play," I state.

I set the boys down. They follow him and wobble off toward the living room.

"Christie, can you watch the twins for a minute? Mommy needs to change, and I want to talk to her," Riggs says.

Christie's face turns more serious. "Okay, Daddy."

"Good girl," he commends and kisses her on the head again. She runs off, and he pulls me into his arms, murmuring, "Missed you."

I've only been gone for three days, but the feeling is mutual. I reply, "Not as much as I missed you."

He slides his arm around my waist, leading me through the house. As we pass the kids, he says, "You're in charge, Christie. We'll only be a minute."

She puts her hands on her hips and nods, watching the twins like a hawk.

Not that much can go wrong. Riggs has our house on lockdown. As soon as he learned I was pregnant with Christie, he installed locks at the top of the doors and childproofed the entire place.

He also installed cameras so the TV is on with the kids in full view even when we're in the bedroom.

We step inside our suite. He spins me against the wall, slides his hands over my cheeks, and tilts my head. His lips press against mine. His tongue slides into my mouth, flicking me with an urgency that weakens my knees.

I murmur, "I missed you too."

"How tired are you?" he asks, his blues gleaming with mischief and also a hint of darkness.

My core stirs further. I reply, "I slept on the plane."

He assesses me. His erection pushes against my stomach, and he finally states, "Good. Lucy's coming over after dinner to stay the night."

Butterflies erupt in my stomach. "Oh? Why is that?"

He slides his thumb over my lips, studying me.

I wait, my heart racing faster, loving everything about this man and our life together. He's given me everything I could ever want, including things I never knew I needed.

He states, "I miss having full access to my wife without the dog or kids distracting us."

I bite my lip. Somehow, he always knows how much I need the same thing he does. And it's all I've thought about for the last month.

Our lives are crazy between my tour schedule, his company that's now the largest in the world, and our family. And we always manage to have our time together, but a night without any interruptions is just what I've been craving.

He announces, "There's an outfit in your closet. Put it on when you get dressed tonight. I'm taking you on a date to Club Indulgence."

I hope that you loved Riggs and Blakely's story in The Auction and The Vow. Ready for one last heart racing bonus chapter to see what else is up Riggs's sleeve for Blakely?
Click here to read their bonus chapter.

If freebie chapters aren't your cup of tea, and you're ready to read some more super steamy Maggie Cole, download Ruthless Stranger, a dark mafia romance!
Click here!

CLUB INDULGENCE-STEAMY BONUS CHAPTER

Can't get enough of Riggs and Blakely? Want to read one last steamy scene? Download this bonus chapter! Click here!

If you are on a paperback go to: https://dl.bookfunnel.com/okr9m6wnr2

If you are having any issues downloading this, please contact pa4maggie@gmail.com.

Come back when you are done and read the prologue from Illicit King, the first book of Mafia Wars Ireland.

ILLICIT KING

MAFIA WARS IRELAND: BOOK ONE

He wants to destroy my father's throne. I should avoid him, but I can't keep my hands off him.

Brody O'Connor is tall, rugged, and hell-bent on obliterating my family. He seduced me on purpose, and now I'm paying the price.

He's my sworn enemy--part of a rival clan.

But no matter how much I try to shake him, or our heated encounters, I can't.

Every step I take, he's there, lurking in the shadows, studying me, waiting for any chance to undermine my efforts to become my father's successor.

Brody says I'm naive--in the dark about Da's true dealings. He's screwing with my head.

Da is cruel, but he's not capable of something so heinous.

Or is he?

If Brody's right, then where does that leave me?

Where does it leave us?

Illicit King is book one of Mafia Wars Ireland. It's a forbidden love, enemies to lovers, age gap, dark mafia romance.

Click to get your copy of Illicit King, Mafia Wars Ireland Book One!

ILLICIT KING PROLOGUE

PLEASE NOTE - THIS BOOK IS CURRENTLY BEING WRITTEN. IT HAS NOT BEEN EDITED SO PLEASE EXCUSE ANY GRAMMATICAL ERRORS. THANK YOU!

XOXO - MAGGIE

Brody O'Connor

Overhead bins rattle above my head, making me grip the armrest. My heart pounds harder against my chest cavity, and I clench my jaw.

"Is that all you've got," my brother Aidan shouts, his eyes wild with excitement.

"Dumb arse," my other brother Devon mutters, white as a ghost. A loud screech fills my ears, and the jet teeters unsteadily for a moment before the wheels skid on the pavement. We slide down the runway before coming to a brief stop.

"Sweet mother, Mary! Now that's some flying!" Tynan, my youngest brother, declares.

I lift my sweaty hand from the seat and wipe it on my pants, grumbling, "All of you shut up." I release my belt and glance out the window, pissed I'm not back in Belfast. I've got a dozen things to do, and none revolve around an emergency landing in England.

"Don't get your knickers in a twist," Aidan reprimands.

I point at him. "We've got shit to do. None of which involves this place."

He shrugs. "Relax. A bit of extra time away from Belfast won't kill us."

"So typical," I scowl. As the firstborn O'Connor son, it's not a secret that the responsibilities of the family are all on me. Plus, we spent more time in Italy negotiating new arms deals with our allies than I anticipated.

My brothers have it easy. They get to fuck off and not worry about the future of our empire. That scenario is all on me. And lately, our business is getting harder to grow, never mind maintain.

For the last year, the O'Leary's have increased their power across the U.K., even impeding on our territory. We've lost men, money, and part of our future. So my father made it our job to come across the pond from New York and reestablish the power of the O'Connor clan.

Nothing about it is proving to be easy, including this current situation.

Maureen, our flight attendant, slowly rises, her cheeks a bit green. She puts on a brave face and states, "Welcome to London."

The door to the pilot's cabin opens, and Shea steps out. "Sorry for the rough landing. I think we're going to be here for the night."

I curl my palm into a fist, gritting, "Isn't it premature when the mechanic hasn't assessed the damage?"

Shea shakes his head. "There aren't a lot of parts lying around for this old of a plane."

I curse my father in my head. I've told him to upgrade our equipment, but he's too stubborn. He insists we use everything until it falls apart since our operations here aren't doing well.

I reach for the door, push it open, and a cold gust of wind hits my face. I stomp off the plane, pull my phone out of my pocket, and call New York.

"Brody," my father answers.

I bark, "Guess where I'm standing?"

"Don't have time for games. Spit it out, son."

I spit, "London."

The line turns silent. I move further from the plane and stare at the smoke coming from the back of it. My father asks, "Why are you there?"

I accuse, "Because you refuse to give us a plane that isn't a hundred years old!"

"Don't be so dramatic. It's only thirty," he states with an amused voice.

It angers me further. I remind him, "I don't have time for this shit. Plus, we could have died."

He grunts. "How long until you're back in the air?"

"Pilot thinks we're here for at least the night."

A moment of silence passes, and he replies, "Well, all things happen for a reason. This is your lucky day."

I rub my hand over my forehead, not into my father's antics, demanding, "How's that?"

He informs, "We've got a problem in London."

My pulse pounds hard between my ears. I gaze at the grey sky and inhale a deep breath of smog.

My father continues, "Go check on Aaron Potter. Things are off."

The hairs on my arms rise. Aaron's been the head of our gambling operations for decades. This is the first I'm hearing of anything wrong in London, and I don't need any more tasks. I question, "What do you mean off?"

"Off. Don't make me spell it out," my father instructs.

I tug at my hair and stare at my brothers, who all move toward me. "Since when?"

"A while."

"And you said nothing?"

He grunts. "Aaron said he could handle it."

I lock eyes with Aidan and shake my head, sputtering, "You should have mentioned something."

The sound of my father lighting his cigar fills the line, followed by him taking several puffs. He states, "I am now."

I grumble, "If you want me to clean things up over here, I need to know everything that's going on."

He scoffs, "Stop whining. Go find out why Aaron can't handle the situation. That's an order." He hangs up.

I glance at the horizon, attempting to calm my frustration. This is typical of my father. He has everyone on a need-to-know basis, including my brothers and me. All it does is create more problems for us.

"That, Dad?" Devon asks.

A private car pulls next to us, and I yank the door open, ordering, "Get in."

"Can't wait to hear what Tully had to say," Tynan mutters.

"Just get in," I repeat.

My brothers obey, and I follow, slamming the door. "Fucking England," I mutter, my knees hitting Tynan's. While I love our motherland of Ireland, I miss New York and SUVs. The vehicles in the U.K. are smaller, and I'm always squished inside them.

"Where to?" the driver asks at the same moment, a text arrives from my father with Aaron's address. I relay it and close the divider window.

"We going to Aaron's?" Aidan questions.

"Yep."

"Why?"

I deeply inhale, my nostrils flaring, staring out the window. "We've got problems."

"What kind?" I turn to Aidan, repeating my father's words, "Don't make me spell it out."

His eyes turn to slits, his face dening. As much as all the responsibility is on me, none of my brothers like what's happening in the U.K.

We stay silent as the driver weaves through the heavy London traffic, pulling up to a run-down apartment building. We get out and make our way inside, stepping into the elevator.

It creaks, slowly rising, and my stomach flips. I've had enough old things that take you high into the air for one day. Put me in a fight against the most savage of men, and I'll thrive from the adrenaline alone. But something about heights makes me think about my mortality.

Not that I would advertise my phobia.

The lift opens, and I step out, glancing at the numbers on the wall and quickly finding Aaron's unit. I bang on the door, and a skinny guy I haven't ever met opens the door.

He inhales his cigarette and asks with a thick British accent, "What do you want?"

I nod at Declan, the guard standing next to him. He would have looked out the peephole and seen it was me to let this moron open the door.

I shove past the idiot, ignoring the other men counting money, shouting, "Aaron!"

The skinny guy tries again, "Mate, you can't just—"

"Shut the fuck up," Aiden warns, following me.

"Aaron!" I bellow, turning the corner.

He steps out of a room. "Brody! What are you..." He scrunches his forehead. "All the O'Connors in this shithole? Never thought I'd see the day."

I point to the room. "We need to talk."

His face falls. He nods and spins, retreating into his office.

My brothers and I step inside and shut the door. Since I'm not into wasting time, I demand, "What's going on?"

Aaron shifts on his feet and answers, "It's the O'Leary's. They took over the horse track a few months ago."

Tynan booms, "How could you let that happen?"

Aaron's face turns red. "I told your father we were losing ground. It's that damn Alaina's fault."

"Alaina? Jack's daughter?" I question.

Aidan seethes, "You let a woman take the horse track from us?"

Aaron holds his hands in the air. "She's not just any woman. Her three brothers are thick as shit, but not her. She's the brains of the operation. And ruthless as they come."

"Sounds like you have a crush," Devon snickers.

I snap my head toward him and leer.

He closes his mouth and stands taller.

Aaron adds, "She turned four of our guys. Men who'd been loyal to the clan their entire lives."

Anger rages through my blood. Nothing is worse than a traitor. I seethe, "Then kill them."

"She already did," Aaron announces.

I arch my eyebrows.

Aaron crosses his arms over his chest. "The minute she got control of the racetrack, she took them out."

"Serves the traitors right," Aidan snarls.

Aaron steps closer and lowers his voice. "When I say she took them out, I don't mean she shot them in the back of the head."

"No? What did she do?" I question.

She had her men beat them while she watched. Then she took them as close to Buckingham Palace as possible before dousing them with gasoline."

Devon blurts out, "Bitch put her men in danger just to make a statement."

Aaron sarcastically laughs.

What's so funny?" I question.

Aaron's face falls. In a non-emotional tone, he states, "Alaina O'Leary is the one who lit the match."

The room turns silent, with all of us processing this new information. I heard stories of Alaina's involvement in her father's business and how most people fear her.

Yet this is another level of barbarity. I don't know any woman who would risk their life to get caught by the metropolitan police. Doing so would result in charges of treason against the royal family.

Hell, I don't know many men who would take that risk.

It almost makes me respect her.

Almost.

She's an O'Leary.

There will never be respect for any O'Leary.

Aaron opens a file cabinet and thumbs through it. He pulls several large photos out and hands them to me. "That's her."

I glance at a photo of a petite redhead with oversized sunglasses getting into a hired car. I peer closer, but the zoomed-out photo doesn't reveal much, so I flip to the next one.

My chest tightens. Adrenaline races through my veins, igniting a buzz that builds with every passing second.

Alaina O'Leary is a knockout.

I don't know how Aaron got this photo, but she's staring straight at the camera. Her emerald eyes gleam with a confidence and mystery I've never seen on a woman. Her plump lips match her maroon hair, and her skin's so pale it resembles fresh cream.

Jesus.

She's an O'Leary.

"Let's kill her," Aidan seethes.

"Agree. Bitch needs to die," Tynan declares.

I tear my eyes off the photo, ordering, "No one touches her."

My brother's eyes all turn to slits.

I add, "I mean it."

"She needs to be taken down," Aidan warns.

In my most authoritative voice, I assert, "She's going to get taken down."

"How?"

I answer, "By me. No one but me touches her. Got it?"

Another moment of uncomfortable silence passes. My brothers finally nod.

I toss the photos on Aaron's desk. "What time does she get to the racetrack?"

"Eight on the dot. She's not scared of routine. Every night, she's there, running the show," he answers.

I step in front of the window and stare at the buildings, trying to push the vision of her eyes out of my head.

"What are you going to do?" Devon asks.

I take another moment and then inhale deeply. I spin and vow, "Make Alaina O'Leary wish she was never born."

Are you ready for the O'Connors in Mafia Wars Ireland?

Illicit King (Brody)- May 1, 2023
Illicit Captor (Aidan) - June 1, 2023
Illicit Heir (Devin) - July 15, 2023
Illicit Monster (Tynan) - Sept 1, 2023

READY TO BINGE THE ORIGINAL MAFIA WARS SERIES? GET TO KNOW THE IVANOVS AND O'MALLEYS!

He's a Ruthless Stranger. One I can't see, only feel, thanks to my friends who make a deal with him on my behalf.

No names. No personal details. No face to etch into my mind.

Just him, me, and an expensive silk tie.

What happens in Vegas is supposed to stay in Vegas.

He warns me he's full of danger.

I never see that side of him. All I experience is his Russian accent, delicious scent, and touch that lights me on fire.

One incredible night turns into two. Then we go our separate ways.

But fate doesn't keep us apart. When I run into my stranger back in Chicago, I know it's him, even if I've never seen his icy blue eyes before.

Our craving is hotter than Vegas. But he never lied.

He's a ruthless man...

"Ruthless Stranger" is the jaw-dropping first installment of the "Mafia Wars" series. It's an interconnecting, stand-alone Dark Mafia Romance, guaranteed to have an HEA.

Ready for Maksim's story? Click here for Ruthless Stranger, book one of the jaw dropping spinoff series, Mafia Wars!

CAN I ASK YOU A HUGE FAVOR?

Would you be willing to leave me a review?

I would be forever grateful as one positive review on Amazon is like buying the book a hundred times! Reader support is the lifeblood for Indie authors and provides us the feedback we need to give readers what they want in future stories!

Your positive review means the world to me! So thank you from the bottom of my heart!

MAGGIE COLE

MORE BY MAGGIE COLE

Mafia Wars Ireland

Illicit King (Brody) - May 1, 2023
Illicit Captor (Aidan) - June 15, 2023
Illicit Heir (Devin) - Sept 1, 2023
Illicit Monster (Tynan) - Oct 15, 2023

Club Indulgence Duet (A Dark Billionaire Romance)

The Auction (Book One)
The Vow (Book Two)

Standalone Holiday Novel

Holiday Hoax - A Fake Marriage Billionaire Romance (Standalone)

Mafia Wars New York - A Dark Mafia Series (Series Six)

Toxic (Dante's Story) - Book One
Immoral (Gianni's Story) - Book Two
Crazed (Massimo's Story) - Book Three
Carnal (Tristano's Story) - Book Four
Flawed (Luca's Story) - Book Five

Mafia Wars - A Dark Mafia Series (Series Five)

Ruthless Stranger (Maksim's Story) - Book One
Broken Fighter (Boris's Story) - Book Two
Cruel Enforcer (Sergey's Story) - Book Three
Vicious Protector (Adrian's Story) - Book Four

Savage Tracker (Obrecht's Story) - Book Five

Unchosen Ruler (Liam's Story) - Book Six

Perfect Sinner (Nolan's Story) - Book Seven

Brutal Defender (Killian's Story) - Book Eight

Deviant Hacker (Declan's Story) - Book Nine

Relentless Hunter (Finn's Story) - Book Ten

Behind Closed Doors (Series Four - Former Military *Now International Rescue Alpha Studs*)

Depths of Destruction - Book One

Marks of Rebellion - Book Two

Haze of Obedience - Book Three

Cavern of Silence - Book Four

Stains of Desire - Book Five

Risks of Temptation - Book Six

Together We Stand Series (Series Three - *Family Saga*)

Kiss of Redemption - Book One

Sins of Justice - Book Two

Acts of Manipulation - Book Three

Web of Betrayal - Book Four

Masks of Devotion - Book Five

Roots of Vengeance - Book Six

It's Complicated Series (Series Two - Chicago *Billionaires*)

My Boss the Billionaire - Book One

Forgotten by the Billionaire - Book Two

My Friend the Billionaire - Book Three

Forbidden Billionaire - Book Four

The Groomsman Billionaire - Book Five

Secret Mafia Billionaire - Book Six

All In Series (Series One - New York Billionaires)

The Rule - Book One

The Secret - Book Two

The Crime - Book Three

The Lie - Book Four

The Trap - Book Five

The Gamble - Book Six

STAND ALONE NOVELLA

JUDGE ME NOT - A Billionaire Single Mom Christmas Novella

ABOUT THE AUTHOR

Amazon Bestselling Author

Maggie Cole is committed to bringing her readers alphalicious book boyfriends. She's an international bestselling author and has been called the "literary master of steamy romance." Her books are full of raw emotion, suspense, and will always keep you wanting more. She is a masterful storyteller of contemporary romance and loves writing about broken people who rise above the ashes.

Maggie lives in Florida with her son. She loves sunshine, anything to do with water, and everything naughty.

Her current series were written in the order below:

- All In (Stand alones with entwined characters)

- It's Complicated (Stand alones with entwined characters)
- Together We Stand (Brooks Family Saga - read in order)
- Behind Closed Doors (Read in order)
- Mafia Wars
- Mafia Wars New York
- Club Indulgence Duet
- Mafia Wars Ireland

Maggie Cole's Newsletter
Sign up here!

Hang Out with Maggie in Her Reader Group
Maggie Cole's Romance Addicts

Follow for Giveaways
Facebook Maggie Cole

Instagram
@maggiecoleauthor

TikTok
https://www.tiktok.com/@maggiecole.author

Complete Works on Amazon
Follow Maggie's Amazon Author Page

Book Trailers
Follow Maggie on YouTube

Feedback or suggestions?
Email: authormaggiecole@gmail.com

- twitter.com/MaggieColeAuth
- instagram.com/maggiecoleauthor
- bookbub.com/profile/maggie-cole
- amazon.com/Maggie-Cole/e/B07Z2CB4HG
- tiktok.com/@maggiecole.author

Printed in Dunstable, United Kingdom

65672509R00234